Four of a Kind

A Women's Historical Fiction

Vanessa Russell

ISBN: 1497348935
ISBN 13: 9781497348936
Library of Congress Control Number: 2014905249
CreateSpace Independent Publishing Platform
North Charleston, South Carolina

When a woman like that whom I've seen so much
All of a sudden drops out of touch
Is always busy and never can
Spare you a moment, it means a Man.
Alice Duer Miller, in *Forsaking all Others*, 1915

Contents

RUBY March 1964

Jesi is lying in a coffin and I haven't the faintest clue why. "Move on, Mama," Bess whispers, rustling a stack of papers. Why papers? "You're holding up the line." Very well. My daughter sees it and she doesn't seem to question it. My granddaughter, Katy, is beside her and she doesn't seem to question it. But my great-granddaughter is lying in a coffin and I haven't the faintest clue why.

At least they're crying, so they haven't totally lost their senses. But accepting it is beyond my comprehension. I want to scream, *Someone, somewhere has made a terrible mistake*, but honestly, having the next two generations watching my every move, anything I say is taken the wrong way so I'll simply clam up and write this down. I clinch my teeth and cling to my handbag with all ten fingers as if its calf leather is Jesi's arm. I see Bess' arms extend into the coffin and lay the stack of hand-written pages to the side. I point a trembling finger to question this but my shoulders are firmly pushed and I step forward.

I take one step and then another, forcing my body to turn away from this horrid lure as I might from an automobile accident, its image staying in front of me like a photograph. I turn to see all these faces watching me and I detest having eyes on me, always have. I look down and not a moment too soon, my shuffling takes me out of that stifling room.

My question still hangs there, ready to submit to Bess. Finally I can be still no more. "Are we heading back to the dining room table?" I ask. I should know better than to speak my thoughts. Bess annoys me again by whispering to Katy - about me again I'd wager. Something about an embarrassing old-timer's disease.

Yes, I'm old. And forgetful. I'll grant them that. I may not know why we're here but I remember where we were. Last I recall, the four of us were sitting around the dining room table writing, and I know we haven't reached the end of our story. I want to go back. But then, what else is new?

And I have another question: Is this how Jesi ends her chapter of our story? She wasn't very cooperative in writing. Perhaps she wants to show us instead. She's played tricks before. Why one time not long ago I remember her face painted white, her long hair painted black and blending right in with the wisp of a black dress, its fluttering layers cut like the outline of a spider's web. Her teeth had looked dingy in comparison to the white around it as she grinned at my hand at my throat in alarm. Did someone die and she was in morbid mourning, I had asked her? "Relax, G-G," she had said, calling me by my nickname, short for Great-Grandmother. "It's Halloween."

What a ghastly holiday, I've always thought. What in the world is there to celebrate in being frightened to death?

Could today be Halloween, too?

My mind connects one question to the next until it becomes one long train rumbling so loud, I can't hear anything else.

Suddenly I find myself outside this monstrosity of a church on the top step. Below me is a sea of black pavement bobbing with black hats and coats and black shiny roofs. I fear I'll drown in all this black. I stop and won't budge, like an old mule.

"Where are we going?" I ask.

"For God's sake, to the graveyard, Mama," Bess says, but I don't like her tone. She seems exasperated every time I open my mouth. Mercy. I declare I'll seal my lips and dry my ink well if this keeps up, and then she'll never get the ending to my story.

White faces surface in front of my eyes and then submerge, always with the same grim expression and glass bottom eyes. "She was so brave ... what a tragedy, the papers say ... murder really ..."

Black ... white.

"The world is not black and white," Jesi has shouted to me, to her mother, Katy, and even to her grandmother, Bess. "If it were,

I wouldn't have so many bitchy mamas and I'd have a daddy-o." Well, I wish she was here to see all these ghastly black costumes and white faces bobbing around me; she'd see she was wrong all over again.

But then she does make one point; these "mamas" are getting on my nerves, too. One on each side of me, hands clamped to my elbows, they force me down, one step at a time, leaving my great granddaughter behind. Elbows as bony as wings on a fat-breasted bird, nonetheless I wish to flap and fly away. Well, isn't that a fitting ending; I've been that way my whole life.

I hold my breath and go down for the count.

RUBY 4 months earlier, December 1963

Not a man to our name. In spite of that, or because of that, our four generations of daughters shall meet here each night to write "our year of awakening". All of us with heads bent, writing diligently, as if our lives depended on it. I suppose it does, with so many sacrifices notched into the lines on our faces like a soldier keeps score of enemy kills. All in defense, of course – I believe we women only act in defense, believing all are good, until offended.

I wish I could capture this dining room circle on a photograph; me in sepia tones I fear, faded with age with my Gibson-girl bun and high lace collar, my series of diaries ready to tweak a recessed memory. In contrast sits my daughter beside me, sixty-four-year old Bess in her no-nonsense starched white blouse and black skirt, as straight and narrow as the Prohibition Days she endured, stacked at her ready are clippings and diaries. Her vivacious daughter, Katy, sits across from me captured in 1940s Technicolor with a cut-short bold red hairdo (where do you suppose she finds this color of dye?), looking older these days than her forty-one years, and a mysteriously pockmarked leather journal by her diaries. Then there's our rebel Jesi, Katy's daughter, my great granddaughter, at age nineteen sitting on my right with one sheet of paper in front of her, yet no diary at all. Long hair not pinned up, hanging loose as a noose, all in a quick flash of Polaroid with the colors stirred up in a tie-dyed T-shirt. She rebels against our old-fashioned ways of woes in womanhood. We must look so dull to her in today's times.

The harsh fluorescent light of nowadays where so much is exposed; no longer the old ways where lives were softened and

4

shadowed in some secret of mystery and romance in that day's flickering light of candle and gas lamps. We're always in daylight these days it seems, tiring my faded blue, eighty-two year old eyes.

Eighty-two years. I've outlived my husband and lost four children to war and disease. Only we women remain. This saddens me too, and yet, how do I explain to you in my simple uneducated way that if I had a choice (which thank God we never do) and could see into the future (which thank God we never can) I would choose this same table of company to churn old memories into a solid journal. For only these ladies, my legacy, can branch out from me, understand me completely, can continue my story, painful as it may be. It is for this reason that we gather, each to tell our own personal year of awakening and link to the other, like an intricate braid or necklace; or better yet, a perennial ivy that links and binds, to bud and grow, its stem to curl and link past to future, its glossy leaves living only in the present to have its moment of beauty and then fall away leaving its roots of strength to pass on to the next in line.

As if reading my mind, Bess leans over to me now and says, "Remember, Mama, tell all, exactly as you remember it. And, yes," she adds to my raised eyebrows, "I shall do the same."

"Well, mercy, Bess, you can't start dictating—"

"We all will, won't we?" she says to the other two, bless her heart, always needing to orchestrate. She narrows her eyes and stares at them intently, waiting for agreement, the only acceptable answer.

Katy laughs easily at her mother and nods with a puff of smoke, saying "Be careful what you wish for!"

Jesi has stopped writing, her arms folded like a mutineer, her leg's metal brace clanging rhythmically against her chair leg. "Hey, man, you're not tricking me," she says to scattered papers. "You're just doing this to try to get the scoop on my scene. You're all too prim and proper to have anything juicy to say."

(Which brings me to wonder: Are we here to write what we know or to read what we don't?)

Ah, Jesi, if you only knew – but of course she doesn't, no, how could she? There are things we've never spoken of - too prim and proper, indeed! She must be told that we all rebelled in our own ways.

Yet we contrast, age I suppose does that and the different eras in which we rebelled. Older ones feeling superior in believing our generation was the best and thinking the next has deteriorated somewhat. Always making those on the bottom rung, like Jesi, believe they'll never reach the top, born too late with too little, so why bother. We should be more honest with her and with ourselves. Truly look at our lives and try not to inflate and paint and exaggerate to give us more meaning. Funny how time softens the hardships of the good ol' days; makes churning butter nostalgic when in fact it brought on blisters.

We all want to make our mark. I disobeyed by marching in that parade of long ago, yelling at an octave I'd never used before - even to scold my sons - holding a sign high saying "Fight for Women's Right to Vote!" My strength came in numbers, in my ladies group where we pretended to have a tea party when in fact we partied the historic Bostonian way (metaphorically of course) by using the Ladies Tea as a platform to campaign for women's suffrage.

(Really, why did those cowardly men disguise themselves as Indians and only throw overboard a woman's drink? Pray tell, where was their whiskey?)

Ah, I digress as old women often do.

Bess on the other hand stood on her own terms. Spoke openly and aggressively – as I was forbidden to do (but I had my moment in the sun, yes!) – in front of many a microphone and man, and helped win the women's right to vote in 1920. She seems impersonal, yes. Many don't like her - which I take full responsibility for. I pushed her out there at the ripe old age of twelve as an extension of my weak arm, without love of man or money. She proved me right, she proved me wrong. I've never told her this, but I admire her strength – why have I never told her? What a personal tragic loss my daughter bore, and continues to carry like a load of dirty laundry. Sometimes I want to shake it out of her. There, I've said it.

Then there's my granddaughter: spirited idealistic Katy, who followed in her father's footsteps and found herself in her mother's shoes. Something happened in her year away in Georgia, opening a birth control clinic. She came back here cussing like a sailor, smoking like a chimney, and looking ten years older, just dropped off on the street by "an old coot named Jerry". Sometimes I hear a cry in that brassy laugh of hers.

And then there's my great-granddaughter, Jesi. I typically sigh around her, sometimes provoked, sometimes not. She fights against us all, resenting our battles for women's rights, yet creating her own. Her story is the saddest one of all – if she will talk about it – her handicap, I mean. I'm assuming that's why she refuses to marry. I have yet to meet a beau of hers, though she's pretty enough. Very sad. Why must she break all the rules? I see chicken scratches on her paper, lines crossed out, two lines remaining. She does disappearing acts and I wonder if Katy knows? (Katy now throws down her reading glasses and taps Jesi on the arm to *sit still!* and I catch the glare Jesi returns. Oh I do hope someday they come to terms- they seem so detached from one another.)

Which makes me look over all these years through sepia lens and tea-stained lace and wonder: With all the freedoms we fought for and earned, there came a price, a dear price that stripped us down to my great-granddaughter's raw nudity, emotions exposed with no sensibilities, no secrets, no coyness ... no femininity. Somewhere, in winning our women, we lost our ladies.

Ah, I'm rambling again and I'm not even sure Bess will type what I've written thus far. Suffice it to say I have no regrets, just occasional melancholy.

So! Sitting around this table, I realize – we have come full circle! I shall begin where Jesi is in her thinking – in the raw. I'm not to be outdone – I have some fight in me yet. The men are gone so I shall throw my propriety to the wind! I'll begin my sentimental journey with the "seed" of how it started: My wedding day in 1898 and its conception of my daughter. How shocking! But this might perk Jesi up … which will make Katy go red in the face … which will feed into Bess's aggravation. Oh how I do love my girls!

I lean toward Jesi and say, "I'll tell you things that will make your hippie hair curl into a bun!"

April, 1898

Memories of my wedding ceremony are little more than blurred images. Of Robert perspiring, his wide mustache quivering, his hand shaking as he slipped the thin gold wedding band on my finger. Of my surprise that he might be as nervous as I. Men slapped him on the back as if he'd accomplished some great deed while women gave me sad teary-eyed hugs, contradicting their happy-for-me remarks. I remember the scratchy lace collar of my light blue wedding gown (women did not wear white those days, which is odd because they were certainly more virgin than women of today. Forgive me, Jesi.). The gown loaned by my mother-in-law, I remember my mama teasing me as she took in the seams around the bust that a few children under the belt would fill in above the belt. That was basically her birds-and-bees talk, along with a reference to the Bible that I must be submissive to my husband. "Your husband will teach you what you need to know."

Mercy.

Vivid even now is the wedding night. Smells and sounds come first; of the buggy's leather seat, the horse's heat, his clip-clop on the bricked street (I rhymed!), his snorting, the rattling of his harness, smells and sounds that are long gone but can still trigger nostalgia. Next is the sight of my mother-in-law's home as we pull up out front. I can still feel that grip of fear as I suddenly realized we were alone for the first time. All I had with me was a small carpetbag; his mother thought it best we wait until after the wedding to bring in my wardrobe. Neighbors might talk, she explained. Like mother, like son, Robert hurried toward the front door, me trailing in his steps, his eyes on the windows of the neighbors' houses as if an unwelcomed audience is watching. This paranoia became contagious for it wasn't long before I believed our verandah was center stage, and only came out when necessary for years to come.

How quiet I remember the house, the ticking mantel clock sounding louder than usual as if demanding more time. I wished it to be so; why, the dongs of the clock only chimed seven times when Robert walked up the stairs to the bedrooms, my bag in hand. I watched helplessly as he reached the top. Looking down at me he cleared his throat and said, "Well, you're not waiting to have tea with Mother, I hope?" I could only shake my head and scratch at my itchy collar. "Then come on up the stairs. Mother is not here, I assure you." His tone became cajoling, as one offering a present to a child. "You will get to see the *upper floors*."

And that's when I learned to take it one step at a time.

When I reached the top landing he said to me, "There now, Ruby, that wasn't so bad was it?" And that's when he began those famous last words. How many times did I hear him say that?

I remember the window at the far end, its outside light barely visible at the end of its day. Funny. I lived more than thirty years in that house and could walk all over with blinders on, yet this first image remains most impressionable upon my mind. It's as if this were my only way out, unreasonable to escape from there, the sun setting beyond as if closing a curtain.

He pointed to two closed doors on the right, his room and the sewing room, and one on the left, "Mother's chamber". He turned and pointed up the stairs. "A large room is up that way, currently used for storage. Mother said it could be made into another bedroom someday." Taking a handkerchief from his back pocket, he wiped the perspiration from his forehead. I wished we were on the cooler first floor having tea with his mother. Perhaps he did, too; he was fidgeting more than usual.

I wondered what hid beyond those doors and what they had in store for me, and then I wondered if I really wanted to know. It all seemed terribly unknown.

Unknown to me as well was a man's body. The mortification I felt when he pulled down his trousers! Thank goodness he had the decency to turn down the gas lamp. Then and there, in the stifled dimness of his bedroom a wave of homesickness overtook me. I longed for the familiarity of my childhood bedroom of seventeen years. I'd known no other and these rooms were strange to me and Robert was a stranger. How could I possibly share a bed with a stranger? Worse than a stranger, he was my husband and that day's ceremony had cut off my umbilical cord for good; I could never go back to my home. I was no longer Ruby Johnson; I was now Mrs. Robert Wright. This comprehension of its vows and the loss and what I'd gained gripped me and I in turn gripped the doorframe. He hadn't noticed that my life had changed in that moment.

He only noticed I hadn't moved. He asked, "You don't plan to sleep in my mother's dress, do you?" To save myself from fainting I hurried off to the sewing room as directed, to change. He'd dropped off my bag here (he'd already planned this out, the scoundrel) and so with muted light filtered through the window blind, I found my nightgown, sewn by my dear sister, Opal. Opal. Well, I have much to say about her later.

I was soaked in perspiration as I unsnapped the many snaps of the whale-boned corset in nervous jerking motions, bittersweet to be released from its clutches, yet feeling I'd collapse without it. Fearful yet forced to move quickly, eager to depart the stifling heat and cramped room. Ah, how comical I must have looked at first, with my nightgown on and ruffled petticoats protruding from the bottom. I had to smile when I looked down and saw what I had forgotten. But when it all came off, I hugged around my breasts feeling ashamed of my nakedness. All my life I was told not to show so much as an ankle and here I was, well, never mind. I desperately longed to wash but at a loss as to how to ask Robert for a water bowl and soap. God only knew how indisposed he might be at that moment. It was then I heard the bedsprings squeak through the wall.

That was telling, nonetheless I called out to him. "Robert?"

"Ye-" he cleared his throat. "Yes?"

"May I wash?"

There was a pause, and then the bedsprings squeaked a release. I heard the porcelain pitcher click from its bowl and return with a louder scratch.

"There is no water here, Ruby," he called out. "You can do that tomorrow."

The bedsprings squeaked again.

I folded my arms and leaned against the doorframe of the sewing room with another realization. Hard work and constant effort were ahead of me in living with a pampered only son of an overprotective mother.

The effort began immediately as we entered his bedroom (this room was to become yours in later years, Bess).

Mercy, here I am losing my nerve, Jesi, I must confess. I've never spoken of this. Am I being disloyal to Robert's memory? He would die again if he knew. Except that, is not my loyalty now to my womankind? Is this not what I longed for all those years – to be able to come out into the open and speak my mind? Perhaps it will be easier to write it down, one word at a time.

Tell all. Yes. Well.

With the curtains closed the room had turned to a murky darkness. Grateful of the darkness I lifted the sheet and slipped under in a hurry, bringing the sheet up to my chin, stiff as a board. He kissed my cheek for the first time since being pronounced man and wife but this didn't help matters, not with the erratic breathing in my ear. I felt like one big question mark as his hand lifted my gown, roamed and explored, eventually finding an opening I myself did not know existed. This must sound terribly naïve or stupid these days but at the turn of the century, our Victorian morals were highly cherished, to our own detriment I must admit, preached in the pulpit, and protected even by such laws as the Comstock, such ridiculous censorship of any literature dealing with sex and birth control methods. Even to teach. (Katy knows this better than anyone, poor thing). So what was I to do but resist: clamp my knees together and grab his wrist?

Naturally, he resisted that. "Don't," he said and continued on his breathless expedition.

Quite suddenly I found him looming over me and flattening me, his male odor overwhelming my senses. Some rigid thing was trying to push and enter between my legs. He was hurting me and I told him so.

Dead-set on his task at hand, he pushed harder. "Help me. Guide me in."

"I don't know what you are doing!" I said breathlessly, but for a different reason than his; I was suffocating under his weight.

Lifting himself, he placed my hand on something that reminded me of the wooden crank on the wringer washer. I thought seriously of doing what I knew best but my touch was enough to make him gasp and jerk and the crank became a wet fish. My sense of touch became most alive at that moment. As if that wasn't enough, he collapsed on top of me for a moment before rolling onto his back.

My body remained still, but my mind was racing. Why hadn't Mama told me about this? I made a silent commitment then and there that when this at last resulted in children, I would prepare my daughter for her own wedding night.

But then I wondered how pregnancy could occur this way – certainly not through the belly button (I had some sense to me). I quietly wiped my abdomen with the sheet, quietly longed to wash. Was this it? I could just about make out the outline of him lying on his back. He appeared to be asleep, but sleep was not to be had just yet.

From the darkness he spoke, in words I remember clearly. "You are a virgin. So am I. But I do know that I am to enter you. You must not resist or I am forced to release my seed where it does not belong. I cannot provide you children this way. This I know for certain. Next time you must relax and open yourself to me. Never again move my hand or close your legs to me. Can we agree on that?"

I stared at the ceiling. The meaning of those words moved across my mind and projected clearly onto the ceiling dark pictures of the demand on my body. But strangely relief came as well in knowing what would be expected. The unknown, I realized, carried more fear. "I am sorry I have disappointed you, Robert. I was frightened."

"Have I ever hurt you?" he asked.

"No."

"Did you not promise just a few hours earlier to love, honor, and obey me?"

"Yes."

"Do you think your way of behaving tonight showed me love, honor, or obedience?"

"Please be patient. I'll do better next time, I promise." My submissive voice sounded like someone else; someone no longer in control and calling the shots as I had in our yearlong courtship. I had now become a stranger in a stranger's bed.

"We'll see, Ruby." Robert rolled to his side facing me. "Remember. Relax."

All I can say here is that I took a deep breath and endured. Endured the probing, endured his testing of my promise.

"I'm ready now," he whispered. "Open yourself to me, Ruby."

I did as commanded and was split in two, with blood on the sheets to prove it, *Virgin's Sheets*, my friends had whispered. I had passed that test, too. I sewed myself together into a different woman, one who'd lost some stuffing and became lumpy, one whom he tried to pound and smooth into the woman he needed. Years down the road I was to break my promise and try to mend again, becoming yet again a different woman.

"No!"

"Yes!"

Opposites that continued to meet in the middle, only the bed squeaking shamelessly as his mother listened from her room across the hall. His mother who took those virgin sheets I had washed in vain had tried to hide, the red stain now a gray half moon that looked to me like a turned-down mouth, and she displayed them proudly on the backyard clothes line, upside down so that the moon would smile.

For the second time that day, he said, "There now, that wasn't so bad, was it?"

My last sense of the evening was awakened: the taste of tears.

December 1963

Mercy, I hope these pages stay in our own family archive and don't see the light of day. If Robert was here, or Victor – just like his father – oh their cold scorn and rebuke! But my dear little son, Jonathon, with those tender brown eyes that reminded me of my brother's dairy cows, would he have – oh but I shall not write another word about him or I shall cry. I surely would.

I hope you're happy with this, Bess.

I am not happy with this, Mama. This is decidedly NOT your year of awakening. Please read again the definition, written clearly in large bold letters on the chalkboard on the wall of the dining room. It says: *We all have a pivotal moment that changes our lives. Symbolically a year of 4 seasons, where the spring seed of an event is born, grows, matures, and becomes winter wisdom as a life-changing realization. Write about this year of awakening.*

I shall allow your "April 1898" as part of your introduction or else I risk being called (once again) a dictator. However, please proceed with your Chapter One here.

Yours Truly,

Bess

Ruby's Chapter One -- December 1963

O h dear, it appears that I must write more. Bess has placed a bottle of wine at the center of our table and poured me a generous amount, to calm my nerves no doubt. My first chapter - or whatever Bess calls it - almost did me in, I do believe. Mercy, I think I've already told too much, and Bess has my pages and her flushed cheeks to prove it. We're not supposed to read each others' remaining chapters until the end, thank goodness.

As I think back over the many years to my "year of awakening" I'm apprehensive in how much to tell. I glance discreetly over at Bess' profile – tight French bun, furrowed brow (those striking crow-feet prints tell me you're not as far behind me as you might think), pinched mouth and distant stare, and my eyes fall to her fast-paced pen writing furious slashes across the paper, telling all, (or so she claims, for she has said so little in the past about her past). Very well.

I have a shocking revelation but, one step at a time, I shall now take you to the first day of my year of awakening, a day like no other before it, when my four gray walls came crashing down and in their place stood five strong women, erect and as promising as a rainbow.

1910 Spring's Seed

I was in a perfect state of mind to learn about women's suffrage, thanks be to my whale-boned corset and to my husband, Robert. One had me trapped within my body and the other had me trapped within his home. The corset forbade me a deep breath, Robert forbade me some fresh air just for a walk to a tea with my next door neighbor, Aimee. Too late for the latter; I had already accepted her invitation and now paced nervously for her arrival in a parlor that had been sanctioned only for occupancy by my husband and his mother.

Ill-prepared, with my petticoat showing below my ankle-length brown skirt - if you can imagine such fashion - safety-pinned at the waist and compounding my uncertainty.

Not only my appearance but my surroundings troubled me. Fear gripped me when I saw a tea cup under the settee, and then peered around the parlor's red flannel curtains for any approaching visitors and saw only the streaks on the glass, or when I tried to breathe in despite the corset bones, only to smell the coal heating and gas lamps.

Suffocating in various ways, I breathlessly took the teacup to my kitchen. The worktable, sideboard and sink pump still showed signs of baking bread that early morning. There was no time to tidy; Aimee was already thirty minutes past due.

She wasn't coming; I could feel it in my bones.

How close I came to staying put inside the cocoon I was outgrowing, with what I could do with my eyes closed, with my duties, my routine. How that one moment of indecision could have changed the path I longed to take, and affected not only my life but Bess and … I wonder, where would we all be now? Even after all is said and done, I shudder to think!

Instead, in that one moment I heard a robin's call to spring. As I tugged irritably at a broken whalebone pinching my side, I entered the dining room through the door-hung drapes (*they are called portiere, my dear, please remember,* echoes of my mother-in-law remind me). Outside the large window the robin fluttered and hopped on a tree branch, looked straight at me and called again. Beyond her perch was Aimee's home and the robin flapped her wings and flew in that direction.

I grabbed my shawl and found myself on my verandah stair, going from dark to light, like being turned inside out, my three-story dwelling casting a shadow behind me. In hindsight, I can't remember the steps there but I believe some force brought me there; mine, God's, the robin, it doesn't matter. There's always something there to lend you a hand, if you take that initial step, I believe.

The brown scalloped-patterned shingles reminded me of day-old fish scales at the market; thick posts and abundant scrollwork were too dark and overbearing; the brown and green painted railing made me think of prison bars.

I smiled, feeling the same freedom as a once-upon-a-time little girl heading toward the candy store. Chores could wait for my return. As long as I was home prior to my children's return from school, everything would be fine. I had a sudden desire to run and skip, but ever conscious of my mother-in-law's teaching of watchful eyes in neighbors' windows, I kept myself in check by pulling my heavy woolen black shawl around me a bit tighter.

Black shawl; my goodness, I still have that around here some-where, put away by one of the others, forbidden anymore to wear it. I had soaked this and my dress in a vat of dye the year prior for my mother-in-law's funeral.

Quite a sacrifice when you realize I only had three dresses. The mourning period was but a few months, unfortunately the heavy wool with its full skirt and tight bodice was to last much longer and was now my day dress for the one day a week to the market (*head down, dear, to meet another man's eyes is brash*). I had hemmed the dress to a few inches above my boot, allowing outside wear where it wouldn't drag through the muddy streets. Practical, without loose sleeves that might catch and snag on baskets. Bone buttons decorated the front. Black cotton gloves without so much as a frill.

Regardless of practicality, I wished for a lighter one. While brush-ing dust and lint from my dress that morning, I had asked Robert if some light-colored cotton fabric could be purchased for a summer dress, tired as I was of dark colors my mother-in-law had insisted I wear because darker colors disguised the dirt and because heavier wool could be brushed instead of laundered. Yes, of course, laun-dering was backbreaking work ... ah, but a light green cotton frock would be perfect for afternoon teas with my newfound acquain-tances. I promised him to keep the dress simple, not too ornate. Hot summer weather was another reason I gave Robert for the money. He didn't approve.

My first thought that morning upon rising was my invitation to tea received the day before. I was surprised to be asked by someone I was not related to. I had kept to my side of the fence, as had Aimee. But speaking to another woman older than my eleven-year old daughter was too tempting. I was rushing about the laundry on the line before a rainstorm, when Aimee invited me over to the fence and gave me a calling card to Cady Pickering's home. Aimee's description of the group was sketchy, but enough was said to know they were called *Ladies Legion* and used terms like "women's inferior status".

I silently agreed that the frustrations I dealt with in this household were less than desirable. I had not questioned my duties before. At least not out loud. No woman had told me before that I was permitted to question this. My mother and then my mother-in-law told me I was a wife and mother first, a woman last. Was it wrong to want more? No, there had to be more than endless chores, with no time for thoughts of my own.

All I knew was that I wanted to know more. What did these ladies intend to change and how, being only women? Did they ever feel like sinners, or that they were doing something wrong, since Robert said men opposed so strongly to their cause? For the first time, I had skimmed through Robert's newspaper that morning, hoping to find clues, but found no articles on this subject.

I amazed myself for wondering such things. How inspiring to realize one's own sentiment! Life was accepted as it came - until now. I had no idea what other women thought, except perhaps my mother, sister, and mother-in-law. Even then, their discussions never touched intimate feelings, or questioned their role in life. I knew my mother-in-law's beliefs best through ladies' books of etiquette, from which she used to quote often. Her favorite was from a copy of *Godey's Lady's Book: Hair is at once the most delicate and lasting of our materials, and survives us like love.*

No wonder I felt unaware. I was born, raised and married within an eight-mile radius.

Yes, born and raised on my parents' dairy farm just on the outskirts of town, the school I attended literally grew as I did, up to grade ten.

The remaining grades of eleven and twelve were academic or technical, designed for the boys' furtherance to college or trade school.

I met Robert in the same shoe store he inherited from his father and then, as Robert's health deteriorated, passed down to our oldest son, Victor. I had just turned sixteen. Robert was twenty-four. Mama introduced him, having met him during her previous visit to town. She insisted I splurge a month's savings on an adorable pair of red velvet slippers, and then shocked me speechless by inviting Robert out for Sunday dinner the next day. I wouldn't have noticed him otherwise, yet after dinner, in whispers to my sister, Opal, I described his eyes as warm chocolate drops. She quite agreed and right then I believed I had met my husband.

That Sunday was his first – and last – courting.

I view the following year, up to our marriage, as a series of callings. Every Sunday afternoon, Robert arrived on my front porch, hat in hand, asking Papa if he could call on me. His mannerism was quiet and courteous, winning Papa's approval as a decent young man with good intentions. His presence alone was enough to win my little sister's heart. Opal gazed up at him as if he were a god. He joined my family for dinner, joined me for a walk in the evening, but alas our lips never joined as I wished they would. There was only a brush of his lips across my cheek as he said goodnight, and off he would ride his horse into the sunset, quite literally.

On many Thursdays, I walked from school to his home for afternoon tea – what became our home - where he lived with his mother. On those days there was still no departing kiss, because his mother never left us alone longer than a trip to the kitchen, reckoning it only appropriate that she chaperone faithfully, reminding us of the neighbors' constant vigil.

Rarely a living day went by for his mother that she didn't remind me the house remained hers. You see, on my wedding day, I simply moved from one parents' home into another. And just as my own mother told me what to do for the first seventeen years, Robert's mother told me what to sew, what to wear, what to cook, and how to clean, until her dying day ten years later.

As I stepped down from the verandah stair, I glanced up at her former bedroom window, the same bedroom where Robert was born, and then his five children.

Life is an endless cycle, his mother had said over the birth of Bess. *Birth, death, rebirth.* She had pointed to her ringed finger. *This wedding ring, this circle, symbolizes this cycle, you know. Endless.* The year before, on the day she died, she reached a trembling hand to me and dropped her thin band into my hand. *First time I've taken this off,* she whispered. *Pass it down to Bess.*

Back then I was so quick to nod, always wanting to please. But pleasing made me feel like I was emptying my vessel into others without allowing me to quench my own thirst first. This last year had helped me slowly evolve into my own woman with her own thoughts. Surely there was more than a ring to pass on to our children?

I recalled this as I hurried next door, refusing to look back, but continued to look down. I knocked on Aimee's door.

The knocking had created quite a stir from inside. Padded feet could be heard running, a dog barked, and children called out to their mother. I peeked through the chipped screen door toward the commotion, and then stood back, embarrassed by my poor manners. My visit was not expected and my mother-in-law would have been aghast. (*Remember how to present yourself in public. You do not wish to become a blot upon nature.*)

I turned to walk back down the porch steps when the front door opened. Only slightly. Aimee remained in its shadow. The screen door stayed closed. Her head peeked around the edge of the door.

"Oh my … Ruby! I had no idea. I thought it was another peddler, was going to send him away."

"Hello Aimee. I must apologize - but your invitation for tea - was it today or …" I felt dreadfully uncomfortable by now. I was not accustomed to visiting outside my home and now on my first social outing in years, I'd already made a discourteous move. I wished to flee but the desire to be steadfast was stronger so that instead I heard myself stammer, "It's the day of the tea, you see. I-I will come back another … or p-perhaps you could come over …"

"Oh no, the tea, of course! You just caught me in an inopportune time is all. A sick child, you see." Aimee waved her arm toward the interior of her home. The curtains were still drawn and the inner room appeared gloomy. Just then her door was opened farther and I saw a young toddler pulling it while reaching toward the screen door. Aimee stepped forward, clearly clad in her nightgown. She snatched her toddler up, scolding "no, no" and retreated back into the shadows.

But not soon enough. I saw Aimee's bruised eye and red swelling on her right cheek.

My stomach twisted. The houses on this street were only ten feet apart; windows opened often year-round to air the coal and gas, the smoke from the fireplaces, and the cooking smells. That's why I had heard a man's shouting voice, loud slaps, and a woman's cries. On one such night, I rose from bed and asked Robert if we could go next door to offer assistance. He refused and forbade me to go.

"This is strictly between a man and his wife," he had insisted. "It is none of our business how he sees appropriate to manage his home."

Aimee held tight to the child squirming to get down. "Another time perhaps. I really should get Anthony out of this draft." Her tone was subdued. Without waiting for an answer she closed the door.

I felt my face blush, decidedly rejected. But then I realized I was on my own and could do as I thought best, better yet, as I wished (odd to think but it seemed that in simply knowing there were women out there thinking more freely, gave me permission to do so, too). I raised my hand to knock again, to offer assistance this time. After all, Robert wasn't here to hold me back. But then I lowered it. Perhaps I was intruding. Hadn't I embarrassed my husband and his mother's spirit enough for one day? Besides, Aimee looked embarrassed enough already. With reluctance, I turned away.

The sun had come out, but I felt as gloomy inside as Aimee's living room. For lack of knowing what to do, I returned home; at least here I knew well enough.

Our front door squeaked like the lid of a coffin. A longing from deep within surfaced and bubbled in my ears like the soapsuds in my wash water. As much for myself as for Aimee was the desire to reach out to a friend. We needed each other. The secretariat against the back wall of the parlor gave me an idea. A note! I would write a note to Aimee and slip it under her door.

With shawl and boots still on, I rushed over to the desk, pulled off my gloves, pulled out the paper and pencil from their cubbyholes, and wrote carefully in my schoolgirl hand, "Dear Aimee, I wish to be your friend. I am only a moment away, if you wish to talk. I've decided to come out into the sunshine. Please join me. Ruby."

I read it twice and hesitated. Before losing my nerve altogether, I folded the paper and walked back to Aimee's door and slipped the paper under. Aimee's parlor windows faced the front, her house being in a similar design to ours, so I hoped that Aimee could see me approaching and might spot the note at once. At any rate, hopefully Aimee would find it before her husband arrived home from work.

I walked along the boardwalk toward home feeling lighter, in at least making an attempt.

Now that I was a free-thinker in its infancy, I became so bold as to actually stop on the street and openly examine the houses there. To the right, past Aimee's house, the cobbled street stretched into a dirt road which if followed for about eight miles led to my family's dairy farm. On my left, the street eventually reached the center of town. At the end of my block was the blacksmith's shop, which was slowly converting into a motor car garage to repair those "mechanical beasts that were invading the town" as Robert expressed it.

I noted very few other changes here the last twelve years; two houses across the street with empty fields on either side; nine houses on my side of the street. All had wood siding painted in white, yellow, or blues; only Robert's home remained in the darker greens and browns, as if sitting there in a bad mood amongst the bright and cheerful. All had wide front porches or covered verandahs, some which wrapped around one side. Fortunate owners decorated their front yards in welcoming flowers and shrubs. I was taught if you're going to work at a garden, make it work for you. Thus only a vegetable garden in the backyard was permitted; my only flowers were lavender bushes along the back yard fence that I dried for oils and sachets.

Construction on these homes had begun some thirty years before, during the building boom following the Civil War. Many who lived here were the original owners, as were my mother-in-law and father-in-law, Margaret and Jonathan Robert Wright. Jonathan had been a cabinetmaker in his living years, and had built all the cabinets and staircases on this street. Our staircase, with its intricate scrolling on the landing post, was the finest in the area, or so my mother-in-law used to tell me (told to her by her husband, no doubt; she wouldn't have known any other way).

I wanted to know if this was true; I wanted to know the intricate details of someone else's life, I wanted to know if other women felt as I did. Surely I couldn't be alone with all these other homes around me.

"If I've come out into the sunshine, I can't very well go back into the shadows, now can I?" I said out loud. I found myself walking past my house toward town.

Why not go to the tea on my own? I will reach out to these ladies as I am asking Aimee to do with me. They may well be the light at the end of my tunnel.

Cady Pickering's home was only a few miles away, the Beauchamp Manor, known to be the town's prettiest. I longed to see its inside. The address was on her calling card.

The sun touched warm on my face and urged me forward into the daylight.

"Ruby, wait!"

I turned to see Aimee running down her steps toward me, her hat in hand, her cape unbuttoned.

"Thank you for the note," Aimee said when she stopped, winded, beside me. She began tucking blonde flyaway curls under her floppy hat, her crystal blue eyes shining. "It was what I needed to get me going. I can't stay hidden forever. And it is a warm sunny day!"

I looked at the hastily applied face powder highlighting the blues and purples, at once feeling happy and sad. The sun may be warm, but it can be harsh.

23

We didn't stop walking or talking for several miles, not until we stopped outside the white gate of a two-story manor.

The vast elegance of this estate was overwhelming in those days. The white-washed colonial brick house gracefully adorned several acres of lawn and gardens. A red brick walkway winded its way to the whitewashed porch, its landing armed on each side with a large white column. Two white wrought iron chairs sat to one side, separated by a matching table displaying a potted geranium.

I halted, intimidated. "Aimee, what is the proper etiquette for a tea nowadays? It will no doubt be a formal one, from the looks of this place. I'm not suitably dressed!" I touched my hair with nervous fingers. "Mercy, I'm so pale! Do I still have dark circles under my eyes? I tried this new hair design this morning, from *Harper's Bazaar* magazine, a Gibson Girl hairdo I think it's called, some sort of pompadour, but my hair is too thick and long, and oh dear, look at the straggly ends coming down!"

"Oh Ruby, you mustn't worry about such things," Aimee said, moving her own frizzed hair away from her eyes. She was slightly out of breath from our fast walk and constant talk about children. "If these women worried about such trivial matters as appearance, they would be society's proper ladies clinging to their own homes, serving tea to other properly behaved wives. That is not the purpose of this tea. Why, I see them as hardy soldiers prepared to fight for their rights as women!" She linked her arm with mine. "Besides, we are all pale this time of year and you have such pretty blue eyes and shiny brown hair, nothing else matters."

This image of soldiers charged me. I hadn't a clue regarding women's rights or the lack thereof, but I willed myself to appear ignorant and ask. One thing I knew for sure; Aimee and her friends would surely understand my own invisible prison. I felt my downturned mouth slowly turn up into my own defiant smile. I lifted my chin and walked up Cady's walkway ready to right my world.

The ladies were assembled in somewhat of a circle so that one could see all. I couldn't say they were unattractive, but there was a certain austerity that seemed to infiltrate into a statement of take-me-as-I-am. The various shapes and design of white blouses and simple black skirts established their uniform of mixed travels, yet all roads led them to this unity. The air about them sang out with a mission. One on the outside had to fight hard not to feel further intimidated. I wiped my clammy hands on my skirt.

I hoped they wouldn't notice these clammy hands, as they shook a how-do-you-do. Their extended hands took me off guard - I had never been offered a handshake before. Was this socially acceptable now among women? It seemed so manly.

Although hosted in various homes, they had an orderly routine that they adhered to, their time together hard earned and must not be squandered. The meeting had come to order when we entered the front parlor. As unassuming as possible, I sat on an overly stuffed sofa colored in rich hues of flower patterns, and sank deeply into its upholstery. It was not easy to sit comfortably in my tight corset, suddenly understanding why my mother-in-law's cushions were less generous. I moved to the edge to straighten my posture and from there I could see the high tin-plated ceiling stamped in diamond patterns. A colored housekeeper delivered to the center table a shiny silver tea tray laden with cookies and small cakes, before joining me on the sofa. I was shocked they allowed her to sit with us, as if she were white.

Soon the sweet tinkle of chatter mixed with teacups was replaced with one voice. That of Cady Pickering. With surprise I recognized Cady as a teacher at my children's school, and wondered why she was not teaching that day.

With teacups quietly resting on our laps, Cady quickly captured the attention of the others. I was awed by Cady's self-confidence. Her tone was neither loud nor overbearing, yet its soft consonants filled the room. She controlled the agenda as a teacher would her classroom. She read from a paper the topics of discussion from their last meeting.

I could not be attentive for long, not with these elaborate surroundings distracting me. I had not seen anything like it. The two vast windows took my breath away. The window dressing was layered in royal blue brocade satin and white sheer under-panels. The matching blue valance was draped and trimmed in tassels and rosettes. The chairs placed under each window were in the same fabric, a marble table and a golden oblong mirror between the two. From my vantage point, I could see beyond the two open doors of the parlor to the main entrance hall's winding staircase. Midway up the stairs, above the landing, was a stained-glass window throwing in rainbows of colors onto the lightly stained wood of rosettes, beading, wainscoting, and spiral spindles.

Suffice it to say that truly my head was fairly spinning, consumed with the overwhelming peculiarity of having tea with these infamous ladies right here in a manor house.

Cady finished reading the paper (I couldn't recall a word of it but noted her hand was trembling). She took a deep breath. "Ladies, it is time we take charge and face our enemies."

My birdbrain still hadn't absorbed the importance of this meeting. I simply noted the perfect postures of Cady and Eunice, their spines not touching the backs of their chairs.

Eunice was as thin and straight as the pen she held poised over clean paper, ready to record today's discussion. Her black hair was parted down the center and brushed back into a tightly rolled bun, her spectacles on the end of her nose giving her a young granny look.

The others waited expectantly as Cady took off her spectacles. She had generous sprinkles of freckles on her hands and face. The small streaks of gray through her light brown hair only added to her persona of wisdom. Her hair hung loosely knotted at her neck, threatening to unfurl. She took a deep breath, eyeing each lady with purpose. "Ladies, we have a dilemma. I must be frank here and say we will be required to gather our strength from within, and from each other. We must move forward from our homes into the light of open scrutiny. We have nothing to be ashamed of. Wrapped in the warmth of camaraderie, we must take a stand."

Her eyes rested briefly on the lady across from her. Phyllis' white hair, further highlighted by the sun's patched rays coming through the parlor windows, gave her a halo. She sat relaxed with knees apart as only Phyllis could get away with and I saw her slightly nod to Cady as if to encourage her to continue. Cady's eyes shifted to the window behind and I recognized the yearning there; that longing to push forward, beyond the walls.

Cady continued, her voice shaking with conviction. "We must stand publicly, or else we all stagnate in our stillness."

The housekeeper, Lizzie began rocking her upper body next to me, humming ever so softly, her dark brown hands resting on her knees, weathered to leather. I recognized the tune, *Shall we gather at the river?* No one else seemed to notice.

Cady paused, clasped her hands together in her lap, and then she smiled. Her tone raised in an announcement. "Ladies, the Women's Rights Convention is now set!"

The humming stopped, Eunice's pen stopped. The rocking chair across from me, occupied by Aimee, stopped.

"When? Where?" Aimee asked, her pink cheeks pinker, a furrow deepening between her eyes. Her finger froze on her temple, where she absent-mindedly twirled a loose blond curl.

"July eighteenth, in the year of our Lord, 1910, right here in our little town of Annan, New York."

Others remained frozen in time.

Cady forged ahead. "Seven o'clock in the evening. I have spoken yesterday with the principle of the Franklin High School, Mr. Whiting. He has graciously agreed to our use of the school auditorium, since the school will of course be closed for the summer holidays. We discussed the afternoon, but as we all know, the auditorium can become very warm. An evening hour should bring us a cooler temperature."

Still, no one dared move.

Placing her left hand on Eunice's back and her right hand on Lizzie's shoulder, Cady leaned forward toward the others as if to bring them closer into a huddle. "If Mr. Whiting, as opposite gender, is willing to take such risks, how much more should be expected of us, as the women whose rights we fight for? We are called to arms, ladies! We must each go forth openly and publicly; even to the point of speaking before an assembly. This convention will permit us to bring our lights out from under our beds and into the open where we may shine and show others the way. We can do it, ladies! You each have unique talents to share!"

At this, I suddenly felt I was back outside looking in. I slightly shook my head. I had no unique talent whatsoever. And public speaking? I hated so much as walking down the church isle to my pew; all those righteous eyes judging my tardiness, or wrinkled clothing, or untidy children.

This did not go without notice; such was the unique talent of Cady. She could look directly into one's heart, as if pinned on one's collar. She gazed at me, heating me to pliable. "You are *all* hardworking women who have learned to work hard with your hands, but long to work hard with your minds. Now here is our chance!"

Cady returned her hands to her lap and leaned back against her chair. She lowered her voice. "I also know that to speak publicly at this convention may create tremendous hardships in your homes. Our battles are not only public but also private. Our husbands and family all voice various levels of opposition to our quest for women's rights; either from a religious perspective where they say women are subservient. Or from a political perspective where they say the Constitution states only men were created equal. Or yet again, from the personal standpoint that the man's position as head of the household is being threatened."

Her voice tapered off here. She sighed, forcing a smile. She waved a hand at the group. "Of course we know none of that is really true. The most important thing here is to believe in what we are doing and speak out boldly. After all, we're not breaking a law. I shall retreat off my soapbox and turn the meeting over to you for discussion." She opened her arms to all. "Please. Open your thoughts."

Lizzie waved her hand toward Cady. "That's right, honey, you got to *believe!*"

"Will repercussions really be that bad?" Aimee blurted out. She looked around the group for help. My heart went out to her - Aimee's husband was enemy enough.

Phyllis raised her hand. "People can be cruel, and I don't know a man that's for it," she said, her bluntness going along with her chipped nails and relaxed posture. "What I recommend is, we test the waters. See how much support we have, before going out into a den of lions. To test I mean to petition. To go out and canvas other women, explain our cause, and ask for their support, their signatures. I've started writing a mission statement to carry door-to-door and I'll bring it to our next meeting."

"Well, perhaps I could …" I said with much hesitancy. I had gone to one neighbor's home today, I could possibly go to more. Maybe these ladies would like me more, too.

Lizzie patted my knee and chuckled. "I said to myself when I saw you there at the door, now here is a little lady who is on a mission!"

"A mission? Well … " My eyes darted around to the others, their return stares making me nervous. I calmed when facing the colored woman's moist brown eyes. "I *am* tired of watching others suffer and yet … I am helpless. I *am* tired of working all day and yet remain … dependent. I *am* tired of sending my children to school, yet *I* feel ignorant. I *am* only a spectator. I'm standing still while everything else is moving around me, watching life through my window."

Cady's head went back in an easy laugh, and to my blushing delight, her hands tapped together in applause. "That was a touching speech and one we must write down to convey at the convention. See how easy it is, ladies? Do not under-estimate yourself. Women can be their own worst enemies." She tilted her head and studied my face, as a teacher might read a student's. "You have talents that only need to be dusted off – "

"And aired out!" I finished, remembering the winter's coal heat and gas lamps. They all laughed and I felt bonded to other adults for the first time in my life. Most of all, I admired Cady and the way her spectacles enlarged her intelligent light brown eyes slightly, eyes that were fully focused on what I had to say, as if what I had to say was important.

But still I feared to commit. Robert would kill me – if he knew.

"Ruby, perhaps I can convince you if I explain our purpose," Cady said. "First, we must work effectively and in a peaceful manner for our cause in the suffrage movement. Secondly, to inform ourselves of our history. If we better understand where we came from, we may have better foresight into where we are going ..."

I'm uncertain as to whether or not I should go into detail here. I believe women should be more aware of their history, yet over the years I find their eyes begin to glaze over when I talk of such things. They become suddenly interested in their child's game or a passing bird. This can become quite frustrating because women have accomplished so much and yet sometimes show so little interest in those outside our inner circle. Perhaps we have too many immediate demands on our presence to pay much attention to past or future.

Let me see if I can summarize efficiently and effectively.

It comes down to this: The first Women's Rights Convention was in 1848 with one of the twelve resolutions in the Declaration of Sentiments being the right to vote. It took us seventy-two years to win that right. Incredible when you think about it, such a basic right really, to be recognized as a person. It still lights my fire to think of it. Only then did we have a voice in improving our rights in education, employment, owning property and our own children ... and even then it took years, or more to the point, is taking years - Bess and Katy can tell you better than I – no Equal Rights Amendment has been passed. Perhaps when Jesi reads this history – where was I?

Oh and in marriage, think of it! In my time, men had the absolute authority. Unfortunately they were not required to prove they were fit to be trusted with absolute power in marriage, as they might be in other institutions. There are different grades of good and bad men and if a woman marries a good and loving man, she will not suffer abuse of power. But if she marries a bad one, she has no escape from his brutality. Law does not punish for domestic oppression.

You might ask, "Then why get married at all?" Well, think of it. Marriage was the only choice for so many, for without our own education and profession, we remained dependent on a man's income, whether that be our father, brother, or husband.

I remember my naivety in asking Cady in this first meeting, "Why won't men let us vote? It seems harmless enough."

She explained that the main challenge was our politicians. Many opposed women voting, for it simply complicated their agenda and here was why. To win a vote, they must address issues that the voters are concerned with. Women are concerned with issues that can be quite different than men's, such as better education and cleaner schools for their children, purer meat and food processing, and child labor. Women are the ones who make the choices in raising children and preparing food, so naturally they are the experts. But men do not know enough about these issues to lobby for them so they had the power to treat them as trivial.

That's when Lizzie said, "That's why we're here, honey! To speak out for what we believe in! When Lincoln freed the colored folk, he forgot about the women folk!"

At any rate, that afternoon tea was how it all started for me. Those precious friends added a log to my smoldering fire and I'm proud to say it's not out yet.

Speaking of domestic oppression in marriage, I shall tell you what happened on my return home that eventful day. Trouble started when the Ladies Tea ended. That was when I met Bess's future husband, Thomas Pickering. A slender, handsome gentleman in a light linen suit, with careless blond hair falling onto his forehead, entered the parlor smiling broadly. He called out, "Where's my lovely wife?" and went straight-way to Cady, who stood instantly and smiled just as broadly back, both clearly happy to see the other. Thomas offered to drive Aimee and I home, since we lived farthest away. He explained that the water boiler in his new steam automobile was adequately heated from his drive home and would be a cinch to restart. Aimee hastily declined stating she had other errands to run, and ran down the walkway like a frightened rabbit. However I wasn't that wise and had become aware that there was insufficient time to walk the distance before the children and Robert arrived home.

Thomas ran ahead of me to his car like a child being let out to play, obviously eager for an opportunity to drive his carriage again.

This was my second reason for accepting his offer: I had never been in a horseless carriage before. I thought, *What a perfect way to end a perfect day.* Mercy.

He stroked the hood of the big black machine as he waited for me. "I named her Fizzie," he stated proudly, "because of the hisssssing noisssse the boiler makesss. Just like a woman, eh?" He chuckled at his use of words as he opened the door for me, and then he disappeared under the hood. A moment later he trotted around to the driver's side and slid in behind the wheel. He clutched the large metal steering wheel and looked over at me with green eyes and a white smile.

"Isn't she a beauty?" he asked.

"Yes indeed!" I nodded, looking around the interior, inhaling strong scents of oil and leather. The two tiny round dials meant nothing to me, but the heavy frame and padded seat made me feel quite safe. I would explain this to Robert. I settled my handbag in my lap and folded my gloved hands on top, prepared for the adventure. When I told him this was my first, he said, "Well, then, we shall take the scenic route!" He released the brake and the carriage jerked forward.

The worry and regret came rushing at me head-on. Robert would wholly disapprove if he knew I was alone with another man, and he would be outraged to discover the drive was in a steam carriage. He was convinced this new invention was a four-wheeled cannon, likely to explode at any given moment, killing its unfortunate cargo. We had no means of transportation, excepting our God-given legs. Not since our old mare, Blacky, was retired to pasture on the dairy farm. Blacky was employed on the daily milk run, first by my father and then by my brother. After many hard years of labor, she was replaced by a younger mare, and thus given to Robert and I to hitch to our small old buggy, another remnant from Robert's mother. Blacky was kept in the stable behind our house, accessed by a dirt alley in the back that ran parallel to our front street. Robert decided the cost of the feed did not equate to the need of the horse. Blacky was given tearful goodbye hugs from the children, and I was given promises of new transportation by Robert. That was two years and many walking miles of shoe leather ago. "I mend shoes," Robert had said. "What is the problem?"

Thomas recognized my furrowed brow I do believe. He patted the dashboard affectionately. "This lovely lady will have you home in moments - under the control of these steady hands!" He raised his leather-gloved hands as proof of his strength.

As he pulled out onto the bricked street, I turned and waved at Cady. She had remained standing on her front porch, the home's slate blue shutters and inner lighting framed around her, the potted geranium beside her. The dusk gave it soft dream-like colors.

"You ladies must have cheered the ol' girl substantially!" Thomas said as he slowly manoeuvred around a plodding horse and carriage. "She felt quite poorly when I left this morning. I came home early to check on her and here she is having tea, smiling brightly."

I looked at him in dismay. "Oh I had no idea! She never mentioned any such thing." I shouted, or so it seemed, in order to be heard above the motor's noise.

"Nor would she. She rarely complains." Thomas waved it off. "Nor does this girl."

I looked to see whom he was talking about.

"Her performance is astonishing going as fast as a galloping horse, when I can find a long paved road. I hope the roads improve soon, but I recently did some research and wrote an article for the newspaper saying there are only about eight thousand automobiles out there and only about one hundred miles of road so far. She'll have to settle for town roads for now."

It seemed to take many years before folks stopped referring to their motor cars as another species, like a winning racehorse, as if still needing that attachment to flesh and blood.

"So, are you joining my wife in her crusade?" He turned and looked at me intently until I pointed ahead. He saw my concern and suddenly swerved around a bicycle.

"It's safe to say yes with me," he continued, noting my hesitation. "If women aren't 'for the people, by the people', then what are they? But I'm the lone wolf in this town. Jump on the wagon and give her a hand; she needs the help."

Admittedly, it was this man's endorsement that made it valid and made up my simple woman's mind. I prayed Robert would be as understanding. I nodded in acceptance, my attention more on the road.

I can still recall my fascination in watching the houses and people go by at such a swift pace. It appeared we were pulling up in front of my house in the blink of an eye.

I reached out and patted the dashboard approvingly. "Good girl! Thank you so much. It was quite delightful!"

"My pleasure, my pleasure!" Thomas remained grinning like a Cheshire cat.

I found the door handle and pulled it gingerly but not enough. He reached across me and pulled the handle harder, simultaneously pushing the door open. His arm brushed across my breast and I held in my breath to give more space between, my face feeling hot. He appeared not to notice. I quickly turned my back to him and lifting my skirt above my boots, stepped out onto the cobblestones.

As I straightened, I saw my husband walking toward me, still a few houses away. We both froze as one spotted the other. Before I could gather my thoughts enough to ask Thomas to wait for introductions, he had closed the door behind me and drove off. I listened to the engine fading away, longing to be back inside its safety shield with someone with happy thoughts. Robert was not happy. He adjusted his collar and then resumed his approach. I did not take my eyes from him. Like a trapped raccoon, I stood wide-eyed and waited.

He glanced around to see if neighbors were peering from their windows. "Come inside now!" he hissed. He turned on his heel and headed toward the front door.

I followed his brown suit silently; sorry to leave the warmth and laughter behind me and enter the dark anger Robert would fill the house with.

He loosened his necktie and paced the parlor. I tried to appear calm and composed but my hands shook as I hung my shawl on its hook in the entranceway. I had learned it best to say nothing so I headed toward the kitchen to begin supper. I tensed as I walked past him.

In the doorway, he grabbed my arm.

He jerked me to him and brought his face close, nose almost touching mine, eyes as hard as dried mud. "I will not give you the courtesy to explain yourself, woman!" he spat between clenched teeth.

With his other hand, he reached down and unbuckled his belt and pulled it from around his trousers. I instinctively pulled back, trying to get out of his steel grip, but the grip only tightened. He being only a few inches taller than my five-foot frame, I was surprised at his strength.

"Oh, Robert, please, the children are expected home any moment!"

He eyed the parlor window with slanted eyes and for the first time ever, he looked like a mad man.

I truly became frightened of him. He had whipped the children in this manner and I had tended to their bruised legs, but of course I was not a child and felt deeply humiliated that he treated me, his wife, the same way. I had always tried to be obedient after he had successfully "put me in my place" by a face slap early in our marriage, and such punishment hadn't been necessary.

But then I had never ventured out on my own before without his permission.

His hesitation allowed me to try again. "Robert, please don't let them see us like this!"

There were no children in sight and he looked at me accusingly, as if I was trying to trick him.

He swung out the belt and brought it back hard against the back of my legs. He struck again and again, emphasizing with each strike, each word, "Don't....you....ever....disobey....me....again!"

Each time I stifled a cry, each time I tried to break free of his grip on my arm, but it did no good. The folds of my skirt and petticoat prevented serious pain; nonetheless I felt my body shrinking inch by inch with each strike, until I became very small and worthless. He pushed me away then, and I collapsed onto the floor.

I watched him tread heavily into the dining room, clenching and unclenching his fists. The belt landed loudly on the floor, as if he'd killed a snake and couldn't tolerate touching it. He stood there for a moment, breathing deeply through his nostrils, and then returned to where I sat in a small heap. I flinched when I felt his hands come under my armpits from behind. He lifted me to my feet. I kept my back to him as I wiped my eyes with the back of my hands. I straightened my spine and walked silently into the kitchen to return to my duties.

Bess, that is as far as I can go for now. I don't know where this is going; I've walked backward into the past before and it always leaves me feeling as if I've lost my way. I know too well that if you keep looking behind you, you forget where you are going. Writing this has upset me and I shall lie down for a rest while you, Katy and Jesi finish your Chapter Ones. I'm feeling quite looped from the wine (is "looped" the appropriate word here?)

Be happy,
Your Mama

Bess's Chapter One -- December 1963

What is happiness?

Yes, Mama, I realize I'm supposed to be happy. I've heard that all my life and I did my best to please you. For a woman who claims to be powerless, you've had incredible influence on those around you.

My year of awakening began when I saw that you had that power, that deep root in home and family, and I felt no more than tumbleweed. I had imagined you and me marching side by side down Main Street but once again you weren't there, with Papa your usual excuse. Your fifth child is born and that is that. Push me out into the world and that is that. All of a sudden Papa is your main focus and for years, until he became bedridden, you spoke rarely about the suffrage movement, and then, only in low tones, as if talking about sex.

I found myself instead in Tennessee, with an ending and a beginning. For it was there where we won the women's war on suffrage but I lost some common sense. What happened after that changed my ways, my life, my love, and began my year of awakening.

So much happened in such a short time and I have the right to blame Mama for much of it. After all, it was her shameful sin that I have to wear. Let these writings reveal it.

Katy my daughter, I realize I am at times considered cold. Perhaps even in today's terms, a bitch, yes, Jesi? In reading this, you'll understand why. Believe it or not I was far worse in my younger years. Yet I discovered a womanly side to me - dare I say sensual? - that I'll reveal when the time is appropriate.

Remember, Mama, you were the first to open *that* chamber door.

But before I begin, you must understand: Women didn't have much choice in those days, since the war, World War I that is, had picked off men - including my beau, Billy - like lined ducks in a shooting gallery. Remember, too, that I was heartsick at the time. I believed Billy's spirit sat there on top of my heart slowly squeezing it down into a thin slice of liver. Or so I thought at the time. I was to learn differently during that year.

I firmly believe it's important to document our years of awakening, and I hope that much will be revealed, and questions will be answered. And now, after reading Mama's explicit first chapter, I've decided to do so without reservation, without attempting cuts that may embarrass me or upset Mama. For what is a smile when teeth are missing, regardless how genuine? You'd only remember that there were gaps.

Yes, Mama, I will shock you with what I have to tell, but my daughter and granddaughter should know their roots and I could never speak of such things. I can write it, though, I can write it all. And I can hope *you're* happy with this.

1920
Summer

August; Tennessee. Floating along in the movement for nine years, I suddenly found myself in the rapids and having to dog-paddle fast.

I had just returned from a march in Rochester and owed notes of gratitude to the Mayor and police chief for ensuring a peaceful demonstration. They were not always so, but the last several months were bringing about less animosity, or at least more apathy, toward our cause. Our constant display was no longer a novelty and we either received quiet support, or silent scorn. But apathy from your enemies is your best defense, I learned. We had reached new heights when no one was looking, and it became more difficult for the anti-suffragists to bring us back down. States were ratifying the

Nineteenth Amendment that would guarantee women the right to vote in all elections, and I had spent countless hours traveling to meet with state legislators and writing letters to state government representatives.

Endless ... and then suddenly it came down to thirty-five states had ratified and thirty-six were needed to pass the amendment and Tennessee's vote was due, and the telegram came. We descended on Nashville en masse.

Eunice was there at the Nashville train station as promised by our suffrage leader, Mrs. Carrie Chapman Catt. And, as expected, Eunice appeared solemn and stern, severe bun and the part in her gray hair so straight as to look painful. She had been part of Mama's original *Ladies Legion* and Mama had told me years ago that Eunice was a divorced woman whose two children were lost to her husband's custody. But this slice of her life did not fit into her demeanor at all and I always pondered this when in her presence. She never spoke of this part of her past with me, but then her divorce was more than ten years before, and her children would be grown by now. No, Eunice did not look like a mother, but could only be imagined with pen and paper in hand, not holding a child's hand. These thoughts were only my own, of course.

We arrived in front of the State Legislature building amidst a mass of people, motor cars, horses, policemen, reporters, cameras - utter chaos. The street was packed with sounds, smells, and slogans. The sultry air was charged with rumors flashing like lightening. Everyone jostled and pushed, verbally pummeling each other. The anti-suffragists had also flooded into Nashville to lobby the General Assembly and they took their mandate as seriously as we suffragists did. Eunice and fellow suffragists who had arrived a few days earlier had been lobbying, passing out flyers, meeting with reporters, and ultimately in the face of anyone showing the slightest bit of interest.

We squeezed our way through until we reached inside the large hall. There by the door, tables were displayed, suffrage and the anti-suffrage, yellow roses on one, red roses on the other. The signs told me readily which I should choose and a yellow rose was pinned to my jacket lapel. Those wearing the red glared at me openly, as I did them. Black looks were part of the warfare yet I found it ridiculous and ironic that those I glared at were women like myself, but were misled into believing that suffrage - meaning the right to vote - was not in their best interest. Ignorant women!

Eunice led me to our suffragist leader, Mrs. Catt, waiting outside the Senate chamber with many others of our own. Mrs. Catt was noticeably nervous, her exact measures of calm and strength almost visibly quivering. Her smile came and went as she shook my hand too firmly, thanked me for coming and then stated, with some deprivation in her tone that this moment was exactly why she did not rejoice when the Nineteenth Amendment was passed by the House and Senate.

"They are in a tie, ladies. Many of the legislators on our side have fled the coop, either out of town, or to the opposition. The anti's knew this and moved to table the Amendment, thinking their votes would win, but they had miscounted. The political maneuvering is continuing amongst them and then they shall vote again. All we can do is stand helplessly to the side and wait."

And that is what we did. We entered the side door to the engorged chamber, two hundred men or so sitting or standing in its center, the woman's future in their arena. Lines of women standing around its periphery, out of bounds, out of control. We watched, whispered, and waited while these well-suited gentlemen, their lapelled roses picking sides, waved their arms high, while keeping their voices low, mingling, meshing, speaking their superior minds. It appeared from where I stood, that the red roses prevailed. I could understand the anti's rationale that they had more than a chance.

"We are in for a fine agitation," I said and Mrs. Catt and Eunice tittered stiffly at my timely usage of Susan B. Anthony's popular quote.

"Yes, indeed we – " Mrs. Catt moved aside as much as possible to allow a gentleman into our tiny circle, people bumping our backsides. "Miss Wright, let me introduce you to Mr. Jere Phillips. Jere has proven to be an excellent activist on our behalf, as well as my driver and protector years ago. Mr. Phillips, this is our fellow warrior, Miss Wright."

"Proud to meet you, ma'am."

I nodded and forced a smile, not particularly wanting a stranger, and a man at that, standing in such close proximity to me at such a moment that I may wish to cry or display myself foolishly, depending on the vote. The lighting being poor behind the massive pillar where we stood caused his face to be shadowed, but his wide smile looked friendly enough.

"Mr. Phillips, by your accent, you must be from 'around these parts' as they say?"

"That's right, ma'am. Just an hour's drive up into the hills, when my truck's running alright. Hard to believe now. It wasn't that long ago, a trip like this by horse was nigh on a full day."

He stood a foot taller than most men with hair longer than most and tucked behind his ears. He seemed to notice our disadvantaged heights as he looked at our heads and then toward the center of the chamber, many people in between. "Ladies, why don't we poke on up to the second floor balcony, where we can look down on these politicians for a change?"

Mrs. Catt agreed and we spent too much precious time weaving our way up to a space along the balustrade. We arrived just as someone from below was banging a gavel, ordering that the meeting is now in session. I watched them, while Mr. Phillips watched me. Finally I turned to him and said, "Sir, you are staring." I noticed then his distinct Indian features, with skin darkened by more than the sun, black hair penciled thinly with silver.

He blinked several times as if clearing his mind. "Sorry, ma'am, but you look very familiar to me. What did you say your name was?"

"Miss Bess Wright. And I don't know you, sir. Nor do I wish to." I turned back toward the proceedings thinking what unusually blue eyes he had. *The better to see you with my dear,* said the wolf. Well, I knew the outcome of that story and this wolf was not going to come close enough to eat me. I had fought off big bad wolves before.

The fateful roll call began, and I truly tried to concentrate, but Mr. Phillips would turn his attention to below, then back to me, then to below, and then – well it totally distracted me, him standing so close beside me and making his attention so obvious. I felt my face flush and become increasingly warm, to the point that perspiration rolled down my neck, behind my ear. I stepped back and behind Mrs. Catt. Soon enough Eunice turned and gripped my arm.

"Oh my God, Bess," she hissed. "It's tied with one vote to go!"

I stepped back up to my place at the balustrade – oh, this is all still so vivid to me! - and watched below as a very young-looking man stood up to a hushed audience. He turned toward me and I gripped the railing – he wore a red rose! Oh no, it can't be! A lady and gentleman standing amongst our small upper mass of anxious spectators hugged one another in anticipated celebration, crushing their wilted red roses, I hoped fervently. The tiebreaker below us said nothing for what seemed like ages and then patted his breast pocket.

"What is your vote for the state of Tennessee to ratify the Nineteenth Amendment, Mr. Burn?" The speaker called out. "Do you vote yes or no?"

Mr. Burn cleared his throat. "I vote yes."

Such an uproar around us and below us! I couldn't believe it at first, until those closest to me, Mrs. Catt, Eunice, Mr. Phillips, were hugging each other and me. Mrs. Catt looked happiest of all, tears flowing freely, all reserve gone for now, declaring that every day of her forty years of fighting for this had been worth it, for this very moment. "Now I can truly rejoice!" she cried. Many others were approaching Mrs. Catt to congratulate, to extend their appreciation to her. I was so happy to be a part of this that I simply returned the kiss that Mr. Phillips planted fully on my mouth. He appeared as elated as Eunice and I, and I didn't understand his connection to all this, but at that moment it didn't matter.

The Nineteenth Amendment had become law. Mr. Burn's vote ended seventy-two years of aching struggle and Mrs. Catt told him so some hours later, on the steps outside the building. Mr. Burn seemed a cautious sort, but was obviously impressed by Mrs. Catt. He patted her on the shoulder and with a boyish grin said, "Please. Call me Harry." He brought out a letter from his breast pocket. "I know that a mother's advice is always the safest for a boy to follow." He read a portion of this letter to us: "'Dear Son, vote for suffrage and do not keep them in doubt. I know some of the speeches against and they are very bitter.'"

Bitter indeed and I saw the anti-suffrage movement continue to delay official ratification for several days through their legal tricks and by holding massive anti-suffrage rallies. We stayed away from this and from the Hermitage Hotel where many were posted there on sentinel duty in the front lobby.

Instead, we worked around the anti's noise, as a farmer might in the midst of a thunderstorm. We knew the rain would desist soon and the sun would come back out. It did when Tennessee reaffirmed its vote, and on August twenty-sixth, 1920, the Nineteenth Amendment was officially added to the U.S. Constitution.

We attended celebratory parties and dinners for several days, with Mr. Phillips as our escort and transportation. He seemed humble and appreciative of my attention to him, which I tried to limit, but he was persistent and at times irresistible with his chatty charm. I was not aware I was heading into his snare until it was too late.

One such night we met in the dining room of Mrs. Murphy's boarding house where Eunice and I shared a room. A glowing evening, with candles and festive spirits and hearty laughter. The more generous the pouring of Mrs. Murphy's prohibited port (this was during the Prohibition Days), the more funny things seemed. Mr. Phillips had joined us for dinner and he came suitably dressed in a black deacon's coat, matching trousers, and a clean white shirt. I would even go so far as to say he was handsome with those piercing blue eyes (even though his age must've been around forty at that time). Eunice surprised us all by being quite coquettish. Something about Mr. Phillips' down-to-earth friendly banter eased her ramrod posture and by dessert she was leaning over her plate with napkin to her mouth, squealing in delight to Mr. Phillips' stories, strands of hair enjoying this moment of slack in gaily dangling about her ears.

He and his brothers were pranksters in their younger days, Mr. Phillips told his captive audience, and they showed no mercy to one another.

"We loved to play cowboys and Indians. But us being half-Cherokee, we all wanted to be Indians, which of course can't be because then you don't have anyone to shoot at. So I made up a contest ..." And so on and on he went, quite open really, a man being most charming when in a self-deprecating way. The evening filled with such stories and I admit I got caught up in it.

Upon retiring to my room, it suddenly struck me - too late I might add - that the ladies had not shared their own stories, stories of marches and picket lines and why we were celebrating in the first place. We had allowed a man to dominate the women's victory! Did we need the man's spark to warm and relax us? I pondered this for some time that night.

Mr. Phillips appeared on my doorstep early the next morning with the day's newspaper. A picture of Alice Paul, president of the National Woman's Party, appeared on the front page, draping a flag from her balcony in Washington DC. The thirty-sixth star, representing Tennessee, had been added to the thirty-five others that she had sewn on as each state ratified the Nineteenth Amendment. I longed to be there to celebrate with her in the nation's capital. There was where the heart of the matter was; victory removed government road-blocks placed in front of suffrage for the forty-five years the amendment had been repeatedly reintroduced to Senate committees. The heartbeat there must have been deafening! Nashville lacked the luster I needed to radiate, as I sat with Mr. Phillips on the front porch swing reading the paper together. Other newspaper articles were local, and praise and ridicule focused on Harry Burn much more so than on the successes of women suffrage leaders. "Please spare me this boring diatribe," I said with a yawn.

I became increasingly restless and fidgety, which Mr. Phillips clearly noticed. Would I like to go horseback riding, he asked? I said no, thank you. Mrs. Catt would want me to write letters, and newspaper articles for Annan's paper but she betrayed me by saying, "Take a day off, you're working too hard. Lighten up and stop being so testy!" I forgave her by knowing she remained elevated in victory and would soon enough return to earth and assign tedious tasks to me, so I took the day to play and soon found myself on a prancing mare heading toward the meadows. Mrs. Murphy's picnic lunch bounced on the side of the saddle, her twinkling and winking eyes still fresh in my mind as she pointed out to Mr. Phillips that she had made his favorite cornbread - highly unusual with her being such a rotten cook. They were all in on this, I believe, to get me and my snapping judgments out of the house. Well, all but one.

I suspected Eunice had hoped to be the one on this horse. Strangely this made Mr. Phillips more appealing to me. I'm certain my smug smile said so. This smile increased with the warm breezes and cloudless sky. I hadn't been in a saddle since my teen years; there was little or no need of these or their attached buggies, what with the regular supply of motor cars now. The sense of freedom one has when riding such a powerful animal flowed through me, and combined with liberation in winning the vote, gave me exhilaration hard to describe. Mr. Phillips apparently interpreted this as enjoying his company and was inspired to kiss me while finishing our picnic lunch. I returned the kiss; why not? His soft lips were warm and comforting. Relaxed and basking under the sun and under his tender gaze, I laughed with carefree abandon at his anecdotes and leaned back on my elbows looking up at the blue, blue sky and Mr. Phillips' blue, blue eyes. He was quite charming in that confidant male sort of easy manner I've always envied.

I had come so far as to appreciate the deep creases around his eyes and mouth as more like decisive lines of wisdom, a man of purpose. The most pleasant surprise and one that drew me close to his side was that not only had he been Mrs. Catt's protector and driver for several years while she traveled through many states on behalf of suffrage, but he appeared as her speaker at many of the lecture halls, assemblies and women's conventions. He articulated very well that being half-Cherokee made him understand what it was like being in a minority, with prejudices being assumed because of how you were born into the world, be it race or sex. I felt thrilled to find this camaraderie in a man.

I had nothing to lose in indeed enjoying his company and I let my barriers down, guardedly at first, yet without reservation by the end of the day. Soon I was telling him my own stories, just as I thought I should have done the night before. He listened carefully with a tilt of his head, eyes focused on my face as if each word had significant meaning. I had not been so open since Billy and it felt liberating to just chatter! Another meeting of the lips and this time I closed my eyes and allowed the kiss to linger with a sense of a new open-mindedness in a freethinking world. So many tingling counter emotions ran through me: to hold him or to run freely through the meadow; to kiss him again or to prattle; to speak of emotions or to talk more on politics. My reserved nature won out and politics were exhausted. He was good-natured about it all and seemed to take whatever the day and I had to offer. Much later than anticipated, we were on our way back to town, both expressing what an enjoyable day it had been.

The early evening hour found him again at our doorstep with hat in hand, here for supper again, invited by Mrs. Murphy. She fussed around him as if he was head of the household and Mrs. Catt made it clear she thought the world of him. I told myself I was outnumbered and did not tell him to go away.

Mr. Phillips noticeably grew under this praise, as a plant would when placed in the sun with moist soil. Their attention and Eunice's pining gaze further bowed my thoughts of him to a positive way, neglecting the negative view I had carefully fostered of men. Wasn't it time I moved on with my life? I rationalized. The war of women was over. When men ended a war, they returned to home and hearth. Where was I to go? My title and rank of suffragist was no longer valid or necessary. My home base, the Lighthouse, served only a wayward station; abused women came there in transit to decide what to do and where to go. It was never intended to be a permanent residence for anyone. Not even the homeowner, Thomas, actually lived there (not since his wife, Cady, died anyway) but only checked in periodically.

And I would certainly be too old to return to my parents' house. I would feel as a failure – worse yet, Papa would view me as a failure. He once told me I wanted only romance, not responsibility. "What is wrong with romance?" I challenged. Mama lowered my raised eyebrows with, "You have to work in the dirt, to get the flowers." I supposed they were right. I needed to settle, to root; I needed a home and a hearth of my own.

These were my thoughts as Mr. Phillips proposed to me late that starry evening on the front porch, and I said yes.

What is love?

At this point and for the first time in my life, I questioned my intelligence. I knew not where we were, where we were going, and knew little of this man I was to call husband. He knew little of his reluctant bride. I had told no one of our plan to marry, but only made excuses to Mrs. Catt and Eunice during my farewells at the station that I would take a later train to Annan. Mr. Phillips must have wondered why this secrecy but he remained silent, only his searching eyes and deep parenthesis around his down-turned mouth expressing his disappointment.

I didn't wish to make a big deal out of buying rings and so I had insisted on him slipping my grandmother's wedding ring on my finger – the same ring I had previously worn on a chain around my neck.

I did not try to analyze but merely recognize that a clandestine and unceremonious marriage at the courthouse was important to me, exciting in the beginning, frightening in the end when I realized the price to pay was that no one knew where I was any more than I did. I was completely on my own.

If someone had asked me for directions, I might have said, "Turn left, and head straight up toward heaven". Although heaven sounds misleading, for I didn't think it was heaven at all. Not in the joyful way one would think of heaven, but this plateau on the top of a mountain was "pert-near" as the mountain folk would say, close enough certainly to wave to those who had passed on to that heavenly shore.

Below us were endless rolls of hills, like giant men with fat bellies, stretched out and snoring clouds of mist.

I looked about me as I climbed down from the truck, wondering where the cabin could be in this wilderness and worried that the truck hood would blow off from all that steam rolling out around the edges. Mr. Phillips fanned the hood with his hat as if shooing a large black fly that wouldn't go away. Fortunately it didn't; I would have detested the three-mile hike back down to the main road. I stood and waited impatiently for further directions, seeing no further road.

Finally I could stand no more of the hot sun and the heated truck. "Really, Mr. Phillips, this is a poor sign of hospitality. What are we to do from here – hitch a ride on a passing deer?" Sarcasm yes, but justified; the startled deer was the only living being I'd seen for several miles.

He walked to the back of the truck. "This is where we hoof it." He pulled out my trunk and headed toward a small path, a dirt line marking the way further up through the trees.

Not knowing what else to do, I grabbed my handbag and stepped in behind him, marching in step as I had done many a time down many a street for a cause. I just didn't know what that cause was this time, however it came to light soon enough.

We walked through last year's leaves, swishing noisily, grateful I became for the cool shade offered by the birch and maple trees. After a few hundred feet I could hike no more of the uphill climb. My heart knocked loudly on my chest wall and the heat threatened my face. I stopped. There to my left, sticking up behind a small crest was a red-bricked chimney. Curiosity overcame my shortness of breath, shuffling me forward.

On a plateau some feet below where I stood, sat a quaint sort of log cabin. A porch protecting its humble faded-gray front, had been painted in red to match the window shutters. A large well-tended garden stretched out to the right of the cabin, framed in cedar fencing. A clothesline connected the left side of the cabin to a shed of some sort, too small for a barn, too large for a tool shed. This structure leaned toward the clothesline, as if the weight of the many garments hanging there was more than it could bear. Spread out here and there on the grass laid bleached sheets, towels and rags, appearing as if spring's thaw hadn't finished yet. Blotches of white bright light caught my eye from the sun's reflection on a creek flowing behind the cabin. Rows of lavender bushes lined the aged cedar fencing around the shed and along the side of the cabin, stirring a little homesickness for my mama's backyard with its long row of lavender along the white picket fence. Here, somehow, around the wild of woods and daisies, the planted purple blooms looked out of place to me, like a prop on the stage of a play.

As Mr. Phillips headed down the slope toward them, children of various ages and sizes, feet bare, dogs nipping at their heels, were running toward Mr. Phillips calling "Daddy, Daddy!" In the center of all this remained one girl in her teen years, standing at the fire pit in the front yard, her sad face gazing over at her daddy, then up to me, then quickly back down to the black pot hitched over the fire.

I saw all this from my elevated vantage point, remaining observant as if I were here only to enquire, and then walk away to write a newspaper story.

Mr. Phillips called me down to meet them all, seven children there were, or at least he called them his "kids", yet two of the boys looked older than I. The girl at the pot appeared younger but obviously in charge. Petite in her torso, unusually broad shoulders, and her arms were visibly muscular in her short-sleeved calico housedress. She simply nodded when introduced as Mary Sue, and only then pulled her frown from me to a younger brother when he shouted, "She's the bossiest!"

Mary Sue's first words were "Daddy, the pig's tail stopped curling."

To Mr. Phillips these words meant something significant; to me this was a sign that I was someone Mary Sue didn't want to reckon with.

He paused in his tickling a toddler and scowled at Mary Sue. "How long?"

49

"Loooong," she drawled. "You been gone a long time." She met his eyes and then quickly diverted her sad light blue ones to the pot. Inside this, laundry soaked and she stirred this with a broomstick. She had my sympathy. Without the aid of today's machinery and electricity, laundry for seven children would be a burdensome task.

He released his hold on two young ones, picked up a crawling toddler he called "Ruby", and approached Mary Sue. "Two weeks is not a long time, honey. And I stayed here two nights of it."

She brought the broomstick out, thick with dripping white garments like boiled noodles and dropped these into another pot of clean water. "I was asleep when you came in at night, I was asleep when you left the next morning." She said this in a monotone voice, her face void of emotion.

"Well, now, whose fault is that?" Mr. Phillips asked her, his scowl deepening. "Besides, I just wanted to make sure everything was alright. And it was. You and the boys look after things just fine." He reached over and pulled me over to stand beside him. "And now I'm back for good and with a new mommy for you. That should make you happy, Mary Sue."

That was my first indication that he hadn't told his children beforehand about me. I wasn't the only one who had held this knowledge in the dark, uneasy that exposure would show the cracks and flaws. They were handling it well, as if it were to be expected along with bad weather.

Mary Sue shaved lye soap into the boiling pot of water. She was either concentrating or ignoring, her expression difficult to read. "Hey you two!" she called out as two boys ran by her in chase. "Help me wring these out and then go pour this rinse water on the flower bed. And don't forget after supper to come out and pour this hot soapy water onto the porch so I can give it a good scrubbing."

Mr. Phillips sighed. "I'm going to go check on the pig to see why it's sick, I guess. One of you boys take Bess's trunk to Daddy's bedroom. Bess go on in and make yourself at home, I'll be in directly and Mary Sue can cook us up some green beans and new potatoes fresh from our garden."

He squeezed my elbow and smiled that bright smile of his until I bared my own teeth. That was the best I could do. I had convinced myself that I was accustomed to large families; my aunt Opal and her eight children, my uncle Jesse with his six boys, a woman would find her way to the Lighthouse with her long line of ducklings trailing behind her ... but this ...

The worst of it was, I was afraid to think. Thinking created questions and I was already in way over my head, and questions would only prove that. As a sleepwalker might, I aimed numbly toward the front porch, toward some unknown goal, something inside me hoping I'd wake up.

I did wake up but at the most inopportune moment, for it was just before bedtime.

The four boys had gone up the narrow staircase to their attic beds; the three girls were in the next room, their shared bedroom, whispering and giggling loudly. I was exhausted – 'dog-tired' I was told - and completely ill at ease as to what to do. The flurry of events leading up to this moment had (at last!) quieted and I sat with my own thoughts on the edge of Mr. Phillips' bed.

In my mind's eye seven children's heads surfaced from dirty bath water; crying, crawling, needling, runny noses, arguing, pushing, and one talking over another. I saw again Mary Sue's helpless expression as she attempted to keep these four small rooms and the attic clean.

Supper involved a long process of stoking fire in a horribly old-fashioned stove I hadn't seen the likes of in years, snapping beans, peeling mounds of potatoes. They had exactly eight chairs crowding around the pine kitchen table and thus a bumpy armchair with exposed stuffing was dragged from the front room into the kitchen where I was forced to sit as 'New Mommy', my chin only a few inches above my bowl of beans. I thought this chair befitting to my situation - I was out of place. Washing supper dishes passed to the children, but I had a sinking suspicion this was only because I was new.

The second part of my New Mommy title would bring great expectations tomorrow. They didn't understand how invalid this was - I could not be a 'Mommy', but a parody of one. I couldn't begin to guess where to begin as I was thrust into the middle of these lives. How could I go forward with them if I didn't know where they've been? Heavy thuds from the upper floor persisted, matching my aching head. If he – if we – were man and wife, he would expect marital relations, but that would bring more children. How would seven others of different blood treat mine? I was twenty-one; suddenly, clearly, too young to begin … such painful nonsense! And it would be painful. I'd heard too many pitiful stories at the Lighthouse from battered women of abusive husbands. I had helped deliver my baby sister, Little Cady, and had seen the seizures of pain and surges of blood, only to witness her death a year later. I would not subject myself to this!

These were my thoughts as Mr. Phillips came into the bedroom from the washbowl on the back porch. His hair hung wet and loose, framing his face, and he smelled of soap. His white shirt now off, he wore only a leather vest and trousers showing off his tanned muscular arms. His bare feet frightened me the most.

I stood up quickly, as if the bed had caught fire. I backed away from his outstretched arms and slow easy grin.

"Come here, honey," he said in a low, playful tone.

"Don't touch me!"

He stopped and dropped his arms. "What's wrong? What happened?" He looked around for some concealed child, but finding none, returned a confused gaze at me. "You're frightened of me, Bess?"

"No, I-I'm just not ready."

"I'll be gentle. I promise." He took another step toward me.

I squared my shoulders and breathed in deeply for strength. "I simply can't, Mr. Phillips."

He folded his arms across his chest and studied me carefully. "You simply can't – what? Sleep with me tonight? Call me by my first name? Tell me what it is you can't do."

"I can't live here."

He shook his head and stared down at the pine floor planks. "I may not be rich, Bess, and I know the kids can get a bit rowdy, but deep down they're good kids and I'm a good man who'd be good to you. I can build on to the cabin if you think it's too small. Is that it?"

"This may sound as a paradox, Mr. Phillips, but on the contrary, this small cabin is too much for me. This cabin and all it entails is simply overwhelming. I must have been mad when I said 'yes', but I wish – well I wish to take it back. It's a mistake, a huge mistake. I wouldn't make you happy – I don't know how. I don't know how to be a mommy either. I've been a suffragist, since the age of twelve. That is all I know. Now that we've won the vote, perhaps I believed I needed a new life, a new beginning. But not ready-made!"

The hurt on his face was undeniable. I bared my heart, not my body as was expected. I could not pretend otherwise. I had been taught to speak my mind but my battles had always been with the government, or with other women, always beyond arm's reach. Now here was someone reaching for me and he – and all that he entailed – attempted to enter into my personal world, my breathing realm. I gasped for breath and backed up to the wall, hugging myself instead, tears flowing. I hated myself – and him - for it.

"Alright, Bess. I hear you, loud and clear. I just wish you'd said 'no' sooner … like at the courthouse before we made vows to God!" His voice became increasingly louder as he spoke. He bit his bottom lip and sighed. "Look, you sleep in my bed and I'll sleep on the couch and we'll talk some more tomorrow."

I felt hugely relieved and my shoulders relaxed. Smiling gratefully, I stepped away from the wall and reached out a hand but he only turned and walked out of the room, closing the door behind him.

Now saddled with guilt, I sank heavily onto the bed. My intentions were not to wound but as always I had said too much too quickly. I certainly thought I could care for him but something inside had blocked the way. Conceivably, too much time had been spent trying to break down women's wall to equality, and I suppose I used those leftover bricks to build a defense against men. Maybe the wall was too high for any man. Where was the love? Not here, where my heart felt as diminutive as this cabin, and that thought cut me to the core. Why did I allow this to happen? I thought myself smarter than this. Tears returned but I brushed them away angrily.

I was spared this night but now what? Making my toilette would give me some time to think. But there was no running tap, no sink, only a basin of water on a roughly made cabinet with a small door. Inside I found frayed but clean rags and a hand towel. My blouse off, the scarring on my wrist and arm looked grim and brown in this light, the skin puckered and wrinkled in spots like it needed a good ironing. Another reason not to expose my body; another reason not to live here. I was terrified of the type of old stove they used here. When I was eleven, the sleeve of my dress caught fire trying to cook from one at home, causing this scar. During that one summer, Mama had been petitioning and marching for suffrage, leaving home duties to me. I had since stayed away from wood burning stoves as much as possible. No one knew about these scars, save perhaps Mama and her guilt, and long sleeves were always there to cover.

My nightgown on, I felt more at ease and could notice my surroundings. Mr. Phillips' wife had died a year or so ago, but her woman's touch remained in the room. A hand-stitched quilt stretched over the pine-posted bed, crocheted doilies on the bureau. Lined along the back of the bureau, the mirror reflecting their backsides, were several hand-carved wooden birds: a cardinal, a robin, and a dove. I inspected the cardinal, then the robin and put them back, but the dove I kept in my hand, not able to let go. Something about its red-colored eyes, gems like ruby that looked oddly familiar. I carried it over to the oil lamp next to the bed for a closer inspection and held it under the light. Yes, I had seen one very much like this, but where was it?

Then I remembered that at about age fifteen I had discovered one hidden in the back of Mama's wardrobe. With the help of her coveted key I had snooped amongst her personals hoping to borrow one of the beautiful dresses Aunt Opal had fashioned and given to Mama. Same size dove, same smooth head and neck, with intricate etchings in the tail and wing feathers. Did he sell these and how would Mama – but then I remembered him saying that he had driven Mrs. Catt to my hometown of Annan about ten years ago during a women's convention, around 1910. I thought back to that year and recalled how Mama had allowed me to go to the convention with her. I had a vague recollection of the speakers but at my height I could only get a glimpse here and there and then Papa made me leave. Yet now I remembered an Indian there. A younger version with longer hair, pulled back in a ponytail – I dropped the dove. Him. Deep laugh lines were etched here now; gray streaks in shorter hair that tucked behind his ears, but this had to be the same man.

And another memory linked: Right after my stove accident, I remembered calling for Mama from my bedroom and when she didn't answer I came down the stairs looking for her. As I stepped into the parlor, the window revealed a strange sight to me. Mama stood on the boardwalk several houses down, talking with a man next to his horse. I thought he might be the same man who spoke at the convention. As I watched, he gave her something brown, yes, about this size, which she enclosed in her hand and clutched to her chest as she walked back to our home. Intuitively I understood I wasn't supposed to see this - something about their movements appeared too private – and so I slipped back up the stairs before she returned. Of course I wouldn't dare ask her about it, and eventually the scene faded in my mind, but obviously not entirely, because for the first time since, the scene had refocused. Mr. Phillips knew Mama and had given her a dove. Why? *You look very familiar to me,* he had said in our introductions. Indeed – I looked very much like Mama!

I could not sleep that night for thinking. I finally gave up in the early morning light and dressed. Slipping out the back door, I walked around the cabin and along the fence, breathing in the delicious scent of the lavender. They reminded me of home and of Mama's lavender sachets and lavender oils, and her scent always of lavender. It made me wish she was here – and then I froze.

"You're not running off already, are you?" I felt his breath on my neck when he said that, and I was startled beyond reason.

"Really, Mr. Phillips, is it necessary to sneak up on me like that?"

"Sorry. I'm half Cherokee. I sleep light, I walk light."

I stepped away from his closeness and waited for my heart to return to its rightful place. Reaching for the lavender blooms, I pinched one off and turning to him, held this up to his nose. "Who does that remind you of? Anyone we know?"

He closed his eyes for a moment, inhaling deeply. The rooster's crow broke the silence somewhere near. He opened his eyes to that, and to my condemning posture. "I think I'm searching for someone else through you. Are you related to her?"

I nodded. "I'm Ruby Wright's daughter."

"Oh dear Lord. I honestly wasn't sure and I was afraid to ask. If you don't like the answer, don't ask the question, my Daddy used to say." One hand reached out tentatively and touched my hair falling around my shoulders, not yet combed back and pinned. "This morning you look so much like how I remember her from ten years ago, only your hair's a little lighter I think and hers fell down to her waist." He spoke softly, the light from the rising sun behind me accenting his native features of square jaw line, wide mouth, prominent nose and cheekbones, giving his face a red-man glow. I was shocked in wondering when and how he saw Mama's hair down; I had only seen it so at her bedtime.

"She had such beautiful long hair."

"You bastard," I said, slapping his hand away. "I'm leaving."

He raised that same hand in peace. "When I saw you here in Tennessee, how was I to know who you were? I just thought God was giving me a second chance to be with the one I love. And you have not only her looks but also her spirit. I couldn't pull myself away from you."

"You married me because you want to be with my *mother*? Do you have any idea how that makes me feel?" I trembled from this revelation of being a second-hand rose. Wings of anger that I hoped had settled around my shoulders as a suffragist, were now flapping hard enough for me to lift ground.

Another thought jolted me like a bolt of electricity (which is perhaps not a good simile because there was no such thing as electricity 'in these here parts'). "Ruby! You named your youngest daughter after Mama?"

"Well, it doesn't matter now, does it? You were leaving anyway."

I refused to allow him to get off that easily. "If I wanted to stay, didn't you think I would have figured it out? After all, you would eventually meet my parents!" My composure gone now, my trembling had raised my vocal chords up a notch or two. "Or was that the whole purpose? A reason to be around Mama again?" I threw the lavender down and walked further away. This was just too much.

He silently followed me up to the grassy knoll I had stood on the day before, surveying my future home. Seemed like a month before. This time I stood there with my back to the cabin, facing the trees, ready to run, only more questions kept me in place. I folded my arms across my chest and faced him, ready to attack again. "And Mama! Was she in love with you too? Was she?"

Pain was plainly there on his face and I was inflicting it and happy to do so. I behaved as a jealous woman.

"It's not right that I speak for Ruby."

"Did she tell you she loved you?"

"That's for your mama to say, not me."

"Did you seduce her?"

He raised his eyebrows in surprise and then frowned. "Good Lord, woman! Remember who you're talking about. Ruby was a good woman! You should know that better than me."

"Fine, Mr. Phillips. I'm a woman; she's a *good* woman. As you said to me last night, I hear you loud and clear. It's ironic, isn't it? I lived my life to please her, to do what she couldn't do and stand up for women's rights. Now I find someone else who couldn't shake her. And she calls herself powerless! Well, you should be happy to know that Papa is very ill." I waited for that last bit to sink in but

Mr. Phillips was better than I at keeping his emotions in check. He simply watched as if waiting for further instructions.

So I decided to give him another stab. "And as for you, for *us*, this marriage is over. It was never consummated and it never will be." I wanted to say more but I stopped. Drained of emotion, or numbed by too much emotion, but at least my mind stopped questioning and I prepared to move on. I smiled bitterly at that one. I did what I was trained to do. Trained to stand and fight, trained to state my position, and then move on. I was not a lavender flower like Mama, growing roots, but much more like tumbleweed, moving with the wind.

Mr. Phillips insisted we have breakfast with 'the younguns', before heading back to Nashville. He said he would also need some time to try to repair whatever went wrong with his truck. I relinquished; what else could I do? I was dependent upon this traitor or march the twenty miles back to the Nashville train station.

My armchair, or my 'throne fit for a queen' as his boys called it, still sat in the kitchen and I obediently sat in it to face biscuits and gravy. Giggling and whispering continued around the table from the night before, as if no time had passed in between. While chewing my biscuit, I suddenly realized that they were deliberating how their father and I had done something naughty 'in Daddy's bed' and my face flushed crimson.

The baby, little Ruby, I nonetheless found enduring, perhaps even endearing, for when I smiled at her, she hid her eyes behind her hands shyly. When I removed her hands and said, "Peek-a-boo!" she gave a glorious, straight-from-the-stomach cackle. It was this child who took her mother's life in birth. I empathized; she would no doubt have this taunted at her by her older siblings as she grew up, giving her personal blame.

I looked around the table and wondered how they would fare without a mother here for sometime longer, perhaps forever, since their father, with his drawn face and shadowed eyes, would likely not attempt this again, especially since his heart was evidently not in it.

I gave credit to Mary Sue, a great deal of credit as I watched her stir and serve and scold. She was their mommy now, and although she made it known this was a burden, she carried the burden well; her shoulders squared for whatever life threw at her. All the more reason to admire her and I did. What better hero than one who didn't want to do it, but accepted the responsibility bravely? And she would rather do it all, then to pass it on to a stranger, someone who didn't belong here. She became my heroine for that short time at breakfast. Could I somehow reciprocate and bring light into her tired disappointed eyes? Naively, I resolved to help her but in my own way, through my own strengths. Goodness knows, I showed only my weaknesses 'in these here parts'.

Not to mention, revenge would be sweet for Mr. Phillip's and Mama's deception.

Mary Sue looked across the table at me and I gave her a promising smile. Her eyes hardened and she returned a look that could kill.

I returned to Annan with my tail between my legs, my virginity intact, my mouth shut. I started where I left off and joined in the celebration for winning the women's vote.

Like I said, I was supposed to be happy. I walked in my place in the celebration parade, smiling and waving, tiny pieces of paper falling down around me as if the white fluffy clouds above me had burst. But with the chill in my heart, they might as well be snow. I wanted to step out of line but I didn't know where else to go, so I did what I always did and followed behind the others.

"Okay, Mama, I'm here," I muttered through clenched teeth, truly hating her. I hoped my face favored a smile, and while doing so, wondering how to get even with her. I didn't want the other women in my group to think I was unappreciative. After all, we had worked hard for this. Yet, the one woman I struggled through this for the most, didn't show up yet again. She made it clear to me under no uncertain terms that it was my duty to march in her place. But to *marry* in her place – that's a bit extreme. I had gone as far as I would go with that woman – damn hypocrite!

Yes, I festered, even with such festivity, complete with the high school band, zigzagging, tooting, booming, some blowing so hard into their wind instruments, their faces were red and blown round as beets. All were celebrating something that many in our midst had fought hard to prevent, or at the very least, had scorned and mocked.

I was reminded of the Henny Penny story where she could find no one to help her plant or harvest the wheat but plenty showed up to eat the bread.

My fellow suffragists looked genuinely happy, some letting white doves out of baskets along the way. We all wore banners that declared boldly, "Women Won the Vote!"

How many times had I petitioned for this moment? After nine years of hard lobbying, if my group knew how I felt now, if Mama knew how I felt … well, it couldn't be helped – my heart wasn't in it. Mama had spoiled my one day in the sun.

Elizabeth Cady Stanton predicted rightly when she wrote, *This is winter wheat we are sewing and other hands will harvest.*

This was harvest time and women were finally declared as people, but instead, my head inflamed with complaint. In solace, I wrote a speech and was asked to give this speech after the parade. Poor timing.

In remembrance of Annan's first Women's Rights Convention of 1910, we used the large gazebo in the City Hall Park for the open-air ceremony. We 'women-folk' sat along the back bench, taking turns in speaking. The crowd numbered five hundred, I'd say; another implication of 1920's open-mindedness to women's advances.

Yet this gazebo also felt like poor timing for me in that while I sat inside there waiting my turn, I pictured us as colorful birds trapped in a large cage, while many people sauntered by looking at this strange species of females.

I had been instructed to speak for three minutes on my favorite topic of Susan B. Anthony, with the purpose of reminding our audience of sacrifices made, and to end this on an inspirational note.

I did this. And then ended it in writing, "As my mama wrote ten years ago and I sang so proudly here as an eleven-year old, 'Women are people too; we are no less than you. Equal rights will see us through; to share where freedom reigns!' To my mama, Ruby Wright, who could not be here." I paused dramatically. "To the Ladies Legion, to Mrs. Catt, to Miss Anthony, to so many others, many of whom *are* here today, thank you for your courage. For standing strong. Now we must move forward. Don't let us stand still. Ladies, be sure to cast your hard-earned vote in November!"

That was the last of my written speech and I should have stopped there, but the crowd's standing cheers spilled over into an act of foolishness. I shouted like there was no tomorrow, "The *corset* of social injustice has been removed, so you must continue to remove *all* that binds you! Be free, ladies! That is the law of progress. Be passionately interested in yourselves. We must catch up to the men because our rights are not as developed as theirs. We must fight against child labor, women's low wages, and men's superiority, to name a few. Women no longer cling to the old separation of 'charity and church work for women, politics for men'. We've waited seventy-two years for this! Celebrate our victory and our freedom!"

The crowd became more and more subdued as I rattled on, with only the rebel women left standing at the end of my speech.

Pearl had her fun with it as we walked home. "Oh dear sister. You said the word 'corset'!" She placed the back of her hand to her forehead and pretended to faint, right there on the boardwalk. Such a public display made me wish we had taken a taxi to Mama's rather than walk there for dinner.

"Behave, sister." I cautioned.

"Well, it is an undergarment," she said, wrinkling her powdered nose. "'Remove all that binds you'. I love that line. Sounds like we should now walk nude in the streets. And this comes from someone worried about my knees showing. You are just too kippy!" Her bright red lipstick spoke louder than her words. She tucked her bobbed hair behind her ears and slowed her pace beside me, her bangs oddly concealing her forehead. Why she wanted to look boyish passed all my understanding. I remained quiet, awaiting her theatrics to end.

She shook her head. "You don't know if you're a reformer or a stiff, do you?"

"Pearl, when I spoke of freedom, I did not mean it physically. I meant freedom of choice in occupation and economic independence. That should clearly be our goal."

"My goal is not so high and mighty," Pearl said. "I'd be happy if I could just earn a decent wage at that textile factory I sweat in. Ohhh, a dincher!" She bent down to a half-smoked cigarette and picked it up daintily from the grass with two red fingernails.

"Don't you dare, young lady! We're almost home. Are you trying cigarettes, too? Next thing I know, you'll be drinking alcohol. And don't bend like that. You're displaying more than your knees in that loose sack you call a dress, sister." The waistline dropped to her hips and her chest looked flatter than before, from the loose fabric, I supposed. That was before I discovered she tightly wound her chest with strips of cloth to hide her womanhood. She dropped the dirty thing and straightened to face her foe, someone who no longer knew her, and she no longer knew.

"Yes, I'm a smoke-eater. You know, sister, while you've been preaching on future freedom, us common girls have been living real times. Sweatshops, penny pay, and men bosses with roaming hands. I don't live for the future, I live for today. And I'm going to have fun. And that includes hootch and smokes and petting parties. Damn the Prohibition, is what we say! You duds don't dance! Do you think I'm going to live like you? A stuck-up Ritz living Mama's dream? Don't criticize my life until you get one of your own!"

Mr. Phillips came to mind and I thought, *Oh and you only know the half of it.* Pearl walked off ahead of me, her shoulders up, her hips swinging angrily. Familiar with her temper, I simply waited until her shoulders relaxed and she slowed her walk. We were soon walking side-by-side again. I hid my hurt – part of what she said was true. But I worried about her careless live-for-today philosophy and told her so.

She shrugged her shoulders. "No need. Soon enough I'll marry a snuggle pup and live happily ever after." She quickly changed the subject. She extended her leg to show mesh stockings and slip-on shoes. "Aren't I just fluky? How do you like my dog kennels? I told our dapper dad he should rename his shoe store from Walk Wright to Dog Kennels. Wouldn't that be the cat's pajamas?"

"Speak English!" I said, having enough. That seemed more than she could do at the time so she fell silent.

We arrived at our destination and Pearl pointed toward the front verandah of my childhood home, brighter nowadays, recently painted in pastel blue and yellow, gone were the brown and green colors. I wondered briefly how she could convince Papa to make any changes around there. Mama sat there in her eternal rocker. "As long as I can remember, she has sat out there rocking, rocking, rocking. I think I was born there."

Mama must have heard Pearl. "I'm out here where it's quiet," she said as we walked up the verandah steps. "Your papa listens to that radio constantly." She clapped her hands together and squeezed, her face lighting with a grin. "Hello my suffragist daughter!"

"Just call me Henny Penny," I answered glumly.

She paused, looking puzzled, but I waved it away.

She pointed toward the wicker settee. "Sit and tell me everything. Did you notice? I'm wearing my *Ladies Legion* colors today. My original white blouse and black skirt to honor our victory! Can you believe I kept it all these years? I remember cutting up a white sheet for the pattern and using the bone buttons from your father's old vest. Isn't it the dog's pajamas?"

"Yes, I believe it is," I said dryly. The blouse was ill-fitted and worn thin at the elbows and cuffs, and had yellowed a bit from old age. Thank goodness she hadn't shown up for my speech in that garment.

Pearl rolled her eyes. "It's *cat's* pajamas."

"Pardon?" Mama once again looked puzzled, as if now both her daughters spoke in another tongue.

"It's cat's pajamas, not a dog's."

Mama waved the comment away, just as I had done.

Her grin came back quickly. "How did your speech go? I wish I could have been there. Perhaps you will recite it for me later. Women make the best speeches, don't you think? We're more timid and decent, and less bothered with the obsession for public speaking."

My attention shifted to Pearl, expecting her to cackle over my inappropriate public verbiage, but she was either repentant over her earlier tantrum or more docile now at home. She only smiled sweetly and sat still. Mama's eyes sparkled with anticipation as I described the ratification and final countdown in Tennessee and the speeches of today, having decided to leave out my personal drama until we were alone. She always delighted in hearing of my conversations with Mrs. Carrie Chapman Catt, whom Mama had idolized since her own days of suffrage campaigning.

"Mrs. Catt asked about you, Mama. She said that during the early days of suffrage, women such as you were the backbone to the cause. Her words were 'we needed more women like your mother, Ruby, because she could communicate to the common woman, whereas the educated woman was difficult to understand when coming to the masses.'" I paused for affect. "It's a shame, really." I enjoyed twisting that knife of guilt once in a while.

As Mama slowly took in my meaning and grimaced, Pearl's eyes dulled and she excused herself to check on Papa. She paused at the door. "Be prepared for Papa, Bess. He blames me on you."

"Yes, let me guess," I said. "The suffragists, those men-haters of the world, have degraded and spoiled those green seedlings of female youth who needed a role model to light their way, to grow, but instead received the rain of dirty rhetoric and dark clouds of hot air blown about by hot-headed women who do not understand their place is in the home, caring living breathing for their husband, that master of the house, that god of good and godly greatness." I said this last with my hand over my heart, breathless at the end.

Pearl laughed loudly in only that careless way Pearl could, doing a little dance step and wiggling her hips - then resumed her hunched over position, poor posture – likely my fault too – from non-restrictive garments and no corset to keep her straight. "Yes, but you're so *good* at dirty rhetoric!"

"Thank you," I said stiffly.

My nineteen-year old sister was the antithesis of Mama's Victorian mind-set with those ghastly knees showing. Where was I in this social change? Somewhere between the old and new.

Which was why I missed the point, caught in this gray blur between mother and sister. The contrast was too profound for my exhausted state and the shortsighted side of me could only focus on the more tangible comprehension of Mama and Mr. Phillips. I needed to ask Mama The Question and for this reason she and I went for a walk, turning right on the boardwalk and walking past the house next door where Mama's old friend and suffragist had lived until about nine years ago, right after the Lighthouse opened. At that time she and her several children hid in the Lighthouse, bruised and frightened, until arrangements could be made to transport her to her brother's home in Pennsylvania to live. Her drunken husband had beaten her for the last time, she had announced.

"Have you heard from Aimee?" I asked, not quite ready to talk Tennessee turkey.

"Yes, she rang me a few weeks ago to say her husband had been found dead from a liver disease, somewhere in New York City. Drank himself to death. Another reason why Prohibition must stay. Women have pushed hard for this because scores of men cannot control their liquor, it's as simple as that. Now Aimee can move back here; he can't haunt her home any longer. It will be wonderful ... like the old days."

She crooked her arm through mine. "It's different now, isn't it? I think your work is harder, more exciting. My suffrage days were in a peaceful time in the world – no recent war – almost thirty years since the Civil War. Battles were more in the home. Your work is in the aftermath of war. The Prohibition, I'm sorry to say, has caused political scandals and crime. The old ways and the new ways are clashing. Battles are outside the home now. I see one commonality: We both saw women suffer as a result of putting the campaign on hold for the men's wars. They did so for the Civil War and for the Great War."

"I'm impressed, Mama, that you keep up on this. But one suffragist said it well. Mrs. Emmeline Parkhurst said, 'What is the use of fighting for a vote if we have not got a country to vote in?'"

Mama laughed softly, erasing that nostalgic yearning-for-the-old-days gaze I saw more and more often. She spent too much time alone. "Do you think women can vote peace into the world now?"

"Not many men left to have another war anyway, Mama." I didn't mean to be flippant about it. After all we lost my brother, Jonathan, to the Great War. But I preferred to generalize. Something I had become good at over the years. "The U.S. mobilized four million of which one hundred twenty six thousand died and two hundred thirty four thousand more were wounded. Worldwide, sixty six million fought and eight million died. Not many bachelors left for lil' ol' me."

"You've always remembered the details," Mama said with a laugh. "I suppose you need to, to win the argument. You told me once that you were raised to rant and rankle, and you asked me then, 'Who would marry such'? Do you still believe this? Billy would have married you."

I sighed. Mama's irritating talent has been her ability to bring me back down to her personal level. "Don't be ridiculous. Billy never asked me to marry him. I accused him more than once of sitting on the fence in his commitment to me. Ironic isn't it, that he died when he landed on a picket fence after jumping from his burning aeroplane." Only one month before the war ended.

"Mercy, Bess, what a comparison!"

"Ranting realist, that's me. You've made me the bitch I am today."
I wanted to get mad enough to get the nerve up to bring up her and
Jere. But she didn't bite back.

She dropped my arm and looked away. I knew I hurt her and
I knew I didn't care.

"About Billy," she said, still looking away. "There's something
I should tell you—"

"I did meet another bachelor in Tennessee, though," I said, purposefully interrupting her. "Well, a widow actually, but unmarried
just the same."

We were nearing the end of the paved street; only a dirt road
from there, the wagon tracks of carts and buggies indented like
sunken railroad tracks. She would want to turn around soon. I hesitated and then practically exploded with the question, "Do you know
a Mr. Jere Phillips?"

"No, why?" she said, without a qualm.

I stopped in my tracks, old anger once again flapping about my
shoulders like tired wings. I felt extremely disappointed in her reaction. She had lied to me and that was unforgiveable. In studying her
face, I saw no surprise or blush as expected - that was the least she
could do in hearing her old lover's name. How adulterous! I had
never known her to lie before and now I wondered how many other
lies had she told? How many of her fictitious stories had I believed in
and followed? My life felt all the more wasted, groundless. I felt glad
I'd said the word, "bitch". Suddenly longing for something solid,
I turned and walked the other way, snapping back at her over my
shoulder, "I'm going back to visit with Papa!"

Thus jumping from the kettle into the fire. Papa sat propped up
in bed half dozing, looking so frail in his nightclothes that I longed
to see him dressed in his usual three-piece brown suit. His supper
tray to his side remained untouched, the radio droning on. The
large cabinet of the radio replaced his bedside table so that he could
reach the dials. His eyes opened upon hearing my greeting. I watched
from the footboard as he struggled to sit up more attentively. Mama

came rushing into the room behind me and began rearranging his pillows. *He's not a cripple,* I thought, *but Mama's making him into one.*

The room had grown dark in the early evening so Mama pulled the overhead chain hanging from a bare light bulb, reminding me of their recent installation of electricity. They could afford such luxuries, plumbing included, when Papa sold his shoe store to my brother, Victor. He couldn't deal with the business anymore, not since his heart attack, and he became weaker after word came that Jonathan had been killed in warring France. So much had changed here in their world and even the bright light in the room made me gloomier because of the shifting changes and his shadowed raccoon-like eyes.

Papa cleared his throat. "Good evening, Bess. I understand you have much to be happy about."

I sat on the chair offered by Mama. As I expected, she wouldn't meet my eyes, her expression looking as gloomy as I felt. "Yes, isn't it wonderful? Women can now vote for their president!" I could pretend, too; I'd learned from the best. I smiled artificially at his pale sullen face.

"Yes, women are taking over, I understand," he said, turning down the radio's volume, me noting the shoe-dye stains forever on his fingers. "It's all in here." He patted the cabinet as if it visibly held the evidence. "Your leader, Miss Alice Paul, is running for president." He shook his finger at my raised eyebrows. "Don't pretend you don't know anything about it. She chained herself to the gate of the White House screaming for equal rights until President Wilson relented. He wants peace and a fair race. There's not much time between now and November so of course she can't possibly reach enough voters to win. But what could he do? She threatened not to eat until they put her name on the Republican ticket. There's a large group of those women there now, pounding on the White House door, saying they're coming in like witches from the night to clear out the cobwebs of Victorian thinking." He waved his hand weakly as if seeing such a cobweb. "They want to be the president's cabinet. Said they've worked long enough in the war factories making guns and aeroplanes and now they want to make laws."

He had slid down his pillows a bit and struggled to sit up more, leaning his head toward me. "And here's the worst part: No more women in the homes, the children and husbands must be fed in the town halls and everyone will wear uniforms."

My eyebrows must have been meeting my hairline by then. These were serious statements so I dared not laugh. My eyes darted to Mama but she had resorted to her needlework, her concentration on a flower keen.

"Papa, you can't believe everything you hear on a radio."

"Do you think this great country of ours would release lies on the air waves for all to hear?"

"Some people like to pretend on the radio, just like they do in vaudeville," I answered. "Some people even like to pretend in their homes," I added pointedly.

Mama jerked her head toward me, a scowl between her eyes. I glared at her openly and saw hurt and confusion plainly on her face.

"I wouldn't listen to such trash, Bess," Papa said. "And I hope to God you aren't seen in such places. You have enough to clean up as it is. Look at the mess you've made with the young women of this world. You and your liberated women. Pearl is wild as a rabbit now, won't eat, says she must diet away her hips, she cut off her long hair, goes to those jazz dances and speakeasies I hear about, washes all over every day of the week, obviously trying to wash away her sins."

"Can't dance forever to the Blue Danube waltz, Papa," Pearl called in from the door. She looked at me and winked. "Supper's ready."

"Those dances are too loud," Mama said, laying down her needlework. "The modern girl can no longer hear the excitement of her own heartbeat, what with the noise of the music and motor cars." She kissed Papa on the forehead. "Get some rest, Robert, and don't worry. Women should be able to do something in the workaday world."

"Well, with a flapper girl as president," said Papa, "I'm wondering why we men fought the war in the first place. Let me see what else you women are up to."

My goodness, I thought as I sat there watching him turn up the volume to hear more 'truth', my mother is a liar and my papa is a believer in the lies. That must be their secret to a successful marriage.

Katy's Chapter One -- December 1963

My year of awakening? I'm pretty sure mine's not pretty. If I was a Sleeping Beauty, that sure as hell was no prince who woke me. Mama Bess and Grandmama Ruby will be shocked to know the truth; their stories will sound homesick and homespun I suspect. They're tight-lipped anyway so I can imagine they'll only write about their greatest love: the women's movement. It'll be like reading a newspaper article. They didn't have it nearly as hard as I did. They had loving husbands and children that weren't crippled. I had Uncle Joe and — well, all I can say right now is, here's what I'm supposed to write about: *We all have a pivotal moment that changes our lives. Symbolically a year of 4 seasons, where the spring seed of an event is born, grows, matures, and becomes winter wisdom as a life-changing realization. Write about this year of awakening.* Mama has written this in big block letters on a chalk board and hung it here in the dining room, replacing the painting of Papa's Georgia plantation house. This action alone makes me think about change – as long as any of us can remember, that painting has hung there, and the newly exposed lighter shade of paint behind it proves it.

What if that *seed* was planted in a Georgian cotton patch – and it wasn't cotton? I mean that in so many ways. Mama does like symbolism. So does my thorny daughter, Jesi, with her peace signs and Bob Dylan obsession. Amazingly, Mama has asked *why* I at last opened that birth control clinic in 1944, and the reasons involve Papa and his kin, a family Mama had refused to talk about. But does Jesi need to know everything? A truth that will possibly change her outlook and worse yet, change her inward belief in who she is and where she

71

came from? I haven't been honest with her but I haven't yet decided if I want to be. The truth might set me free, yet as President James Garfield said, "but first it will make you miserable." Mama would love that and I mean *that* in so many ways.

I'll start with this:

My father died before I was born, long before I knew there was one. This corresponding male part surprised me about Mama. I thought she could do everything. I must've thought of her as all encompassing, a hermaphrodite of sorts. But instead she had a negative force to charge the positive, opposing qualities with stamens and pistils that somehow connected - sounds much more proper than saying the vagina and the penis coupled, doesn't it? I had to look some of that up in the dictionary.

Oh hell, I'm just going to write it like I talk it and stop trying to use big words like Mama. She wouldn't approve any of those metaphors anyway. How's this: It was like looking under the hood of a car for the first time and finding the engine, too, makes it run as much as the frame, tires, wheel and key. She'll like that and even now her say-so is important to me. For years I was enclosed in her womb, all-consuming, hearing only one heartbeat, one Madonna above me, female life wrapped around female life until I was ready.

It's Autumn, 1943. I'm ready now. I think. I'm standing at the door. But as I did in departure from my mother's womb, I cry now in departing from my mother's home. I'm afraid I'm premature.

"Katy?"

"Yes, Mama?"

"It's time."

I head toward the car, inspect the tires, scoot in behind the wheel, Mama hands me the key.

Mama. Always there pushing. Feeding me the food of the female: *Eat with care, take in that which is good for you, speak out that which is good for others. Walk straight, never slouch – the hunched back is subservient. Take caution with men, those with forced laughter have no respect for themselves, those with heated eyes have no respect for you. Give the day your best effort and the night will give you its best rest. Every woman has a purpose....*

She stands beside my window, silent yet her life-long words linger. Her strength is now a part of me.

"Don't worry, Mama."

I turn the key in the ignition and the male beast under the hood awakens and roars.

Pickerville, Georgia 1943

"Where the hell is your mama, girl?"

I lick my lips, still tasting the Georgia dust, red and metallic tasting, like blood. How ironic. My uncle is as white as his bed sheets, looking like his own land is draining him.

"Well, you see Uncle Joe, Mama is awfully busy at home in New York and Grandma Ruby is sick and needs looking after—"

"Is she dying? Because if she ain't - and I am - then who should come first? Now you just answer that, little lady." His head returns to his pillow with a plop, eyes closed, energy spent.

"That's why she sent me, Uncle Joe. I'm your true kin, your real flesh and blood." *Happy to donate some to you, Uncle.* I pat his hand, trying to warm up to him which is hard because he is indeed the bellowing blow-george Mama warned me about. His sagging jowls work with what I said, his jaw moving back and forth as if chewing on my last words.

"Hell, I shouldn't be surprised," he says in an I'll-give-you-that-much tone. "Bess run off from here like we were boll-weevils and she was a fluff o' cotton. That was back in 1921 and she just sneaked out. About broke Harriet's heart, God rest her soul. You'll learn weak hearts run in this family. Your daddy died of one and your Aunt Harriet fell dead in the chicken coop. And now me."

He opens his blue eyes, colored like over-washed denim overalls, and points a thick-knuckled finger at me. "But I ain't gone yet and I ain't gonna go until I get this plantation settled. So don't go getting your hopes up that the only place you have to put me is six feet under. My heart ain't just going to quit but sort of sputter and run out of gas. I reckon I'm about on a quarter tank now."

I give him my best exposition of teeth. "You're not a car, Uncle Joe. This is the forties and doctors can help you. You'll be fine." I pat his arm, my tanned hand touching what looks like the skin on raw chicken meat, belying what I said.

"My Lord, you look like your daddy when you smile." He stares, mouth open, until I feel blood rise to my cheeks. Seems I have enough of the red stuff for the both of us. A strange thing happens then: As he continues to eye me, I start feeling drained, like he is indeed the vampire of the Deep South I'd read about. Oddly enough, his cheeks flush, something definitely passes between us, perhaps only some level of understanding but it feels like more, like something is taken from me.

It's Mama's fault really; she had set me up to expect the worst from this man, for whatever reason she wouldn't tell me. My rebellious nature comes in to save me and I withdraw my hand, raise my chin, laugh a silly sound and say, "Yes, I've seen his picture so I'll take that as a compliment. It's terrific to be here where Papa grew up; I'm quite excited about it all. Can you believe I drove down here from New York all by myself in Papa's old Duesenberg?"

He raises himself up onto his elbows. "You have her *here?* Ah, what a pretty thing she was – does she still have that wide-eyed look?"

"Who?" I blink at him thinking that his mind is going before his body.

"Duesy that's who! That ol' auto had a classic beauty – still sleek and black I hope? With overhead cams? The only auto of its kind that operated four valves in a cylinder. 265-horsepower. Damn! You would've had no problem, girl, in that, unless your mama gallivanted in it all over the place. Where's she at?" He slides a leg over the side of the bed, struggling to get up.

I grab his elbow to assist. "I told you, Uncle Joe, Mama is at home in Annan—"

"Not her you fool! I'm talking about Duesy."

His frame rises two feet above me and then his two-hundred-pound-plus flesh leans into me, his forearm against my left breast until I readjust our positions. "Help me to the window, girl, don't just stand there. She's more than twenty years old; that was a 1921 model I recollect – how'd you keep her that long."

"Mama rarely drove it – I mean, her. Mostly just taught me how to. Too many memories for her, I guess, I really don't know. The only thing wrong is it's got a dent in the trunk hood, but Mama said that was your fault – I mean that it happened down here."

Again he studies my face and again I feel I've given him something, too much I think for it's as much as I know. Mama would be disappointed already but I can't help it. Here's the biggest difference between us: She reveals nothing and I tell all.

His window faces the gravel driveway in the front of the plantation house and this we shuffle to, me moving the heavy brocade curtains aside to give us a view of "Auto" as Mama calls it, me thinking she meant "Otto" when I was younger.

"Now that's a Duesy," he breathes. His mouth remains open, his jowls jiggling at this close range, his eyes alight.

I can't help but laugh, regardless of Mama's teachings. "My goodness, Uncle, you'd think you were looking at an angel."

"It's like looking at your daddy himself, it is," he nods. "He loved that vehicle as much as I do; looks like he should be getting out of it, just doesn't seem right that he's not. I kept her here as long as I could, until your mama got up enough nerve to take the train back down here to get it. Brought her brother with her for a bodyguard I reckon. Anyway, I kept her clean and hardly ever took her out of the pasture here where I kept my other vehicles I bought and sold. Could've sold her a hundred times over but didn't want my brother to haunt me. He wanted you and your mama to have it."

"He didn't know about me," I breathe out, sounding as nostalgic as Uncle, me, too, wishing Papa could step out of the car. "And I only know he died of a heart attack."

He shakes his head. "Get me back to bed." We shuffle back across the wide room and he crawls into the ornate four-poster bed's lace and satin coverlet, looking at odds, like a dog dressed in a dress. "Damn your mama," he mutters. A few thin wisps of white hair, about all that remains on top, fall onto his forehead and my hand automatically raises to move it back but when he says those last words, I change my mind. I swallow down my homesickness.

"I'll come back later. My bags, see." I thumb to them sitting by the door. "I'll take them on to my bedroom if you don't mind. And freshen up, rest up … or something." Anything but stay in here a minute longer. I have an urge to sleep in the car, like I did the night before, something familiar.

He closes his eyes, his coloring gone again. "I've got a lazy darkie in the kitchen that comes with the place. Go find her and tell her to show you which bedroom is yours. There's five of them; this is no small place you'll be inheriting, just remember that. Come back before supper. There'll be someone here I want you to meet."

I step out into the hallway like stepping out into fresh air and sunshine.

Her name is Clary and I find her in the kitchen. Her back to me, her focus on stirring vigorously in a big ceramic bowl, her broad back-end moving in a dance, she jumps when I call a hello. A warm smile but cautious nature as if on guard all the time, her small brown eyes take everything in quickly, her chocolate skin glistening in this kitchen heat. Out of habit, I look at her arms and neck and sure enough there are tell-tale signs; old bruises, new bruises, scarring, one wrist bone raised as if a broken bone hadn't mended properly. Of course some marks are to be expected from popping hot grease and heavy-duty housework, but I know there's another story here. I've seen battered women come into Mama's Lighthouse all my life, even if this one is colored.

"Honey-chile, you's here already!" she says loudly, drying her hands on her apron. "Did you ring the bell?"

"Oh yes, about an hour ago, and when no one came, I stepped into your entrance way, and when I saw I had to turn left or right, I turned left, went through the living room and found Uncle Joe's room. I guess if I'd turned right and gone through the dining room, I'd have found you."

"I swan, I never heard a thing. I's so sorry, honey. My hearing's almost gone, don't you see, along with my peepers, so you's got to be loud!" She looks around for other ears and then lowers her voice a tad. "Don't seem to be a problem for your uncle."

We laugh and I like her right away, her deep-throated chuckles loosening the knot in my throat.

Three bedrooms beyond the kitchen are pointed out, the last one requiring a small staircase to reach it. Rooms were restored or added on after the Civil War burned part of it down, she tells me. It looks like they'd started with the entrance way and just kept building to the left and the right of it, angles and rooflines giving the house a train-on-uneven-tracks look but somehow I like the spontaneity it gives, as if up for anything that comes its way and can bend with the wind but not break. I can relate to that.

I was tickled to see that the last room, the biggest one, is mine, with two large windows facing south, showing off the lawn's one magnificent weeping willow tree, and a smaller one not far from it. Where I'm standing is a high bed with its own stepping stool, and a thick feather mattress and four of the fluffiest feather pillows I've ever seen. I can't resist the invitation and so I flop down in its lap and lay my head on its pillow chest, the white cotton swelling around me protectively. I straighten up to Clary's laugh.

"Miz Harriet – that's Mr. Joe's deceased wife – she made feather pillows and ticking for a living. You won't find any better anywhere, I wager," she said as she carried my suitcase over to an ancient wardrobe, not liking where I sat it by the door I'm guessing. I make a mental note to keep things tidier than my habit, as I observe the wardrobe, the sink, and large soaking tub that line other walls. But most importantly is the small desk and bookcase, which sits like magnets and I'm the paperclip. I vaguely hear Clary say she'll let me know when supper is ready, me giving a faint nod as I pull out *Tale of Two Cities*. How I love Charles Dickens' first line, *It was the best of times, it was the worst of times, it was the age of wisdom, it was the age of foolishness ... it was the spring of hope, it was the winter of despair ...*

How fitting for the way I feel in my small world, in my potentially new home, and how fitting in the big world, with the horrible war going on over in Europe. I put it away with a promise and reach for more, Mark Twain now, an autographed copy of *Following the Equator*, pages dog-eared, funny sentences underlined in ink, like *Be good and you will be lonesome.* I have weak eyes for reading and I can't read for long but I love what time they give me before tearing. I kick my shoes off and settle back against the bed pillows. I feel my shoulders relax and I sigh, wishing to stay here until tomorrow.

This is not to be so. "Mr. Joe summoned the girl" – these are Clary's words with a wink, not mine. And then just as Charles Dickens predicted, it is the "spring of hope" when Uncle Joe tells me that I won't be eating supper with him in his dreary bedroom but in the dining room. Which quickly becomes the "winter of despair" as I am introduced to a man who came earlier than expected and would be joining me there.

He stands tall and confident at the foot of the bed, his hand around the bed's post like he's holding a king's scepter. His smile is infectious, truly a weak point with me, full of white teeth, straight except for the eye teeth that are a bit pronounced but this only gives him an earthy rugged look that I read as sincere and sincerely good-looking. Eye color doesn't matter at this point and difficult to determine at any rate because of the low lighting. Even so, his blond hair glows as if catching every meager ray the lamp throws out. Outside my mother's watch, on my own now, a grown woman of twenty-two, I boldly approach him, hand outstretched and shake hard with a back-at-you sincere nice-to-meet-you and flash my own smile, one I know the boys like.

"She's such a pretty puppy," Uncle Joe says to him, "I decided you'd want to meet her sooner, rather than later. Now here's what I want you to do," he declares, looking pleased at our coming together as we stand at the foot of his bed facing him. "I want you to go with Clary and she'll serve you up her mouth-watering sweet-potato casserole and whatever else she fixed. You young folk will enjoy yourselves more without a sick ol' man around." He waves his hand weakly. "Now go on, like I told you."

I open my mouth to protest; I'm still rumpled and dirty from the long drive and this dapper fellow in his light green linen suit will see my messy dress in the bright chandelier lighting of the dining room. Besides, I'm not in the mood for the flirting game but only to go back to my room and read some more, soak in that tempting tub, and sleep away many hours of driving. This man, this Will Tom something-or-other is cute but he isn't as tempting as a bath. Others look better when I look better, plain and simple.

But my elbow is grasped before I can say Joe's-my-uncle and he pulls me away and down the hall and through the living room and through the entrance way, me stepping foolishly in tiny stiff geisha steps to keep up behind his long determined strides like he is heading into battle, me wondering if he is going to stop in the dining room long enough to eat. We finally come to rest at the table and I call out, "At ease, soldier!"

He grins but says nothing, only pulls my chair out like a gentleman would, sits in his own and proceeds to eat with the gusto of a hound dog. I think of that because Uncle Joe has three such beasts outside whose constant barking reminds me.

"Ever body calls me TJ," he finally says as he sops up the melted butter with his biscuit. "Just remember that."

I'm eating fast too, I suddenly realize, both of us seeming to want to get this part over with. My stuffed belly is making me sleepier. "Why?" I finally care enough to ask.

"I knew you'd ask that."

How does he know that?

"Because my full name is William Thomas Jackson the Third. That's a mouthful." He wipes his mouth, full and red now.

I sip my iced tea, wishing I can be more alert but my eyes feel heavy-lidded after such a big supper. "Then I shall call you William," I drawl slowly.

"Why?"

"I knew you'd ask me that."

He snorts softly, giving me his best part, a leisurely lopsided grin. His eyes come alive, blue, green, it's hard to tell, with tiny speckles of gray. I smile dimly, trying to soak in his rays but I need darkness and sleep to restore me before I can appreciate the sun.

I stifle a yawn during his story of who's who in Pickerville and Savannah, not able to concentrate or comprehend or care, and he pauses and leans back in his chair, looking at me quizzically.

"Sorry," I say, knowing I've taken this trip as far as it can go today, "but I've had little sleep in the last two days, took me that long to drive from Annan New York, so if you'd excuse me ..." I stand clumsily, my napkin dropping to the floor. I don't bother picking it up. I only want to pick up my bed sheet and crawl under. I look at him for mercy.

His lips thin in disapproval - poor Southern hospitality on my part I suppose - but he manages to smile again. He bends, his head disappearing under the tablecloth and I flinch as fingers squeeze my ankle. He comes up waving the napkin as a surrender flag and I smile in spite of his advance.

"Get your rest because tomorrow night we'll be dancing our shoe leather off. We've got a local band that is hot to trot to play for soldiers, sailors, and sots like me who haven't signed up yet." He grins a lop-sided one with a wink on the same side.

As he chucks my chin and walks away, I can easily imagine him as a poster boy for Uncle Sam. He has that I-want-you look. What he wants though I'm not quite sure.

As I run bath water for a long soak the next morning, Clary comes knocking.

"I thought I heard you up," she says, walking past me. With her customary one arm extended with a limp wrist, as if on the ready to grab something, she hurries over to the bookshelf. On the second shelf she moves books to the left and right and behind there I see a small door. "You were too pooped yesterday so I waited til you was rested to show you this." She opens the door and I see it's a safe with a book inside. She pulls this out and hands it to me. "I found this in my cleaning frenzy before you arrived. It's your daddy's."

The book is actually a brown leather-bound journal. Inside, in small, neat handwriting better than mine, in vivid blue ink with little scrolls at the end of some words, is Papa's talking. His own words! For the first time I believe he really existed. I run my fingers over the surface of the page, feeling each indentation from his ink pen, goose bumps rising on my arms in feeling his proof of presence in his marks on these pages. I look down at the wood plank flooring, see dents there in the dark stain and wonder if he'd made those, too.

He was here. Ate here, slept here – could I have been conceived here? I'll never know.

Never have I felt so close to him, yet suddenly do I recognize how very little I know of him. Mama rarely spoke of him and only if I questioned her. When I did, her expression would visibly fall, like a curtain coming down, her eyelids at half-mast. Small, cryptic answers and then she would raise the curtain with a smile and bring on more work for the both of us. That taught me to stop asking questions and told me enough to understand why she never remarried.

I touch his pages again. Papa must have been something. I strip, not even knowing when Clary left, and sink slowly into the hot water and open the journal to page one.

July 10th, 1921. I'm writing this from my childhood home, in my childhood bedroom, so many memories, yet all are boxed in here and summed up in my pondering by the window, for there is where I spend so much of my time. No difference today. I sit here now watching with sympathy the lawn's great weeping willow tree droop wearily to the ground in the summer heat, no strength to so much as move in the breeze. I feel as one with this life form, our roots digging ever deeper in the rich Georgian soil, searching for something to quench our insatiable thirst, yet this search is contradictory in only taking me down deeper, where I can never again move on from here as the wind and a good news story would take me.

The only difference is my room is nowadays shared with my new wife, my dear Bess, restless, ready to move on, her roots are not here, I'm not sure they are anywhere, even in her hometown of Annan, New York. Still a suffragist at heart, wanting to right the world of women. Cady, ah Cady, my first wife, my first love, a true love, is smiling from heaven at my wise choice. Sickly with consumption, yet she marched right on up to God.

I am supposed to be happy. Bess has told me so. She tells me she is supposed to be happy too but cannot be unless I am. I have an idea: I'll plant another weeping willow tree out here with her name on it and perhaps then she'll grow roots here and we'll both be happy where we are.

My poor Bess; she knows so little but knows enough to know she knows little. I've kept much from her; don't know why really. She's not a weak woman, but tall, erect, chin up as if expecting the worst, yet those lovely ink-blue eyes hopeful for the best, like the sea looking for the sun on a cloudy day. I'm afraid I'm her sun, storm on the horizon.

Her firm footsteps can be heard now, one stair at a time, sure and steady and rising to me. It is my wish that I'll always be here at her summit, but it doesn't look good.

More to come.

I close the journal and close my weak eyes and listen to the many bubbles around me, whispering secrets I wish I knew. For some strange reason I feel myself on the cusp of something and I envision that I'm standing in the wings and I'll soon step out and do my part, but I'm frightened and don't know my lines. I breathe in deeply and out slowly and, yes, I hear it, over and over in the little pops of bubbles, *Papa, Papa.* Yes, that's it, Papa will tell me what to say. I decide to read one entry a day, wanting to savor and absorb Papa's words and imagine his presence as he's writing that day's events, when he and Mama lived here twenty-two years ago.

I read his entry again until my eyes begin to water, and then I rise to a new place.

After breakfast in the kitchen with Clary, I'm summoned to Uncle Joe's bedroom. He's a crackerjack, is all I'm saying right here.

"Alright, girl, here's what you're going to do." He partially lifts himself on his pillows and clears his throat in an important-announcement way.

"It's Katy."

"What?" He looks at me like I've interrupted him.

"My name is Katy, not 'girl'."

"Well, I beg your pardon, missy," he says, but without sincerity. As a matter of fact, I detect some sarcasm. "Look. If you and I are going to get along, I suggest you not start with those high-and-mighty airs of your mama's. Do you understand me?"

"Uncle Joe, I assure you I'm quite different from my mama, but she *is* my mama, and would you want your mama talked about in a bad way? I don't think so. And all I'm asking for is that you call me by my given name, Katy. It's a pretty name and Mama named me Katydid because katydids was all she heard every night while she lived down here with Papa. Now what's so high and mighty about that?" I run out of breath, my cheeks burning from being so outspoken but really, I'm not accustomed to taking orders from a man and I'm having trouble liking this one, kin or not.

He narrows his eyes at me. "Well, now, did she really?" But it isn't really a question, so I keep my mouth shut. I am smart enough, though, to give him a tight smile.

"Alright. Now we know what your Mama *did,* let's see what *you* katydid, diddle-do, Miss Cat and her fiddle." He cackles at himself, more like a cough, and weakly slaps his leg.

I sigh and simply nod, wishing now I hadn't told him about the 'did' part. I'd heard enough jokes in school and now just went by the name, Katy. ("Katy did, didn't you Katydid?" "Katy *did* that mess ..." and so forth. Really not so funny, is it?)

"I want you to dress up pretty tonight for TJ and behave yourself like a proper lady should."

"How'd you know he asked—"

"That boy's got money in his family, a cotton plantation that makes mine look like a hobby farm, so you be real good to him and show him what the Pickering's are made of. I don't know how people act up North but down here we don't take to poor white trash so I hope you've had a good upbringing."

What better opportunity than to call Mama right after this meeting, my hand cupped over the mouthpiece in the living room, believing by this point that Uncle Joe had listening devices in all the lamps.

"Mama, what in the world have you gotten me into?" I murmur into the phone. I laugh lightly to let her know it's nothing serious but to let her know it's something.

She's quiet for a moment. "Katy," she finally says, "he's still bed-fast, isn't he?"

"Oh yes, but that doesn't keep his mouth from motoring."

I hear her sigh as if relieved. "The doctor says it won't be long, or else I wouldn't have sent you down there. If he ever becomes well enough to step away from his bed unassisted, you call me. Do you understand?"

"Sort of." Mama's obscure explanation as usual.

"You being there makes sense, Katy, for your future. He simply requests that he spend some time with his only niece, his only close kin, before he dies. In so doing, you inherit the plantation. It's not a bad arrangement, not when you look at what's on the horizon."

I'm not so sure it's that simple, and that horizon looks kind of cloudy to me but I readily agree, wanting to sound grown-up and less worrisome to her. It's time I grew up, past time really. So, I say nothing about William Thomas Jackson the Third or about Papa's journal. Instead I do the usual: I fill in her blanks with my rambling. I blather on and on about my road trip and the flat tire and the night's sleep in the car, making it all sound so carefree and easy. And she does her usual: Listens. I can almost picture her head tilted into the telephone receiver, her expression focused, her hands handling paper, writing notes, opening mail, stuffing the cubicles of the messy roll-top desk. So, I should be prepared for her final statement.

"You have an appointment Monday with Ellen Whitman. I have her address here for somewhere in downtown Savannah."

I groan in spite of myself. "Mama," I whine, sounding like I used to when she told me to go to bed.

"Yes?" I can hear the chatter of women along with the clatter of dishes in the background. The Lighthouse sounds busier than usual, but then post-holidays and all that that entails, sends women bruised and crying to Mama's haven. I feel ashamed of myself.

"I'll go talk to her," I say. "But a birth control clinic is a long ways off," I add. My goodness, I have to have some control in my life.

William (also known as TJ but I hate initials for names) arrives precisely at seven, running into Uncle Joe's room like it's to beat the band. I dressed up "pretty" for what that's worth. William doesn't even notice, so absorbed he is in showing Uncle Joe he's on time. He's rewarded with money I'm not supposed to see, but William drops one of the bills on the floor and Uncle Joe rolls his eyes at him. I pretend not to notice but I have to choke down a giggle; their expressions of I'm-a-klutz-He's-a-klutz are so telling.

Uncle Joe offers Duesy to William to drive as if he now owns it. William seems pleased. They discuss the route downtown and what time to have me home. William heads out the door and I follow behind him like an obedient dog that remains unacknowledged until he opens the door for me. Like a treat he gives me his easy grin and an easy compliment and I surprise myself by feeling grateful. I slide into the passenger side like a good girl.

That's the good part. The rest of the evening goes downhill from there. The country road is long and bumpy, the stories of who-owns-what is boring and braggy, the dance hall called "Bottom's Up" is an everybody-knows-everybody joint, except me who they don't want to know but take a lot more time wanting me to know them. Now I know that sounds negative and maybe that's why I'd stayed single up to this point but I'm put off by that I'll-take-care-of-you-kid wink, especially when he doesn't.

There's too much beer and not enough food, too little talk and too much kissing. I say William is moving too fast; he tells me I'm moving too slow. I tell him to take the fast-track back home then, I've had enough. I slam hard the car door in Uncle Joe's driveway, hoping to make a point, until I realize he's driving away in my car, gravel spitting back at me. I stomp my foot in vexation.

Thankfully, Uncle Joe's light is out and I tiptoe up to my room. I'm too agitated to sleep with the roaring in my ears from too-loud music, too-little dancing ("Teeee Jay only dances when his pants are on fire," a lady-friend had called across the table, her drawn-out pronunciation of "fire" sounding like it had three i's in the word). TJ – I mean, William – singing in my ear along with *You made me love you* while we shuffled across the floor didn't come close to "dancing our shoe leather off" as he'd promised. I can swing dance with the rest of them even if the South did come up with it in the first place, I replied to the boasts. That line at least did catch me a skinny fish by the name of Joey or Boy or something -oey, who swung me across the floor with some fair boogie-woogie footwork. Okay, I'm not good with names but then neither is William; I must've called out "William!" a hundred times and he didn't answer until I elbowed him. It's like he doesn't even know his first name. Daft.

Jesi's Chapter One -- *1963*

The answer, my friend, is blowing in the wind
The answer is blowing in the wind.
Bob Dylan
Signed,
Go-with-the-flow Jesi

Jesi, please insert your Chapter One here. And do enter more than two lines!
Yours Truly,
Grandmama Bess

Here goes, Grandmama Bess (aka GB!):
Come writers and critics
Who prophesize with your pen
And keep your eyes wide
The chance won't come again
And don't speak too soon
For the wheel's still in spin
And there's no tellin' who
That it's namin'
For the loser now
Will be later to win
For the times they are a-changin'.
Bob Dylan

Bi-dah, bi-dah, bi-dah, that's all folks!
GB, do your own thing and don't worry about mine.
Peace and Love, Jesi.

Ruby's Chapter Two -- 1910

A t Cady's Tea and what followed that summer of 1910 were "mind-blowing" as Jesi would say. I felt I had entered a woman's world, one where there was an openness amongst these women that intricately wove a connection in and around them that was as delicate as lace; durable and colorful as needlepoint. Each life, each story, brought a different color, another scene to the mosaic. Oh God, how I loved that camaraderie! Each meeting with the Ladies brought me more understanding of what was happening around me, in what I came to know as my community. I was amazed (and at times horrified) at how different other women's lives were. How different they were and yet somehow the same, all being able to listen attentively, cry easily, or laugh deeply as their intuition saw necessary.

Contrary to criticisms, we all believed in three basic principles: the institution of marriage, protection of children, and a firm belief in God. They simply wanted to be able to stand up for these beliefs and be counted. As Lizzie stated more than once, "Ain't we people too?" More surprisingly I learned I was not alone in my frustrations as a wife and mother. I had only looked inward before knowing these Ladies, only to find my thoughts sometimes dark and aimless. The Ladies Legion brought light into my mind and a purpose to move outward. Each woman had been brought to the meeting place through calamities of her own, where her rights as a woman had been violated. That's what brought them here. But what kept them here were each other.

They shared their stories as best they could, beginning at Phyllis' Tea. I can still recall Phyllis perched on a footstool looking dwarf-like, resembling one of her lawn ornaments in her fairy-tale garden out front, thus explaining her weathered skin and hands. Animated, straight-forward, lots of exclamation – "Oh my! I'm a midwife but I wanted to be a doctor!" Her hearty laughter bounced both her white-haired bun and un-corseted belly. (While I hated the corset, I believed without one I would fall in a heap looking much like the pile of laundry I'd invariably left behind.) She said she had wanted to become a doctor ever since she'd heard her own heart beat through her uncle's stethoscope. Her heart proceeded to quicken at such a bold thought and she followed its excited state as far as she was allowed – which wasn't very far, as you can rightly guess. She was repeatedly shooed out of her uncle's clinic but wasn't reported to her father until she stole one of his medical books and asked him to assist her in applying for the one Female Medical College in Pennsylvania. Her uncle and father demanded a meeting, enforced with their own book in hand titled *Sex and Education* by Dr. Edward Clark (quite popular in those days because he wrote that a girl could learn, but not without uninjured health, and could suffer from uterine disease, hysteria, and other diseases.)

"I was told I must marry soon," Phyllis said, her hand over her heart as if to be reminded that it still beat on. "My father said that next thing he feared he would hear would be me joining that petticoat rebellion of women wanting to vote. He was wiser than I gave him credit for at the time!"

That wasn't to happen for many years later, she went on to say. Her uncle knew of a widower whose dying wife he had doctored. Phyllis marrying him would kill two birds with one stone: this would ease her uncle's conscience in the first wife's death (too much opium prescribed!) and would ease her father's conscience in public criticisms over his unmarried daughter. Lucky she was, or so they said, to have eight ready-made children and a man willing to marry a bookworm.

"A sweet heart but an old man!" she cackled. Yet she proceeded to have seven more children, mixed blessings that came with a midwife who taught Phyllis how to become one. She began work in a hospital and again attempted medical school only to be told that the American Medical Association barred women from membership. So she attempted nursing, only to be told that women nurses there were rare to none. They hired primarily men because the hospital board believed it improper for ladies to feed and bathe men. "And in men's beds!" she added with a snicker. "A lady seeing a man's nakedness would only add discomfort to an already sick man and could hamper wellness. Now think about that! An art that for centuries was considered a woman's domain was now considered for men only!"

She paused in thought. "It seems," she finally said, "that the more education is required for medicine, the less need there is for healing." She did not exclaim this but looked more deflated and reflective. The room became very quiet.

After a few moments silence, our colored comrade, Lizzie, patted Aimee's knee and spoke. "Well, now, my testimony is short and sweet. I don't talk much about my past - it becomes too real, too dark. I'll just say this: I was born into slavery in Georgia. When my papa found out that our master was selling him to another plantation, he ran off and escaped on the Underground Railroad up here. Mama told me after the war that he had gone to a station up here in the town of Cicero, to the home of Matilda Joslyn Gage. Mama said Mrs. Gage was a brave woman with four children of her own who signed a petition saying she would face a six month prison term and a $2000 fine rather than obey the Fugitive Slave law. This law made criminals of anyone assisting slaves to freedom. I wanted to go there, too, but Mama said Papa was supposed to come back for us ... but I never saw him again.

"My mama and I had nowhere else to go, so we stayed on the plantation long after the war set us free. Free from cleaning for the white folk for free, but only free enough to earn small wages cleaning for the white folk. You see, that was about the only difference, because schooling was not provided for colored women. And without learning you find yourself right back where you started.

"I just want to say, I thank the Lord for Cady taking me in the way she did. She taught me to read and to write, and showed me how to stand up for myself, or else I'd never know how. That is why I am here today."

The room became quiet once again.

I looked expectantly to Aimee now, next in line on the sofa to speak. She tugged her blouse sleeve down over her wrist and folded her hand over top of the bruised hand.

"I am thankful to be here," was all Aimee would say.

Cady diverted our attention to her announcement: We would march in the Fourth of July parade, carrying banners and signs and advertising our July eighteenth convention.

A cold wave of fear hit me with that one.

"Did you say, *march?* My goodness, in *public?*" I cried out. I just couldn't imagine it. "My husband, you see, he will know then, and my children. Shouldn't they come first? He forbids me even to attend these teas. But once I've started, I can't stop. It's like cleaning your stove, isn't it? Once you get started cleaning, you get dirtier and dirtier, and you wonder why you didn't leave well enough alone. A stove is black anyway, who would know it's dirty. Only you do, and that is enough and so you start cleaning and finally you work through the grease and the grime, until your arms feel as if they will fall off with the effort and the time. Finally you stand back and you say, yes, the stove does shine! It will work much more efficiently now. And you feel better for your efforts, and you know deep down you've done a good day's work, the best you know how!" I exclaimed just like Phyllis had done, breathless from saying so much out loud.

Cady said, "Thank you for your testimony, Ruby. I like that metaphor."

"Is that what that was?" I asked. I was that naïve and they all laughed knowingly.

Cady was so clever in what she said in answer. "Your first priority is to your home and family. There is no creature fiercer than a mother protecting her cubs. If it were not to defend her rights to her home and children, what would give her the reason? Why, the reason that brought our Legion together in the first place was this very thing! A student of mine was wrongfully separated from her mother and I saw first-hand the child's withdrawal—"

"You may say who it is, Cady," Eunice spoke softly. The room once again fell into silence. I finished my cookie, reached for another, and gulped my tea, wanting more of everything.

In contrast to Phyllis, Eunice spoke in a non-emotive tone, except at the end of most sentences when her tone would rise as if she were questioning what she just said. Or perhaps she needed validation for her bitterness and resolve-filled statements – validation we often gave in nods and smiles.

"My husband of nine years told me last year that he wanted a divorce – I was shocked? Hurt? Frightened? I asked if I could remain in our home to raise our children and he said I was no longer required to do so because he had made other arrangements. Other arrangements? I told him I was not leaving without my children. He showed me how wrong I was? That same evening a lady appears on my doorstep introducing herself as the new housekeeper. She had been Mr. Pickering's secretary. Young, well put-together? While she takes the children upstairs to their nursery, my husband enters our bedroom, throws some of my things into my dress case, and sets the case outside. He takes my cloak and wraps that around my shoulders and says to me ever so calmly to leave quietly - so as not to disturb the children?"

Eunice remained stoic, posture straight, only her thin hands clasping and unclasping, knuckles white, giving her away. "From my mother's the next day, I walked to the sheriff's office and reported what my husband had done. In tears I could hardly speak, clutching his arm. He brushed me off by saying any divorce was for the courts to decide and there was nothing he could do. My home was legally my husband's home and his to decide who lives there. I walked by many times looking for life, for I felt dead, but saw no one. My life as I knew it had ended, inconsolable for weeks?"

Her lips began to tremble and Cady took over, finishing the story by saying that the court ruled in the husband's favor because Eunice had deserted them. Since Eunice didn't have a proper home and the husband complained about her influence over the children, she was not yet allowed visitation with her children. She came to Cady at the school and they arranged visitations at lunch periods. "Her story is what sparked a long-time idea of mine to formalize protests for women's rights," said Cady. "I had already experienced chauvinism when I was limited to teaching only grade school level, higher learning being saved for men, by men. But, rather than fight it, I met Thomas and settled down." Her arm about Eunice's shoulders, she gave her a squeeze and a smile. "Eunice is what got me going again."

I wondered what in the world Eunice must have done to her husband to force him to do such a thing. Was she a bad cook? Disobedient? Neglectful mother? She didn't look like the wifely type so perhaps it wasn't in her nature to be a good one.

I learned the hard way what Cady meant by her last statement of the day: "Many of us are not aware of the law until we are affected by it. Its realizations can be quite frightening, particularly to a woman."

Mercy.

I worried that Robert would find out about us petitioning. Door to door we went, dressed in our black and white uniforms. I had proudly sewn my blouse from a bed sheet and stolen buttons from an old vest of Robert's. White represented the woman's non-violent and nurturing soul and of all white women shackled in men's laws. My black skirt no longer spoke grief for only my mother-in-law but for all women's oppression, including all Negro women.

Together we had finished Phyllis' draft of her Seven Reasons Why We Fight For Our Rights. We asked women to sign this. How I came up with the nerve to petition for signatures is still beyond my understanding. And Aimee and I had become clever enough not to petition on our street. Word might get to the husbands quickly. Time was limited to afternoons when husbands would be at their workplace, thus allowing wives' participation. Many feared doing so however, and with the word "demon" on their lips, doors were slammed in our faces. Others viewed us as angels or at the very least, were curious. If we could get our foot in the door, then we were in and our petition was signed.

One lady stays on my mind even today because she couldn't remember her own first name. I remember her answering the door, children orbiting her as if in their own solar system. We followed her waddling steps into her cluttered front room, consisting of a mixture of parlor and kitchen chairs, scratched tables, and a small bed draped with a large fabric, pillows along its back wall to declare it a sofa instead. Strong mixed smells of cooking beans and onions and urine hung heavily in the crowded room. Many children with their accompanying clutter was common-place for most of these homes, I fast realized.

With tin cups of coffee in hand, we read aloud our Seven Reasons, having previously learned that many women could not read. This lady sank her ample frame heavily into her rocker and eyed us curiously, laughing quite openly when we finished reading about women's lack of rights. "Rights to the law? I am the law here," she said, sitting a baby on her lap. This action pulled the others to her as if attached by one long string. "Here there's no vote and I do not allow fighting for rights or anything else. Land and property? We're thankful we have a roof over our heads and I can't work outside to keep it any more than my husband can work inside to maintain it. And pray tell, what would my husband do with custody of nine children? He treats the kitchen as his hallway to get out back. They would all surely starve without me."

We were inexperienced and at a loss for words, Aimee and I sympathetic with these natural roles of husbands and wives. "But one thing you said hit home," she continued. "And that is, the right to my body. I have had a baby a year since I was married at barely fifteen. My husband is Catholic and large families are expected. Would you believe I'm only twenty-five?" She did indeed look forty-five. We watched as she flipped the baby onto his back and won any contest for changing diapers. Her oldest daughter was sent off to the outhouse with the soiled one. She wiped her hand on her apron. "Where do I put my X on this petition?"

"I'll spell out your name first," I said. "What is it?"

"Mrs. Henry Watkins."

"What is your first name?"

"My first name?" She seemed confused. "I can't recall. Even my husband calls me Mother." After rummaging through her bedroom a minute or so, she could find no paperwork or documents with her name. "Oh, I'm so frazzled today, but it'll come to me eventually," she said, wiping a toddler's nose with the ever ready hanky. We were running out of precious time and had no recourse but to end the visit with her placing an X by "Mrs. Henry 'Mother' Watkins".

No, Robert didn't discover me petitioning door-to-door. Marching down Main Street in the 4th of July parade is a different story entirely. Everyone goes to the parade, well, everyone except Robert who didn't appreciate crowds, thus I thought it would be safe. Town businesses and shops were closed for the holiday, including Robert's shoe store, which meant Robert would be home. But that meant I needed an escape route. Aimee and I hatched a plan. We told our husbands that we were asked to bring food downtown to the park, and prepare picnic lunches for the needy. I received the necessary grunt of permission from behind his newspaper.

Two-miles at a clipped steady pace released some of the tension of the morning, and the small clouds of fog gave everything a positive dreamlike appearance. I became ready and willing by the time Aimee and I reached City Hall Park, the group already gathering under a cluster of gnarled oak trees. Cady and Lizzie had brought supplies of large white cardboard and black paint and we immediately went to work writing out our slogans. Cady knew that keeping us busy was vital. The parade was a big moment and regardless what Cady preached, we were only simple women. Repercussions were inevitable.

Our signs declared boldly:

Equality for Women!
Rights for All!/Change the Law!
Give us a voice!/Give us the vote!
Come hear 7 reasons to fight for Women's Rights!

At the bottom all the signs read: 'Women's Rights Convention, July18[th], 1910, City Hall Park'.

City Hall Park was a last-minute change in location. Cady announced at our last meeting that the Franklin High School auditorium was no longer available. Mr. Whiting, the principal, apologized with a vague explanation that the auditorium had already been booked, before his commitment to the convention. Cady believed there was more behind the cancellation than he was telling. There were rumblings among the school staff that the school should not be associated with a controversial political agenda. Parents opposed to the convention believed that its influence would seep into the children's education and would not present the proper ethics of a learning institution. Cady heard through the educated grapevine that there were supposed threats of children being pulled out of the school, if the Women's Right's Convention was held there. She did not wish to create a dilemma for her colleagues, or be at fault for hampering the children's education. Thus, to prevent further conflict, Cady moved the location of the convention to the park grounds outside City Hall.

The large white gazebo centered in the park was used as a stage for public outcry every Friday and Saturday night, from various male citizens who wanted to be heard when injustice rained on them. People out for an evening stroll would gather around the gazebo to listen, some to learn of current issues, some to be entertained, some shaking their fists, some shaking their heads, some wandering off with disinterest. Orators protested the fall of corn prices, property taxes, job loss from the local textile mill, or a gripe about a neighbor's wildstock. Anyone was allowed to speak, as long as he waited his turn with respect to the speaker before him. When he finished, he handed the megaphone over to the next, and exited the platform. Only one speaker at a time was permitted on the stage. A mounted sheriff's deputy was usually close by in case the complaint erupted into a fist-fight. Freedom of speech also permitted those "not quite right in the head" to ramble about their own views, whether that be sightings in the sky, or the government being seized by some foreign entity.

Never had the ladies witnessed nor heard of a woman walking into the gazebo to speak. It was normally considered loud male buffoonery. Cady realized that the Ladies' credibility would have been much stronger if supported by the school's institution. But they were left with little choice. On the bright side, Mr. Whiting pledged his continued support by promising to speak at the convention. He was an excellent orator and we drew encouragement from his pledge.

Cady paced around us women bent diligently over our signs, offering suggestions and encouragement. She finally tapped her hands together rapidly.

"May I have your attention, please! Ladies! Stand up and hold your signs in front of you…let me read them now…excellent! Now shoulders back, stand tall…yes! Now I want to see you smile! Beautiful! Remember as you walk two-by-two, stand proud of who you are and what you represent!"

Our signs were visibly shaking from trembling hands. Cady clasped her hands together at her chest and continued pacing in front of us. "Do not worry about the crowds! Do not hang your heads! I believe our march will receive the attention we need. To be heard! To bring in more audience to our convention! Remember why we march! As we gain support, we gain strength!" Cady pounded her hand with her fist. "Our government can no longer ignore us!"

I suddenly felt I was going into battle. Panic seized me. I became thankful my shaking knees were hidden within full skirts. The thought of knees reminded me of eight year old Jonathan's knobby knees in the early morn, and I felt remorse for snapping at him to go back to bed. I'd left Bess behind to wash all the pots and pans, standing on a small cricket bench at the washing pan. *Please God*, I prayed silently, *tell me I am doing the right thing. Not only for my sake, but also for my children's sake.*

The thought of my secure home with its familiar tasks sounded mighty comforting at the moment.

Then the marching drum began its beating rhythm to sound the beginning of the parade.

"Ladies, formation please!" Cady called out loudly. She picked up her own sign.

Our Ladies Legion had grown to ten women now thanks to our petitioning. All were in uniforms of white blouses and black skirts. Two by two we formed a line and marched into our assigned place behind the school band.

Behind us rolled a wagon pulled by a team of four horses. The wagon's sides were covered in chicken wire with many carnations of red, white, and dyed blue, strategically placed in the holes of the wire to depict the United States flag. Four people were standing in the wagon, dressed to look like George and Martha Washington, and Abraham and Mary Lincoln, each one waving their own small flag. They stopped waving when they saw us. Their shouting complaints about following "non-patriotic petticoats" were finally drowned out by the band's horns. I was relieved to see the smiling clowns on unicycles stay at our sides, and the town sheriff and his ten deputies who led the parade on horseback, each carrying a large American flag. The mayor and his wife drew up next in a buggy colorfully decorated in flowers and streamers, their horse draped in an American flag. We were surrounded by red, white, and blue, and admittedly our black and white looked, at the very least, non-participatory. At the most, like radical fanatics.

The parade moved slowly away from City Hall while the band played *All Over This Land*, surging us forward in marching step. It was such a rare treat to hear live music!

The procession snaked right onto First Street where spectators were beginning to form.

I had hoped to be more hidden. With some trepidation, I looked from the corner of my eyes to each side to see the smiling waving onlookers. There I noticed some faces form into frowns, some were pointing their fingers at our group, two heads were shaking. I blushed crimson when I heard a woman from the sideline call out "Shame on you!" Another yelled "Men-haters!" - the voice of an angry man with a clenched fist. It was best to focus on the straight narrow back of Cady, and the slight hunched back of Lizzie, leading the group. They held a six-foot long, three-foot high banner between them. Printed in large bold letters on white silk were the words:

Take the Shackles from Women!

We slowly gyrated onto Main Street, then Annan's longest street. The sparse gathering of spectators had flowed into crowds. The band now played *The Star-Spangled Banner*. Flags waved everywhere. The noise was getting louder. The drums seemed to be beating from within my chest. The ground pulsated. I hadn't prepared myself for all the many eyes, let alone eyes holding condemnation. But then I met Aimee's eyes and hers were shining, and she appeared confident, smiling, returning waves, and I felt better. Three teenaged girls joined in beside Aimee, and began waving cheerfully to the crowds, their brightly colored ribbons and calf-length dresses adding rainbows to the little black and white group. One shouted "What is right for the goose, is right for the gander!" A few women on the sideline laughed and applauded and their confident exuberance flowed over me, as if brought over by a breeze. My fear dissolved to my feet. I picked these feet up higher and higher, as if to kick off fear's burden.

The sounds were alternating between applause and booing. The response was amazing - far more outcries and applause than the Ladies ever supposed in the confines of our disciplined, peaceful parlor meetings. To be able to create such a stir made me feel so strong! I moved my sign up and down, up and down, chanting, "Fight for women's rights! Fight for women's rights!" to the rhythm of the band's song, *America the Beautiful*. Aimee looked over at me, obviously surprised and delighted. She joined in the chant and raised her sign higher. The three teenage girls yelled the chant too. I could easily imagine Bess marching with me in a few years and this inspired me further. By this time, I could no longer feel the ground beneath my feet, so high was my energy.

There we were chanting as our parade snailed past the bakery, Robert's shoe shop, the shops of the dressmaker and the tailor, the flower shop. What fun it was to represent something so large that could evoke emotions from opposite ends of the spectrum! I felt elevated, protected in our righteous cocoon of black and white. And then the cocoon slipped away, and for a brief and beautiful moment, I had the sense of a butterfly, weightless, free to fly. For a brief and beautiful moment, nothing else mattered.

It was at that moment that I looked over to the crowd on my right and saw Robert and my children. My mouth froze in mid-chant. They had a clear view, a perfect shot. It was too late to hide behind my sign. Bess had her hands to her mouth in surprise and then was jumping, pointing, leaning to Pearl and the boys, still in her calico housedress of early morning. All four children waved frantically, shouting, "There is Mama! Mama! Mama!"

Robert did not wave. He only stared at me hard and long. His eyes were large in surprise and then slowly became smaller until they were slits in his face. I had no choice but to continue to walk slowly by with a pasted smile and a nod as if I always marched in the 4th of July parade, flapping my hand to them like a damaged wing.

Continuing down the street, I wondered at my stupidity in thinking I could join a march such as this without Robert knowing about it. My shoes became heavy as if his sole repair had added lead. The band blared noise. I no longer worried about the crowd's eyes, only Robert's.

I tried to focus on Aimee's eyes, eyes who were looking at me, her mouth saying, "Ruby, are you alright? You've grown so pale! I saw Robert, too!"

I shrugged my shoulders, more to brush off Robert's angry stare on my backside, than to show indifference.

Seeming now never-ending, on down Main Street the parade continued. The sun that shone bright a moment ago, now felt hot and burned into my straw bonnet. My face felt flushed, my heart was racing; I surely thought I would faint but the greater fear of attracting more attention kept me upright.

I had not known before that so many emotions could happen moments apart: nervousness, elation, comfort from a woman's timid wave, fear in remembering my husband's stone face and it seemed now that all men in the crowd had that hard look.

The band played *Daisy, Daisy, give me your answer, do!* as we passed the steel fencing of the textile mill. Two newer members of the Ladies Legion practically screamed their chant and shook their fists as we passed the mill's entrance gate. These poor ladies worked there and had informed our group of their twelve-hour days in the intense heat of the machinery. The scale of stingy wages depended on the whims of the owner and the level of tolerance to his abuse.

Finally, finally, Main Street at last, ending at St. Mark's Catholic Church. The parade slowly disbanded and streamed out onto the church's expansive grounds as if nothing had gone wrong.

The blister rising on the bottom of my foot compounded my dread of the walk home. I would've kicked myself for being in this predicament if I could have lifted my legs. Obviously Robert hadn't followed me but where were he and the children? I prayed fervently to the church window's stained-glass Jesus that Robert hadn't vented his anger onto the children. How could I forgive myself for that?

Aimee intuitively knew that my day had ended. We would not stay for the picnic lunch we brought. We went in search of Cady to tell her of our departure and found her amid a group of women and men. Thomas had his arm around Cady's waist. He looked very cool and comfortable in his off-white linen suit. I could only dream of such support from Robert and at that moment I coveted Cady's husband, as bad as that may sound.

We joined the group as a gentleman's voice was asking, "Thomas, do you agree with your wife? Does she have your permission for such a display of outlandish women's politics?" I recognized him as the proprietor of the Rose Cafe. He had puffy cheeks and a full beard that contrasted his tiny eyes. His mustache was waxed on the ends and curved upwards into handlebars. His rounded stomach pulled hard at the buttons of his vest. His fat fingers held onto his coat lapels. He was quite full of himself.

"Yes and no," Thomas answered, appearing unraveled by the provoking. "I see both sides. I see myself as somewhat to blame, since I am of the same gender that directs these hardships that my wife and her group speak out against. Yet I understand some reasoning behind our laws. I believe many of the laws were designed to protect our women - they have enough on their plates as it is. Yet those men who wish for more power have abused these same laws. Our government might benefit from women's higher moral standards. But men do not like to change, and therefore they resist. And no, she has not disobeyed me. Any married man knows that husbands and wives learn by discussion and argument. If I told her to be silent, truth between us would no longer exist. She has my unabashed respect for her beliefs. She has a sound mind and excellent control of her faculties. I'll not stand in her way."

He raised his index finger. "However, I do not stand too far away because there are those, I understand, sir, that vehemently oppose the ladies' sentiment toward women's rights. Why this anger, I do not know." He looked down at the ground and shook his head but the accusation was directed, nonetheless. He continued. "I am concerned for my wife's well-being and admit that I asked her not to take such an active role. This was the same as asking these birds in the trees not to fly. Or like asking you not to question. You both have the right, am I right?"

The gentleman grew red-faced. The ladies were smiling and nodding. Cady looked at her husband gratefully and that's when I noticed for the first time how tired and pale Cady looked. Dark, recessed circles had formed under her eyes and Thomas's arm was holding her waist quite firmly, as if more for physical support than moral.

The gentleman cleared his throat and spoke loudly. "Sir, surely you are not upholding women's rights to vote! Most are unversed in political or financial affairs. Many are not even educated."

Thomas raised his head and confronted the gentleman as if accepting a challenge. "To say that a woman cannot vote because she is uneducated is a moot point. First of all, a voter does not make the rules but simply votes for those men who can, hoping that his own personal interests are regarded. Secondly, women are uneducated through no fault of their own but are oppressed by the very men who criticize them for what they are lacking."

The gentleman shook his head at the applause of the ladies circling around him. "You make men sound as tyrants. I am a married man who provides well for my wife, my mother, and my daughters. Men are perfectly capable of representing women. They take their beloved's best interests to heart. Regardless what legal position may be out there, women's actual conditions are quite good. We are not barbaric, inflicting misery and suffering!"

"Yes, this is true for many but not all," Thomas said, "If he so chooses, he has the power to subordinate her will to his whenever they argue. You must admit that, at the very least, if you exclude her from being heard then she is in danger of being overlooked."

Thomas looked down at his wife, concern furrowing his brow. "We must go," he said, studying her face. "She has *agreed* to go home for a rest. She had a big day. Good day." He tipped the brim of his straw panama hat to the circle. With his arm steadfast around Cady, they walked away.

Outside the earshot of the others, I asked her if she was ill. She answered by asking if Aimee and I would collect the signs and bring them to her carriage. She pointed to the steam automobile that I'd had the pleasure of riding in earlier that spring. It reminded me of the whipping I received because of it, and of another whipping that could happen again today. I had to get home.

"And one more thing," Cady said. "Would you please lead the group through the picnic on my behalf? Give them some encouraging words. You all did beautifully today! Would you do that?"

"Of course!" I would walk through fire for Cady. Robert's wrath would have to wait.

The ladies were all in good spirits, looking content and at ease sitting on the grass, the white table cloth spread, the vase of daisies and pretty dishes giving just the right inviting touch that only a woman can do. I couldn't possibly be the only one with trouble brewing at home like an overheated teakettle? I would simply have to forget myself for the afternoon.

I thought of what Cady would have said if she were still here. "We have achieved much today!" I exclaimed to all. "You did a beautiful march. Well done, ladies!"

"We will read about this in the paper tomorrow!" one exclaimed. "I saw a newspaper photographer!"

"Right is might!" another shouted, her fist in the air.

"The convention can only be a success!" another cried.

But at what cost, I wondered gloomily as I, with Aimee in silent tow, finally headed back home in the late afternoon sun, my empty pie plate clutched in clammy hands.

I walked slowly up the steps to my front door. The growing blister protested painfully and perspiration soaked the back of my blouse, collecting inside the corset.

The house was unusually quiet for this time of day. The boys should be outside playing in this sun. I turned the doorknob. It was locked. I tried again, thinking it was stuck. It wouldn't turn. Robert normally locked the doors only if we were going away overnight. He held the key and he made such decisions.

Walking over to the parlor windows, I shielded my eyes with my hands to look in but saw no one. Perhaps Robert took the children to the Rose Café for dinner? Highly unlikely that he would spend that kind of money, but then his appearance at the parade was out of character.

I sat stiffly on the wicker settee, back straight, hands folded in my lap and waited, but soon my fatigue and summer heat gave me a slouch, my skirts hiked immodestly to my knees, my stockings rolled down. To heck with the neighbors - our house wasn't built on a stage! To prove the point, I boldly removed my boots and stockings and sat there as barefoot as a baby.

Thirst drew me around to the back of the house where the water pump stood at the center of the yard. Moving the squeaky handle up and down as I pumped the water sounded noisier than usual and I couldn't shake off that something was strange but I couldn't quite put my finger on it. I normally kept the back door locked from within but I tried unsuccessfully at any rate. I also made use of the outhouse, glad for once that we didn't have an inside toilet with a flushing water tank. Then there was the vegetable garden and as my mama always said, "wasted time should be a crime", I began pulling weeds diligently to pass the time in waiting for my family's return.

Such a beautiful garden and I loved this one chore above all others in seeing my labors come to visible fruition and could proudly display this as eventual sustenance for my family. My lavender bushes along the fence were my other pride, the oil good for mosquito bites, the leaves for a digestive tea, the fragrant blooms for sachets. Wood ash my secret to their growth … I could have spent all my time in the back yard if allowed. Outside the monotony of cooking and ironing, gardening was a learning experiment of when to plant, what to plant, how much to plant for canning and preservation.

Hence, the next time I looked up, it was close to dusk and I was dusted in dirt, my feet caked in it and enjoying this rare solitude in the outdoors. In rising off my knees, some movement caught my eye in the third-story bedroom window. The curtain stirred but nothing was there. This was all very odd. The sun was setting quickly and the house took on a quiet gray gloom.

I returned to the front verandah and felt relieved to see the lamp on in the front parlor window. I knocked and knocked on the front door but although I heard footsteps on the interior stairs and muffled voices inside, no one came to the door. I became completely exasperated. Walking over to the parlor window, I at last saw Robert sitting in his chair, as plain as day, reading the newspaper as if he were deaf and dumb.

"Robert!" I whispered loudly, tapping on the window and caring for once that the neighbors didn't see me. How embarrassing to be standing outside while your husband cannot simply answer the door!

He looked up from his paper slowly and deliberately, and focused his eyes on me. No, I take that back; he was boring his eyes into me. So, he was still angry. No more secrets, I had decided in the vegetable garden. I would tell him everything. I wanted a relationship like Cady and Thomas had. Perhaps Thomas could come over and talk to Robert ... I flinched as he threw his paper to the floor and rose from his chair. The front door opened and he came outside, closing the door behind him. He folded his arms across his chest and stared silently down at me.

"Robert, I am sorry. I can explain everything."

"No need. I wouldn't believe you," he said, low and calm. "You lied to me.

You lied to the children. Worse yet, my mother would turn over in her grave if she saw the state of this house. Dishes, dirt ... look at this shirt, Ruby. Look at it! Two buttons are missing. I came downstairs this morning to find little Bess standing on a bench trying to wash pots bigger than she is. We had strawberry pie for breakfast *and* lunch. I had to take the children downtown to actually *buy* something to eat and that is where I found the disappointment of my life. My own wife marching with men-haters. Which can only mean that you must hate men, too. Which can only mean that you hate your own *husband*. Worse yet, I will be the laughing stock among my customers. But you are not concerned with my life, are you Ruby? Nor with my children. You are not a good wife. You are not a good mother."

He purposefully eyed me up and down. "And look at you. A poor seamstress with that cheap blouse you are wearing. Cheap and dirty, for all to see. And my God, bare feet as filthy as a beggar. You shame me. My own mother and father built a decent home and reputation in this neighborhood, only for you to tear it down. You ridicule the government for not looking after you when you can't even look after yourself, let alone your family."

His words bit deeply, stripping me of my essence as a woman. All I could do was stand there raw and crying, retorts jammed in my unworthy throat. His cold eyes met mine and did not waver. "My children do not need this sort of upbringing. They deserve better, Ruby." He pointed his thumb to his chest. "*I* deserve better, Ruby."

He took another look at my feet, making them feel adulterous. This seemed to decide my fate. "Filthy liars are not welcomed here. This has always been a Christian home. It will remain so. You are to leave my home and these premises." He turned his back to me and opened the door.

I didn't understand. I reached out and clutched his shirt. "Robert, what are you saying?" I suddenly thought of Eunice and how everything became a question when her life turned upside down. And of how I had judged her harshly from my secure roost.

"Is that Mama? Where is Mama?" cried Pearl and Jonathan from somewhere within.

"Go to bed!" he yelled around the door to the inside. "I already told you to stay in your rooms and away from the windows! Now GO!"

I made an attempt to step around him to get inside, but his arm shot out and he pushed me hard so that I fell against the rocker and onto the floor. With a fleeting look at neighboring homes, he quickly stepped inside and slammed the door hard. The click of the lock echoed over and over in my ears.

I could only sit there in shock.

More shouts and cries from within pulled back to my feet and I pleaded through the parlor window. "Oh my God, please Robert don't take this out on the children!" In an absolute frenzy I ran back to the door and banged there. More cries, more shouting. I stopped banging. I was causing my children's hysterics and whippings and hadn't I done enough harm already?

I collapsed into the rocker in tears and prayer, landing on something hard. I reached under and brought out the pie plate. I stared dumbly at the leftover crumbs as a new wave of sobbing shook me and the pie plate fell with a loud rattle to the wooden floor. The parade and the picnic seemed like years ago.

"It's all my fault," I whispered, banging my knee with my fist. "I hate you, I hate you! You are a bad woman, a bad, bad woman! How could you be so selfish? How could you do this to them? To your husband, to your children? You don't deserve such a loving family! You've been told how fortunate you are but you wouldn't listen to your own sister, to your own mother! How will you face Opal and Mama now?"

They all seemed so far away. Everyone who loved me. Would they all stop loving me now? I choked and cried and finally the tears subsided. I wiped my face with the sleeves of my streaked blouse, trying to think of what to do, where to go.

Then, the light went out in the parlor and left me in darkness. Only the fireflies came around to offer their pitiful light. I desperately hoped for one brief moment that Robert would open the door on his way up the stairs. The house had become so quiet that I could hear the creaking of the inner stairs as he climbed to his bedroom.

Fresh tears came as the impact of his words and the cruelty of being left out here in the dark began soaking in. I wrapped my arms around me as the cool night air stirred around me, and I began rocking slowly.

"I hate you, Robert," I whispered. "How could you do this to me when I have obeyed you every day of our married life? Well, at least until this spring. I cooked you hot suppers every day. I boiled and scrubbed your soiled underwear, I ironed your shirts, I cleaned your house, like the servant I am to you. And never once did you thank me or tell me you loved me. You, your mother, you both only made me feel that *I* am the one who should be thankful. Well, your mother is dead, Robert, and you need to bury her once and for all. She's starting to stink around here!"

Believe me, I tried hard to still the storm of hateful words to him, to me, tides of anger rising and falling. I had to think clearly about where to go. I looked over at Aimee's dark house. I could be jumping from the pan to the fire in facing Aimee's husband, judging by her bruises. Asking for Aimee's aid any evening with her husband home, was out of the question.

Nor could I walk out to the farm at this hour. It would frighten Mama to death. And the blister wouldn't permit the three-hour journey by foot.

As my tears dried with the dirt and sweat on my face, I felt a hardening. A hardening that penetrated through and through. I began thinking logically. I resolved that I would eventually find my way back in. Here was where I belonged. Robert remained my husband, who, whether I liked it or not, I took an oath to love, honor and obey. He made an oath, too, to love, honor and keep me, though he needed to work on the 'keep' part. These were my children, my own flesh and blood. They were my responsibility. But I would take more control of my life, and of my children's lives. I had been too trusting of my security within these walls. I would make sure I was never so vulnerable again.

Suddenly it dawned on me what women's rights were all about. Now I fully understood for the first time what I was marching for. What I was petitioning for. Before this, I had been only a student going through the motions of class participation. Now I was living it. Now I could sympathize with what the other women were saying in their testimonies, and the scars that brought them to the place to fight back. How law must be changed to protect women from the anger of men. In such an exposed state, I saw what they were fighting for so clearly. Robert's cruelty only strengthened my resolve to support the Ladies Legion all the more.

"If he is attempting to teach me a lesson," I whispered, "he will be surprised at what I've learned."

I would take it one step at a time. First step: find a place to sleep. I stopped rocking and looked over at the wicker settee, its thin cushion offering little comfort.

"Mercy," I muttered.

Lying in a fetal position, I was thankful for the first time today for my wool skirt and petticoat layers, for my long thick hair that I unpinned and loosened around my shoulders and arms, for my stockings.

Once back in the house, my mind continued, the first thing I would do is have another key made. Yes that was it.

Take it one step at a time.

My exhausted body finally pulled my mind down into sleep.

I walk down a long empty street. Snow begins to fall, blowing around me, through me, blowing up my skirts, billowing them out like a storm-swept sail. I bend my uncovered head against the wind and push my torso forward, my feet and hands become frigid with colds, leaving only my teeth limber in a wordless chatter. The snow piles quickly as I push my legs, stockings wet and stiff. I must keep moving. My knees rise higher and higher to stay on top of the rising white but I'm moving too slowly. The wind chills my lungs as I breathe in heavily, its release a cloud that looks like something else to have to walk through. I am losing strength. I plow my body through again and again, the icy flakes all with their individual pattern packs into sameness-snow that is now as high as my knees. Keep moving, I repeat over and over. If I stop, I know I will become buried in these cold drifts. No one will ever find me. I push on, the snow now up to my hips. I look beyond the white mounds down to the end of the street. There is no end in sight, just forever and ever. I bring in my shoulders and push forward. Keep moving! The snow is now at my chest that I claw away with stiff unprotected fingers. It is of no use. The snow is only mounting higher. My body is becoming numb to the cold. I'm getting sleepy. It doesn't seem to matter anymore, this struggle. Why do I struggle so? But the question causes doubt and the doubt causes me to stop, if only for only a moment. A moment I immediately regret, because the snow quickly covers my ears, eyes and last my head. I can only see the white crystals before my eyes. I can no longer be seen. I'm suffocating. Why did I stop? I cry. Tears freeze on my cheeks. I will die here. No one will find me, now that I stopped the struggle. To keep going would have made a trail for my daughter to take safely. I am so angry with myself but it is too late. Why did I stop, why did I stop?........out of the distance, I hear Papa's voice. "Ruby, Ruby, wake up! Get up!"

"Is that you, Papa? Papa?"

"No Ruby, it's Jesse!" My brother was shaking my shoulders hard.

"Jesse?" I mumbled, trying to climb out of my dream. I rubbed at my eyes, crusty and hard to open.

"Ruby, why are you out here?" Jesse's voice sounded troubled, scolding, like I had lost some sense and had chosen to sleep out here.

Memories of the night before came rushing back and with it more tears. I sat up and tried to focus on Jesse who was leaning over, looking intently at my face, his hand still on my shoulder.

"Ruby, what happened?" His voice was softer now, filled with concern.

Good ol' Jesse, steadfast and true, always there for family. I couldn't say any of this.

"Did Robert do this to you?" He shook my shoulder again. "Did he?"

I betrayed Robert and nodded.

"Why?" Jesse asked. He stood up straight and said, "Well, it doesn't make any difference why, anyway. No kinfolk of mine is left out in the cold like some barn animal! No, not even if you marched with the Confederates!" He took off his cap and slapped his leg with it, his thick curly brown hair unruly. "This ain't right, Ruby!"

He paced in front of me, his round face and short nose so much like Papa's, it added tears. His mind made up, he stated matter-of-factly, "Well, you are coming home with me." Without waiting for a reply, he reached down and picked me up as light as a pillow.

His warm arms felt so comforting around my cold exposed body, I accepted all the pity he had. He carried me down the steps and out to his milk wagon. I looked at his face as he did so. I had never seen him at such close range before. His lips were pinched together and his nostrils flared, whether it was from my weight or anger, I couldn't tell. Yes, just like Papa.

He sat me carefully onto the bench like I might break. "Whoa!" he called to the startled horses. "I'll be right back." he said to me. "Don't you move!" he commanded.

I rubbed my eyes again and tried to gain composure. Left with no choice but to face Mama and the rest of them looking like death warmed over, I struggled with my waist-long hair and a clinging hair-pin, but the one pin could not hold its burden alone and my hair fell into a downward spiral that I felt symbolic of my situation.

I looked up startled as I heard Jesse knock on the front door. In the gray early light, I noticed the milk bottles sitting there by the front door and realized it must be six o'clock in the morning and Jesse had delivered our milk as usual. Jesse's morning deliveries had not occurred to me the night before, although they should have. With no answer, Jesse banged hard on the door this time. When the door opened, I couldn't hear what Jesse said, but I could hear the punch from where I sat. Robert fell back against the door, clutching his face in shock. Jesse simply turned away and walked back down the steps, rubbing the knuckles of his right hand. Robert continued holding his jaw as he closed the door again.

I could only stare open-mouthed. Strangely, my first thought was that I hoped Robert remembered to come back for the milk for the children's breakfast. My second thought was that now Robert would know what it felt like being on the other end of an angry hand. In my exhausted state, it all seemed like a gray nightmare.

Jesse climbed onto the bench next to me, flicking the reins, clicking his tongue to get things moving. He and the horses pressed forward, while I looked behind.

I gazed back at my home of twelve years. The memory of my daughter pulling the bench up to the wash pan, and the memory of my son's knobby knees came back to pinch me. Was that only yesterday? They both had asked if they could come with me. I longed for them to ask me now. What would they do without me?

I yearned for a glimpse of their faces framed in their bedroom windows. The blinds were drawn, like closed eyes shutting me out.

"Oh my babies!" I whispered through choked tears. I clutched the bench to keep from jumping off and running for home. But Robert wouldn't open the door again now, for certain. And I didn't want the children to see me like this. Yes, Jesse was doing the right thing.

As we rolled slowly past Aimee's home, I could see her motionless figure, watching from her parlor window.

I shivered against the chilled morning air and Aimee's hesitance to wave, against Robert's cold eyes, against the frigid snow in my dream. A chill pierced through to my soul and I needed the love of family to bring warmth again.

Jesse silently handed me the reins and reached back behind him to the backbench. He pulled out a coarse woolen horse blanket and draped this around my shoulders. Quiet and self-assured like Papa, he was accustomed to spending a great deal of time alone with his own thoughts. And like Papa, early every morning he delivered his farm-fresh milk to the local dairy in the large aluminum cans. In exchange, they gave him clean empty cans and several cases of fresh bottled milk that he would then deliver to assigned homes on his milk run. My street ended his deliveries for the day, on his way back to the farm. I rarely saw him but instead I could set my clock to the sound of his timely footsteps on the wooden planks of my porch along with the clink of milk bottles as he replaced two empties with fresh bottles. Sometimes hand-written notes would be tied to a milk bottle with a string, Jesse's way of passing on news or invitations from the farm. He always refused to take money for the milk. "Nope. Family," he'd say.

"Jesse, you are God's gift, did you know that?"

He rubbed the back of his neck and straightened his cap, in his way of shyness. With that crooked smile and beloved dimple, he said, "Do me a favor and tell that to Edith. She won't be too happy when she finds out I just punched Robert."

"I have more explaining than you do, Jesse. You had cause to do what you did. Robert had it coming and I am glad you did it. I'm sorry I forgot to set the empties out."

"I'll get them tomorrow," he said. "I'm sure once I knock on the door, Robert will bring them right to me."

We both grinned at that.

"I'll make it up to him," he continued. "I'm delivering eggs starting next week. Edith's eggs are selling for twenty-two cents a dozen."

I turned to him in surprise. "What a marvelous plan, delivering eggs with milk!"

He shrugged. "Edith's idea. She can tell you all about it when you get there."

Like always, it was like pulling teeth to get him to talk about the details.

A long stretch of silence ensued with us listening to the occasional snorting and jingling of harnesses and the sounds of the horses' hooves plodding over the cobblestones and then sounding more muffled as the road reduced to hard-packed dirt outside of town, the wagon wheels creaking over the deep pits and ruts.

"Jesse?"

"Hmmm?"

"Thank you for looking after me."

"Papa would turn over in his grave, if I didn't look after his girls."

I remembered Papa's voice in my dream, and what Robert said about his mother turning over in her grave the night before. *That means I've disturbed two dead ones in short order. How can I bring peace back to the living and to the dead, and still want to live myself?*

Bess's Chapter Two -- 1920

What is honesty?

Not only my parents but the newspaper redefined 'truth' in those days. The agony I felt when I saw on page four the most unflattering portrait of myself. The photograph showed me standing at the podium during my speech, my mouth wide open, my wide-brim hat a bit lopsided. I should have had no modesty by now and I certainly did not agree with my schoolteachers who believed women should not find their names or photographs in the press. Of course this was silly, when publicity was exactly what I wanted. But feminine vanity prevailed, and I would have preferred to be caught in the act of smiling sweetly. It was so easy to get your name and photograph in the paper – common women got more advertising for saying anything publicly, than did popular male candidates for election. It was such a novelty.

The editorial page was worse. A cartoon was drawn of a woman in only a camisole and old-fashioned petticoat, rising into the air, corset and other garments falling away. She held a sign reading, "Free, Free, Free; Me, Me, Me!" Her arms extended above her toward a man's leg, covered in trousers and shoes. I recognized this as a mockery of the last rambling portion of my speech. My words came back to me: *corset of social injustice; be free ladies,* etcetera. A letter to the editor written by a Mr. Edrite Formen (that couldn't possibly be his real name) expressed the mockery more clearly.

Good News, Men! Now that women have won the right to vote, we men of drudgery and dirty battles can relax into our easy chairs for the remainder of our callous irresponsible days. Women will clean up our mess and right the world once again. A rebel spirit has been born, shedding herself of all responsibilities of the pure woman, and instead wants to 'move forward' and make the world a decent place to live in. Oddly she must become interested in herself to do that. Internal muses will save the external. If we dastardly men only knew the power of the vote we once owned as our own, why think of what we could have achieved before the women came along to save the day!

In their naiveté, I will kindly take this time to remind these new freedom fighters that achieving their goals through political action is like running a mule in a horse race. The mule doesn't belong there, she has no prior training to run, and although she may make it to the finish line ... eventually, by then the winning horses have gone on to other races.

I was livid and immediately carried my anger and this article to my old friend, Thomas Pickering, the editor of the Annan News and also the owner of the Lighthouse. I met him at the front door to his office, he as usual heading the other way. He had a smile that could charm a squirrel from its tree limb.

"Bess, my dear, just the person I wanted to see! Amazing you would come here today of all days when I have a job offer for you."

As in the past, I had to resist moving his careless hair from his forehead. He invariably appeared as if he didn't have time for such foolish vanity. The color had become more gray than blond but again something he likely was unaware of. He'd been a widower of ten years since his wife, Cady, leader of Mama's *Ladies Legion*, passed away. He'd traveled extensively since then as a reporter and did so for the war, and only recently stayed more in place since his promotion to editor. Most of the rooms of his manor were handed over to the Legion for their Lighthouse upon Cady's death. Only the master chamber had been sanctioned off and its double doors locked. He rarely visited the Lighthouse, preferring to live downtown. Lizzie and I and the many battered women whom we had cared for at the Lighthouse, were eternally grateful.

Which was why I was so aghast at the article.

Incensed I met him with a shake of the newspaper in my hand. "Why would you let such trash go into your paper?"

He returned his hat to the hook on the back of his door. "Free speech, dear. You believe in that, surely. Besides." He pulled open a desk drawer and waved a stack of letters back at me. "I printed the decent one. There were worse, believe me."

I slumped into a chair unlady-like. "All we heard before we won the vote was that men dreaded the change women would make in politics. Yet now I think they will be disappointed when the change doesn't come as fast as that. One married suffragist explained it like this: Men imagine us housecleaning politics in the same manner as they saw their mothers spring clean in a frenzy by beating carpets and scattering dust and children everywhere. Actually women just plan on cleaning one room at a time and the men will hardly know the cleaning is going on."

He sat in his own chair and stretched. Hands behind his head, he looked at me for a moment, his eyes squinting in thought. "You've consecrated the cause. Give it up."

"That reminds me." I pointed to my paper on his desk. "Can you print this for me?"

He placed wire spectacles onto the end of his nose and read. He finally looked up at me over the top of his lenses, his green eyes intense, his countenance all business. "The suffrage movement has changed you. You are entirely radical now." He took his spectacles off and gave me a level gaze. "Don't be so hard on the southern cotton mills. As you know, I was born and raised in the south. The only reason they used child labor after the Civil War was because the hands of the adults were too callused from working in the fields. Only children could do the delicate operations necessary for a mill-worker. I also know that if we print this, we are going to get antagonistic letters from our local women's union. There are talks of unfair practices in the factories and I wish there was something I could do about it."

"But as you said, 'free speech, dear'." I smiled, enjoying the challenge. Billy had called me a radical suffragist too, when I argued once that I didn't believe in that printed pap they fed me in school about civil government, all ruled by men.

Thomas didn't return my smile. "I'll print this on one condition: you come work for me. I'm being bombarded with requests for advertisements for any consumer goods you can think of. More and more electrical gadgets, motor cars, shampoos, washing machines. Demand for goods has grown since the war. The factories are more than happy to accommodate since they no longer manufacture munitions. People no longer must put aside personal needs for wartime. Now they want to indulge in luxury and convenience. Simplify tasks. Travel more now that many families own a motor car. People want to celebrate our peacetime and go to movie houses and be entertained. You could appeal to the liberated woman. Women make most of the purchasing decisions of the household so we would do well to direct our advertisements to them. I give you the product, you write the advertisement, and I'll pay you five dollars a day. Deal?"

I desperately needed a purpose in my life. I felt depleted and distant, unsatisfied with fate's offerings. Not even when Miss Gail Laughlin (President of the National Federation of Business and Professional Women's Clubs no less, and a well-known woman lawyer I'm proud to say) approached me to write an article on the recently conceived Equal Rights Amendment proposal and submit this now to Thomas, did I feel any sort of nourishment. This would take care of today, but what about tomorrow? There were many other members of our chapter of the association who had also lost their enthusiasm once the Nineteenth Amendment was passed, and Mrs. Catt talked about closing the National Association of Women Suffrage for good. There were many more battles to be won, we all knew this, but taking these issues to task were tedious and anticlimactic at this point. Only a handful of suffragists brought legislators to civilization, inch by inch.

And now we needed to introduce these same war-weary women into the political sphere. But women wanted to go back home and mend fences, make peace with their chicken soup.

"I suppose I could try advertisements. I'll take the job on one condition: You agree to come to the Lighthouse for dinner tonight."

He returned his attention to me with such an unabashed gladness that I could feel my face redden. "I would love to!"

"So you will publish my article for me?"

His smile dropped and his business mask came back. "As long as you understand there will be repercussions."

But like an old war-horse smelling cannon fire, I only felt at home.

Thomas was twice surprised when he entered the Lighthouse that evening: Firstly with my hello kiss on his cheek at the door; secondly, with my request to go out after dinner.

"You? Jazz music?" he asked.

"Yes, while it may be hard for you to imagine me kicking up my heels and having fun, I believe I can."

He laughed as if the whole thing was preposterous. "Have you before?"

"Yes, well, once … with Billy. It wasn't jazz music but the orchestra was lovely."

"Do you know what these speakeasies are like? Illegal—" He cut himself off and looked at Lizzie, shaking his head.

"My sister asked that we meet her and her boyfriend at Hullabaloo's. It's all set. You're a worldly man, Thomas, you can handle such an establishment, can't you?"

He leaned toward me and grasped my hand, those green eyes warm with mischief. "I wouldn't miss this for the world."

Lizzie stooped over with a grunt and picked up Thomas' scarred leather brief case. She could no longer walk upright, but in a permanent bend, her cane now as natural an appendage as her arm. She motioned me to follow her ever-constant black dress and unfashionable petticoats to the back parlor. I thought to ask how she felt but Lizzie's pride was intolerant of sympathy. She wouldn't take it and she wouldn't give it. Brought as a former slave by Thomas and Cady when they first married Lizzie was as much a part of the house as the staircase.

"Why do you want me back here?" I asked as we entered the back parlor. Papers and books were everywhere; the typewriter, desk, and chairs practically hidden by the collage. The walls were covered with posters, announcements, and letters thumb-tacked anywhere within reaching distance. But there were no women there to blame or claim credit for it. The vast old house was unusually quiet; especially considering it wasn't that long ago that our chapter of the National American Woman Suffrage Association met here regularly. The well-worn furnishings and marked floorboards proved many women harbored here. This became my home away from home when younger, and now my only home. A harbor for others, a haven for me.

Lizzie's dark brown lips protruded in deep thought. "What did I do with those letters?" she mumbled. She remained still, her small black eyes skimming the room as if suspiciously waiting for such papers to announce their hiding place. She shrugged, while I silently agreed with her that it would be hopeless to find specific papers here.

"You've got work to do," she said. "People are complaining about your speech and you need to answer their letters. Besides. You have no business asking a man, and Cady's husband at that, to take you to a sinful place."

Deceased ten years, Cady still lived in this house it seemed. I felt rebuked and shameful, and by a colored person at that.

"Know your place, Lizzie. This is not your concern."

I walked over to my roll-top desk and read again the words of my heroine, Susan B. Anthony, before her death. *When it is a funeral, remember, that I want that there should be no tears. Pass on, and go on with the work.* This yellowed clipping from a newspaper article, was pinned below a fading photograph of the aging spinster, hair severely pinned back into a bun, her thin spectacles framing eyes that revealed fathoms in determination, intelligence, and sorrow. I had met her once, while she was on one of her cross-country campaigns, and will never forget it. She had died in 1906 without seeing her dream realized.

I had seen the dream realized and had woken up. I had nothing now to say. I now wanted to live. The many papers' scrawled writing, bold typing, red underlines, seemed to be shouting at me like a mother with too many demanding children. I decided not to answer to any of them, including Lizzie. I walked out of the room, seeking out Thomas as my temporary refuge, leaving Lizzie alone with the parlor and its past.

After dinner, we said our goodbyes to Lizzie, her furrowed brow letting me know her deep disappointment. I made a mental note to discuss her role as housekeeper and for her to keep it at that. Besides, I was tiring of writing speeches and articles, only to be accused of dirty rhetoric. Thomas was right; I'd consecrated the cause and should just give it up. But I didn't know how because I didn't know what else was out there to do. As Pearl had said earlier, during her invitation, "Step down off your soapbox and come see how the other half of town is living."

"I warn you, you're going to feel simple in that dress," Thomas said, as we headed toward the door.

"What is wrong with it?" The white Peter Pan collar and dark brown cotton fabric belted at the waist were slimming when I last looked in the mirror. The length fell to about mid-calf.

"Nothing is wrong with it, but, well, you'll see."

I certainly did see. Pearl's sack dress was like so many others in the crowded and poorly lit Hullabaloo's – short to the knees and one even above the knees. "She rouges her knees for that dress," Pearl confided, her hand beside her mouth as if telling a secret. No need – she had to shout this twice, the trumpet and drums were so deafening. Women were decorated with ornate beads and feathers and holding cigarettes as if all understood they were at a costume party. In comparison, I felt dressed to take notes as the stenographer. I watched one lady across from our table smoking a cigarette as if kissing her lover, her eyes closed, her lips puckered to inhale and exhale slowly. Obviously the fashion was to cut one's hair short and put in waves; I was the only bun in the place. I got the message and decided to let my hair down - literally. Thomas glanced over at me, looked away and then his attention snapped back to me with a surprised look. I awaited his disapproval but his face creased into a big grin and he nodded.

Pearl's boyfriend wore his hair slicked back and black with a matching clipped mustache. One jacket sleeve hung empty as like many men, ravages of the war. He acted as if he wanted Robert to think he was older than he was, enjoying calling out to and openly flirting with other women by their first names, his dark eyes squinting as if from deep thought, but I think it was more from cigarette smoke. When he agreed, he used one word: "Pos-a-lootly!" I found him far too forward and presumptuous with Pearl, kissing her hard and long, keeping his one arm possessively about the back of her neck and shoulders. She was quite brash in return and I felt embarrassed that my sister behaved in such a way in front of Thomas. I conveyed as much to her via shouting into her ear across the table but she pretended she couldn't hear me.

Conversation was difficult but enough words and signs were given to follow David and Pearl into another room upstairs, leaving our half-finished sodas behind. "I know the password," David winked and another nail went into his coffin-according-to-Bess.

Upstairs displayed a larger band playing the piano, trumpet, saxophone, banjo, bass, and drums. The strong rhythmic music beat in my chest. This rhythm traveled down my spine and into my legs and feet. Many were dancing fast steps, their energy and pounding shoes vibrating the floor. As I followed Thomas to our table, I found myself walking in rhythm to the beat, marveling at the dancers.

The dim lights went dimmer still as a voice spoke through a microphone, "Ladies and gentlemen, give a loud clap to Lady and Her Tramps as they perform her hit number, Razz-Ma-Tazz Jazz!" The lights flashed blue onto a small stage where a lone figure stood, her silhouette a very womanly hourglass in the shadows. A spot light suddenly shone bright on her to reveal her long bare legs and bare arms. Her costume had less fabric than a man might wear to the beach, except for exposed garters holding up her net stockings. Three men appeared and danced with her in such an intimate way that I flushed in the smoky dark.

I glanced over at Thomas who was watching me. He burst out laughing so I closed my gawking mouth with a snap. A glass was placed in front of me. I sniffed it and looked at him quizzically. It was whiskey. I leaned over and loudly whispered in his ear, "What about the Prohibition?"

"It's still illegal," he shouted with a grin, his face too close, his breath already strongly illegal. "Drink up. We don't want to be here too long."

I took a small sip, the burning in my throat taking my breath away. What if someone recognized us?

Too late. Several approached Thomas and knew him by his first name, including some scantily-clad females – I dare not say ladies – who were quite pleased to see him. He shouted introductions but I missed the names in the noise. I could only nod and smile. I took a large sip to swallow down the rising jealousy and this caused my eyes to water. I watched him chatter and envied that confidence he exuded in any situation I'd seen him in, whether it be editing the newspaper, calling out orders to his staff, stepping onto a speaking platform, or answering confrontational questions from the public and reporters. And now in an illegal establishment he appeared as comfortable as at our dinner table. With his jacket off, suspenders and white shirt glowing in the dim light, he looked distinguished and casual at the same time. I hadn't quite seen him like this before and felt proud to stand beside him.

I took another sip. I wondered what kind of life he had been leading. Had there been other women since his wife's death? Most certainly, I scolded myself. A long-time widower would know other women. One here wished to know him, if she didn't already (why else would she call him 'sweetie'?); touching his arm at every opportunity, speaking low enough so that he must bring his head down to hers to hear her. I took another sip and slid my arm around his. *He's my date tonight, sweetie,* I smiled to the woman on his other side.

The music slowed its pace and the dance floor slowed with it. The saxophone played a mournful sound, the banjo giving it a swaying tempo. I swayed with it. I could dance with that, I decided. I took another sip and brought down Thomas' handsome gray-blond head to mine, interrupting his sentence to others who didn't matter. I was learning the sultry side and feeling warm all over.

"Dance with me," I said into his ear. I expected raised eyebrows and another surprised look, but he only nodded and held firm to my elbow as we weaved through the crowd and onto the squared-off dance floor below the band of colored and white men, their perspiration and instruments glistening in the blue light. We stood facing each other, our eyes locked and his arm slid around me. He held me so close I became breathless. Such warm, green eyes, such an earnest smile, I longed to kiss him. Instead I gave him a heartfelt smile of my own and laid my head on his shoulder as I'd seen others do on this patch with their partners. It felt so nice here, swaying and moving our feet, his hand clasping mine tightly, that I giggled. I looked up at Thomas, feeling self-conscious at my outburst, but he hadn't heard.

Instead he said, "I love the way those beautiful blue eyes of yours light up like that. I wish they'd do that more often."

So did I and I had all the faith in the world that as long as we danced, he would keep them lit. I kissed his cheek and he gave me his sheepish half-grin.

"Now, now, girl. Behave."

Why should I? I had been behaving all my life. Wasn't it time to let go this corset and slip on a garter? That thought gave me another giggle that I hid in his shirt as we continued to shuffle along.

I was sorry to hear the saxophone wind down and cymbals end the song. We had no recourse but to return to our table. David and Pearl were standing there, Pearl's eyes darting about.

"We didn't want to make a scene by dragging you lovebirds away from the schmaltz," said David, "but you've got to kick out of here. Someone tipped the police off and you being here, Mr. Pickering, has given this more juice. Here comes the owner."

"Hello, Mr. Pickering," said a short, thin man, shaking Thomas' hand. "Follow me, sir, I'll show you out the back door."

I waved a goodbye to Pearl and David, glad to be rid of the Siamese Twins. Our departure meant a blur of squeezing through people, descending down a dark staircase, and breathing in foul air in a trashy alleyway. The owner shook Thomas' hand again, saying "Become mayor and pave these muddy streets."

A white blinding flash made a loud pop and I brought up my arm to protect my eyes.

"Jack, give me that camera!" shouted Thomas.

White spots blurred my vision but I could see well enough to recognize one of the newspaper reporters.

"Sorry sir," Jack said as he obeyed. "I didn't know it was you. I only heard that a prominent politician was here."

"Now you know different." Thomas took the roll of film out of the camera and handed the camera back. "Now move on out of here." Jack looked down at his gaping camera and his missed opportunity and shook his head. Thomas must have noticed the angry look as I did. He patted the young man's back, saying, "Good detective work in coming out here, son. Nice touch waiting in the alley. But save it for a day when you have a good story. I'll see to it you get one. Nothing going on here tonight."

We scurried through the alley for two blocks to his new Duesenberg. I was out of breath by then and sat in the passenger's seat waiting for my heart to calm down. I felt oddly thrilled by it all. Thomas took note of my rapid breathing, my hand over my heart and my guilty smile. His hands left the steering wheel and clasped my face. He looked into my eyes as if trying to read my thoughts from there. Likely reading my dormant desire for him, he gave me a deep and long kiss. Delicious enough that I wanted more. The warmth that began earlier had heated up a few more degrees.

He started the engine. Looking straight ahead he asked, "Would you like to go to my apartment for a coffee?"

This was not goodnight as yet! "I would like that very much." I said, smug in being so audacious. I would see his apartment!

Taking turns swigging from his flask of yet more whiskey, we rode into the center of town and parked outside a large gray stone building. A statue of a lion was posted on each side of the stairs leading to the entrance. I patted one's backend as I walked by. "Swell butt," I said and giggled.

Feeling more than a little lightheaded as a doorman tipped his hat to "Mr. Pickering, sir", I stifled another giggle. Pleased to be holding Thomas' arm to keep me steady, I attempted to straighten my posture and my long climb to his third-floor apartment. I was grateful that he asked me to sit down. His tweed sofa felt scratchy, his living room looked sparse.

"Looks quite different from the Beauchamp Manor's front parlor, doesn't it?" he called from the tiny kitchen tucked into the corner of the large room. The only lighting came from there.

"Beauchamp Manor?"

"Yeah, where you're living, the Lighthouse, didn't you know? When we first bought the place, it was known as the Beauchamp Manor from two generations of a French family who had lived there. My wife, Cady, included this on her calling cards to give a better indication of where we lived. The name seemed to die out as the Lighthouse took over."

He said "we" twice. This irritated me. "Oui, oui, monsieur," I called out jadedly. I watched, fascinated, as the coffee table swayed to the left and then to the right. A scratchy record player was playing *Second Hand Rose* somewhere. I hated that song. It finally ended and a cup of steaming coffee appeared.

"Straighten up, Bess. You're slouching." He sat next to me and peered into my face, his hand on my knee. "Are you feeling okay?"

I smiled back at his sweet mouth. "Fine and dandy." I licked my lips, feeling as brash as my sister. I wondered where she and her boyfriend had gone off to – was I supposed to be their escort? But when I opened my mouth to ask Thomas, I couldn't remember what her boyfriend's name was.

He continued to look at me intently as he took a drink of his coffee, his thick brows shadowing his thoughts. I followed suit, taking several sips into my parched mouth.

He snorted into his cup. "Your eyes crossed when you looked into your cup just now. I think you've had too much hooch."

"So much for looking like a sultry flapper girl," I said. My low voice was meant to sound sensual, but the smoky speakeasy had reduced it to a hoarse whisper. I cleared my throat and took another drink.

"Here, give me that cup, you impetuous thing," Thomas said. He placed his cup and mine on the coffee table and returned his hand to my knee. He gave me a light kiss, the coffee's bitter taste lingering. We kissed again, his hand sliding up my leg, under my dress. He pressed me back and further down to where he suddenly appeared above me, his weight on me, the toes in his sock removing my slip-on shoes, his knees between my legs. I gasped for air and reached for another kiss, a wetter one, on my lips, my ears, my throat. He moved his hips against my pelvic and I moaned for a deeper touch. The room began spinning and I gasped again, unsure if this was because of him or the hooch.

"Thomas?" I whispered into his hair.

"Yes, darling?" he muttered into my neck.

I began to feel nauseous. I tried to breathe in deeply but his mouth came down on mine again. How could I be ill at a time like this? I debated what I wanted more – to breathe or to be kissed. His hand massaged my thigh. We were moving too fast, or the room was. It seemed exceedingly warm.

"Thomas, I'm becoming dizzy!"

He slowed his motions and brought his hands to my hair. He studied my face for a moment and then kissed my nose. "No, not like this," he mumbled, more to himself than to me. His half-closed eyes looked into mine, sending tender affection. "I won't take you like this." He smoothed back my hair and kissed my forehead. "Raise up, you'll feel better."

We rose together, smoothing down our hair and laps. Another wave of dizziness came over me and I heaved to his toilet in the nick of time. A few moments later as I remained leaning over the bowl, a cool wet cloth softly landed on the back of my neck.

"You'll never be a flapper girl at this rate," he said.

"Darn." I moved the cloth around to wipe my face. "Oh well, the dresses wouldn't become me anyway."

Such a disgusting bodily reaction to alcohol was sobering – and humiliating to say the least. This introduction to the social scenes was very telling to Thomas I was certain; so much for appearing worldly. Lizzie would be so pleased. More than ever, I was relieved Pearl wasn't there to see how quickly I had been despoiled.

He poured water into a glass and handed this to me. "Rinse out. I'm taking you home."

My head now sitting straight, I glanced around the room and noted that the only enviable piece of furniture was a chunky walnut cabinet, its dials, knobs, and panel telling me it was a radio, just such a one as I hoped to purchase some day. Was he happy living here when so many more of his earthly treasures were at the Lighthouse? It hardly seemed fair that his existence was reduced to this on behalf of women's plight.

As we were leaving, I grabbed his hand and stopped until I had his attention. "Thomas, it's your home too, you know."

"It will be a home for me again someday." He motioned around the room. "This place is certainly no home." He placed his felt hat on his head. "I don't know what I was thinking by bringing you here." He gave me his sheepish grin. "That whiskey made me sick in the head and you sick to your stomach. No wonder it's illegal."

Katy's Chapter Two --1943

That next day after that first date, I face down Uncle Joe to get my Duesy back.

"Now, little lady, that's the last thing you need with all those wild soldiers running loose and free on furlough. Traipsing around Savannah alone can only get you hurt. I protect *my* kin," and here his fat thumb points to his little heart, "or I'll end up having to answer to your daddy. Why, his ghost would come around scaring the living daylights out of me, and I don't have many daylights left." He chuckles to himself.

Boy, is he funny.

"I thought I was here to look after you," I say, trying to sugarcoat.

"You might if you weighed more than a hundred pounds, but you don't." He eyes me slowly up and down my body until I blush and take my hands out of my pockets and fold my arms across my chest. His eyes actually wet with a lusty shine. "You couldn't whip your way out of a paper sack," he said. "No, I've got Clary to help me around here; she's better than most niggers. What I want you to do is to make up with TJ. And don't you roll your eyes around with me, missy. I damn well heard you yelling 'so-long' in nary a sweet tone and then abuse ol' Duesy by slamming her door. What else was TJ to do but to take it away until you cooled down? We southern gentlemen don't take well to whores or to you sweet young things with temper tantrums. You be careful with her from here on out or I'll take it away from you for good. What you need to remember is, they stopped making automobiles two years ago, thanks be to the war effort needing steel and rubber."

He raises his hand to my open mouth. "Now, don't get mad. I'm sure TJ had it coming, but he means well." He drops his hand as if that's too much. He leans his head back against the pillow and closes his eyes. He uses a softer tone. "I just want you to be hospitable to him is all, when he comes over tonight. Can you do that for your dying uncle? That's all I'm asking of you."

I want to ask, *Why is this so important to you?* But I just sit there watching him go to sleep, not really wanting to hear him talk.

So here TJ pulls into the driveway again that evening. In my car. He steps out like he owns it and everything around him. He brings irritation to settle on me like dust in the air and I fold my arms across my chest again. I kick at the gravel with my scratched oxfords and say nothing.

I hear the gravel crunch as he walks closer. "Go to a flick with me," he says.

"Why?" *Why is he interested in me?* is what I really want to ask. I'm no lady, well, not like my mama is a lady, with good posture and dresses up every day of the week as if the mayor might just drop in.

"Cause I love going to the movie house more than anything," he says, starting to circle around me. "Cause I'm buying the malted milk balls." He pops his head over my shoulder from behind. "Cause it includes a newsreel on what's going on in the war." He comes around to face me and lifts my chin to look at his casual grin, his head tilted to the side as he watches me closely. "Cause I know you'd love this new one just came out."

Ouch, he got me in my weak spot. "What film?" I say, against my will.

"'Meet Me in St. Louis'. They say it's a smash." He says that last part like he's tempting a child. He is, and I also love Judy Garland. I'm weakening.

"Besides the fact that the Office of War declared movie flicks essential morale," he says, boldly placing his arm around my shoulders and pointing to Duesy. "I can't very well leave your car here if you can't take me home. And, while we're out, we might as well see a picture show, don't you see? Then you drop me off at my place and everybody's cheery."

Everybody's cheery, most of all William, and I quickly learn that is the most important thing in the world. When I drive him home, even his mother, Marge, says so. "I do hope that picture show made you cheery, TJ," she says, handing him a glass of iced tea. She hands me mine with a wink and a smile. "He's been in some sort of snit here lately. I thought I was going to have to sic the dogs on him and his big brother the other day, they were battling so. I don't know whether to call the sheriff or call the Army. Is it warm out here to you?" She blows down into her pink sleeveless blouse and manages to plop gracefully into a wicker chair, her silver hair glowing from the lamplight coming through the window.

The white-sided two-story feels so homey with the front porch as wide as the house and the overhead balcony almost as wide, like arms open wide saying **Welcome**. Its pretty hostess plays the part of the charming southern lady wholly, with her healthy complexion and that silver hair styled and waved without a glitch. I like her and her home so much, I start liking William more.

"I am more accustomed to dressing for New York's cooler nights," I say. I hope this explains why I'm dressed in long sleeves and ankle socks. A woman can't get stockings nowadays with war time, and truth be known, I have hairy legs that I hadn't tended to. I cross my ankles and tuck my legs under my chair. "You have a lovely home. And I love that old oak tree with all that Spanish moss hanging from it. It sounds like a choir of birds in there."

"Thank you, honey, that's sweet. It's a wonder we have any birds in that tree. Thank goodness TJ outgrew his sadistic slingshot. He killed about all these birds' ancestors. Where did you say your home was?"

"It's a small town you never heard of, in New York, Mother," William pipes in. "Don't start getting nosy. Let me guess what's next: you'll bring out a picture of me as a baby, naked and being washed by my mammy, to ensure my complete embarrassment."

"And would it make you terribly un-cheery if I asked your friend where her home is now?" She says this softly but her eyes carry a big stick. She doesn't wait for his answer but turns to me for mine.

"I'm staying with my — "

"She's staying with a friend of her mother's," William interrupts. "It's on the other side of town, on the outskirts of town, and no, you don't know her, or her family, or where their grave plots are."

I open my mouth to correct him but he locks his eyes with mine and I can't seem to get any words passed that stare. His mother seems the same way, although she has a right to be angry at his rude retort. We both just sit there looking at him. I'm asking myself why he doesn't want her to know that I'm staying with Uncle Joe. Does she know him? Is his reputation so bad that William is protecting me? Would his mother think less of me? I certainly don't want that. I finally nod. "Clary is her name," I say, the first name that comes to me, and at least this name is true to where I'm staying. I can meet her eyes that way and look confident. "Clary and my mama go way back," I say, and then stop because I'm not certain if Clary was here when Mama lived here with Papa. I blush in spite of myself. I've always been a lousy liar.

Something in her eyes and stiff lips tell me that I've lost some points with her and I'm sorry for that but William had dug our hole and I'm going to have to sit in it.

He slaps his knees and stands. "Well, thank you for the drop-off, Katy. Come on, I'll walk you to your motor car and give you directions on how to get back to … your …"

"To Clary's?" I fill in for him. I narrow my eyes at him in mischief. *Keep up; you started the lie.* I give him a big smile and he has to smile back in spite of himself.

I'm grateful for his mother's forgiving hug and invitation to return and I tell her I hope to come back. This seems to cheer William up and she notices that straight away and then she cheers up and now everybody's cheery again. I can reckon easily that this baby of the family is the sun in his mama's world.

We walk over to my motor car and William leans against the door handle with his arm up over the roof. He's so casual in his moves, he makes me stiff. We listen to the front door close as his mother goes inside.

"Thanks," he said. "For helping me out back there. Mother is far too nosy." He gives me his lazy grin and holds my chin between his thumb and finger. "You're fun. You're a lot like me. We make a great team. We should get married."

"And have matching slingshots?" I ask, thinking he's being flippant.

His eyes squint in that intense way of his. "I'm serious."

"*What?*"

"You heard me. Marry me."

"Look, you're cute, copacetic and all but—"

"Don't 'but' me. Just say yes."

I slap his hand away, the fingers now pinching my chin. "I'm not saying anything."

He sighs. "Okay. Don't say I didn't ask." Like I'll be sorry.

"I won't mention it if you won't," I say, giving him a slight push so that I can reach the door knob.

He laughs and moves aside. I get in and close the door. He leans into the window opening. "I could love you, I think. And somehow I'll convince you to marry me."

I relax again, now that I'm in my own space. "And would it make you terribly un-cheery if we don't?" I ask, imitating his mother's soft southern drawl.

"Yes," he says automatically, and then pauses as if thinking about it. He nods. "Yeah, I think it would. I actually like you. A lot. Which is a bonus; I didn't think I'd like you this much." He gives me a peck on the lips. "Like my daddy says to Mother, I'd walk through hell with gasoline underwear on for you."

"*Liking* someone you ask to marry is a *bonus?*" I ask. "Is this a southern custom along with dowries?" I laugh and wave away his malarkey. "And like my Grandmama Ruby says, I'm off like a bride's nightgown." I put Duesy into reverse and back away from him, feeling like I have the upper hand. I wait until I've reached the end of his laneway before I give in to giggles.

Sadly I thought we both were being funny.

I can't sleep that night. I grab Papa's journal and snuggle into the deep feather bed to read his next entry.

July 28th, 1921. This morning I promised Bess we'd look for a place of our own in Savannah and I'd apply for assistant editor to the Savannah News. I think I've lied to her. I have no desire to move from here. I asked her: Only my brother and his wife live in this big house, a good size plantation, why don't you want to live here? I know her reasons, but I put her on the spot anyway, if nothing else but to have a feisty dialogue to get her dander up. She's restless, listless. Hard not to be in this heat, but it's more than that.

My cousin, Jimmy, telephoned today. I haven't told Bess about Jimmy but here's the truth: Jimmy and I go way back, him being my Uncle Willy's son on my father's side, and my Aunt Marge's son on my mother's side. Not incest as Bess would read into it; just two local families that married brothers and sisters. As double-first cousins, Jimmy and I attended the same family gatherings, sharing the same grandparents and relatives. (Exception: I didn't claim his younger brother as kin; one of those midlife "oops!" babies. More on him later.)

Anyway, Jimmy tells me that brother Joe owes my uncle money and plenty of it. Seems they made some sort of bootlegging deal.

Which brings me to this: Bootlegging is bad business but mark my words, Prohibition is worse. When I was editor of Annan News in NY, we wrote plenty of articles on the damn Prohibition and all the problems it's caus-ing. Passing the 18th Amendment in making alcohol illegal was supposed to stop men from beating their wives during a drunken stupor, or so said the Christian Women's Temperance Movement.

Well, how ironic is it that both the 18th and the 19th Amendments (whereby women are allowed to vote in Federal elections) were passed last year? Congress was too fucking busy but I can say without a doubt that neither amendment will be successful or enforceable in my humble opinion (of which

Bess would say those two words don't belong together in my vocabulary). Both amendments go against the nature of the man and woman. Consider these comparisons:

–One takes away rights in order to give to the other. It's as if Congress has only so many rights to give out and if some go to one group, then others must be taken away. Right now I'd give up my own right to vote for a strong drink.

–Underground saloons are renamed speakeasies because you have to whisper the secret entry code. Above ground, parlors are no longer for tea, but for shouting women wanting more rights. It seems to me that the more women shout from their parlors, the more men whisper underground. Reliable sources say that speakeasies in NYC alone have grown to more than 100,000, which proves my point.

–Corruption began with the 18th; Interruption began with the 19th. Now you may think that's funny but there's some truth in it.

–They say alcohol is the devil's advocate and that Prohibition is the noble experiment. Then I say, Suffrage is the angel's advocate; winning the vote is the mobile experiment. Women's roles are now shifting around like sand on a high tide.

–Both Amendments are unenforceable; men still choose to drink, women still choose not to vote.

–Men don't obey their government; bootlegging has increased crime by 75%. Women don't obey their men by staying in the kitchen and voting with head-of-household. Divorce has increased 25%. Motto: Poorly fed men with guns are dangerous.

–I've heard it said that Prohibition has succeeded in replacing good beer with bad gin, since it's easier to transport hooch (or make it in the bathtub – I'm not naming names here). I'd also argue (underground) that the Right to Vote replaced good women with bad marriages.

Now I realize that writing about another woman would not be as hurtful to Bess as the words I just wrote. But, hell, I can't help my cynicism any more than Bess can help her criticism. I don't roll with the punches like I used to. I was a helluva good reporter, and rewarded well in my day, in seeing both sides and writing an objective article, while still standing straight at my first wife's Women's Rights March and Convention. Well, to be honest – and what else can I be when I'm writing to myself? – I was doing more than seeing both sides; I was living two lives.

If Cady had known that it was I who had written that editorial titled <u>Evolution: Girl, Government, or God</u>? after her march in the 1910 July 4th parade ... why, she would have died sooner. That's something I never told a soul, no, not even to my then-mistress whose scruples in those days gave her no right to judge – but such beautiful bee-stung lips! She cared only in how to please a man - until she tired of my false promises. In revenge she moved in with my arch enemy, George, thus kicking out his wife, Eunice, who was also Cady's friend – whew! That felt good to get off my chest! Here's some irony: As a result of their separation, Eunice lost custody of her children to her husband and this injustice is what got Cady in gear to begin that damn ladies suffrage group. So I only have myself to blame for Cady's involvement. And get this: It was George who ultimately beat me out of becoming mayor of Annan. What a tangled web we weave. What a cad am I! If I were a Catholic, I could be absolved of such sins; instead here I am carrying them all these years on my way to the grave.

Even Bess would hate me now for that long-ago article. (And even more so for the one I wrote later attacking Bess for her speech that - I'm ashamed to say - I knew would bring her to my office ...). I justified writing this first article by thinking that Cady would read this "Edrite Formen" letter in the newspaper, become frightened of repercussions and quit the women's group. I should have known her resolve would only become stronger. But the other side is, I hid like a coward behind a pseudo-name of Edrite Formen in order to be able to give the male perspective, or, more to the point, my perspective, the only way I could and still keep peace with Cady, and then with Bess. Is it my fault that I'm surrounded by do-gooders?

Except I'm tired of it all now as I sit here on my memory bank, like looking at a post-party mess of deflated balloons, dried cake and dirty (soda only!) glasses, with no energy left to clean things up. Like my own worst enemy, I've had enough of me. I reckon, too, that Prohibition has put me in a very bad mood. Whatever my reasons, I must hide this diary as I must hide my flask. I've sat here and drank the whole damn thing.

More to come.

More to come, alright – a lot more when Mama reads this and finds her husband deceived her. But it'll be easier on the eyes to read my writing than to read his writing; his last few paragraphs really got sloppy. After reading this entry, out of respect for Mama, I didn't read more of his entries for some time, not wanting to know any more details for awhile. But I should've been reading – so much happened and I stayed in the dark. Papa became my flashlight – but it shined on a crime already committed.

Jesi's Chapter Two -- December 1963

Where have all the young girls gone, long time passing?
Where have all the young girls gone, long time ago?
Where have all the young girls gone?
Gone for husbands everyone.
When will they ever learn?
When will they ever learn?
Where have all the husbands gone, long time passing?
Where have all the husbands gone, long time ago?
Where have all the husbands gone?
Gone for soldiers everyone.
When will they ever learn?
When will they ever learn?

I think of My Mamas when I hear Peter, Paul and Mary singing that one. I don't want to make that same mistake if that Vietnam thing takes off; I've got a high school friend over there now flying helicopters and he wrote me to say that with both our president and the Vietnam president assassinated last month, we're in Deep Crap.

My Mamas don't like me not finding a husband but I'm just telling it like it is with that song.

They say that you create your own reality, so here's mine: I live my life through songs, man, and Bob Dylan is The Coolest. And that's all I have to say.

GB hands this paper back to me and tells me to write more. For a grandmother, Bess is a pain in the ass. I don't know what she wants from me. I don't care about women's rights and I don't have anything to add to their war stories on Equal Rights Amendment bullshit. With this bum leg, I couldn't march in their damn parades anyway. They're out of it. They may be pure and always right but that's easy when you're not with it.

It's Civil Rights, where it's at. Let's just say I'm not their Equal but I can be Civil – real Civil. Do you get my drift, man?

Anything I've done – that I can talk about – is done here and I can do this in my sleep I've done it so much: changing countless sheets, washing and hanging endless panties, more women and kids coming in with the same sad stories. And no matter how hard I work, *Jesi Messy*, is Mama's nickname for me. Where is the love, man?

And speaking of love, where the hell are the men? I don't get it, why My Mamas make such a big deal about birth control clinics when they never do anything to get pregnant. Women Only: there are enough sanitary pads around here to choke the old well out back. I love men, man. Just call me *Jesi Yessy*. Thank God for The Pill.

I had my awakening and it wasn't here. And that's all I have to say, period.

GB hands me back this paper a second time. THIS IS GETTING OLD.

"Write more," GB says. "I'm tired of your insolent attitude. You've contributed nothing thus far." I write down just that, just what she said.

"Why are you staring at your Grandmama Bess like that?" Mama says to me, referring to GB. "Be respectful! And sit up straight, stop slouching," I tell her I'm just thinking, but I'm really just waiting for GB to say more so I can write it down. What I'm really thinking is, Why does Mama sometimes look at me with hate in her eyes? Not Cool.

"Leave her be," says GG. "At least she's writing something." For a Great Grandmother, Ruby is groovy.

"As long as she's not writing about Bob Dylan again," Mama says, taking a long draw from her cig and making me wish I had one. "That long-haired beatnik can't carry a tune in a bucket and that's all I hear her record player playing. He sounds like somebody is stepping on his tail."

"'It ain't me, Babe, no, no, no, it ain't me, Babe, it ain't me you're looking for, Babe,'" I sing softly as I write my Dylan's words.

"How do you know what she's writing about?" GB asks Mama. "No one is supposed to read the submissions except me. I have the papers locked in my wardrobe."

Mama blushes and lies badly. "Shit. It's not hard to figure out."

"Just. For. You." I stab the air with my pen with each word. "I wrote a Peter, Paul and Mary song just for you but it still isn't good enough," I say. "What I do is never good enough." I start singing Bob Dylan:

"*Come mothers and fathers throughout the land/And don't criticize what you can't understand/Your sons and your daughters are beyond your command/Your old road is rapidly agin'.*"

"Katy, would you please stick to our agreement?" GB says to Mama, ignoring my off-tune. "Why must you go your own way and then learn things the hard way? And your language is trash ever since you returned from Georgia. ("Here we go again for the thousandth time," Mama mutters.) For once do as I say," GB continues, "and please stay out of my locked wardrobe."

"Don't we have enough damn secrets around here?" Mama snaps back. "I thought the whole point—"

"The whole point is to write exactly what's on the chalkboard," GB interrupts (it's so cool to call Grandmama Bess by her initials – she hates it).

GB gets up and leaves the dining room and soon returns with tonight's second bottle of red wine. Between you and me, I think they've all had enough and I don't know how they can drink something that looks like blood and tastes like vinegar. There are better things out there to make you Feel Good.

"Mercy, Bess, my head is swimming from the first bottle," says GG, reading my thoughts – or is my great-grandmother being sneaky and reading my paper? She goes on with "You need to be careful of how much drink you take. It's not good for your nerves. And what is another word for clothesline?"

"My nerves are fine, Mama," GB says with a sigh, always in that it's-hard-to-tolerate-you voice. "String. Another word is clothes string." And when GB talks to my mama, Katy, she uses that voice that says I'm Superior. And when GB talks to me, I feel about five years old.

She refills their wine glasses but leaves me out. By this point I could use the buzz.

"Then why is there an empty wine glass in your room every morning?" Mama says to GB in a syrupy southern drawl. We all blush to that even though I'm thinking the same thing, especially since I'm the one who usually makes GB's bed.

"I'll forgive you for that, Katydid," GB says to Mama after a moment of silence. Mama flinches at the down-low of hearing her whole name. "I realize that asking you all to write the truth exactly as it happened may have opened a Pandora's Box – it's causing you to be far too outspoken. But I simply won't hear anymore." GB stands and gathers her papers. "If you want to say it, write it down. I'll finish my chapter in my bedroom." She picks up her wine glass and then reconsiders and sets it back down. She leaves the room with her head in the clouds, Miss Mount Everest.

They had said all that too fast and I'm writing it down as quick as I can. Now it gets quiet.

You know what? We're all yappy poodles that nip at each other but never sink our teeth into any meaningful rap; that's where it's at. Maybe it's because we hear enough sad stories from the down-and-out women who come in here that we've become like clams, man, so that none of that irritation will penetrate. Whooa! Deep Thought.

"Jesi, you started this," Mama says, drumming her pen on the table. "If you'd be more cooperative—"

Uh-oh. This lecture has lasted a lifetime.

"Leave her be!" GG says in an exasperated tone. "As Jesi says, just go with the blow!"

I laugh for the first time today. "It's go with the *flow*, GG, not blow!"

Mama laughs too. It's easier to do when GB leaves the room.

I start fidgeting, my leg brace clanging against the chair leg, waiting for somebody to talk.

Mama gives me a flash of her overused <u>irritated look</u> because she hates me reminding her that I wear an ugly brace - which of course is why I do it. She stands up in a hurry, gathering up her papers and drinking down the rest of her wine. "Maybe finishing my chapter in the bedroom isn't such a bad idea. Nor is taking a glass of wine up there with me." She grins at both of us as she refills her glass. "I got her that time!" She walks out in her knee-high "kinky boots", a look-alike to her heroine Cathy Gale in *The Avengers*. Lucky, lucky.

"And don't forget to turn out your light!" I call out, mocking GB. Mama leaving her light on all night drives GB ape-shit.

And Mama has such a cool smile, when she wants to. Wish I'd gotten that from her but they tell me I have more of a solemn look like my great-aunt Opal. That's kind of freaky. In that old picture, Opal looks about a hundred years old and she had about a hundred kids. And we know I ain't never having kids.

GG and I sit there for a few minutes writing nothing. She has her hands in her lap and giving me her own cool smile; I guess that's where Mama got hers, skipping generations (GB didn't pass down a smile, that's for damn sure). Like I said, GG is such a groovy great-granny.

I lean toward her and whisper, "Are you really telling it like it is?"

"I'm shocking myself!" GG says with a laugh. She leans in too, and whispers, "You may find a key under a china vase on a bedroom mantel right next to *the* wardrobe. Go find out for yourself. But you didn't hear that from me."

I probably shouldn't write that down since GB will read this but what the hell. She won't give GG a hard time about it, no matter how she puts on The Bitch. In this family, shit only rolls downhill.

"Are you reading what we write, GG?"

"Mercy, no," GG answers. "My eyes are too weak to both read and write, so I save them to write. Besides, I love surprise endings!"

If GG's story is as juicy as she claims, maybe sometime I'll write some real happenings, man, like, The Truth, if nothing more than to entertain myself.

Ruby's Chapter Three -- 1910

By the time my brother, Jesse, and I reached the farmyard I thought my heart was going to squeeze in two. Like an invisible clothes string wrapped there and its other end strung to my front door. The farther we plodded, the tighter the string became. I could barely breathe from the pull when Jesse at last heaved back on the reins between the dusty red barn and the weathered-gray backdoor of the farmhouse. Scattering chickens and dogs announced our arrival, cows and the horses made their replies, the screen door squeaked and slammed, and I simply tried to adjust myself into a presentable human for the onslaught of family fuss.

Edith came out drying her hands on her ever-present apron. "Why, Ruby, what on earth!" Although close to my age, I looked at her as being much older. Thanks to Jesse, her once-thin figure had thickened permanently in the middle from nine pregnancies, six of which produced large healthy boys. Her hair grayed like their back-door, but more than that it was those penetrating brown eyes that held ancient wisdom. She gave me a hasty hug, always in a hurry. "You're as pretty as you ever were," she said in her habit, scrutinizing my every inch, her eyes asking, *Is everything all right?* She patted my cheek with a callused palm.

Mama trailed behind, the arthritis in her hip causing a slight limp, her height shrinking, her back bending a bit more each time I saw her, like gravity was having more effect on her than years were.

"Ruby, honey, what is wrong?" Mama squeezed my arm, making sure I was alive. "Has one of the children taken ill?" She wiped her dish towel at a dirt smudge on my sleeve. "Did something catch fire in your kitchen?"

I didn't know what to say and afraid to cry, I cast a helpless glance over to Jesse who was off to the barn lugging milk cans, and then I looked down at Edith. She continued to watch as if she were studying tea leaves in her tea cup. This was her nature until she knew what to do. She seemed to hone in on reading action, not words, a necessary skill for her boys' storytelling of who was right or wrong. "Boys, say hello to Aunt Ruby and go back to your breakfast," she said without wavering her study of me. The boys had swarmed to the screen door and jammed there. They disappeared one by one back to the kitchen.

Without so many faces staring at me, I breathed a little easier.

"Child, come in and eat." Mama said firmly. One thing Mama knew for sure and that was that good food soothed the heart of everybody.

But I was humiliated enough with my story, let alone of my appearance. "Could I wash first?"

Besides, I needed more time to think of how to tell them. The dirt soaked in to sin and I suddenly felt unworthy of my Christian family. I knew very well how they believed that the woman's place is in the home; I'd been fed that as a side plate to the good food.

I went up the backstairs and knocked on sister Opal's door. She answered with a mouth in an o-shape of dismay but quickly recovered. "Ruby, your hair! My goodness, I haven't seen you wear your hair down since we were in school. You look so young!"

"Yes, it is the latest fashion, along with wrinkled clothing," I said dryly.

She smiled at that as if doing me a favor and returned to her mirror still holding her hair in place and finished pinning the complicated braided knot that only Opal could create. She topped it off with a comb trimmed in opal stones, a gift from Papa before his death. That same Christmas he'd given a similar comb to me with rubies, and one to Mama with her namesake of garnet stones, all to represent "Papa's gems".

She had dressed for an outing in a cool silk taffeta day-dress colored in light rose. What a lovely dress it was, with lace she'd sewn on the sleeves and around the neck, and long lace strips were sown in even intervals from the waist down to the hem. Longer than fashion to her ankles yet Opal was such an excellent seamstress, she could design dresses that could become the fashion if she'd wanted to. She knew how to distract from her own large bosom and thick waist.

As she rustled past to fetch me water for the basin, she left behind a scent of rose water. Without meaning to, she diminished me down to a lump of barn dirt brought in by the boots of the boys.

I worried needlessly about how to tell them of my participation in the 'devil's workers', as our preacher called the suffragists. As I entered the kitchen hitching the too-long skirt of my sister's loaned house dress, I saw there on the table in plain view a newspaper. On the front page was a picture of my group in the parade with me clearly recognizable. Worse, I looked angry, my mouth open, my sign lifted above my head, one knee lifted high showing my white petticoat and scuffed boot. Headline above the picture read, '<u>Evolution: Girl, Government, or God?</u>', written by a Mr. Edrite Formen.

Jesse had brought this home without a word about it to me. I now understood what he meant by his "not even if you marched with the Confederates" statement. If only such unconditional love would be contagious with the *women* of this household.

The three female family members sat silently at the other end of the long wooden table, coffee cups in hand, looking at me with shock, confusion, and yes, I believed with some awe.

I lowered myself heavily onto the first chair I came to and pulled the newspaper over to me with both hands as if the words weighed more than the paper they were written on. Resting my elbows on the table, I involuntarily brought my hands up to my forehead to shield the oncoming stares and began reading. Below the picture was a short paragraph describing the parade, its participants and its path. The text referenced editorials on page 6, one of those from a Mrs. Thomas Pickering. Cady's letter! I couldn't continue the day or any discussion without reading this. I read as hungrily as I ate; eggs, biscuits and coffee sliding into my peripheral view.

Cady's letter had a precursory clause that stated the newspaper upheld the constitutional right to freedom of speech and thus published said article with the understanding that the opinions of the author were *not* those of the publisher.

Her letter assured the public that we were the same steadfast and dedicated wives and mothers of always, continuing to love our husbands, fathers and brothers, living and dying for our children. "We do not wish to *be* more, but simply *do* more," she wrote. "An evolution of government is required. Enfranchisement of women is the next logical step in improving government thinking regarding domestic life. Our government must be brought up-to-date to harmonize with the present social conditions." She went on to talk about reform required in laws for marital rights and the workforce, covering all our discussions during our secret teas. I was neither surprised nor alarmed until the end when she announced the July 18th Women's Rights Convention. Robert would be sure to read this and would now know about it. And it being only two weeks away and I'm totally out of reach here at the farm, my lady friends would think I had deserted them when they needed me the most.

Waiting for Robert to cool down – or to tire of Bess's inexperienced cooking – was going to be grueling.

I looked up at my family staring at me as if I were a stranger. I suppose I was one - they'd had no warning.

"You must read this to understand. Cady Pickering explained it better than I ever could."

Opal forced a token smile. She stood up suddenly from the table. "I apologize, Ruby, but I must go. Jacob is due here soon and I've got to pick some garden goodies for a gift basket to his parents."

"Jacob?"

"You're not the only one with surprises. Jacob is my fiancée." That explained her light rose dress and pink glow. Her rounded face reminded me of a cherub.

I glanced at Mama and Edith but they didn't seem to show the same glow. Mama's written notes to me referred to their neighbor – and now fiancée - as 'Amish-Jacob-Penn' as if all one name.

"Has he been courting you?" I asked.

"If you call courting wearing a path down between the back door and the orchard like you and Robert used to do, then the answer is yes. Is he still such a creature of habit?"

"Let's just say, if I moved the furniture, he'd be lost."

"Oh you girls. Shame on you Ruby for criticizing your husband!" Mama said, slowly lifting her heavy frame from her chair. She looked upset over this Jacob.

Opal glanced over and saw the same thing. She sat down and fiddled with an empty cup. "Jacob's a decent man," she said. "Recently, he came around offering to help Jesse. Jesse was short-handed with the dairy business growing like it is and gladly accepted. He worked for several hours a day for a week. Jesse then attempted to pay him a week's wages, but Jacob would not accept payment. He asked that instead he be permitted to call on me and begin courting. Can you imagine?"

This isn't the dark ages, my scowl told her.

Opal quickly added, "He's very shy you see."

"Let me understand this," I said. "He worked into the good graces of Jesse in payment to court you? What about *your* good graces? What do *you* feel for Jacob?"

"I'm touched by this, Ruby. And naturally he would go to Jesse for permission. After all, Jesse is head of the household now that Papa is gone." Her tone sounded defensive. "Furthermore, since we are not Amish, Jacob was concerned that Jesse would forbid it.

"He had great difficulty asking me to marry him, especially with German being his mother tongue. I didn't think he would ever get the proposal out of his mouth. And do you know what he gave me with his proposal? A mantel clock!"

"Was this symbolic?" I asked. "Did he mean that time is quickly marching by on your way to being an old spinster?" I smiled but Opal was in no mood for humor.

"No, it's Amish tradition. But time is marching by, Ruby. Is it not part of God's plan that we marry and have children? And here I am twenty-five years old, for goodness sake. You were married at seventeen! And God will know me in that church as well, won't he?"

It sounded odd to me. "What does Jacob's family say about this? Does he have their blessing?"

"Yes. Of course they told Jacob that I must be baptized into the Amish faith and join their church. I am now reading the *Ordnung*, which is their written set of rules for daily living."

Mama and Edith busied themselves with the dishes but I knew their volume was turned up. Now I understood why Mama looked so upset. Opal must leave our church. I'd miss Opal not sitting in our customary pew, but it would be harder for Mama not to have all of us there. Sometimes I thought Mama lived to go to church and was dying to rest in the church cemetery next to Papa. Eternally in her one church dress of dark green wool, its high collar pinned with her garnet brooch.

"Your heart matters here, too, you know," I said.

Opal licked her lips and her misty blue eyes finally met mine. "What would you have me say? That I love him? Love, I believe, comes with time and ... and ... children. Living with one another, learning one another. How do you know a man before marrying him? Our courting is no different than yours and look how well you faired."

Who said, *Silence is golden?*

"You are right, Opal. I am in no position to question your decision. However, may I just say that a wife's obligations are many. I admit I find these difficult at times. A man's needs..."

Mama and Edith both turned and looked at me open-mouthed. I hesitated but if I was going to talk in front of a convention, I'd better start practicing now. In spite of my heated face, I continued. "... are often. And you worry when he is meeting his needs that conception will occur. And conception means childbirth. And childbirth could mean death, for you, for the baby. And it repeats itself. And sometimes, it seems...there is no end..." They all looked so shocked, I couldn't go on.

"What hogwash, Ruby," Opal said. "I only want the married life that you have and no more. Why isn't that enough for you?"

"Look, little sister," I said, sounding angrier than I intended. "I only wished to prepare you for the worst. I only wish you the best. There are some scary moments ahead of you that you should know about. It is no wonder women never speak of it."

"I will not allow any more of that talk in here," Edith said, her back to us. She was pumping water at the sink faster than normal, filling a large washtub stacked with fresh-picked green beans.

I was outnumbered. "Congratulations, Opal," I conceded, trying to sound calm, although I trembled inside and wished to cry for some strange reason. "Can I help you with your wedding plans?"

Opal stood and shrugged her shoulders. "What little there is to do. Amish folks have a very simple ceremony at their homes, from what I understand. I should know more today. We're going to his house to discuss the wedding with his parents." Poor Opal had always talked about having a big church wedding, wearing her own wedding dress creation.

Mama began stacking jars into a large wicker basket. "I'll go outside," she announced to no one, "and have one of the boys help me start the fire to sterilize the canning jars." She waddled away under the basket's heavy load. Edith followed her and called out to one of the boys to come quickly and help grandma with these jars.

The day's work had begun, just like every other day I could remember. They would be grateful for the extra pair of hands. Yet I felt out of place drooping here in an oversized dress, like a half-sack of year-old apples that no one quite knew what to do with. I settled at the table and listened to the many sounds around me; the ticking grandfather clock coming from the front room, the dripping water from the sink pump behind me, the outside voices of boys, dogs, commands from Jesse. Keeping his boys busy doing their chores during the summer months was a challenge. At the core of it all hummed the softer resonance of Mama and Edith, tones of harmony that knew their parts by heart in working the summer-long task of food preservation.

Everything around me felt distant, like I wasn't part of the living, but only a ghost wandering old places where I once belonged. My place was in my own home with my own chores – my garden, my children. How long must I wait before Robert called me back home?

I laid my head on the table at this juncture of my self-pity and that's when I spotted the Annan Newspaper editorial by Mr. Edrite Formen, titled *Evolution: Girl, Government, or God?* It read:

4ᵗʰ of July. Celebration of our Independence. Independence that granted us freedom. Freedom of religion. Freedom of speech. Freedom from being subjects of a king, from monarchy, from burdening taxes to royalty. Celebration of the spirit of man. Of self-government. Celebrate the men, the real soldiers who fought for our liberty. This is a time to celebrate democracy as we know it: the best government, the best society in the world.

'Yet, best is not good enough for some amongst us. We, in our peaceful town, were abruptly confronted with a group of women marching like soldiers in uniform, carrying banners of protest through our serene streets, as if marching to war. Who are her enemies?

While the band played America the Beautiful, these female fighters of disruption seized the opportunity to sew strife amongst us, to turn us against ourselves, man against his wife, to attempt to divide us so as to tear at the fabric of our families, to conquer us back to the era of cave men. Evolution of Girl? I think not. Devolution, perhaps.

This legion of women carried a banner saying 'give us a voice'. I ask this: What are they going to say that we haven't already provided? America the beautiful has the best system of governing in the world. Our democracy is a vast improvement over any former system of government. I thank our forefathers who struggled tirelessly to prepare our constitution. I thank our fathers of today: state governors and our mayors, who work to provide us with effective government. The issues of the day are complicated and difficult. It is foolhardy to have female fighters voicing opinions to further complicate today's issues and delay governmental proceedings. With such angry female voices in our legislature, we would not get any laws passed! They ask to change the law in the institution of marriage. Yet women have the choice to accept or deny a man's proposal of marriage. When she says yes, she is accepting the rules that protect this institution. The old adage applies here: 'If you can't take the heat, stay out of the kitchen!' Evolution of Government? Not required. I say 'If it's not broke, don't fix it!'

'This legion of women asserts to change the order provided by our God, but I ask you, who are they to improve on God's work? They advocate that men and women are created equal. Have they not eyes to see? Do they not know that the contents of men's britches differ from the contents of women's petticoats? Do these female fighters not see that men naturally carry the seed of life, women naturally carry the child, and women naturally nourish the child at their breast? Can they not see that men and women are not created equal, but are complimentary? Do these women pretend that they will fight to defeat nature? Evolution of God? Read your Bibles, ladies: 'He is the same yesterday, today, and always'.

It is unnatural for women to fight. These legionnaires who fight against our established order, God's order, against good government and good family, are fighting against our children growing up in the images of their parents. It is right that a son should grow up in the image of his father, and a daughter grow up in the image of her mother. From an early age our children start to assume their proper roles. If these female fighters are successful in their battle against government and God, then our whole order of society will be tossed upside down. Our children will not know what is expected of them. They will not know what path to follow through life.

'The Ladies Legion, as their group is called, have chosen to fight Our Father, our forefathers, our fathers, and to fight the natural order of hierarchy of family and state. It is no wonder they are also called men-haters.

Fueling my doubts first planted by Formen's article, I wandered out to the front porch and around to the backyard, long ago memories running through my mind like a nickelodeon, showing me what family is supposed to be. The scene in the backyard and beyond to the garden stopped me in my tracks, so much like an oil painting, so much like my childhood here. Opal was off to my right in the distant garden, her large pink bonnet shading her face from the bright sun, walking, bending, stooping, basket on her hip. Edith stood in the center of the scene, bent over the large black iron kettle, a hungry fire licking around its grate. She was dappled in sun and shade from the trees behind her, her face flushed, her bonnet dangling down her back. Mama sat on the left of the scene, on her red chair with the cane bottom, her favorite place to sit in the shade by the back door, churning butter, her hand moving the thick handle up and down inside its clay crock without notice. Her attention stayed on Joey who was chasing a chicken.

"Now grab its neck, Joey," Mama called out. "That's it. Now hold on tight to the neck and spin it in the air, like I showed you. That's it!" She cackled loudly at Joey's beaming expression as he looked down at the severed head and neck in his hands. The chicken's body ran in circles back down on the ground.

The only thing I could relate to was the chicken.

I joined Edith at the fire and Mama called out to me, "Do you remember that little poem you wrote when you were young about all the chores?" She started reciting it and Edith and I joined in:

>Monday wash my sins away,
>Tuesday iron out my wrinkles,
>Wednesday knead my cares all day,
>Thursday mend my crinkles,
>Friday cook a pot of love,
>Saturday buy more trinkles,
>Sunday pray to God above,
>That Monday I don't stinkle!

They both cackled like that was the funniest poem they'd ever heard. That's what planted the seed - I'd write a poem for the convention. As I spent the rest of the day washing and hanging boys' clothing on a line that seemed eternally to suspend the same apparel, I created and memorized rhyming lines. And as the clothing dried, so did my doubts dissipate. My womenfolk had no idea that their sameness made me want change.

It wasn't until suppertime that I realized that no one had prodded me as to why I was there.

Opal had returned from the home of Amish-Jacob-Penn and quietly took her seat at the supper table. Her pink glow had faded into
cream. Her clear blue eyes looked ready to cry. A face accustomed to
the simple life that was suddenly becoming complicated.

I had my own difficulties swallowing food past the lump in my
throat. Sitting there with Jesse's boys around me silently shouted
that my own children were not present. I longed to see my boys
cajoling with their cousins, forgetting their manners, talking loudly
with their mouths full. More so, I missed watching Bess and Pearl
watch the boys. Bess did so attentively, only to roll her eyes in mock
disgust when their teasing directed toward her. I think Joey actually
had a school-boy crush on her and I meant to warn her about it but
didn't know how to broach the subject.

Jesse signaled the end of the meal by scooting his chair away
from the table. He pulled out his small leather pouch of tobacco
from his shirt pocket. He glanced around the table and then cleared
his throat. Edith jumped to her feet removing his plate and bringing
him a cup of coffee and a battered tin plate he used for tapping his
ashes.

He concentrated on the small white paper within his fingers as if
tending to a delicate insect, crumbling leaves into the paper's fold.
I looked forward to the aroma of the smoking tobacco, often wondering what this smoke tasted like. Men obviously became relaxed
and derived pleasure from its inhalation.

"Boys, your Aunt Ruby is staying here awhile, and her boys and
girls may show up any day now," Jesse announced.

I understood his logic and my spirits lifted. Robert could not
abandon his shoe store to stay home with the children, and they were
out of school for the summer. Soon they would need fresh bread
baked and Robert had never picked a vegetable in his life. Jesse's
explanation seemed to satisfy any curiosity, and the boys one by one
left the table as evening chores were assigned to each by their father.

"Ruby, really, what is going on?" Opal asked, in no mood for
mystery.

"Robert left her to die on their front porch," Jesse answered.

"My goodness!" Mama and Edith chorused.

I had planned to start from the beginning and explain my way to the parade, but now I would have to go backwards from the night before, thanks to Jesse's dramatic opening.

"It's not all Robert's fault," I blurted. "He-he didn't know I would be in the parade, well, I told him I was going downtown for another reason. I had to. He forbids me to do anything with the Ladies Legion. He was quite upset, you see, and for a good reason."

"So he leaves you to sleep outside, like some cat?" Jesse asked. "And that was the right thing to do?"

It was coming out all wrong.

"You lied to Robert? Is that what you are saying?" Opal asked. "This is wrong if Robert forbids it. Remember what Preacher Paul said: the husband is the master. You made a vow to obey him."

I sighed audibly. They were all going to be upset with me for their own reasons, no matter how I explained it.

"The Ladies Legion only wishes to protect women through better law. And I know women who need protection."

"Ruby, these women you speak of, are they Christian women? Because I don't think this would happen if they went to church," Mama said.

"Mama, that is unfair. You don't know what it is like to be mistreated. You were fortunate to marry Papa. He was a good man. He protected you," I said.

Mama's weathered hand, bumped with arthritic nodes along its fingers, smoothed down the tablecloth in front of her as she thought about this. Her eyes of light blue film, looked up at me finally, eyes that were looking into her own past and it pained her to do so. "He was a good man because I was a good woman to him. I carried his children; three to live, five to die. I fed him three hot meals a day. I worked by his side and I prayed by his side every day of our married life."

This stung. Was Mama implying that I deserved what Robert did, because I was not a good woman?

Opal leaned toward me. "What Mama is saying here, Ruby, is that God is the law in a Christian home. And we know our places in our home. Why, without God in a marriage, I suppose the woman could dress in knickers and rule the roost! What is this group of women going to do next – ask that the *law* be changed, so that men would bear children, too?" Opal shook her head and smiled.

I hated Opal's superior tone. "Really Opal, if you'd come to the Women's Rights Convention with me, you'd understand."

Opal sat up stiff and sniffed. "Right is what the Bible says—"

"Girls, girls" Edith said softly. She had a way of soothing and reproving at the same time, clicking her tongue, drying her hands. She had continued cleaning since Jesse's meal ended, and now the dishes were washed and stacked for drying.

Jesse uncrossed his legs and stood up slowly. "I have only this to say, Ruby." He ended the smoking of his tiny paper cylinder by squashing it into the tin plate. "My home is your home as long as need be. But when you go back to town, be careful. I've heard talk in town, and men don't like it – they say these women are getting all womenfolk riled up over nothing. So just be careful, is all I'm saying." He put his cap on by the door, tipped his cap rim to his own womenfolk, and headed outside.

"Did you hear Jesse, Ruby?" Opal asked. "Is this worth risking your life over? This is a man's political world we know nothing about. Nor do I care to. You weren't raised to believe this way either. What in God's name are you wanting, when you have it all?"

Was I 'riled up over nothing'? None of my family were listening to me and maybe that was because I didn't have anything really to say. I didn't have a cause for complaint. Admittedly my problems with Robert didn't begin until I started holding the cross for other women's woes. Was it worth all this? This judgment? I could see disappointment in Mama's eyes, disapproval in sister's eyes. I remembered Robert's eyes the night before, burning with condemnation. I closed my eyes to it all and lowered my head into my hands, all energy spent.

My prayer to go home was answered the next morning by way of a note tied to an empty milk bottle. Jesse's expression looked sad as he handed the folded paper to me and walked away. I read the note and ran to the back screen door, calling out to him.

"Jesse, can you take me home today? Robert says that Bess is not feeling well and I'm needed at home!" I waved the paper at him, as if he hadn't seen it already.

He continued his walk toward the barn; his only sign of hearing me was his backward wave.

"I must get my things together!" I called out as I ran up the back stairs. I felt excited, worried, and nervous all at once.

Opal sat at her sewing machine, her slippered feet moving rapidly up and down on the black iron pedal to keep the sewing steady. She'd been here since dawn.

"The clothing you wore here is cleaned and hanging over there on the hook," Opal said without looking up. "Fresh water is in the pitcher for washing. I'm taking in my dresses to give you a better fit, they're all yours. And my ruffled and lace petticoats, too. I have one petticoat you are going to love. Eleven inches from the hem are three rows of beautiful white lace. The other petticoat is cotton with a silk ruffle at the bottom. Wear the two together and your skirt flares beautifully and your waist shrinks like magic. You could use some flare - you look like a poor orphan girl wearing my housedress."

She stood up with a measuring tape in her hand. She measured my length of limbs in almost a feverish way. "Silly me fretted about how much time and money we needed in order to sew my lace and pearl wedding gown. No need to worry. I found out yesterday that not only do I dress too extravagantly now, but my simple wedding dress will be of blue cotton – I can choose the shade. Don't you think sky blue would go best with my eyes?" Opal talked on quickly. "I will also make my newehockers' dresses. Newehocker means sidesitter in Amish. That dialect of German they speak. You know – bride's attendants. Which will be Jacob's sisters. Anyway, it won't take long because the dresses are unadorned, without trim or lace, or train. How simple! Jacob's sister told me this dress would also be my Sunday church dress. I will also be buried in the same dress. Isn't that practical?"

I noticed even her pink and lace nightgown had pearl buttons. She was the best seamstress in town, creating the prettiest of wedding gowns for so many young girls.

She laughed but it sounded bitter to me. "And do you remember how much trouble I always have making button holes for buttons? Well, never again, because all Amish clothing only have hooks and eyes. Simplicity at its best!" She took a deep breath. "Which means, of course, there is no longer a need for these costumes of colors filling my wardrobe. I don't mind really. It is a small sacrifice to give them all to you.

"Why is it that you got Mama's small waist, and I got Mama's large breasts?" Opal asked. "Seems hardly fair."

"I've heard it said that Mama was a beauty in her younger days. Farm life and babies take their toll," I said. Opal seemed not to hear the intended warning toward her upcoming marriage.

"Well, she is forty-five years old, Ruby. We can't stay young-looking forever." She patted my elaborate braided updo that she'd clinched with her opal comb. "Your hair is holding nicely after that thorough wash with egg whites last night. Continue rubbing your lavender water into the roots. The braiding should be good for another month. And remember, a woman's hair is her glory."

She sat back down at her machine. "I'll continue sewing while you wash. I promise I won't look. Now I need to know what length you prefer in your skirts. The instep length is appropriate for shopping; the clearing length is one inch longer for general street wear; then there is the round length, for visiting with the ladies for tea. Now if you host the tea—"

"It doesn't matter to me," I interrupted. I took down my corset from the hook. It had been brush-cleaned and aired outside, by the smell of it. I slipped my arms through it and began the tedious job of sucking in my stomach and squeezing together the many hooks and eyes.

"Ruby, you are a walking contradiction," Opal said irritably.

I stiffened at the words and tone. "Whatever do you mean?"

"You wish to socialize with the ladies of the town, yet you wish to dress like a farmhand. You wish to be free as a bird, and yet you can't wait to get home to the very chains that bind you."

I stared at Opal's back for a moment. Could this be true? I watched Opal gently handling the sleeves of a light green frock trimmed at the sleeves and neck in dark green velvet, its many yards of fabric flowing over the side of the table onto her lap. As if tending to a child.

"Perhaps you're right," I said softly. "Perhaps we both are contradictions. Or perhaps we both are willing to make sacrifices to do what is right. Or ... perhaps we have no other choice?"

Opal stopped, her head down. Then slowly she nodded, and resumed her work.

Finally dressed, I bent to Opal and gave her shoulders a tight squeeze. Her hair was smoothed into a uniquely braided bun. "Keep the dresses and wear them as long as you can," I whispered.

"I'll deliver these dresses myself," she said, as if I hadn't spoken. "Poor Jesse must feel like a mailman at times." She handed me a note she had written: *Hebrews 13:4. Marriage is honourable in all, and the bed undefiled: but whoremongers and adulterers God will judge.*

I sighed and said nothing. What would be the point?

Mama was waiting for me at the bottom of the stairs in the mudroom wearing a worried frown. "What is wrong with Bess do you think? Send me a note tomorrow with Jesse. Why do you suppose Opal sent a note this morning to Robert? We've packed up some eggs, butter, soap, and a fresh-killed chicken for you. All you need do is pluck it," she said, patting my back. "Remember, you are in my prayers."

Edith came in with their basket of goodies. She, too, looked worried and sad. *But then when did they not?* I decided. I picked out the chunk of soap. "Oh I forgot about the soap making at spring cleaning. Do you still do that? Why, you can find wonderfully fragrant hard soaps now in town, in all sizes and shapes, even heart-shapes, for only pennies. And soft soaps you add directly to your washtub. Making soap is such hard work!"

"I was worried when you moved into town, Ruby," Mama said, "that you would be forever tainted if exposed to city ways and radical thinking. Remember Sodom and Gomorrah? You need to come to church more!"

Opal suddenly showed up, to join in Mama's tune. "Why do city women want to vote?" she said loudly, as if busting at the seams. "It's ridiculous! What business would I have at the polls, talking men's politics when my place is in the home? Where I want to be! If I voted, I'd simply vote the same as my husband to support him. I would certainly value his decisions on such matters, more than mine, just as I would expect him to value my advice on matters, such as, well, canning tomatoes, or birthing babies!"

Mama shook her head adamantly, and for a good moment I thought she was going to scold Opal. "I just can't imagine! Sinners they are! If this group of women thinks like men, what's next? Will they start dressing like men as well?" She began rearranging things in the basket.

I could be quiet no more. "Really, Mama! They are simply asking that all women have a right to be heard and counted."

Opal shook her head adamantly. "I hear you, Ruby, but it makes no difference in the end. The results are the same, for the wife should follow the husband in what he does."

Edith held the soap under my nose. "Isn't this the sweetest smelling soap of any in town? I got the idea from you and your dried lavender. I crushed some lilacs and some dried herbs and started experimenting. Pennies go a long way toward feed and farm tools. Making soap costs nothing and uses up all that ash and grease from the winter."

"Well, anyway, you be careful out there with those city women, Ruby," Mama said. "Mark my words, girls. We are nearing the end of time when we see the devil move from men to women. Another Eve in our garden."

Bess's Chapter Three -- 1920

What is love?

Ladies, liberate yourselves from the drudgery of dirt! What you long for is a picnic amongst the rabbits, so why stay indoors with the dust bunnies? Ease your burdens and take the rest of the day off with this time-saving Home Washing Machine. For only fifteen dollars this machine will take away your worries and red hands and do the work of mothers and daughters. No rubbing or beating – soiled garments are whitened without friction - so consequently no injury. The currents of water passing through the fabrics cause no wear. Boiling water and a good soap is all that is necessary. The base is made of sturdy pine and the crank is easy to turn. While some labor is required, any intelligent woman will find this a labor of love. The Home Washing Machine promises to be to the housewife what the motor car is to the husband.

I dropped my pen. What tacky tactics! No substance; like soap bubbles without the soap. No mission except to convince naïve women to buy yet another product. Hardly a cause to work hard for. But work hard I did because frankly those wages came in handy to replace those weathered and worn travel clothes I previously lived in. The remainder I gave to the Lighthouse household account. It was time I started giving back. So I treated each working day as a means of collection to earn my keep. This form of independence I was unfamiliar with. Funding from the suffrage association had paid for my trips and lodging with fellow suffragists for years, and upkeep and menus for my home in the Lighthouse were covered by monthly checks from Thomas to Lizzie.

I was accustomed to taking orders from a woman, so to repeatedly be ordered about by Thomas' assistant editor, Mr. Shilling (or
Chilling, or Shivering, or Shelling I liked to think when perturbed
by him), proved a difficult transition. I was given one badly scarred
wooden desk holding one drawer underneath, and a typewriter on
top with sticking letters of R and T (the most commonly used letters
of course), and a barely productive type ribbon. *Dare* may read like
dave, if you dared read it at all. I was in a long room with all-male
reporters who were quite filled with smoking breath and cursing
shouts. These men were a crude species and I only had hope for my
man-kind when Thomas approached my desk. I gave him a justified
smile one such day, when reading over my advertisement for The
Home Washing Machine.

"I told these hounds around you that you smiled. I also told them
you could be witty in a quaint old-fashioned way."

I took back my smile and replaced it with pinched lips. "Yes,
I have a rather mid-Victorian flavor, don't I?"

He perched on the edge of my desk with such comfortable ease,
I felt envious. He looked down at my hair twisted back into a bun,
my back straightened with exaggerated posture, my hands docile in
my lap, and he laughed heartily. "You are a modern lady who just
doesn't yet know how to have fun. Someday I might teach you, but
it won't be today. Today I have an assignment for you. Come with
me."

I grabbed my hat and coat and tried to follow closely to his long
strides, my lengthy straight skirt having me resort to a silly pony gait.

His motor car was parked out front and he opened the passenger
door for me. "A riot is brewing at the textile mill."

I stopped and waited for more.

"Your sister, Pearl, is working there, correct?"

I nodded.

"The United Textile Workers Union is there asking women to
sign up, and it's creating quite a buzz. Get in and we'll motor over."

I obeyed and then waited until he did the same on the driver's
side. His new Duisenberg was a beauty in the daylight, the details of

163

which I'd heard at great lengths on our ride out to Hullabaloo's the other night. It hummed quite nicely as we bumped and splashed along the pitted muddy streets through the rain.

"Do you want me to handle the story?" I asked hopefully, wanting some substance to write about.

"No, I already have a reporter there gathering the facts. I thought you would be interested in seeing how the other side lives and why these women ask for labor laws to protect them. Does Pearl not talk to you about working at the mill?"

I squirmed uncomfortably under such direct questioning. I knew little about her. "Pearl and I lead very different lives, Thomas. I don't even understand some of the language she uses. She's so crude, really, and the way she dresses." I stopped here and shook my head, not able to go on with something I didn't understand.

"She's not so different, Bess. She's searching for answers just like we are."

I was caught off guard by the use of 'we' – he seemed to have all the answers - and changed the subject. "You don't have a Model-T like everyone else?"

"No thanks. Ford doesn't need my money. He makes two hundred thousand a day making Model-Ts and Model-As. The real reason is I'm on the road so much I need more comfort. I was down in North Carolina a few months ago and slept on my backseat because a rainstorm had muddied the one good road to where I sank into mud up to my hubs. I had to wait two days before the road dried enough to continue. The government is offering federal money for highway construction. It will create more employment, increase use of motor cars, and more people will be out traveling, visiting, and spending money. The growing prosperity of this country is because of the motor car. Remember I said that."

"Oh, and I thought it was because of my catchy advertisements." I said, trying to mock his southern drawl, but my words sounded stiff and flat, compared to his soft vowels.

He smacked his palm against the steering wheel. "See, I was right. You *are* witty!"

I glanced over at his profile and felt warmed by his presence. I pulled my eyes away from his mouth and tried to concentrate on the street's next pothole. I didn't agree with his motor car theory. I preferred the train as a mode of transportation myself, its metal tracks connecting the states like no road ever could. How could the government afford cutting and dynamiting paved strips of ribbon through farmers' fields, home yards, mountains and canyons, removing anything in front of them, including houses and villages, only to force families' added expense of private motor cars?

We soon pulled up alongside the gate to the factory, its two-story building no more ornate than a child's building block. A tent protected a long table outside the side entrance. A banner sagged in front of the tent like a baby's wet diaper, reading 'United Textile Women Workers'.

I tiptoed between mud puddles, once almost losing my shoe to the mud's suction and finally made my way to the inner tent, more out of a desire to escape the rain, than of curiosity. Ten or so women were standing about or leaning over the table writing in ledgers, two seated women were deep in discussions. No one acknowledged our entrance. I assumed Thomas expected me to ask questions about the purpose of such a union, but when I approached the table my attention was drawn to the easel beside them. Thumb tacked there was my article on Equal Rights with a thick red X marked through it. Written above it in big bold letters was 'Women ARE Women!" Crude notes were posted around the paper with name-calling I shall not name here. Suffice it to say, my article was not favored.

In my defense, I believed the Equal Rights Amendment would give equal rights to women with men. Yet only with another long uphill climb – many working-class and trade union women opposed it, saying they benefited more from labor legislation that gave a special category of benefits for working women. They had their side, I had mine. Another battle. One I was too exhausted to commit to. So it was with dispassionate belief that I had written the article.

Nonetheless I was livid with the red X, as if they'd used my blood to mark it. How dare this lower working class criticize my learned research and findings! What did they contribute toward women's rights? I recognized not *one* of them in any of the women's parties to fight for suffrage. This was how they supported other women who fought on their behalf?

I leaned over the table, and parroting much of what I wrote, spoke loudly to the two women seated there. "Women are women? This is a common sentimental old argument. What does this mean? Weaker. Defenseless. More susceptible to accidents and disease than men. Mothers or potential mothers, nothing more. We all know that's not true. What about the Great War? Eight *million* working women took over practically every trade formerly owned by men. While men fought the war, more than a million women provided them the ammunition. For four years, they worked long hours in the war industries of factories, mills, shipyards, workshops, and laboratories. Did they complain that they were weaker and defenseless? Of course not. Why are we doing this now? Approximately seven million women are wage-earners – that is one out of four women in the paid labor force. Nearly two million of these women are married, so the image of the only women workers being the wretched virgins fluttering between the schoolroom and the matrimonial altar is a façade."

When I paused for breath, I heard someone to the side of me snicker. "You said 'virgin'."

I turned to scarcely recognize my own sister. Dressed in men's trousers and a tweed jacket buttoned to her neck, collar up, a man's cap completed her ensemble. The sack dress was better than this. I felt terribly embarrassed for Pearl and for me as her sister. I opened my mouth to rebuke her but she beat me to the punch.

"Why are you here?" she asked, her tone not curious but critical.

The rain pattering on the outside of the tent became noticeably louder, as if pounding to get in.

I looked above me hoping to avoid any potential water drops on my wool coat and then brushed some drops off my sleeve. The bigger problem was that I wasn't exactly sure why I was there.

Thomas stepped in. "Pearl, your sister and I just wanted to make sure you were in good form. We'd heard there were altercations earlier."

"Your *sister*?" another woman cried, entering in our circle. Her baggy calico dress and coat looked many years old. Her face didn't look any younger, with pale pocked skin and raccoon shadows around her eyes. "Isn't she the one who wrote that nonsense in the paper about equality with men? Work here lady; I'll show you equality!"

Pearl rolled her eyes at Thomas as if to say, *thanks for letting the cat out of the bag*. She folded her arms across her chest. "Sister, now that everyone knows who you are, perhaps you won't mind explaining what you mean by equality. Before protective labor laws, we were *equal* to work twelve-hour days but not free to refuse it. And take Ethel here." She jerked her thumb toward the baggy coat, "She'll lose her job if they find she's pregnant. How can pregnant women have equality with men? Besides, we don't compete with men. We get leftovers. No man wants these under-paid, unskilled jobs."

Pearl's eyebrows were completely covered by hair flattened down by the cap. I wondered why she spoke good English only when dressed like a man.

"That's right, Miss … ?" Our attention turned to one of the ladies seated behind the table.

"Miss Wright," I said, self-consciously folding my right hand over my left. There was no need as that little wedding band from Jere was long gone.

"Miss Wright, more than one hundred organizations, clubs and unions agree with United Textile Workers that protective law is needed; not for all women, but for all mothers. We oppose the constitutional amendment sponsored by the Woman's Party because it's too dangerously sweeping and all-inclusive. More harm than good will come of it." Because of the tent leaks above her, water dripped unnoticed from the wide brim of her felt hat.

I took a deep breath to prepare myself. I had entered a debate unknowingly and unwillingly but had no recourse. I would lose all credibility if I walked out now. Thomas understandably remained quiet in such a hen house.

"You and I agree that much improvement is needed to further the position of women," I said. "Suffrage is only half the battle. But as long as women are subject to restrictions that do not apply to men, women will only get the jobs men don't want. Under protective legislation, employers are liable to a heavy fine or imprisonment if he keeps a woman five minutes over the nine-hour days. Men have no such restrictions so don't you think men are more likely to be hired? Here in New York alone, thousands of women in restaurants, candy stores, and railroads have been thrown out of work in the name of protecting their health and their morals. If an employer has the choice between a woman who can legally only work nine hours a day – and only during the day - and a man who can work twelve-hour days on any shift, naturally the employer will chose the more flexible of the two. Women's labor laws can actually work against her and give more opportunity for the men. Is this protection or a handicap? Is it protecting women, or protecting men from the competition of women? Is it any wonder men support protective legislation? After all, most of the protective legislation was passed before women had the vote. Equal grounds would give the defenseless a weapon to make them strong. Preaching protection only makes her appear weaker."

They were closing in around me and I began to perspire in this cool September air. I hadn't felt this uneasy since being arrested for disturbing the peace during the Syracuse march for suffrage. Policemen closed in like this but I feared these women more; they had righteous anger.

I stepped back, swallowed, and continued, raising my voice to try to cover my tremor.

"Hundreds of state statutes take away the rights of women. In some, the earnings of the wife belong to the husband. In forty states, the husband owns his wife's work in the home, which means if the wife is injured, the husband can collect for damages for the loss of her services. The woman is put in the same class with children, so she becomes of as little value as a thirteen-year-old child. The amend-ment asks for equal rights throughout the United States. Don't you want control of your own earnings?"

"Earnings?" came a cry from behind me, the thin woman's ran-cid breath reaching me before she did. "What earnings? We get paid half of what these here men do. You suffragists promised us every-thing; a new heaven and a new earth. To listen to you, all women are going to have their own offices in the White House. Well looky around, miss – this ain't heaven and the earth ain't nothing but dirt that these men throw in your face if you don't do what they tell you!"

Pearl stepped in front of her as if to hide her. "Look, sis, when *you* sweep the floor boards, you leave the dirt between the cracks." Pearl's thumb pointed toward herself. "We're that dirt and we're forgotten about. First, we start here and look after our own. We've got to work from the bottom up." Her eyes suddenly squinted in resentment. "But you don't hear me do you? You don't know –"

As if the sky was falling, the tent abruptly collapsed on one side, women squealing and protecting their heads with their hands, all scurrying toward what once was the entrance. Men's voices were heard outside, barking orders to pull out the poles on the other side. Lifting the tent canvas, we scrambled out to see two heavily built chaps working around us like we were nothing more than escaped ants. I followed Thomas over to a suited man standing to the side, obviously in charge of his devilkin.

Thomas extended his hand to the man and said calmly, "I'm the editor of Annan News, Mr. Griffith, and this will make a helluva story."

The man, well-fed and full of himself, sputtered in surprise. "I'm very well aware of who you are, Mr. Pickering. I had no idea you were in the midst of that group of – of traitors and whiners! I'm the owner of this factory, sir, and these so-called union representatives refused to leave private property."

Thomas took out a small pad and pencil from the inside of his jacket and began writing. "So you are opposed to union representa-tion? Women having a voice?"

"If you think I'm going to listen to seventy-five yacking clacking broads with cat claws at each other's backs, think again! Loyalty is what I command in this business. If you want a story, write about my productivity. That's why I'm a successful businessman just as you are. Now let's shake hands so that I can go off and do my business, and you can do yours."

Mr. Griffith extended his hand but Thomas seemed too engrossed in his notepad to notice. Thomas finally tapped his pad and looked up. "Your success would allow an increase in women's wages then, would it not? My sources tell me they make one third of the men's wages here."

The extended hand dropped and Mr. Griffith's fake smile dropped to a frown. "There's no point in discussing this any further. It's unfortunate that you have become hen-pecked. You and that loudmouthed broad that tagged behind you can get the hell out of here. My men are capable of carrying you out, if you like." He walked away waving his arms. "Back to work, girls!" he barked at top volume. I dared not guess whether his bark was worse than his bite. I touched Thomas' arm and shook my head as a way of saying it's not worth pursuing him.

I watched my sister's backside disappear into the dark doorway making me think of a shark swallowing her whole. That was my first inkling of guilt; somehow I felt I had let her down. Somehow I felt too, that this was Thomas' intention.

The next time I saw Pearl, we were on our way to vote in the federal election.

I don't know what I was expecting. A glow in the sky, women flying while singing Halleluiah, tingling sensations, *something*.

"That's the beauty of this kind of day, Miss Bess," said Lizzie. "It will feel like any other day to the men-folk too, but we're just going to sneak up on them, cast our woman vote, and the Democrats won't know what hit them!"

To show her my celebratory mood, I gave her a rare day off to walk to the colored section of town to cast her vote.

I pinched Mama and Pearl, too, as the three of us walked downtown to vote for the next President of the United States. We played the game of the men and dared not divulge our candidate choices; although I would have bet my cherished autographed copy of *The Woman's Bible* that we would vote Republican, just as the majority of this town was known to do.

"Oh, Bess, I feel different indeed," Mama said, her eyes shining. "I woke up this morning remembering how town folks ridiculed the Ladies Legion and there were only five of us in the beginning. But Jesus fed five thousand with five loaves of bread. So five is a powerful beginning and look how we grew and what happened!"

She suddenly snorted loudly, giving me cause to frown. "Of course Robert insisted that I vote on his behalf and not on my own. God forgive me but I was forced to remind him of his last two Presidential choices. William Taft was so obese he got stuck in the White House bathing tub. Robert had installed a tub only a few years earlier and as soon as he heard this, became convinced that tubs could be hazardous. I was tempted to chain our lovely claw foot to the floor in case he had the notion to drag it outside and shoot it. President Wilson has faired worse and we all know his illness is so that his wife runs the White House. Ironic, ladies, when you think about it. Women were not permitted to have a vote on who runs the country, but a woman nonetheless ends this term in doing just that. Imagine what we can do now that we have the vote!"

"Today is a doozy alright," Pearl said lackadaisically. She was gawking at the male driver and female passenger of an open Model-T as it bumped and swayed through the puddles and pits beside us. Recognition and hurt registered on her face but she said nothing. She shrugged it off. "I don't know what you expected, sister. You've been a mouthpiece since I can remember, yelling that the sky is falling unless women get the vote. The sky should be clear now. As Harding said in his campaign, 'Return to Normalcy'."

Her acquaintance with Harding's slogan was a revelation to me. I wondered why she practiced being shallow, when in fact her own 'normalcy' was quite the contrary.

I supposed she was right, although the noise level at the City Hall was up a notch or two to where we felt the vibration of a different day. Women sat at tables taking voter registrations from excitable women who filled out the form as if applying for the President's position themselves. It pleased me to see so many women come out to vote. I counted two men in the long line, leading me to cynically think that such a womanly gathering diminished the man's reasons to be here.

I completed my own form quietly amidst the cackles and cluck-ing, checked the box on the voting slip for William G. Harding, and slipped this into the slot of the glass box on the center table. In doing so, a camera's pop made me jump and I recognized the photographer and the newspaper reporter with him, pen and pad in hand.

"Miss Bess Wright," he called loudly. "How does it feel as a suf-fragist to finally cast a vote like a man?"

Thomas had sent them, I was sure of it.

The high-ceiling and large pillars along the sides of the hall cre-ated echoes and his challenge traveled and quieted others.

"I *man*aged," I said with a smile. "I believe it is *man*datory that all wo*man* do so. It is no longer a man's right to vote but also a woman's. The Nineteenth Amendment states: 'The right of citizens of the United States to vote shall not be denied or abridged by the United States or by any State on account of sex'."

My mind flooded with the many roadblocks and excuses given over the years, many times over. I knew them by heart. I opened my arms to include women standing around me. "And what about the other women here? Did you leave your husbands abandoned and dirty, your children crying, your homes in shambles, to come here and vote?"

"No!" some shouted.

"Did your ballot create divorce, take the place of head of household, or cancel out your husband's vote? Or worse yet, did you only vote as your husband told you to, thereby wasting votes?"

"No!"

"Have you lost your feminine ways? Do you feel corrupted by politics? Do any of you feel like a man, now that you have the audacity to think like one?"

"We can think for ourselves!" called out a familiar voice. Mama blushed when I tracked the voice to her.

"Do you believe we went against God and Government?"

"Certainly not!" another yelled.

"Then all those who resisted us for these many years were liars, and we're here to prove it!" I decided then to use my own slogan from years past. "We're not only here to prove they're wrong, but to *improve* our right!"

Applause sounded throughout the hall and as Mama came to my side and cast her ballot, another picture was taken. I forgave her past transgression with Jere long enough to feel secretly thrilled that she could find a sitter for Papa and get away to be here. I also secretly wished I could be a fly on the wall when Papa saw Mama's picture in the paper.

It was an exciting moment and yet, as I walked away, somehow the whole event was anti-climatic to me. Voting was a personal choice, a human right, a small contribution to democracy, and yet women had to fight hard for such a minor freedom, to be treated as a person. To earn the simple right of checking the box next to a male politician's name. Bittersweet, indeed. I didn't know whether to laugh or cry.

Tired of looking homely or old? Do you want youth and beauty? Rub Fountain of Youth Vanishing Cream well into your face and the wrinkles will vanish with the Cream. The Cream has no oil in it, so next apply your face powder

and that ugly shine will vanish too! It makes all the difference between look-ing commonplace and ...

I drummed my fingertips on the desk. I inked in a white scar chipped into the wood surface. I gazed off through the window to a scattering of buildings and trees of the park beyond. Writing one more falsehood about a product would surely cause me to scream. A simple gadget can do everything except tuck you into bed at night. And of course there's always an elixir out there that can even do that. I had indeed swallowed my pride in taking this job.

My guilt was augmented in a recent visit with Papa. He was hav-ing increased difficulty in distinguishing reality from radio reality. He talked as if he were an amused spectator in all radio events. News, tragedy or comedy, was to him a performance. He believed in all radio advertisements, no matter how farfetched the claim to eternal health or wealth. The more he listened, the more ignorant and disil-lusioned he became. It saddened me that my advertisements with unproven boasts contributed to the nation's hunger for fairy tales. I was further depressed in remembering that it was that evening that I would return to Papa's bedside to listen to the coverage of vot-ing results. Papa had the token radio and for the first time in radio history, commercial radio was broadcasting coverage of election returns. A radio station out of Pittsburgh was going to read telegraph ticker results over the air as they came in. With some degree of agi-tation I resolved to silently tolerate his ravings. I would not argue. These were my thoughts as Thomas appeared and perched on the edge of my desk.

"You'll not guess the offer I just received," he said, smiling so broad his laugh lines doubled.

"You're moving to The New York Times and I'm getting your job here."

"No, but such a presumptuous attitude from a woman reminds me – did you vote today?"

"I find it quite humorous that so many ask me this question. What am I lacking that make others think I would not be thrilled to place a ballot?"

"Passion," Thomas said without hesitation.

"P-passion?" I felt my face blushing and was as mortified by this, as I was by his statement.

"When I would see you on one of your women's campaigns, I had the urge at times to shake you. To say, Bess, wake up! You know that expression, 'he could do that in his sleep'; well you looked to me like you were sleepwalking, saying and doing the right things, but without heart or feeling."

"Well, worse than that, Thomas. You make it sound as if I'm not even aware." I found myself wishing someone would walk by to allow me to smile broadly and say Good day! with feeling. But of course, discreet as usual, he stopped by during our lunch hour and the office was empty.

He placed his hand on my shoulder and looked into my eyes with such intensity that I very much wanted to look away but to do that would give in to what he said. "Bess, don't be defensive. I think you are very much aware, which is why you're the first I wish to share this bit of news with. A member of the city council just moments ago asked me if I would be interested in running for mayor in the next election."

"Mayor! Why Thomas, that is wonderful news."

Thomas backed up and tilted his head at me. "Your eyes literally lit up. I believe I've found the switch, by golly!"

"I think you'd make an excellent mayor, and this town needs a liberal thinker at its helm. Why ... why I could advertise you. Let me do this, Thomas, it would mean so much." A new cause and for my friend, Thomas.

"You mean act as my campaign manager?"

I nodded. "I certainly learned a lot about politics over the years as a suffragist."

"Have you now? Then I do hope that means that you voted for Harding. He was a newspaper editor, like yours truly."

"Oh really?" I said and batted my eyes demurely. "What a coincidence. So is his opponent, James Cox. And both were editors in Ohio."

He did not hide his surprise at my knowledge of this. "Very good!"

His condescending tone irritated me immensely but I wished not to get into a political debate at the national level, but focus on the local level. "Please don't patronize me, Thomas. Look. All we need is a campaign strategy and some necessary campaign stunts."

"Stunts? I'm not a vaudeville act, my dear." He was looking in front of him, twirling a pencil between his fingers, a recognized habit when he was deep in thought. "What kind of strategy?"

"Strategy based on what you believe in, of course. You said yourself you wish there was more you could do about women's equality at our textile mill. And paved streets - I know how much that means to you, and to every motor car owner. And when I say stunts I mean, for example, milking a cow on my uncle's dairy farm to get the farmer's vote, sweeping the streets to get the business man's vote, shaking the mill workers' hands to get the common folks' votes, and holding children to get the women's vote. You need to give the public a necessary ration of affection … of passion." I grinned at this, predicting his reaction.

"*You* are going to campaign passion?" he asked, returning the grin. I laughed easily at this, and Thomas joined in.

He was silent for a moment, still perched on my desk, his one leg solidly on the floor, the other leg dangling and swaying to and fro beside my desk, leading me to think that part of him wanted to stay, part of him was anxious to go. He finally looked down at me with tenderness there, yes there in his green eyes and in the relaxed corners of his mouth. "I don't want to lose that light in your eyes. If it pleases you, I'll do it," he said.

Just when I thought our friendship had deepened into a meaningful partnership, where we could work together for a common cause, Thomas announced that he was heading south to Georgia to visit family and continue research on a story he was writing on the advances made in technology. In line with the machine age, he wanted to know more about the labor unions in the north and south, and to educate himself on the highway construction program. Nothing would please him more than to see the eastern states criss-cross thousands of miles of hard-surface highways. If he was going to be a serious contender for politics, he would have to do his home-work, he said. Thomas was such a modern fellow, traveling without thought to distance as others might do, roving from north to south as easily as the rest of us drove from the farm into town. Many people continued to think of travel between states being a week's journey apart by stagecoach, although paved roads and motor cars were fast becoming the reality.

During this time I received a letter from Thomas. "I have an assignment for you," he had written. "There is to be a large confer-ence to focus on the Equal Rights Amendment. Supporters such as you (you know the type; middle-class professional women compet-ing with men – yes you are, just look around your office) are meet-ing with the opposition – women in lower working class and their unions. Representatives of the United Textile Workers union will be there. I tell you this because your sister is now one of their members (I have my sources). Go there and write a story on it – an unbiased story. Look at both sides. It appears that your suffrage was only the beginning to women's revolution."

This assignment gave me a dilemma. I had previously agreed to attend the conference and speak in support of the Equal Rights Amendment, even though I knew this was in opposition to Pearl's union. A business conflict; a personal conflict.

"Life is such a kaleidoscope," I whispered to Thomas' clearly defined handwriting.

Despite the cold November air, the conference room of the Annan Hotel sizzled like frying bacon. More than fifty women delegates from national organizations or state branches thereof appeared ready to have their say. Contrary to Thomas' instructions, I came prepared as the opposition; opposition I say because the agenda had been built only around protective labor laws that my group opposed.

Following the lead of Miss Gail Laughlin of the National Woman's Party, we planned a campaign of disruption typical of our suffrage days.

In the first day's open session, Miss Laughlin challenged the program because it did not allow opposing viewpoints on labor laws for women. The other delegates overwhelmingly voted her down; in other words, not wanting to hear any opposition. Consequently, with each pro-protective law speaker, our group stood up, yelled, hissed, and clapped our hands. It was all I could do to stand up and hiss, for Pearl was squirming angrily and watching me closely from the back wall.

At last, to avoid another "militant outburst", our proposal was adopted to meet in debate and lively debates they were, beginning with President John Edgerton of the National Association of Manufacturers. He pleaded for women's right to work unlimited hours unencumbered by "legislative poultices" as he called the labor laws. President William Green of the American Federation of Labor opposed him by saying, "Of course Mr. Edgerton doesn't want restrictions in his wishes to employ his women at any hours he wishes."

Miss Laughlin agreed that a shorter workday and sanitary and humane conditions were most favorable, but should be obtained based on the industry, not upon the sex of the worker. She declared that the Woman's Party would not rest from its labors until the goal envisioned by the Declaration of Sentiments in 1848 was realized – the complete emancipation of women.

As planned, she introduced me. Because she hadn't allowed opposition to speak next, I was forced to shout much of what I had to say over the cat-calls, Pearl being one of those standing.

"Many good men sighed with relief when suffrage was won. They said, 'The woman problem is solved; let's move on.' But women have returned to being seamstresses and what, in God's name, do we want now? Why aren't we satisfied with what we have? It is because we're not yet fully clad. We cannot go out on equal grounds in our camisole now can we? We would continue to be viewed as sexual beings and nothing more. We ask for the same rights as the opposite sex receives in being accidentally born a male. As inadequate as these laws and custom are, women are deprived of many of them. Here in New York, fathers control the earnings and real estate of the children. In other states, the father can still will away the custody of children from the mother. In most states, prostitution is a crime for women, but not for men. How many more examples do we need in order to know we cannot make fair earnings, control our income, home and children? We all know this. Why should we only ask for political equality and not for civil and industrial equality? We should be dressed in the same protective law that men have, from head to toe, or else men will always feel superior to our flimsy see-through labor laws. The Equal Rights Amendment will give us the ultimate protection."

Annan was a small town and many in that conference room knew my sister and I, including Mollie Mills who stated she was "outraged" at the Woman's Party's rude antics. She introduced my sister, Pearl, with a vendetta visibly displayed on her expression. Pearl walked to the podium in a conservative light blue wool dress with a wide collar and this was quite becoming.

"I'm not good at speeches. Don't think I've ever made one," Pearl said, her voice weak and quavering. "But I have made my own living, grimy as that may be, so I know what I'm talking about. Miss Wright does not; Miss Wright is wrong." Her play on words brought out a few snickers. My group began hissing in the same manner as the opposing side did while I had spoken.

"A working woman is not equal to a working man; he's stronger and he's meaner, and he could care less about an equal rights amendment. That's way above him and too far away to touch him. He only knows he can lift more than the woman working next to him, so why does she have the job instead of his brother."

I could no longer tolerate my group's interruptions. I hissed at all of them to hush instantly.

"She only has body parts suitable for one thing," Pearl was saying, "and he will do what he can to make those parts work for him. Where does she go when he traps her in the storage room? I tell you – there is nowhere to go."

She paused and for one brief moment her eyes searched mine, and all I could do was nod slightly, silently sending her wishes for strength. She wiped her tears with the back of her hands and then grasped the podium. "That is when you meet non-equality face to face," she quivered loudly, determination in the grim line of her pale mouth. "His above yours shoving your womanhood to where you can't find it anymore. What government law in Washington can reach her in the weeds of a small town? She is untouchable, except to the men around her who think women are to be owned and used like machinery. It's easy to speak theory; it's hard to speak truth, especially when it's so personal." She returned her gaze to me, and I felt as vulnerable as one at the wrong end of a rifle.

"Miss Wright, I've seen you stand up for women for about as long as I can remember. I thank you publicly for that, but you have to start thinking with your heart, and not your head. You've done good with getting us the vote; now use that vote to protect us as you promised to do! Look after your own before you worry about the world." She left the podium giving others no choice but to focus their stare on me.

I wanted to fire back that it was going to be difficult to think with my heart when she just shot a hole through it, but I remained silent, the poison in her words being absorbed. This explained her sudden change to defiance. Why didn't she come to me for help? I knew why. I was up there in the clouds with Billy, perhaps a cloud myself, no substance, just puffy floating air. I had nothing left to stand on. I walked out of the conference room.

This was the second time Thomas had thrown me into the midst of the lower class working women, forcing me to look at both sides.

But I hadn't stayed neutral as I wrote his article. I would be in deep trouble now.

Debate, debate. Pros and cons. Your side, my side. Never the two shall meet. I suddenly understood why Billy sat on the fence. Debates required taking positions; positions in favor, positions against, thus you have a battle. Billy once said that was the difference between us; he refused to argue over anything whereas I agreed to argue over everything. Of course I argued that if he believed in something, he would not be so passive. He only proved his point – and mine - by walking away.

Thanks to Pearl, I became increasingly tired of yelling across the fence and wondered if this was a weakness. I longed for Billy to be here so that I could say: What do you say let's sit on the fence together? I needed something tangible and real in my life. Something true to hold. So I did what I had done for years and turned to Billy. Of course he wasn't real any longer but only a fading memory of brown, perfectly parted hair and a smile that flashed white teeth and lit his light brown eyes. But his smudged letters were something I could hold in my hand and smell its mustiness. This was more real than anything else I touched, including those airy advertisements I wrote daily.

Dear Bess, how's my girl?   *August 1917*

Are you shocked I called you my girl? I must be homesick, wouldn't you say? I can just imagine you right now with that half-smile and one eyebrow raised, saying, "The word 'my' is possessive, my dear."

Just arrived in London last week and there are ceaseless lines of troops here. I hear complaints about President Wilson's "he kept us out of war" slogan and how his 976 days of neutrality has kept the war in motion longer. Now that America has finally declared war on Germany, troops and morale have picked up. Everyone is making preparations for one big quick battle and then it will all be over soon.

I'm training to fly aeroplanes – can you imagine your fellow hundreds of feet in the sky? Probably, since you once told me my head was in the clouds. When you see a bird, think of me. But then your last letter said you thought of me often, so perhaps you don't need a prompt? Now that I see lives being cut short, I wonder, why did you and I waste so many hours playing games? The few kisses, that rare private touch ... remember the moonlight picnic ...

*we should have … Damn it, what I should have done was to have flown you
away from all those radical hens and settled you into a wife and mother. Only
I get the impression that you would want to fly the plane and I'd get stuck as
gunrunner. Speaking of that, I saw my first girl bus conductor today, you will
be happy to know.*

*I hope to be home for Christmas so tell Lizzie to have some of her peanut
butter fudge waiting for me.*

Your fellow, Billy

Dear Bess,   *October 1917*

*I've returned to Blighty as the English say. This means I've come back to
England and wounded at that. Some burns when my aeroplane's gas tank
caught fire from shots. That's nothing compared to the legless ones and arm-
less ones around me. They look unreal to me, like actors on a Civil War stage
in my school days. If a soldier dies here, he's 'gone west' they say and I've seen
a lot of that too. I wish you could meet the nurse who works for the Red Cross
Motor Corps. She has your independent spirit. Christine drives the ambulance
and visits the soldiers. She's cute as a button wearing breeches, high boots,
and service cap. She said her husband would never have let her wear this, but
he's 'gone west' too. Everybody has a war job; it keeps the grief and depression
at bay.*

Yours, Billy

Merry Christmas Bess!   *December 1917*

*Merry Christmas and at this rate I'd better say Happy New Year too. I got
your letters but couldn't write back what with all the flights I've flown between
England and France. This is the place to be on furlough. Music and dancing every night and women certainly know how to dress up for the soldiers.
Christine said it's all part of the game to keep our morale up. She said that in
days gone by, mourning would require a woman to go into black for several
years but now everyone has lost a husband or brother or father and they can't
show their grief in the few days the living soldiers are on furlough.*

*I'm sorry to read that your father is ill. Give him my regards. I wish I had
a photograph of you. I'm having a hard time remembering what you look like,
well, except you have beautiful eyes that burn a blue flame when you're angry*

with me, which is probably right now. And your long brown hair – don't cut it like a lot of women are doing these days. It would be great to see you, a woman with some meat on her bones. All the women here are worried thin.

Sure wish I was home for Christmas but it looks like the war is going to be a little while longer. Ask Lizzie to save some fudge for me.

Yours Truly, Billy

P.S. I was disappointed to read in your letter of your group's latest escapade and of your being arrested and going on a hunger strike, especially since I am surrounded by men fighting for a much greater cause and their hunger is not intentional. Why would your suffragettes call our President 'Kaiser Wilson' in comparing him to Kaiser Wilhelm II of Germany? It's a stab in the heart to say that 20 million American women are not self-governed when we men are dying over here every day for freedom for men <u>and</u> women.

Hey, how's my girl?   June 1918

I thought I'd better be sweet on you, I hadn't written in so long. The war is dragging on and you must be getting tired of the Red Cross slogan, 'Give Till It Hurts'. I know I am because I see so many hurting. You recently wrote about your marches for women's equality but let me tell you, the best way to get equality is to start a war. Women are replacing men everywhere I go. They've had to – I heard that six hundred thousand men have been killed in France alone. Women are harvesting the crops, butchering the lambs, cleaning the engines on our aeroplanes like they were cleaning their stoves at home, opening their homes to billeting all the extra women munitions workers and traveling soldiers. There are women here in the London hospital too (yes, I'm back here with a gunshot wound to the leg but this bird will not be grounded for long) with factory injuries from handling explosives and soldering lead. You'll be happy to know, I no longer think in terms of 'woman's work'.

When my hospital train arrived at Charing Cross, the only lights on at the station were those from the ten or so motor ambulances waiting there in line, to prevent enemy planes from spotting us. It looked like I was being taken to my tomb. Quite unnerving, really, until I saw Christine, and of course the other nurses and sisters. These angels are there every night with their flashlights, waiting for the wounded. Each ambulance holds four stretchers and a nurse or sister to comfort us on the way to the hospital. Wounded German *soldiers are treated the same, except a soldier enters the ambulance with them instead of a woman.*

I know that men's talk bores you but just to let you know I've been in more than 75 air battles and destroyed at least eleven enemy aircraft. I'm an accurate shooter but lousy pilot, so no one would be the wiser if I voluntarily crash my Nieuport rather than have the enemy send me down in flames. In the meantime, my smoking bullets hit every Hun machine I can find and the closer to the hooded pilot, the better.

I've made a decision: I'm not going back to that factory when the war ends. I'm sure I would enjoy being a pilot – it's just that right now the war is taking all the fun out of it. I can't fly from one destination to another without fearing fire. I can't enjoy the freedom of flight without fearing capture by the enemy. Well, hell, my ol' playmate, I should be able to tell you some things about myself without your attention flying away.

Your flying ace, Billy

Dear Bess   *September 1918*

I was surprised to read that you have joined New York City's Motor Corps and have learned to drive an ambulance. Good for you, ol' girl! I'll be sure to pass that on to Christine. And that your entire motor corps marched in the Red Cross procession to raise money for the war! I'm having trouble imagining you in a starched uniform, although your marching in military file I've seen often enough, but now you do so for others. Thousands of men (including me, dear) thank you for your selfless act. I wish to give you a big hug and kiss for it. Oh and for your letters too. It's always great to hear from home. You're my favorite so chin up and all that. Don't worry; you shouldn't have to do this for long. The Germans are retreating out of France and we're bringing in a lot of prisoners from the battle in the Argonne Forest. Remember what they say: this is the War to End all Wars.

Just to keep you up on your interests in women's work, there's a 500-women Motor Corp here in Paris, some of who moved here temporarily from London. The women have their own garage and hotel for sixty motors and manage just about all of it from mechanics to car dispatcher. Motors here have no self-starters, so Christine told me that several girls have had their arms broken trying to crank the bloody things in the cold early mornings. Oh yes, and she asked me to pass on that women over the age of thirty have won the vote this year in Great Britain.

Sincerely, Billy

I received this last letter a week or so after word of Billy's death. I had read it back then through tears, thankful that he knew of my own war efforts and that he still wished to kiss and hug me. Yes, he wrote in small doses but this salve to my lonely soul lasted long. So much was going on in the foreground of my life that he became my background, his past words giving me strength to move forward. Believing he was still alive and loved me was enough. But now ... now, did he love me? I noticed for the first time that there were no words of love in these letters. In reading, I saw them through a different light. Now that the war of men and the war of women were over, the dust had settled and all was quiet, I could see clearly. The romantic hues of him flying in blue skies into pink sunsets were lifted. Stark clear reality with its harsh pen strokes struck me with a force that left me sitting there stunned, the pages of this last letter falling onto my lap. Even I the detached, could recognize passion if presented close enough, but Billy had only brought the flame to me once, in a long-ago moonlit night.

Was it pride or protectiveness? Did I assume he had the same devotion, but little emotion to show it? And here was a question I dared not bring to the forefront before: Was Christine his new love? If I were honest with myself, I had thought little about it. He had always been there, from high school on, in the same group of friends, sort of naturally matched up and comfortable with one another. He listened passively to my current raves on women's subservient position in society and men's abuse of women. I listened not at all or with accumulating anger to his long-winded stories of hunting, factory escapades, and talk of loose women. He grew up with seven brothers, I grew up with righteous women; he was a man's man, I was a woman's woman. I used him as an excuse to not love other men. Here was the thrust of it that stunned me: he was there in mind, but not in my heart. Why hadn't I seen this before?

The letter blurred on my lap. Sniffling, I collected the pages of my once-precious small stack. Stiffly I walked toward the fireplace, my extended arm holding the papers as if they were already smoking. I threw them into the fire but somehow a few pages separated and his signature page landed on the fire screen.

It was just like Billy, to find himself on a fence.

Katy's Chapter Three -- *1943*

With these two men in my life, all of a sudden I have mixed emotions. I love 'em, I hate 'em. What's with all this ego and proving themselves? Living at the Lighthouse with women gave me a simple steady feeling of just being. Here at Uncle Joe's house, I'm more on guard, alert, like needing to keep one ante-up on him, and it's not different with William Thomas Jackson the Third, aka TJ. Nothing's easy and it's a tug-o-war or I'm the ping-pong ball.

"Stop it, I've had enough!" I say to TJ as I'm buttoning my blouse. "I told Uncle Joe I didn't want to go out with you again just for this very thing, and here I am again!"

"Ah, honey, don't get mad at me," TJ says, his voice muffled by my neck. I pull back. His lips look swollen and red from all our kissing, which I can handle with the best of 'em, even enjoy it. And William is a great kisser, the best no doubt. Just ask him. But here's the thing: he can't keep it a simple steady feeling. He's got to make it complicated and mix my emotions up by stirring around my chest and thighs. I'm just not ready for that increased emotion, passion, risk. I try to explain but it comes out sounding whiny and high-pitched and I hate that about us women.

"Can't we just kiss?" I ask.

"For a while, honey, but we've been doing that for a month now, baby, and a man needs more."

We're sitting on pillows in front of the radio cabinet listening to Cajun and bebop music and I'm starting to like it, even though I'm surprised at the Negro sounds he prefers, like Dexter Gordon's sax, because William talks so racist. Plus I'm tired of him making fun of the Glenn Miller Orchestra and besides that, listening to orchestra just makes me homesick for the nights around Mama's radio. But it's hard to get romantic or even want to dance to Queen Ida's accordion.

He lights two Lucky Strikes and hands me one. I'm beginning to get the hang of this, and I blow out a perfectly shaped o-ring. He does the same with his fine-looking kisser.

"You think you're such a big cheese," he says, flicking his ashes with his little finger. "Where'd you get that attitude, when you're no more than a broad?" He's looking at me sideways with a cocky grin and I know he's goading me, so I stay cool.

"If you knew my mother you'd understand; as a matter of fact you wouldn't dare ask that around her. She's framed more than one beau with her questioning. They'd come in kind of pumped up about me, and they'd leave like a flat tire."

"Is that why you're not married?"

"No. I've just never saw the need to marry. I've still got time before I lose my teeth." I give him my Cheshire cat grin to show them off. I'd heard about my beautiful smile all my life. *Your Papa's smile,* Mama once said before turning her back on me and walking quickly away to avoid any further questions.

"You'll marry someday." This isn't a question but a statement he makes so I study him closely. He's not meeting my eyes but is examining his cigarette like it's his invention. I think about flirting with him which I usually enjoy doing, like, *Why whatever do you mean – are you proposing to me, Teee-Jaaay?* But I just can't bring myself to flatter him any more; he thinks he's so hotsy-totsy when I can't get him out of my mind as a drugstore cowboy. You know the type: hangs around on the streets, whistling and trying to pick up dames – sorry, "*broads*". I haven't actually seen him do that, though, and he's harder to figure out than my beaus back in Annan, so I feel all mixed up inside again.

I turn away to the radio and turn knobs trying to get a better station. This FM is one of those big old-timey wooden boxes that sits on the floor like my mama's. I'd seen newer, smaller ones that you can carry in both hands, some in the Sears catalogue even have a phonograph player, but with the war on, it seems like no one is updating anything. Poor William came over with his stack of 78's that I would give my eyeteeth to hear but no such luck at Uncle Joe's where everything looks and smells old. I think again about what I'd do with such a place and where I'd get the money to modernize it. The telephone's five-way party line would be the first to go. I could barely hear Mama, what with all the nosy breathing of party-line listeners, and to reach her I had to go through four operators. I might as well live in Timbuktu.

I find a station with less static and Bing Cosby is singing his *White Christmas.* William groans his "not that again!" and I immediately turn the knob back and forth until I hear Benny Goodman singing, *Take a chance on me.*

In one swell swoop, William's got me down flat and he's on top. "Kiss me again, honey, you know you like it."

I give in to the song until it changes to *Praise the Lord and Pass the Ammunition,* when I have the audacity to giggle during his serious smooch. Nose to nose he murmurs, "Woman, you're killing me." He kisses harder, hurting my mouth.

I'm getting braver with all this testosterone in the house and decide to turn his motor off. I push him off me and roll over. I feel pretty smooth myself as I stand and turn on the other floor lamp.

"Why haven't you enlisted?" I ask, straightening my blouse and skirt.

He's red in the face now as he sits there on the floor with one arm over his bended knee, the other leg straight out, his hand making and unmaking a fist. "My daddy says I have flat feet," he finally answers, staring down the long dark hall toward the bedrooms.

"And do you?"

"If my daddy says I do." He lights another cigarette. "You didn't have the privilege of meeting him when you met Mother. He'd put the fear of God in you to do what I want." As an afterthought, he gives me a just-kidding wink.

"Are you saying he's hard-boiled?"

"Let's just say his group of buddies has their own Army." He's still clenching, unclenching his fist.

I open my mouth to ask more but he steers us away to his immediate needs.

"Stop playing games."

"How am I playing games?" But I know what he means.

"You're a tease."

"I'm not. You're a handsome guy and I like kissing you."

"Then why did you let me touch your breasts?"

I finally meet his eyes. "I thought I'd like it but it just made me … all crazy inside."

"You're crazy cause you don't know how to treat a man."

For some reason this hurts and I want to prove him wrong. I kneel down in front of him. "That's not true."

He stands and stretches nonchalantly and looks down at me as if enjoying seeing me like that. My eyes are level with his crotch and he's still aroused.

"Walk me out to the car. I'll bring it back to you tomorrow," he says with a yawn.

I want to please him, to no longer have him mad - he can be fun when things go his way - so I nod and follow.

Once outside, he opens the passenger door to the Duesy, moves the front seat forward and steps aside. I go to the back seat as if planned and then sit there wondering why. He stoops and lowers himself beside me. "Is it back here where you slept, you know, on your way here from New York?"

"Yes, I did, and you *were* listening," I say with a laugh. It's hard to tell because much of the time he has a distracted look on his face.

"Show me how you laid, and I'll lay beside you." He notices my raised eyebrows and raises his hands. "No hanky-panky."

I lay down on my side, my arm curled under my head and he spoons behind me and remains still. It actually feels quite cozy and warm in this late-night air, and stupid me starts relaxing. It seems we doze for an hour or two before he starts heavy-breathing in my ear. I try to move away from his groping hands but there's less room here to move and his grip is harder around my waist at every attempt. He's more aggressive than ever before, bruising, tugging, out of control, his pants down, my skirt up – he almost succeeds, except I squeal in frustration, kicking the interior car frame, and the hound dogs hear me and start barking.

William jerks his head up toward Joe's bedroom window that faces the driveway and we both notice the bedroom light comes on. He gets himself back together in a hurry. His hands now fumbling with his pants gives me a chance to get out of there.

I don't take any chances this time and I high-tail it directly to Uncle Joe's room. I see the tail lights from there of my Duesy going down the long laneway. I'm not afraid but "mad as a wet hen", as Uncle Joe describes my look when he sees me.

I imagine I'm quite a sight, with my mussed hair and wrinkled clothing. I don't care. I point my finger at him. "Don't ask me again to go out with that cad."

Uncle Joe attempts to sit up a little further in bed and flattens down his few strands of white hair across his head. "What happened?" he asks hoarsely, but I can tell that he knows already by his averted eyes.

"What happened is that I tried to please you by giving William a chance, and then I try to please him by being nice to him, and then I find what happens is that neither one of you is trying to please me."

He chews on this for a minute, moving his jaw back and forth. Finally nodding, he says, "Here's what I'm going to do. I won't ask you again to spend any time with TJ. You're my kin and you come first. You just lay low and I'll give him a good talking to. If I have to, I'll talk to his daddy and TJ sure as hell doesn't want that. Now you go on up to bed and we won't talk about this again."

I feel like there are things he's not saying and I want to question him, but he waves me away and slides back down onto his pillow, turning off his light.

Because of Papa's last journal entry, I can't turn to him tonight or I'll just get mad again. Men! Who said you can't live without them?

I see even less need for a birth control clinic but with William's attraction/distraction seemingly out of the way, I have nothing else to do, hence I call Ellen Whitman and actually drive into Savannah to meet with her. But you may have caught on to the fact that I can't drive just yet because William has my car.

So here's what happens: Two days after I send him home, I go down to the kitchen to have breakfast with Clary as usual. There sits William as pretty as you please. He grins when he sees me, in a kind of, can that be a shy way? It's out of character but so cute I can feel myself soften already. But poor Clary is pecking around as nervous as a hen in a storm. I tease her that he won't bite and he holds his hands up in surrender, yet I spot her look of, can that be loathing? I've never seen that look on her before, not even around Uncle Joe and he talks mean to her. "Just when you think you know someone," I say to both of them and laugh.

A mixing bowl slips out of Clary's hands and splinters across the floor, giving me a jolt stronger than her coffee. I grab William's hand and pull him out of the kitchen, saying that men make Clary jumpy.

"I've been thinking," William says as he sits on the living room sofa and lounges back like he lives there.

"That's a switch," I say, sitting on the edge of the sofa, a seat cushion away.

He doesn't give my retort his customary pinched lips. Instead he chuckles and shakes his head, deploring the ceiling for guidance. "Oh Lord, give me strength," he says.

I reserve another comment so that he can stay focused on what he has to say. I at least recognize a man on a mission.

He puts his arm on the back of the sofa. I notice then the cream-colored trousers, the red cashmere sweater and how it blushes his cheeks and shows off his freshly-washed blond hair. He catches my breath with his casual good looks. "I've come on too fast and too strong, when what we need first is friendship. I know I've been a total cad, but I just couldn't help myself, you're so pretty."

"Okay," I say. "I'm in agreement so far."

I see him struggling with this and I wonder why he wants to be friends with a smart-ass, when he's said more than once that he hates them.

He forces out a small chuckle and nods. "I deserve that." He meets my eyes with that puppy dog look. "I'd like for us to start over again. As friends. Just do things together. We have a lot in common, like movies and music, and I know we could have a first-rate time together, just getting to know one another." He licks and chews a bit on his bottom lip apprehensively. "And I won't even mind that you don't always agree with me." He pulls out a slip of paper from his trousers' pocket and reads, "Too much agreement kills a chat', says Eldridge Cleaver."

"I don't know," I say carefully, trying not to stare at how he made his mouth moist and kiss-ably pink. I decide to hold out for some more groveling; this is entertaining, especially coming from William Thomas Jackson the Third.

"And to prove it to you," he continues, "I've went to great lengths in order to assist you in your business of the day. I'm here at your disposal. Why, I've even gone so far as to meet with Ellen Whitman and tell her I'll chauffeur you to her as early as this morning, if you're open to it." He does his usual and raises his hands to my raised eyebrows. "I know you think I'm not listening but I remember distinctly you telling me that you are supposed to meet with her about some sort of baby clinic."

I let that one pass. I sit there silently, trying to soak this in, this everybody-seems-to-know-your-business town. He must've talked to her after I called her.

"Mrs. Whitman said herself that you could use a male escort around there. To open up this kind of clinic is risky business, now you have to know that." He says this softly, as if he wants to break it to me gently that I could be in danger and he's here to rescue.

So what – maybe I do need rescuing. At any rate I need pushing in keeping this appointment and I owe Mama some effort in research. I just don't feel inspired like she does but I can't tell her my heart's not in it – she'd never understand. I grew up on women's rights the way most babies grow up on Pablum and I'd gotten tired of the same food. Wouldn't Mama be surprised at whom her advocate is; I smile at the irony.

William slaps his knee as if silence is close enough to agreement and he jumps up, grabs my hands and pulls me to my feet. "One more thing," he says. He lifts my chin to meet such earnest eyes, more blue than green today. "I promise not to advance on you again. Not even so much as a kiss. I'll wait til you're ready, and if that's never, then we'll still have our friendship, and I'm still better off than before I met you."

I smile again, which seems to be all I need to do, and we head outside, with my only insistence in that I drive so that I can learn my way around (I also want to get my hands back on my car). "Yes, ma'am," he says as he hands me the keys, with a stronger than southern sound, more like a colored person's acquiesce.

This is my first time outside Pickerville, which according to William is the only hotspot of the south. I say to him that the real reason he doesn't go to Savannah is because of the crummy umbilical cord that attaches Pickerville to its big mama, Savannah, less than 15 miles east. This cord is a road that is a combination of gravel and dirt that hasn't sufficiently filled in the potholes. He laughs and says I'm just thinking that way to get into the mood to talk to Mrs. Whitman about having loads of babies.

That proves it; I didn't think he had been listening.

Anyway I find I need more than that to get into the mood to open a birth control clinic. I'm excited that Ellen Whitman's address is not an office but her own home in the wealthy Victorian District - until I find that many of these great homes have been deserted by the wealthy and have become boarding houses. After driving past many of the twenty-something park-like squares, splashing fountains, canopies of oak trees, statues and cast-iron railing, her whiteboard siding looks drab and some of her windows are boarded up. She has a neglected rose bush and bicycle by her door and a tricycle inside her entrance. Men in uniform are coming down the stairs and she explains that they are her boarders.

She introduces us to her eight children, reminding me of octopus arms going all which way around her, and hence I understand her personal interest in birth control. Ellen is big-boned, looks frazzled and disorganized; her place a shamble of toys, shoes and an indoors-dog of all things, and I sniff hints of urine. William and I have to move aside books and folded laundry to sit on her sofa. Mama would never allow this clutter at the Lighthouse and I immediately feel outside my comfort zone.

I suddenly wish I had asked more questions of Mama before coming here.

Ellen doesn't make me feel any better when she finally sits across from us and hardly looks our way, saying as much as she can at once, as if this is one of a million things on her mind. Her first mistake is that she assumes I know more than I do and she throws me right in the middle of her mess. "I'm glad you came. We've got problems here that are too big for me alone. I need to rent office space but I can't get funding, so you'll need to raise some. The Maternal Health League is on my back to get it going but they won't give me any money. I asked the state to sponsor it and before the war, that would've been no problem. But now churches are stepping in and saying that because of all the soldiers coming in here, venereal disease has spread, and if birth control contraception is readily available, such as condoms and jells, we're promoting loose women who are seeking sexual relations with soldiers. Police are now singing with their choir that prostitution is on the rise, and ... what else ..." She smoothes back some loose strands of diffused hair, removes a bobby pin, opens it with her teeth, and reinserts it in her loose bun. "Oh yes, and the mayor is shouting that immoral, diseased women have brought contagion to healthy soldiers and he doesn't want to lose the money that soldiers are bringing in to his town. I don't know what to do."

Neither do I. I can't even think of the right question to ask and all this sex talk is making me squirm in front of William, and just when he promises to calm down. "How do you know my mama?" is all I can think of to ask.

She answers this just as quickly as her last explanation as if this question was on her agenda too. "I was up in New York more than twenty years ago in the same march she was in and I heard her speak, but we didn't actually meet there. What a scandal she was, in shouting out that women should lose their corsets and be free! I was about the only suffragist left standing for her. Then she was down here for a short term when married to your daddy, but we didn't actually meet here. She stuck to the Pick Plantation and didn't make connections, I hear. I remember reading about them in the papers when your daddy died though. And then they said she vanished into thin air. No, I met her in Nashville Tennessee in 1920 when suffrage was won. Isn't that funny how lines cross? You start realizing after a few years that there's only a squirt gun of us activists out there. I don't know how I did it, being pregnant most of the time. I'm just like a machine – pop another one out and keep going. I met her and her handsome Indian beau at a celebration party. I heard they got hitched but I don't know if that's true. Well, no, that couldn't be true because she married Thomas Pickering, didn't she? A fine-looking fellow your daddy was, with so much going for him. Never at a halt, always travelling. You favor him, you know. I've seen his picture. Pickerville was named after your great grandfather and he also founded the Pickerville newspaper. Now I know *that* because my husband is from Pickerville and he was working at the newspaper when we met –"

"We don't have much time, Mrs. Whitman," rudely interrupts William. I want to hear more and give him a cross look. "I apologize," he says lightly, touching my arm, "but I have to get back to the printing shop soon." He turns back to Ellen. "What is it exactly that you want Katy to do? I'll help her where I can but if it's dangerous, we'll have to discuss it with her uncle. He's very protective of his kin."

"Yes, of course," she says and begins rummaging in a basket next to her chair. She moves aside knitting needles, yarn, newspaper, a rag doll, and pulls out a sheet of paper from a stack of such. "I have found one potential source of funding that you need to go talk to. It's the Eugenics Board of Georgia. They've offered to combine their method of birth control with ours and they're state-funded. It's better than nothing."

I don't want to ask, in front of William, what methods of birth control she's talking about and I plan to look up "eugenics" later. I accept the paper with the Savannah address on it and tell Ellen I'll call them soon to set up an appointment.

She nods, her small rounded eyes reminding me of her children's marbles, taking us both in for the first time. "Just be careful; we don't want anyone getting arrested. Some of this is hush-hush, don't want to upset some people, even though every woman I know is begging for such a clinic. Your mother tells me she is opening up such a place up in New York so perhaps you two could bounce ideas off each other. Of course the south has its own way of doing things and some don't take kindly to northern advice but the north does seem to pave the way, and we southerners do follow – eventually. We're to handle this delicately, like a rose."

"Right," I answer. I have a headache and can't get out of there soon enough. William has ants in his pants and seems eager to get back to his job at the printing shop.

"'Like a rose'" he mimics, as we pull Duesy away from the curb. "Did you notice that dead rosebush? No wonder she can't get a clinic started. And a birth clinic? Don't need it; she's got babies everywhere." He snorts. "My father would die if he knew I was in Savannah."

"Why is that? It looks like a beautiful old city."

"The oldest in Georgia," he nods. "But it went to hell when all the niggers moved in after the war." (I was to learn that whenever anyone in Pickerville referred to the war, they meant only the Civil War.) He continues. "It's half filled with them now and look at all the slums." We're driving past some pitiful dwellings and everything seems to be in primary shades of gray, black and brown as if frozen in old black and white snapshots.

"I've never seen so many niggers before," I say, and then feel guilty for using the "n" word like others do down here. We always described them as "colored people" up north. "Why are they all down here? It's like the Great Wall of China lines the northern border of Georgia. You don't see many in New York where I grew up. Papa had to export one up to our house, an ex-slave by the name of Lizzie who lived with them for many years." William gives me a scowl and I hastily add, "She was their maid." He responds with a satisfied smile but I only feel more guilty.

"My uncle tore down his house here," William says, "and built a brick four-story, and he charges high rents but they stay anyway. Look how lazy some of them are there; they're about as handy as a back pocket on a shirt. And fight with each other like cats and dogs. It's true what they say that Savannah has become a pretty woman with a dirty face. You won't see that happening in Pickerville, I can promise you that. Daddy nipped that rose in the bud." He snorts at himself. He also sounds like he's repeating others' words and has grown to mean it.

I'm not understanding anything since I woke up this morning. I'm relieved when I finally drop him off at his print shop at the port where hundreds of workers are building the Liberty Ships for the war effort. I learn later that that was the smartest thing I did all day.

I'm back in the warm, aromatic kitchen with Clary the next morning, loving our routine. I thought I'd hate any type of habit because of the Lighthouse's rigid schedule, but I fit back into it like a well-worn house-slipper. With just the two of us, Clary is back to her old self and she makes me my favorite of her cooking: sweet potato biscuits.

"Here's some more peckings, chile'; I don't know where you put it all. Did you find what you were looking for yesterday, Miss Katy?" she asks, setting two of these orange biscuits in front of me, the butter melting across the tops making me salivate. I'll tell her anything she wants while smelling this, and so I tell her every "hush-hush" that happened with Ellen Whitman.

"*Eugenics?*" She freezes in mid-scrubbing

I blush at her reaction like I've said a bad word. "Do you know what that is?"

"Of course I know what that is!" she says, for the first time raising her voice at me.

"Oh. Can you tell me then? I don't have a clue."

Her shoulders settle a bit and she resumes her scrubbing. I can see her from the side and she looks upset. "You've led a sheltered life, Miss Katy."

"So?" I say with a mouthful of biscuit.

"So you may have trouble believing some of the things that goes on down here."

"Does this have to do with all those scars on your arm and that badly-healed broken wrist?" I sigh. "I just don't understand why you colored people or niggers or whatever you're called, just can't get along. That's the trouble I've seen down here."

She turns and gives me a glare that glazes her eyes like chocolate pudding. She pulls the biscuits away from my reach to get my attention and puts her hands on her hips. "I've worked for white folk a long time and I sees a lot, so don't you go gettin' your righteous white back up. If you don't know of a woman in your *own* family," she says pointing at me, "that's been treated bad, then you're not hearin' close enough!"

I stand up and reach over, pulling the saucer back to my place. "Come on, Clary, tell me what eugenics means."

"That's a fancy word for a doctor to make a poor Negro woman sterile." She's still using that hateful tone but I let her.

"I'm hearing close enough now, Clary. This happened to you?"

"Yes'm, it did," she says with resolve, as if it's all settled to tell me. "When I was thirteen I'd done had a baby and then was told I was feeble-minded with low morals. A white social worker came to my mother and said if she agreed to sign the consent form, they wouldn't cut her off welfare. After she signed, they cut me where babies couldn't grow again. Then they gave away my baby so I wouldn't try to go on welfare. I got married when I was sixteen and didn't tell my husband for a long time. 'Course eventually he got suspicious and I told him the truth and he left me. I've paid my dues. I've been working here ever since."

"Holy Mother of God," I whisper. Eugenics sounds like something my great-uncle would do to his cows on his dairy farm, but to sterilize other people I can't imagine. Why does government consider this more moral than birth control? At least with contraception, women can have a choice on how many children they want. "Where's the money coming from for this, Clary? I heard today that money is the biggest problem."

"Your friend would know that best of anyone, or at least his daddy will," Clary says drying her hands, and with that she leaves me alone to the whole pan of biscuits.

Jesi's Chapter Three -- December 1963

Man, oh, man, maybe this project isn't such a bad idea. GB - I mean Grandmama Bess - looks all flustered tonight and won't meet my eyes. She must've read my papers from last night. Like Mama said, *Be careful what you ask for!* This just tickles me to death. It's always been such a trip to egg GB on, I don't know why. She looms over me with that righteous white moss of hairdo twist and gives me a hard time - maybe she's like climbing Mount Everest and I just want to brag that I conquered her. Or at least got to her and messed with her head.

So I reach for another rock hold and, with the news of the day agitating my mind, where a colored man was beaten to death in Alabama for marrying a white woman, I say to her, "GB, with all this liberal thinking you got, what's wrong with whites marrying colored? And don't give me that crap about birds of a feather flock together either. You said yourself that, 'women are people too' so don't that smooth everybody out to the same thing? Whitening their skin would just be adding cream to the coffee, baby."

She takes a long drink of her wine and I gotta give her credit for keeping her cool. She picks up her pen and starts writing on another umpteenth lined page like she's the only one with a year to write about, and then pauses. She looks over at me with the same color in her eyes as that bluejean ink scrawled all over her paper. There's not space left on there to say, 'go to hell Jesi'.

She Speaks: "Mama came up with the line 'women are people, too.' Let her explain."

What a shitty cop-out, man. GG's head has a small tremor when she's put on the spot and I feel sorry for her being on this one. She lays down her pen and relaxes her hands on the table, her crooked knotty fingers giving a brush here and there to leftover crumbs from din-din. "It's not only the birds, Jesi," she finally says. Her trembling hand flutters toward the window, her fingers making me think of branches. It's dark out there but I get her drift. "But nature itself teaches you. Like ivy and wisteria on our arbor out there, we can't be of the same vine, but we can grow in the same garden. It's the way God intended."

That's no fun.

I pick up my pen.

So here's the thing: I got to thinking: What My Mamas want from me is something to fight for. A cause seems to be important around these digs. But not the same cause, not like marching for Women's Equal cause, not quite as virgin as that. But still far-out, man. Even if it is *for* a man, if you get my drift. Doesn't matter if you don't; I'm just writing like I was told.

But first let me say: Great-Granny Ruby (aka GG), you are The Coolest! I did what you hinted to. Wow! You're right, The Wedding Night curled my hair into a bun, so I'm not the only one - I thought that *first time* thing was just me. Other surprises too, like Grandmama Bess had more than one husband and did you know, GG, that her first husband loved you more? Probably not – GB sure as hell hasn't told you, not as far as I can tell. Of course, she's The Virgin Bess, and we won't get any good stuff from her love life. But she had to do *something*; there is Mama after all. Maybe Mama was adopted. Hah-hah. And Mama is no better; she's acting all Annette Funicello with what she's written so far. So what, that this William TJ is groping her. What man doesn't grope?

I've been groped, I've been … well, before I go ruining my reputation, I'm going to excuse myself from this table like someone else I know, and write more in my private den. But I'm going to keep these next pages to myself until I read more of the others.

I'm not feeling so low-down, now that I know some secrets.

And …

The less I feel like the dumb cripple around here, the more I'll talk.

And ...

The more I take in, the more I'll give out.

It's the Way of Life, man.

So here's The Truth of Isaac: Last summer I'm sitting in Civics class. You can talk about anything in Mr. Jones' classroom. He has long shiny brown hair all the way down past his ears in this beatnik way, and he likes to have group discussions about local government, what our civic duties are, and how we should get involved. He'd almost preach this in class, but he'd do it in a slow, we've-got-all-day way and the way he'd saunter back and forth in front of the chalkboard with a bit of a hunched back, was mesmerizing to me (plus his family is rich since his grandfather owns the textile mill and don't people listen more to a rich man, thinking money buys brains?). He also had big blue eyes that showed us the red-eye when he was smoking dope. He was So Cool and I was so In Love.

He asked us one day to picture how we see ourselves in our microcosmic world. Was our world at home a democracy, where we have a vote in decisions? Or more of a monarch, where one person rules? Or could it be a theocracy, ruled by religious beliefs?

I snickered, which got his attention. "Miss Pickering?"

"Where's the Matriarch in this?" I asked. Everyone laughed because who doesn't know about the Lighthouse?

"Well, the matriarch is a *female* ruler in more of a *social* system," Mr. Jones said. "What we're talking about here is a more powerful political system, a balance of struggles on he who has the power." He walked past me where I always sat in the front row to stay closer to him, and he squeezed my shoulder.

"Then mine's a monarch with a queen," I said.

"Yeah, well that's the only way a chick will get power of this country," Tyler said, and Florence, his steady, giggled. She and her striped shirtdress and matching head kerchief and long straight legs. I hear they do IT in the park. Who cares what they think?

"Let the Mob rule," Bobby said. He's one of The Hoods, always looking for a fight.

"That's ochlocracy," Mr. Jones said.

"Another name is mobocracy. But if the mob rules, it's worse than anarchy because you still have rules, but the rules change based on the mood of the leader, and what if he's in a bad mood?"

"Then we cream 'em," said Bobby. We all laughed.

"Or you lynch them," said a voice from the desk directly behind me. The room got quiet.

I turned to see all eyes on Isaac Cosman. He stared back at me.

I'd never seen a colored person up close before and I'd never heard this one speak before; he's new to summer school and I'm making up a class I flunked when in the hospital last year. He looked older than I thought they should look for a student but what did I know? Only what I'd seen on television, with cameras more and more on Negroes-in-the-South getting water-sprayed in the streets, drinking from fountains labeled "Colored", entering doors that said "Colored Only" and I thought the "Colored" signs were all messed up because everyone looked black and white on television.

"Go on," I whispered.

"We're supposed to be a democracy, but we can't be at home, because we're angry and poor and take it out on each other. We can't be in our country, because we take away the rights of an entire race. Which is why we're angry and poor, and it goes in a circle you see. We're angry at home because my father was lynched in Georgia when I was a little boy and my mother raised five children by herself. 'Jesus was lynched,' she said. 'He too, hung from a tree, so your dad is in good company up in heaven.' We moved to New York to get away from having to drink from a separate water fountain. It's not that I minded being separate, but I did mind that my water fountain was dirtier and didn't work half the time. I don't mind being separate; I mind being less. But to run away does no good. My mother is still a washerwoman for the white people. Like Martin Luther King said, 'we take necessities from the masses to give luxuries to the classes'. We can't seem to live up to democracy. But do we fight? King says no. He says force begets force. So no mobocracy, no monarchy. No race or sex should rule the rest."

He said all that to me, our eyes never wavering from each other. You could've heard a tear drop in the room, it was so quiet. His voice, man, his voice … there was a sweet tender melody in there, slow and distinct. I'm hooked and would've slow-danced with him right there.

I turned back around to see what Mr. Jones thought about this. He had meandered back up front. He was nodding, nodding, kind of staring at Isaac but not really looking, and then he tucked his hair behind his ear and resumed his teaching as if Isaac hadn't said a word. It was the first time I was sorry I'd lost my virginity to that man.

This was the last day of school and I didn't play kiss-up after class and hover around Mr. Jones, hoping for some attention, a promise, a hurried rendezvous. Instead I walked out with a group so he couldn't discreetly wave me over, but I felt his eyes burn my ass.

I was bent over at my locker, cursing my new leg brace and the blister it had rubbed onto my leg when patched jeans came into view … a sweatshirt that read NAACP … Isaac's face. I straightened up but with my short height – I don't reach five feet – he still looked like the Jolly Green Giant. My height is where I related to his "I mind being less".

"Ho, ho, ho," I said, deep down like the Jolly Green commercial.

Something about his round brown eyes locked me in, deep, searching, as if trying to see what color my soul was. "Come with me to the March on Washington," he said. "For jobs and freedom. A group of us are taking a chartered bus down. We'll hear Martin Luther King, John Lewis, Joan Baez, Bob Dylan."

My head was full by the time we arrived in D.C. and began the long walk toward the Washington Monument and on to the Lincoln Memorial. Six of Isaac's school cronies, two of us white – and hey, I admit that I was relieved to see another white – sat in the back of the bus with the other colored folk. I trusted Isaac for some unknown reason and thankfully he sat next to me, but I hadn't thought this out further than a school field trip and Dylan being there at the end. Economic slavery, racial segregation, discrimination, police brutality, they talked about it all, while I secretly worried about the lie I told Mama about spending the day and overnight with a girlfriend. (My Mamas think that I can't do anything for myself, even refusing to let me work outside the Lighthouse. What else could I do, man, except steal money from your purses for the trip?)

It really wasn't a march as I'd feared would be like My Mamas had marched in, but a far-out flow among the masses of what seemed to be everyone in the U.S. – I couldn't have turned around to go back if I wanted to. Halfway along the concrete pond between the monument and memorial, I had to take a break. I stepped out and reached for a tree as if reaching for the shore. I motioned for the rest of them to go on, each holding signs demanding integrated schools and decent housing (they didn't give me a sign, and for once I was glad to be treated differently). Isaac lingered but I pushed him back out into the swarm. I don't cry in front of anyone. This trip was the first thing I'd done on my own but this was like jumping into the middle of a massive river and suddenly realizing I need to learn how to swim.

I leaned against the tree, hiked up my long skirt, and took off my leg brace and its connecting shoe. Its sole is five inches higher than my other shoe to make my left leg the same length as my right and under this August sun, it weighed a freaking thousand pounds of humid heat. I massaged around the blister that just wasn't healing and that I just wasn't going to tell Mama about. I hate that worried look in one eye, and that here-you-go-again look in her other eye. She doesn't mean to, and no one knows that better than me, but it's like, I don't know, man, like she sees a demon in me.

Without the peoples' squeeze, I could breathe again. I could mellow out while they sang *"We shall overcome ... We shall all be free ... We shall live in peace ... "* and I knew what they were singing about, this sense of being unburdened. I held my leg brace and believed if I dropped it, my body would become weightless and I'd float above this tree and see it all. I imagined I hovered above Bob Dylan and then I wished I was chained to the ground with Isaac as Dylan sang, *And he's taught how to walk in a pack/Shoot in the back/With his fist in a clinch/To hang and to lynch/To hide 'neath the hood/To kill with no pain/Like a dog on a chain/He ain't got no name/But it ain't him to blame/He's only a pawn in their game.* I sat on the ground rocking, singing, hearing voices and music, near and distantly amplified, watching with my mind's eye, until darkness and Isaac came.

Back at the ranch, my Mamas are acting more queer. They're dragging me into heated discussions over their TV show, *Wagon Train.* After years, the show has moved from Wednesday night to Monday, and on a different station, and they're bummed out. You'd think their husbands had left them. They're crowded into the TV room that used to be the 'back parlor', la-de-da. They're dividing the movie star hunks between them: GG gets Bill Hawks because she likes his Indian name and she always, always makes a big deal about rooting for the Indians; GB goes for the dashing scouts, Flint and Coop, claiming they're the cowboy version of a reporter; and the blond dollbaby Scott Miller is supposed to be Mama's but she complains that he says too little and shoots off his gun too much, and besides she doesn't like blonds anymore (whatever "anymore" means). GB says, "Take Charlie, the cook, then. You both make bad coffee." They want me to take Barnaby but *he's just a kid, GB,* I argue, heavy on the *"GB"* part, because, like GB, Mama hates, *hates* me using initials for names.

Out of boredom, I rile them up by saying, *why not the Bonanza boys? The Cartwrights are fine-as-wine for us four of a kind.* GG could have the papa, Ben. I'd give the eldest son, Adam, to GB, and – "Oh no you don't!" Mama cuts in loudly, lighting a cigarette and throwing her arms around like someone gave her a bum deal, saying she's not taking no Fat Cat like Hoss, what am I, *crazy?*

"It's just like you to want that hotheaded Little Joe," she said, pointing her two fingers at me, the cigarette in-between scattering ashes. "Besides, these guys are dangerous for women. Every woman they've loved has been either murdered or died of disease."

Maybe now you can see what a drag it is and why it's so cool that Isaac telephones me just then. Mama hands me the phone with one eyebrow up. "Don't talk long; you need to go to bed. *The Feminine Mystique* is on your nightstand." Of course I say nothing and turn my back to her to *kiss my ass.*

Isaac says he thinks he's found something I can do that won't require marching. Right now I'd agree to march to Vietnam. But then I remember the Washington D.C. march. I stammer into the mouth piece in memory of how I'd leaned heavily on him to get back to the buses lined along the streets, inching along, dragging the walk out. Coupled with that the two-hour search for me in the dusk, when Isaac couldn't quite remember where I'd dropped off. The day ended in us missing the bus and sleeping on park benches because motels were full and *hey, let's be honest*, Isaac said, *what motel is going to let colored people stay where white people are?* It's a bad cold from then on that I'm still having trouble shaking.

Anyway, I want to make it up to him: "Sign me up," I say. He says, "OK" and pretends to hang up. "No, no!" I yelp, laughing, coughing. "Hey, man, you can't do this to me. What did I just sign up for?"

"A sit-in," he says. He explains that he's become a member of CORE, the Congress of Racial Equality. They're arranging a sit-in at the local Woolworths to protest lunch counter segregation in southern Woolworths and other stores. All I have to do is "sit-in" at the lunch counter with a small sign while others picket outside.

My sign reads, "Uphold democracy! Stay out of segregated stores!" Easy-peasy. Isaac and I sit there for four hours with no trouble, getting all the free cokes we can drink, waitresses behind the counter giving me quick, nervous smiles.

"Rehearsal for the Big Sit-In," Isaac informs me as we sip through straws with downcast eyes. He looks so distinguished; all the colored boys who came to protest do, in their white shirts and ties. He reads Yeats poetry to me, *Accursed who brings to light of day the writings I have cast away* (I made him repeat that one over and over, since I'm hiding these pages I'm writing in my bedroom for awhile). The Annan Newspaper takes pictures and that's how My Mamas find out. It's like no other family member had ever been in the paper before. Yeah, right. They give me more hassle than anyone could at Woolworths. Except: As I limped stiffly away from counter, I cringe; not for the bad sore on my leg but because of the whispered *Nigger lover* from a booth.

Ruby's Chapter Four -- 1910

I climbed down from the wagon bench with Jesse's last words ring-ing in my ears. *I won't stand for you being treated badly. If I see you sleeping outside again, I'll do more than give ol' Robert a punch. Let this be a warning!* He handed me my basket from the wagon, tipped his hat to me and rode off, without once glancing at the house.

The door opened then, cries of "Mama, Mama!" came tumbling out with the children.

I ran to meet them halfway, my arms open wide. "My babies!" I cried. I had never spent the night away from them before and after two long days they looked older already. They came headlong into me, forcing me to lose my balance and fall onto the grass. We shouted, laughed and tickled each other.

"Children," Robert called from the verandah. "Would you and your mother stop making such a public display?"

I had made a muddle of my welcome already, and hadn't yet even spoken to him.

I stood up quickly, brushing my skirt off. With twelve-year old Victor and eight-year old Jonathan in hand, and Bess and Pearl tow-ing behind, I walked up the verandah steps to the door where Robert remained standing. I felt happy to see him and a warm hug would've been nice ... but his eyes ... how could I get them from the color of mud back to chocolate drops again?

He and the children obviously needed cleaning; that would be the first thing.

"Robert?" My voice sounded soft and tentative, pleading.

He stepped aside to let me in. The parlor was cluttered with newspapers and dishes. To my left I spotted dirty dishes on the dining room table.

I reached down to Bess and felt her forehead for fever. Cool as a cucumber. "Bess, how are you feeling?"

"Better now, Mama. Last night I wasn't feeling well at all and I asked Papa to get you home to look after me. You would know what to do." She looked up with eyes that longed for affection.

Pearl clung to my skirt, as did the boys. I stooped down and hugged all four again. I looked up at Robert, knowing he saw in my eyes the same longing I saw in the eyes of Bess. He watched us closely, yet staying a distance apart. He cleared his throat and finally looked away, hands in his pockets.

I straightened up and timidly approached him, my ducklings walking in step behind me. I tiptoed and gave him a lingering kiss on the cheek. I noticed the slight bruise on his jaw. Jesse would be pleased with himself.

"And how are you feeling, Robert?"

"Very well, thank you," he answered, nodding. He wouldn't meet my eyes at such a close range. He cleared his throat again. "I'm going to the shop now. Someone had to stay home with the children since you, er ... well, at any rate, I'll be home at suppertime." He looked down at the children, blinking a few times. "Perhaps with something fresh from the bakery for dessert."

Amid the claps and cheers from the children, I sent a warm smile up to him. He was being extravagant! Bess wasn't ill. Bess knew it. Robert knew it. They all wanted me home and they were each showing it in their own way. Tonight I would prepare the best supper ever, starting with the chicken from the farm. Make it festive. And top it off with a shop-baked dessert! Extravagant indeed!

Robert returned my smile and I felt warmed inside-out. He announced we would all go on a picnic the next Sunday afternoon after church, where the boys might fish. The girls clapped their hands and the boys drummed the table with "hurrahs!" Eating out of doors and dealing with tangled hooks and repeated worm baiting with active boys were not activities Robert would relish, and I recognized his valiant effort.

Fishing reminded Victor of a joke. "Hey Papa, how do you communicate with a fish?" He paused for affect and sucked in his cheeks, moving his puckered lips up and down. Jonathan shouted, "You drop him a line!", his dimple deepening with his grin. Victor shoved him for stealing his line but Robert actually laughed out loud and patted his sons' heads affectionately.

He reached over to his hat on the hook in the entranceway where we all remained standing, eager for more. He placed the hat slowly onto his head and paused at the doorway as if remembering something. "Oh, by the way, Preacher Paul is coming over tonight."

"Preacher Paul?" This was completely out of the norm. He hadn't been here since Jonathan was born, his attendance requested by my mother-in-law for prayer, in fear I would die during the long labor.

"And things must be tidy, of course, for such a visitor. I would very much appreciate a clean white shirt to change into before then. And the children ... " he waved this away as if he couldn't be bothered anymore.

"Robert, why— "

"It's good to have you home," he said to the doorframe and he quickly opened and closed the door behind him.

Those words were the boost I needed. I began cleaning. I took all the rugs outside to beat and rub with salt to clean. Once the rugs were out, I scrubbed the wooden floors to rid them of that constant coal dust. Then the laundry – I needed Bess to help; this took all the strength we could muster to agitate the round disc of a wooden dolly stick within the copper pot, built in brick over a coal fire. It took both of us again to feed the laundry through the wringer while the other turned the crank. The dolly stick and wringer were again required for the rinsing, and the attached wringer came unbolted ... again. Then tomorrow I would tend the garden, bring in the cucumbers to begin the twelve-day process to pickle and gather flower spikes from lavender plants and spread on newspaper to dry overnight. And of course the laundry brings about more ironing. And I needed time to bake bread, but that would have to be late at night because the heat of the stove was too great to bear during the summer days. Unfortunately the house hadn't been built with a summer kitchen. Maybe someday. What day was it anyway, because I needed to get back on schedule or –

"Yoo-hoo, Ruby!"

I jumped at the adult female voice and turned around from the clothesline to see Aimee standing at the fence.

"Don't forget our meeting tomorrow. I'm hosting because Eunice had to cancel. She's too embarrassed about the scandal."

I continued to unhook clothespins from sheets, my heart in my throat.

"You know! The scandal about her husband and his mistress, the same woman who'd had an affair with a newspaper reporter? Do you think Cady's husband, Thomas, might know about this?" Aimee sounded light-hearted, as if she had not a care in the world, but I refused to get caught up in it.

I had made a decision during that day's cleaning frenzy. I became determined to work harder at ensuring my family's happiness. To seek my own was selfish. I simply would not attend any more meetings; I would silently withdraw from the Ladies Legion. Its sacrifice was too high, my hopes too high-in-the-sky, only to fall back down to reality and its ensuing battle, with Robert …my mother…my sister. Best to live in this gray cocoon. Its familiar casing could be comforting at times, this I knew.

But I would have to lie. I hated having to do that, especially to one I had once hoped to be my friend. Well, I had made up my mind and it had to be done. I shook my head at Aimee as I remained clinging to my clothesline.

"No, that would be impossible," I answered, as firmly as I could muster. My mind went blank.

"Why?" I hated hearing the cheeriness leave her voice.

Why indeed? I reached for another sheet and folded it, trying to think. "Because my husband...because I...well, *we* do not approve, that's why!"

I was saved by the rain. One drop hit my nose, and I quickly wiped it on the sheet in my arms.

"Really, Aimee, I must go in before these are wet yet again. I really do hate to repeat my work; there's enough to do without duplication!" I forced a laugh. The most artificial laugh I'd ever heard.

I rushed to my back door, ignoring Aimee's call to please wait a moment, to please talk. I stopped when safely inside.

The tears came quickly and dripped unnoticed onto my fresh dry sheets.

"Well! Sister Ruby! Shall we have prayer first?" Preacher Paul said, hiking his rain-damp trousers at his knees and sitting down in Robert's chair in the parlor.

Robert seemed at a loss as to where else to sit, that chair being his only resting place. I picked up my Bible waiting for me in my rocking chair and sat there. Robert finally sat stiffly on the settee.

Whatever else this visit might bring, I decided it would be well worth the rest off my feet. Robert expected the house and children to be washed clean of their sins before Preacher Paul's arrival. Finally, to sit! Not even supper allowed more than a five-minute rest, for as the meal began, so did a rainstorm, and I was back out at the clothesline while the others finished their meal. I ate while walking between kitchen and dining room, clearing up the dishes. Preacher came soon after.

The rain was pouring by now. The children, previously told they must play outside, were now sent to their rooms. Why they couldn't remain here after their preliminary how-do-you-dos, was beyond me. Robert found their giggling chatter a nuisance during adult conversation and were promptly sent upstairs.

Oh well, they might be better off, I thought, keeping my eyes respectfully closed during Preacher Paul's prayer. The Preacher was a sincere man, but he talked loudly and long, as he was doing now, as if his congregation sat in the wings of the room.

"And dear Heavenly Father," Preacher continued, "I come to you today, asking that you give me your Holy Word. Righteous words, Lord, to say to our dear Sister Ruby. Dear Lord, guide me to show Sister Ruby the error of her ways, so that she may be a light to others, so that she may bring love to her family. Dear Lord, help me in delivering the message that a woman's obedience is a virtue and one required by law, by God's law. Dear God, show Sister Ruby that as Christ *is* head of the church, so *is* man the head of woman. I ask this in the name of the Father, the Son and the Holy Ghost. Amen and amen."

My chair became uncomfortable now, for it was the judgment seat. Error of my ways, indeed!

I blinked back tears and eyed them both and waited and rocked, my hands docile, folded in my lap on top of my Bible. If I spoke, I would surely cry, and I would not give them the pleasure of pointing to my emotional womanly ways as another error. Preacher leaned over in his chair, arms on his legs, his small Bible in both hands, looking at its worn black cover as if waiting for words to appear. Robert would not meet my eyes, but folded his arms and looked away, pretending a keen interest in the framed needlepoint on the wall over my head that read, 'Learn to do Good'. Another of my mother-in-law's legacies.

In a slow purposeful motion, Preacher put on his spectacles and opened his Bible to a page marked by a red ribbon. His head rose from his reading, his watery, tired eyes beseeching mine. To me, he often looked as if he had just finished crying or was getting ready to.

"I wish to take you to Titus, Chapter Two." He moved his thick finger down the page line by line until he found his place. "Now let's read verses three, four, and five. 'The aged women likewise, that they be in behavior as becometh holiness, not false accusers, not given to much wine, teachers of good things. That they may teach the young women to be sober, to love their husbands, to love their children. To be discreet, chaste, keepers at home, good, *obedient.*" Here he raised his finger to emphasize, "to their own *husbands,* that the word of God be not blasphemed."

What was he insinuating? "I understand I'm being chastised here, but for what reason may I ask?"

Preacher took off his spectacles and rubbed one eye. He sighed the sigh of a burdened man with a heavy load. Accounting for souls could not be easy.

"Sister Ruby, let me be frank with you. Ever since July fourth I have been praying for you. You have been on my heart and I believe that is God's way of telling me, 'Preacher, show her how she's been led astray.' Why, I was shocked and deeply wounded to see one of my own Christian soldiers, one of my own souls, marching with she-devils! Yes, Ruby, she-devils, marching against God and God's word. Onward Christian soldier, not with the cross of Jesus, but with a banner of bad tidings. My poor wife was crying and praying for you, too. I tried to block it from my memory, saying, no it can't be so, not our little Ruby, who has been going to church, faithful and true, since she was a baby. But then God said, 'Wake up, Preacher!' and He showed me your picture on the front page of the newspaper. Sister Ruby was marching, as part of a God-forsaken women's march. These women dressed in black skirts, are no more than black widow spiders, going against God, the church, venom to poison their own homes and families. Somehow you got tangled up in their web, Sister Ruby."

I stared at my hands in my lap, feeling a blush rise up my neck against my will.

"Word came to me from a God-fearing sister of our church that these spiders are not finished with you. That you'll be part of a convention this summer with a group calling themselves ..." He read from his black book, "...Ladies Legion."

I sucked in my breath, and then prayed that Robert hadn't noticed my reaction. I glanced sideways at him, the scowl between his eyes deepening as he watched the preacher intently. Opal – did she tattletale?

"These *ladies*" he emphasized, "want to *vote*, and to own *property*. And why, I ask, unless they want to be a *man*. Imagine the deserted firesides, neglected children, and forlorn and hungry husbands. Frayed clothing and loose buttons. The babies crying while your wife and the mother of your children is sallying forth to do her duty at the polls. I don't wish to go into politics here, but what if I stood here on God's Holy Ground and said to my brethren to be pure, and to the maidens of the church to be brave? Nature itself teaches you that I would have it in reverse."

Preacher Paul shook his head in disbelief. "Let me just read you what the 13th century Christian theologian, Thomas Aquinas, said: 'Woman was created to be man's helpmeet, but her unique role is in conception … since for other purposes men would be better assisted by other men'."

He paused and sighed loudly and I hoped his sermon was over. He'd preached this warning from the pulpit. *Whether you have sheep, cattle, horses, wives, children, they must have a master and the master must rule and protect!*

"But as the Lord forgives us of our sins, He teaches us to forgive others. I forgive you, Sister Ruby. I am not here to condemn you. Why, on the contrary, I am here to set you free! I prayed to God to forgive you as soon as I saw it, and I walked over to your husband's shop as soon as I could."

"Why not come directly to me, Preacher? As you said, I have been attending your church since I was a baby."

"It is my obligation to know first, if you had your husband's permission in doing such a vulgar public performance. He assured me he had forbidden you to meet with these ladies at all. He was as shocked as I was! Why, Sister Ruby, you outright disobeyed your husband! Now I'm here to tell you as your shepherd, you cannot attend this convention or have anything more to do with these she-devils, do you understand? Don't disobey your pastor, too. You could burn in hell for this!"

Disobey. He kept saying that word last Sunday. I pulled out my notes tucked in between pages of my Bible, notes I had taken from his sermon on Man's Dominion. I had written down what he'd preached: *Every living creature has a role in descending order. Here on this top step is our Almighty God. Next step down is man, next step down is woman, next step down is children, on the next step are animals, then fish, then crawling creatures. To step outside what we are designed to do under God's rule, is to disobey God. Men, you are to obey God; wives you are to obey your husbands; children, you are to obey your parents. Our domain is our household!*

Reading this reminded me of our last Legion discussion.

"To obey my husband would mean my husband is my master?" I asked.

Preacher nodded happily. "Yes, he is the master of his household. I see you *were* paying attention in church," He sounded relieved that he had gotten through to me.

"Then I am his slave," I stated matter-of-factly. "And of course it wasn't long ago that we fought a very bloody Civil War over that very thing. Do you know what Abraham Lincoln said on the subject? Let me find that quote for you."

"Well, now, Sister Ruby, there is no need—"

My legion friends had given me more fodder: I returned from the secretariat while reading aloud from a newspaper clipping, one of several I had saved on the assassinated president and had discussed at our 'tea'. Lizzie was so excited during our discussion, in remembering her sense of freedom as a child when the Civil War ended.

"Mr. Lincoln is quoted as saying: 'As I would not be a slave, so I would not be a master. This expresses my idea of democracy.'" I stopped in front of Preacher Paul and looked at his bent head, his thin threads of gray hair, his pink scalp. "Surely, you believe in democracy?" I asked. Yes, I challenged a Man of God, but I found strength in Mr. Lincoln's words.

He continued looking down at his Bible, his finger still on the Word. "Yes, of course, democracy is a rule of government, for all *men* that are created equal. But God's Word presides over government,

Sister Ruby." His tone was of one talking down to a child and losing his patience.

But I had another quote: "Mr. Lincoln also said: 'Those who deny freedom for others deserve it not for themselves.' How far must obedience go before we are denied our freedom?"

Speaking these words of freedom somehow gave me courage and from deep within I felt a release of my own words, a power. Preacher opened his mouth to speak, but I forged ahead, sitting back down on the edge of my rocker, my elbows on my legs, leaning forward in earnest. My corset pinched my side, sitting like this, but I paid little mind to it - or to Robert and his pinched lips.

"These women you saw me marching with are all good Christian women. But their freedom has been denied. Take Aimee, my next door neighbor, for instance. Her husband, in the name of obedience, beats her. Would you beat your wife into submission? Of course not. But what about the men who do? Must she obey a drunken husband? What if, in his drunken stupor, he told her to rob a bank? Must she obey, and thus break a government law, because God's presiding law said she must obey her husband first? You read here in Titus ... let's see ... here it is ... that women should be 'teachers of good things'. Well, women are not permitted the schooling they need. How can they teach the good things to others, if they themselves are not permitted to learn? How can an aged woman teach young women, when they are forbidden by their husbands to leave their own homes, forbidden to talk to strangers or even their own neighbors? How can I teach my children of life's lessons and struggles, when I myself am not allowed to experience it beyond these walls?"

I clutched my hands together as if in prayer and gave both gentlemen my pleading eyes. "Please forgive me, but I see 'obey' as another word for control or slavery. I see the democratic law not protecting women. And I see husbands not protecting their women." My thoughts were tumbling over one another in an effort to get out and be heard.

"And what else does God's law say? Why do you only read to me what women are supposed to do? Look here! It also prescribes what men are supposed to do. Let us read on here in Titus. 'That the aged men be sober, grave, temperate, sound in faith, in charity, in patience ... young men likewise exhort to be sober minded. In all things shewing thyself a pattern of good works; in doctrine shewing uncorruptness, gravity, sincerity.' And does the Bible not also say, in Genesis I believe, for the man to cleave unto his wife? To love her as Christ loves the church? Well, I say that if man *obeyed* the command- ments and did all these things, then women would be happy to *obey* the man. Because to obey a sober, patient, loving man would not require obedience at all, but many returns of love and honor. She would stand beside him happily and willingly, both man and woman teaching the young good things!"

I was out of breath with these last words, my face feeling hot from my audacity. I swallowed hard, my mouth dry. In the pursu- ing silence, my courage slipped away from me as if caught naked and they'd discovered me. "May I offer you something to drink, Preacher?"

Preacher Paul seemed to be at a loss. He shook his head. His cheeks had become a rash of red. His finger had not moved from his open Bible. His eyes darted over to Robert and then back to me.

Clearing his throat, he returned to the verses. "Well, now, Sister Ruby, you may be right in some things you are saying there, but not being a minister of God, you have misquoted. You see," he shifted in his chair and began tapping on the page of his Bible as if he were trying to keep the words down, "the verses you are reading are com- mandments for the pastoral work of a true minister. If you studied your Bible more, you would know this chapter does not apply to all men." He said this last sentence sounding rather relieved at finding a rebuttal.

I hated his condescending tone. I looked down at my own verses and nodded as if I suddenly understood. "Oh, yes, of course, I see... then that means that the quote about women being teachers of good things, only applies to women ministers?" I put my hand to my mouth as if struck by a revelation. "Oh my! Does that mean that women can preach? For truly, what is the difference between teaching and preaching? And does this mean, then, that only women ministers must obey their husbands?"

Does he think I am stupid and cannot read?

Preacher sat up straight, shaking his head emphatically. His eyes were dry now, heated in anger. "God did not call women to preach!" He shook his finger at me. "Jesus chose only men as his twelve disciples!"

My eyes went wide in surprise. "Surely you are not saying that this chapter only applies to all women, and not all men?"

Preacher looked truly confused, and helplessly directed his glares to Robert.

Robert uncrossed his legs and then crossed them the other way. He looked reluctant to take charge. He cleared his throat. "Ruby, are you questioning a Man of God?"

I drew in a deep breath and let it out slowly. Sitting back in my rocking chair, I attempted to settle, rocking to soothe. I was both amazed and a bit disconcerted at being so outspoken. Where did all that come from?

Well, I started this petition and I will surely have to finish it.

"I do not mean to be disrespectful," I said to Robert. "I am only asking that Preacher Paul, as the true minister I know him to be," and I read again, "to be 'sober, grave, temperate, sound in faith, in charity, in patience' when preaching to me. Preacher, please, in charity, listen to me. I have done nothing wrong! You see me marching for women's rights and neither one of you have asked me why. Without a fair trial, I am judged and on my way to fire and brimstone. And for what? For speaking out for downtrodden women! I *can* speak my own mind, which surprises me as much as it may dismay you."

I stopped rocking and gazed at Robert. He was certainly on his best behavior in front of the Man of God. His hypocrisy made me so angry. "And Robert, while I have the courage to be so outspoken, I don't remember you cleaving unto your wife as she slept on the front verandah."

I stood and extended my hand to Preacher Paul. "Forgive me but I must tend to my children."

Preacher half-stood, nodded his head, and sat back down. He ignored my hand, trembling as it was. He looked dazed and a little upset.

I placed my hand over my heart, feeling the need to make peace, even feeling a little sorry for the two of them. "Thank you for giving me the opportunity to speak my mind. As a Christian woman in a democratic society, I should be able to speak it. Good night, gentlemen."

I walked up the stairs feeling like I understood Lizzie's use of the word 'liberated' for the first time.

I found Bess sitting on the top step, chin propped in her hand, evidently eavesdropping.

"Your mama actually spoke her mind!" I whispered to Bess with a hug.

Bess returned the hug and smiled. "That's good, Mama," she whispered back. We walked hand-in-hand to Bess's bedroom.

Bess sat on her bed and looked up at me. "Mama, why does Aimee's husband beat her? What does women's rights mean? Could we talk about that sometime?"

That's when I saw her immense capacity, her ability to understand.

I smoothed the hair around her face. "There is more to talk about some day. I have so much to tell you. Perhaps some day soon."

I kissed my eldest daughter good night and walked to my room a lighter woman. I wanted to run across the yard and tell Aimee about tonight. And then I remembered I'd cut off all ties to my legion of friends.

The bedroom door slammed hard. I jolted from the washstand, my camisole clutched in front of my breasts and turned toward the door. Robert approached me in three long strides and grabbed my shoulders.

"How dare you be so rude to a guest in our home! I am ashamed of you!" He slapped my face hard with his open hand. "Is it not enough you flaunt yourself in public parades, carrying my name? Now you must do so in my home and shame me?" He shook hard enough that I dropped my camisole. I began to cry.

"Not so high and mighty now, are you?" He pushed me back and I fell halfway onto the bed. I crossed my arms across my exposed breasts, afraid to rise.

He placed his hands on his hips and looked down at my vulnerable state with some degree of satisfaction. "Preacher's last words, before he left were, 'You better get control of your wife, Brother Robert, better bridle her and break her in or she'll just buck again and run off." He pulled his suspenders off his shoulders and unzipped his pants. They fell to the floor and he fell on top of me.

He pinned my shoulder down with one hand as his other hand jerked at my pantalets. Somewhere in my mind I knew they were tearing, but the sound was muffled by my sobs. Foolishly I struggled, until I gasped for air as he pressed down on me harder. He whispered names in my ear, names I blocked out, could not comprehend. He grabbed the back of my hair and held on tightly as if holding onto the mane of a galloping horse, and I felt my braided updo, along with my body, unravel across the quilt. I could no longer sob, no longer breathe, everything melted in my mind, until, finally, he pulled away from me.

He stood and kicked his pants away from his feet, unbuttoned his shirt and threw this onto the floor. He did not look at me but shook his head as if in disbelief. "You are not the woman I married. I don't know you anymore." His voice now weak, shaky, his anger now spent.

I gathered enough air into my lungs to move again, to crawl up to the head of the bed, to puff my pillow, to feel its soft substance. I felt deflated as if his weight had pressed me paper-thin, my only substance being his fluid he'd released inside me. I hugged my arms in my fetal position and faced the window.

"And the man I married is only a dream," I murmured.

In the early morning, I awoke with his words still there, as if written on the window I faced. By the window's light, I wrote in my diary:

"You are not the woman I married." Had I changed? At what point did I become a woman in the first place? When did my smile turn upside down, as if the weight of the world bore down on these muscles?

Was it my wedding night? Did the loss of virginity's blood take with it the naive girl and her dreams of sweet romance (ah, he kissed her lightly, ever so lightly – directly on the lips! – gazing into her eyes as if she was too good to be true!)

No, my naiveté did not suddenly harden on my wedding night. I vividly remember the heated flush, when my mother-in-law returned home the next day from a night at her sister's. How terribly awkward and apologetic I was, as if the residue of my lost blood was visible on my face. That his mother was secretly shaming me for it. And a week later, facing my family. That somehow they were looking at me differently, a knowing smile twitching at the corners of their mouths. How I had trouble, like a naughty girl, looking them all in the eye for months!

Did motherhood, then, bring me into womanhood? Was it my unspoken pregnancy and its public proof of what Robert and I were doing in the privacy of our bed? Why keep it so private, I remembered wondering. What difference did it make if the outcome was protruding obscenely from your belly, as an invisible banner that read, 'Vulgar acts performed here!'

No, I had not changed then, because as the doctor lay my newborn baby in my arms, my first thoughts were the same as when I held my first porcelain-faced baby doll to my six-year old breast: 'Mine, my own'. Its painted cheeks were etched in my memory as clearly as my breathing babies' warm cheeks were. I felt no different, only that this was the next natural step.

Was it gradual then, this becoming a woman? Was it the days, the weeks, the months, the years, that added bits and pieces of womanhood, like the birds add to their nests, one twig at a time, until one day you realize, as you fly toward home with yet one more twig - can't stop, must keep going! - you realize the round nest is there, intact, precariously clinging to its tenuous branch, for better or worse, in windstorms, and in sunshine. The nest is holding four babies, their faces turned up to you expectantly, dependent on you for food and protection. You must keep holding on. Is that what womanhood is all about? Just keep holding on, going on, take your duties one twig at a time, don't look beyond the task at hand. For if you saw the end of the day, and that this day and its efforts only brought night ... and your husband ... in the privacy of your bed ... more pregnancies to labor, more children to feed. An endless cycle. Why ... why would it be worth it all?

Afraid to make noise and disturb the sleeping beast I heard snoring behind me, I had held my bladder but could do so no longer. I slipped off the bed and tiptoed behind the screen to the chamber pot. Sitting down fully on the thin cold rim, I sat practically as naked as my plucked chicken from yesterday. I winced at my soreness and bruises. Merciful Lord, there was my robe hanging over the screen. I was never so happy to see any object. I put the robe on quickly before someone could stop me, could hold me tight as he'd done most of the night ... and during the night, in the blackness, again, more demands ... *spread, on your knees, touch ...* another stranger, and me with no gown, feeling strange and detached like a mishandled rag doll. I hugged my sleeved elbows in the robe's generous protection.

As usual, I would not wash and change until Robert had finished washing, had eaten his breakfast and left for the shop. Accordingly I tiptoed lightly to the door to prepare the morning meal. I could hear the boys' footsteps above us.

"Ruby."

My hand froze on the doorknob. I pressed my forehead to the door. Please dear Lord, he is not going to make me—

"Yes, Robert?"

"About last night," Robert began, and then cleared his morning throat, "I have gotten past my anger and am thinking about some of the things you said to Preacher Paul. You made some good points. I watched in disbelief as someone else spoke passionately through my passive wife."

I turned slowly around in surprise, to see him addressing the ceiling, his hands linked at his bare chest.

"I was disjointed," he said softly, as if pondering it all. "Somehow unassociated with the only woman I've ever known, in the only home I've ever known. Odd. Very odd. Where did these ideas come from?

Ah yes, the parade of women! Well, I must put that all behind us now. You did go a bit over the edge though, when you directed your disfavor of wrongful doings toward Preacher, then toward I, but … well … in all fairness … I reacted inappropriately."

He was apologizing! My spirits lifted in spite of myself.

"Robert, could we talk sometime about – all that?"

The window light had not yet reached his side of the bed and he lay in a long shadow. He stretched and yawned. "I think I've heard all there is to say, haven't I? There is more?"

"Much more." My hopes moved up one more step.

He breathed in deeply and let his air out slowly. "Perhaps some day soon." The same answer I'd given Bess. *Man's dominion, steps of descending order …*

Robert sat up and ran his fingers through his hair. "Please heat some water for my bath. I wish to bathe before breakfast." The sheet slipped away as he moved his bare legs over the side of the bed and I exited hastily.

The kitchen was too warm for summer as usual, the stove still heated from the night before, bubbles popping through the lid of the kettle of simmering chicken bones broth. I opened the window and shoveled red-spotted gray ash from the stove's belly into my ash bucket, fed it more wood pieces, and then added coal to feed its never-ending hunger. I pumped water into the kettle and placed this on the stove. I walked out to the small scullery between the kitchen and backdoor and pulled out the large round gray bathing tub I stored beside the bricked and copper laundry tub. I sighed, hearing the grit of coal dust move across the floor under its heavy weight. I wondered once again if my mother-in-law and Robert had decided the right thing in installing the sink pump in the larger kitchen. This scullery was once used as a back kitchen for washing dishes, and a sink pump would have been handy to wash both dishes and laundry. I started a fire in the grate under the laundry tub to finish that chore.

As I poured boiling water into the bathing tub followed by cold water, he entered the room behind me. I flinched involuntarily in memory to last night. I silently handed him his soap and scrub brush from the shelf above me, draped a towel over the tub and exited. He pulled the cotton curtain across the kitchen doorway and I heard his robe land on the floor.

"Now he is being modest!" I muttered under my breath, already in a bad mood from the heat.

"More cold water, please," he called.

I pumped more water into the bucket and carried it through to the tub. His five-foot-four frame sat on his haunches in the tub, his knees drawn up to his hairy (beastly!) chest, his buttocks not yet touching the water. I didn't wish to see more. I drew back the curtain at the backdoor window to look outside while I continued to pour.

There was Aimee out in her garden! It was so good to see her! She was bent over, appearing to attack the dirt viciously with her hoe, in between her rows of green leaves. Her one long yellow braid had fallen over her shoulder, its pointed end bobbing up and down, threatening to lick the dirt.

"I said, that is enough water!" Robert said from below. "For the love of decency, would you close the curtain? What are you looking at out there?"

I quickly obeyed. "Oh, I see our next door neighbor, Aimee."

"Oh yes. She called to me from her fence one day," Robert said. He was soaping his hands now, his knees still at his chest, his buttocks submerged. "She asked me where you were. She wished to speak to you. Why would that be?"

"We've become friends and visit occasionally," I answered casually, not wanting his anger to flare in this heat.

"Yes, I am *perfectly* aware of your friendship," Robert said.

Yes, all-knowing, all-seeing, I thought, sarcasm dripping like the water from his arms as he washed.

"A friendship that has led you right down the main street of town, parading yourselves in front of God and men alike. Scrub my back, please." Agitation was returning to his voice as he spoke.

I didn't want to discuss this any further but must get him bathed, fed and out of here. My day had brightened, just seeing her out there in her bright yellow frock and large white apron. I exited to the kitchen, cracked eggs into the skillet, and returned.

I lathered his back, making note to trim the brown curls on his neck. "Ruby, you will not remain friends with Aimee. She is an angry woman and her husband is having difficulties enough as it is. I heard her shrieking again, only two nights ago."

"We're no longer friends, Robert," I said softly.

"She will not spread her disease to her neighboring home and into my wife," he continued as if I hadn't spoken. "I will not allow any more of this nonsense." His skin flinched as I scrubbed a bit too hard on his lower back. "Do you understand me, Ruby?"

"I'm right behind you, Robert," I answered softly. I dropped the brush in the water behind his back and left, drying my hands on my robe. *Just let him try to squeeze around in that narrow tub to reach the brush. If he says one more word, I shall surely shriek myself.*

We spoke no more. Finally he was gone. Unfortunately, by that time, so was Aimee. *Not that it mattered,* I declared under my breath. I did not wish to speak to her, to be tempted again, yet, unwillingly I watched for her during my trips to the clothesline and garden.

It wasn't until noon, while Bess, Pearl and I were slicing potatoes and breaking beans, and the boys were pushing the rusty grass cutter through thick grass, that Aimee reappeared on her backdoor step. With a glance toward us, she hesitated as if to go back in, but then squared her shoulders and headed toward her garden, a basket in hand. Our yards were narrow and long. From my working table, I could see Aimee's right eye, swollen and purple, her lip puffed on the same side and bruised. A cut redlined her right cheekbone.

"Oh, Aimee, not again! This is the worst yet!" I cried before thinking, rushing over to the fence. Aimee stopped, quickly turned her left side to me and shrugged. She peered at her back door as if watching something significant going on in her window.

"I apologize, Aimee. I don't mean to embarrass you."

Bess joined me, partially hidden in my skirts.

Aimee smiled a lopsided smile. "Naturally you would notice," she said with a lisp, her attention now on a stubborn weed, the toe of her boot kicking at it. "The lavender here along your fence row smells lovely!"

I couldn't walk away. This was just too much, to see my friend like this. I leaned forward over the fence, longing to hug and comfort, but Aimee only backed away a little. "Aimee, why does he do it?" I whispered. "What drives him to such – such violence?"

"I say it is because he is drinking hard liquor. *He* says it is because I am not a good wife. But this last one ..." she shook her head, "is because of your husband. I deplore you not to be angry with me." She paused and reached for the fence for support. "Two mornings ago, I was bringing in some laundry, when I spotted your husband walking from your ..." she pointed toward our outhouse. "I hadn't seen you since the parade, and I became worried. Silly me ran over to the fence, in a hurry to catch him. I was only asking him where you were. I suppose I shouldn't have been so forward but..." She looked back toward her garden, refusing to look at me.

"I don't understand the connection. Why would I be angry?" I said.

"I was talking with a man, other than my husband, and was dressed unsuitably, to boot." Aimee explained, her tone parrot-like, like she was quoting another's words. She kicked the weed harder and its roots became exposed. "*Your* husband, Ruby!" she emphasized, as if wanting to bring home the point that I could understand, and perhaps would then understand Aimee's husband. "Look, it was morning and I was still in my robe. I was being far too bold." She folded her arms across her chest and kicked the weed some distance away from her. "Do you suppose he was jealous?" Her tone sounded hopeful for some understanding, her own understanding.

"Humph," I answered, also crossing my arms. I turned toward my own garden, not willing to see Aimee struggling so. I could not, would not, justify his drunken temper, no matter for what reason. "Jealous, indeed! Mercy, Aimee, why aren't *you* angry?"

"I was ... I was, but not anymore." She focused her attention on the fence, her fingernail chipping away at the cracked white paint on the fence rail. Her hand was red and chaffed.

I looked down at my own hand, folded across my opposite arm. No different, I realized.

"Yesterday morning," Aimee was saying, "when he sobered and drank enough coffee to rid of his headache, he then noticed my face. I was pouring his coffee and he grabbed my wrist and just *stared* at me. I am a fright, I suppose. I backed away, spilling some, but it was he who apologized. He reminded me that it is partly my fault, for I *do* provoke him and do not always do as I'm told. Which is true ... of course." She attempted a little laugh, but it sounded more like someone had pressed hard on her stomach and forced air out her mouth. "The ironic thing about it all was that if I had been advancing toward your husband with illicit thoughts, it would have been all for naught."

"What do you mean?"

"Because your husband was rather ... un-neighborly. He stopped at your stoop there, and, I believe, *glared* at me! Then he answered, 'Ruby has gone to her mother's for a few days. When she returns, I suggest you remember that the fence is there for a reason. Please keep on your side of it, or I'll report this to your husband!'"

I waved it away and shrugged my shoulders, trying to appear nonchalant. "Oh, he didn't mean it!"

She looked at me in surprise. "Oh, but I think he did!" Then she stared. Then she put her hands on her hips. "And Mrs. Good Wife, why would there be a bruise on *your* cheek."

I had forgotten all about my own situation whilst I was judging hers!

"Neither one of our husbands aim to misbehave, and we all shall live happily ever after," I said.

We both chuckled without mirth, shaking our heads at the irony of it all. It was a fine line from crying.

"I'll forgive you for flirting with my husband on one condition," I finally said, swallowing hard. "Re-invite me to your afternoon tea."

I tell you all this not to complain, not to be disloyal to my dead husband or to reveal private, intimate moments, but to explain, to justify my future decisions, why I went the direction I did, why I turned right and then a very hard left, willing myself toward a greater judgment.

Bess's Chapter Four -- 1920

What is passion?

A s I typed, each word became matter, and this matter began fill-ing me, as water would fill an empty vessel. For the first time I wrote with feeling, and the pain felt good, because at least I could feel something, and it was fulfilling – I now knew the true meaning of that word. Emotion, whether positive or negative, was better than indifference. I felt alive for the first time in a long time. I finished the article with a hard bang of the period key, like hammering in a nail. Pearl must read this before anyone else and Thomas was due back today. With haste, I rolled the paper loose from the cylinder and splurged on a taxi to take me home speedily.

Two children whose names escaped me were playing on the veran-dah indicating to me that Aunt Opal was visiting Mama. Opal sat in the parlor exactly as she did ten years ago when she married her Amish husband, in the same dark blue Amish costume with no buttons, with only a cape and snug white cap to diminish the harsh lines. When I was with her I always had the sense of looking into the past.

I patted her swollen stomach. "I'm losing count, Aunt Opal. Is this the tenth?"

"And last, I pray," she said and smiled that forever-tired smile of hers. In examining closer, I saw that she did not look the same at all; her eyes were a duller blue and her light brown hair had lost its shine. This made me sad, although aging quickly was to be expected on a large farm with breeding her main occupation. It seemed every-thing Uncle Jacob touched bred more, grew and multiplied, and his corn crop and herds of horses, cows, and children were a productive lot. When working about his domain scattering seeds, he must believe he's as powerful as God himself.

"I remember a time," Mama said to her, "when you were praying to be with child same as Sarah in the Bible."

"I didn't know I would continue to have children once I was as old as Sarah," Opal retorted. They laughed easily together, Aunt Opal's hand covering her mouth to hide the missing teeth. There were brown splotches on her once-creamy skin, too. Carrying children was taking its toll.

Seeing her gave me one more reason to believe in my jump to the other side of the fence. Protective law should include protection against unwanted children. I was indeed becoming grounded.

"Aunt Opal, would you have had as many children if you could protect yourself from becoming pregnant?"

"Children are blessings from God, Bess. Why would I protect myself from blessings?" Her eyes welled up with tears – from thankfulness or sadness? I asked her as much.

Tears now flowed down Aunt Opal's swollen cheeks and Mama eyed me oddly as if to say, *why are you doing this to her?*

I didn't have an answer; only more questions.

"You've caught me at a weak moment, Bess," Aunt Opal said as she brought out her handkerchief from her dress pocket. "I came here to cry on sister Ruby's shoulder. I'm concerned that my body doesn't have the strength to carry another child within a year of my last one, and so late in my life. I should have more faith in God, for He knows best." She shook her head as she blew into her handkerchief. "Jacob would tan my hide if he knew I was saying such things."

I wondered who she was more afraid of – God or husband.

"Were you breastfeeding your last one?" I couldn't remember its name. "Breastfeeding is a form of birth control, is it not?"

"Yes, but I dried up within a few months. My milking cows are far more industrious than I am."

"But you knew that while you were breastfeeding, you were decreasing your chances of becoming pregnant, am I right?"

"Yes, of course."

"Then what is wrong with using other means of birth control? Especially when it may well save your life. If I recall, you've come close to death during several of your deliveries. Perhaps it's not as God wishes, but as man demands. Always be submissive to your husband, is that it?"

"Bess," Mama said, warning clear in her tone. "I understand what you are saying and why, but this is not the time nor the place. What is done is done. I'm afraid I've encouraged far too much freedom in your thinking, and now you seem too critical of those who have less freedom."

My own vision blurred but I could see her well enough to know she was taken back by my tears. "I'm sorry Mama. Aunt Opal. I'm far too opinionated and it is easy to judge from my high horse. Pearl convinced me to come down to earth and the fall has been painful, but it shows I can still feel."

"Well, well, welcome to the real world, Miss Serious Spinster," came a voice from the stairs.

I turned to see Pearl hanging over the railing, looking down at me with a wicked smile. This being Saturday, she was dressed for a night out in her sack dress and long beaded necklace.

I waved a paper at her. "I have something I want you to read. If you like it, I'll have it printed in the newspaper."

"Read it out loud to me. I'm on the run. Mama, Papa wants his bath now."

"Tell him I'll be up in five minutes – that's two radio commercials to him," Mama said. "Bess, please read your article now. I don't want to miss it."

I've titled this, *Women's Equal Rights; Ascend versus Descend.* The text goes like this:

> 'The question here is: Do we fight for equal rights for women state-by-state or with one national Equal Rights Amendment? Sound familiar? It should. This was the same argument encountered when fighting for women's vote. Do we heave it from the bottom up

234

at local and state level, or do we push it down from federal level? At the Women's Industrial Conference, I saw both sides and it became clear to me that while the Equal Rights Amendment is needed, we as a society are not yet ready for it. We have too many social customs, sex-prejudices, and strict religious beliefs on the ground floor to work through. As I was rightfully told by my sister, Pearl Wright, federal law is "above him and too far away to touch him". One sweeping federal amendment may throw out the baby with the bath water. We may lose what we have achieved thus far in local protective statutes that address women's issues in work conditions, birth control, preserving the rights of mothers, and protecting children. Let's put our own backyard in order before going to our neighbors.

I returned the paper to my lap and looked up at Pearl, now sitting on the stairs and peering through the railing. My heart warmed at her sincere smile and blushing face.

"This is so kippy after what I saw you do at the conference, sis," Pearl said. "Are you really going to publish that? I think it's great what you're saying but you're going to get a lot of ridicule from your fellow snake charmers."

"I'm ridiculed either way I go, Pearl, so I might as well do it for a cause I can believe in. What I say in this article makes more sense to me than what I said at the conference. Something about that amendment that sounds too big, too much, too soon and it's not looking after our family's needs. Let's work together to fight the system, shall we?"

"I suppose so, Bess, though I'm just a tomato; just a good looking girl with no brains. Not as smart as you, so I wouldn't know what to do."

"Oh, you'll do fine, Pearl!" Aunt Opal said, surprising us all - I would have used her as a perfect example of problems in social customs, sex-prejudices, and religious beliefs. "Yes! I have been forced to look beyond my farm gate, now that my children are in school and I've lost nephews to the war. I used to control what my family ate and Jacob and I were not dependent on the government, but now we see that their decisions can affect all of us."

Mama reached over and squeezed Opal's hand. She seemed to literally light up at what Opal was saying. "You and I used to buy rolls of fabric to sew into clothing and linens. Now the fabrics are sewn by factory machinery. My daughter-in-law does not even know how to sew! And she buys her bread, she doesn't bake it. Now many foods are canned outside the home. I took pride in my lavender oils and sachets and sold them well, but now young ladies turn their noses at them, preferring store-bought products. Advertisements make factory things prettier than homemade. We'll have to become aware of every government decision because more and more, it will affect our home."

It was my turn to light up. "Mama, Aunt Opal! That was very insightful. The four of us should campaign together."

"Oh no, Bess, your father is too ill—"

"Oh no, Bess, Jacob would never permit—"

"Well I suppose I should tell all of you," Pearl said loudly, "David has asked me to marry him, and I said yes."

Would this ever end? "The opposite sex has caused your problems in the first place, and here you are succumbing to the capital Him once again!" I stormed out of the house.

I returned to the newspaper office angry over everything and nothing. I suppose I had hoped for praise and partnership with Pearl. Mama and Aunt Opal would have been a bonus. Instead I departed empty-handed save for the sheet of paper I had waved around the parlor like a surrender flag. Once more, Pearl had gotten under my skin in an irritating fashion. Not that I opposed her upcoming marriage; it was that she was marrying and forsaking all others, including her own co-workers at the textile mill, brushing me off by saying there's nothing she or I could do about the unfair conditions of such a place.

"Men rule, women spool," she said with a shrug of her shoulders.

The day was not getting any better for now I must face Thomas who had returned from the south, and he was motioning me into his office when he saw me coming in. I continued to hang on to the paper as if it had become a shield. *It just might save my life*, I thought, looking into his stormy eyes clouded by thick low-cast eyebrows.

"Do you have a problem working for me, Bess?" he asked, walking behind his desk and slamming a drawer closed. He flattened his hands on his desk top and leaned forward. "Do you? I understand you did not follow my orders but instead followed some damned women's radical group at the Women's Industrial Conference. I shouldn't be surprised but, frankly, I'm disappointed. What do you have to say for yourself?"

His anger needled me. Reminding him of his own words, I answered "Freedom of speech, remember?"

"That's a weak-ass reason, Bess. I expected better from you." He sat down and pointed to a chair for me to sit. "Why have you gone back to such crude ways of making a point? This isn't the first time you ran to the Woman's Party defense. You tried this back in 1916, didn't you? You think I don't remember how you left the NAWSA along with Alice Paul and a group of militant activists and formed the National Woman's Party?"

I sat on the edge of my seat. "I was tired of the sluggish state-by-state plodding to win the vote, Thomas. The same thing is happening all over again with equality."

"Yes, well, militants only brought you arrests and hunger strikes. I worried—well, at least you did return to Mrs. Catt and her older women's peaceful strategies."

He paused and rubbed his mouth in thought. I waited, looking as passive as possible, letting his temper ease. *He worried?*

"Enough of the past," he continued. "Let's look at today's story: the great majority of the working girls today are unskilled because they are so young and because they quit when they get married. They work in crowded, sex-segregated jobs, excluded from most men's jobs. So many competing for limited jobs has created a downward spiral in wages. We need to do something."

Even though I had written an article agreeing with that, I felt rattled by his lecturing tone. "Women needing protection gives us an inferior and old-fashioned view. Women's bodies are not so Victorian anymore, now that artificial methods of birth control, like condoms and diaphragms, are out there, well, if we can get rid of that damn Comstock Law. And then there's the growing clerical labor force giving women a better working environment than in the factory. Oh, damn it to hell, I'm tired of it all!"

Thomas tapped his fingers on the desk, studying me in his intense way. "Why do you debate with me so strongly?" he finally asked.

"Just publish my article, please." I placed the article I had read to Pearl on his desk.

He reached for his reading glasses and read my essay, looking down his nose through his lenses. He shook his head. "Woman, you could start an argument in an empty house." He threw his glasses to the side and rubbed his eyes. "Pick a side and stick with it, Bess."

I drummed my fingers on the arm of my chair and returned his intense stare. "Few men understand women's movement, let alone work for it. Why do you?"

"My wife taught me a great deal. She once said I had enough of a taste for adventure and change to understand women's evolution. In turn, I admired her ability to work in the drudgery of preparation and in the heat of the battle. I have no patience for such detail. As a true reporter, I only wish to move on to the next hot topic. You remind me of her somewhat."

"Oh? Did she also lack passion?" His earlier accusation obviously still stung but I bit my tongue for my poor taste in bringing it up now. I attempted to laugh to soften the blow but he was not amused.

"On the contrary," he said. "I have yet to meet another woman who cares as much."

I care, I wanted to say. But its admission would only add to more poor timing. So I did what I was best at and changed the subject.

"Why must women progress alone? Why can't men and women right the world together? Bring in world peace and better education."

"Are you back to supporting equal rights again?"

"Never mind," I snapped. "Women must have freedom of choice in occupation before we have the power to right the world. Hopefully being able to vote will help us." I thought about that for a moment. "No, that won't work alone. You're right about working girls. Discrimination in women trades is much deeper than in government jobs. It requires many small steps to break down the barriers from the working level. This is the only practical way."

"Finally you got around to my way of thinking," Thomas said with a knowing smile. "Now just stay put. We'll make cleaning up the textile mill and factories around us part of my campaign to run for mayor. That'll do more than any statute or law. You, as my campaign manager, are going to help me do that. We can right our own small world together." He banged his hand down hard on his desk, giving me a startle. "Let's move on with it then!"

That was my last effort on the Equal Rights Amendment for forty years.

I felt manipulated – and needed. I must admit that what made me burst forth and manage the campaign trail as if in hot pursuit was not the end-result - of course I hoped Thomas would win, but I had very little doubt that he wouldn't. He was popular, well known for his accurate reporting, and respected as the newspaper editor.

With my sense of argument feeding Thomas' speeches, and his sense of compassion for those around him, we usually walked away from the podium feeling confident that the audience was on our side.

I enjoyed that, yes, but my enthusiasm came from deeper within. Thomas was more right than he realized; he was righting our world, only our world had narrowed down to two in my vision. I thrilled in opening my eyes on a new day and thinking over the day's schedule of events, knowing that within a few hours I would stand beside Thomas. His intensity and quick decision-making drew me in, forcing me to concentrate on the underlying details. A buzz existed around him, as if he were a honeycomb nesting busy bees. If I wasn't standing beside him, basking in his light, then I felt as drab as someone sitting in the chilly shadows.

Lizzie looked happier too, for Thomas was coming to the Lighthouse several times a week for dinner to discuss campaign strategies with me. He always insisted Lizzie eat at the dining room table with us. I worried about the inappropriateness of colored help dining with us but of course this was not my decision to make.

"Lizzie," Thomas said one night, "Annan is swarming with committees. Rather than one person getting under the load and working it the old way, we need a full room of folks talking about it. Committees begat conferences and conferences begat working groups and working groups begat reports. Two heads are better than one I know, but twenty tongues give us more advice than action. Now I have a committee who tells me that we need to institute a unified system of milk depots throughout Annan that can give out certified pure milk to mothers for their babies. They claim this was done in New York City and the death rate went down considerably. What do you think?"

Lizzie protruded her thick lips in deep thought. "I've been listening to all these issues and how you want to solve them for the people, Mr. Pickering. When I was marching for suffrage, there was one thing I learned about the public and that is they're like a spoiled child crying for more candy. What you'll need as mayor, Mr. Pickering, is to be both parents: the father who lays down the law and the mother who holds the child to her breast. Committee or no committee, you'll be the boss. Now don't take offense to this, but this is where you and Bess come in, because I see you as the mother and Bess as the father. You think with your heart and want to give it all away, but Bess thinks practical, with her head. Now about the milk, breast milk is the best purity one can get, but some women can't and some women won't. Says it's too much of a bother, so they want to give their babies cow milk. Cow milk is for calves. How would a calf grow if we was to give it woman's milk? Not very well, I wager. But for women who can't, we need to help them and we can't very well sit good mothers around town offering up their breasts for babies. So what we need is clean cow milk. So I say, if you want water, go to the well. The tit will talk."

"Lizzie, watch your language with Mr. Pickering!"

"Do you mean go to a dairy farm, Lizzie?" Thomas asked, rudely ignoring my admonition. "We could do that easily enough, with Bess's uncle's dairy farm. Set it up, Bess. We'll take a photographer with us. He can take photographs of me working on the farm for publicity and we can talk to your Uncle Jesse about the milking process. We'll kill two birds with one stone."

When we pulled into the farm yard of clucking, scattering chickens, I half-expected Grandmama Garnet's short solid frame to appear at the screen door. Garnet hadn't approved of my "un-womanly ways", and wondered out loud if I was ever going to settle down with a husband and children, as God had intended. I remembered the last time I'd entered this well-worn living room, its sameness shattered by the open coffin displayed under the window, furniture moved to accommodate, giving it a strange-house feel. Thankfully, the furnishings were back where they belonged, where they'd always been for as long as I could remember. Still, something was amiss with Garnet's absence, like something left unsaid.

Aunt Edith looked as old and gray as Grandmama Garnet used to. Uncle Jesse, on the other hand, had aged more slowly, a deep dimple giving his grin a boyish mischievousness. He scratched the back of his curly-haired head when Thomas asked him for an interview, saying he supposed he could do that, but didn't know if it would be interesting enough to anybody else. No one seemed to care much about farming anymore, he said. He was having trouble keeping help out here, with only one son out of six interested in dairy farming. Two sons had been lost to the war - one was buried in France and the other was never found. Another had been killed in a factory explosion in New York City years ago. The other two had moved on to the excitement of city life, I heard him tell Thomas as they walked out to the barn together.

Good riddance to Joey, I said to myself. I thought it unlikely that Joey was lost over in France, but more likely hiding with some French girl, and would some year show up here again, when he tired of her. I knew first-hand how he felt about girls.

"For a thirteen-year-old, you sure are prissy," Joey said to me. He jumped up to latch onto a barn rafter and swung back and forth. He landed on his bum in the hay beside me.

"I'm not prissy," I said, brushing off the hay he'd scattered onto my lap.

"Yes you are. You don't play like you used to. Why do girls stop playing when they grow tits?"

"I'm going to tell on you, if you keep talking like that," I said, trying to sound angry, but secretly feeling flattered that he noticed at all.

His papa's dimple showed in his cheek, and his mother's deep brown eyes locked mine. "Nah, you'll not tell. You and I are too grownup for that. Besides, you followed me in here."

"I did not. You said you wanted to tell me a secret."

"I do." His mouth moved to my ear. "I think you're pretty," he whispered.

Smiling bashfully, I looked away. "Thanks."

"We're going to start dating people soon. Want to practice kissing?"

"I don't think that is proper."

"I told you, you were prissy."

"It doesn't sound right for two cousins to kiss," I said, avoiding eye contact with his lips. He was too cute for a cousin's own good. I stared down at the entrance below our loft, wondering what Uncle Jesse would think if he walked in just now.

"We're not hurting anybody. It's just pretend. What if you really like a boy someday and when he kisses you, you kiss like a fish." He sucked in his cheeks and gave me a fish-kiss on the cheek. Where did he get such nerve to talk this way?

His closeness gave me goose bumps that caused me to giggle.

"Well, hopefully he's not a shark," I said, watching my feet tap together.

"Just one kiss," he said, moving closer.

242

Just one kiss wouldn't hurt. He smelled like hay and the chocolate cookie we just ate. His eyes locked mine again and his face covered my vision. There was nowhere else to take my attention. His lips touched mine and then pressed.

"Kiss back," he muttered between my lips.

I did. He pressed harder and we remained like this for an interminable amount of time. Just when I was wondering if I was supposed to do something, his tongue slipped between my lips. I tried to back off but his hand held the back of my head.

The kiss, my struggle – something perpetuated a spark in him. In one quick movement, he sprawled my legs and forced me back. He kissed me harder and sloppier and his slobber and heavy breathing repulsed me.

I pulled my head away enough to speak. "Get off me!" I whispered.

His rock-hard pelvis rubbed against mine, and his hand grabbed my breast and squeezed. I pushed him off with a yelp. I sat back up, picking hay out of my long hair and wondering if he was angry with me now, and if I had done the right thing. I had wanted his attention, but not this.

"I'm not interested in fighting off boys," I said, astonished at my own calmness. "I'm going to fight for girls. I'm learning how at the Lighthouse. So don't try that again, cousin." I emphasized 'cousin' to get the meaning across. I hate you, I said silently.

He stood up, his calm matching my own. "You're a queer, and you're a tease. One of these days, a man will put you in your place." He walked over to the ladder and stepped down. He soon paused in his descent, only his head and shoulders visible, his cheeks as flushed as after one of our potato sack races. "You'd better start getting used to this, because those little tits of yours are just going to shrivel up and fall off like rotten apples from the tree if you don't let some man nibble at them. That's what you're put here for."

I watched Aunt Edith take her apple pie out of the oven and test her potatoes, her apron-covered paunchy stomach catching oil and water as she worked, her calico dress the same home-fashioned ankle-length dress of my childhood. I wondered what she would think if she knew that Joey and I had kissed in their barn loft so many years ago. I wondered if she knew she had raised at least one chauvinistic boy. I doubted that 'chauvinism' was a word she would use or understand. Uncle Jesse likely controlled everything.

Poor Edith. I felt sorry for her limited, isolated life here. Such a simple housewife. She had no exposure to the world beyond with not so much as a radio or the electricity to run one. It didn't help her misfortune that when she spoke, her false teeth rattled loosely.

She seemed to read that on my face. She suddenly asked if she could show me her stocks. Edith invested in stocks? She led me down to her cellar where shelf after shelf were filled with jarred vegetables, beans, fruit - hundreds of jars. Pickle barrels, baskets of apples and onions and potatoes sat on the dirt floor. She chatted on and on about how her egg and soap sales were still in good business, and about how she planned to set up a market stand at the end of the laneway, now that motor cars regularly passed by.

I got her message: she had filled her space completely.

Secretly I longed to be the round peg that fit perfectly in the round hole like she did ... like Mama did ... like even Aunt Opal. They had such purpose. I sent out a silent wish to Joey that he, by now, had opened his eyes to all that women were put here for. He needn't have looked beyond his own backyard.

Thomas scooted his chair from the table and gulped down his remaining half glass of prohibited red wine. He had brought up a bottle from the cellar explaining to our raised eyebrows that this 1910 Bordeaux was only going to turn to vinegar if we didn't drink it, and besides, this was a night to relax. He indeed looked as if he had achieved his goal as he looked about the dining room.

"Thank God the ghosts are gone from here now." His cheeks were flushed and his lips were stained a deep red. "When I look around, do you know what I see?" He didn't expect an answer and we didn't give him one. "I see you, Bess, and I see you, Lizzie, and that is all. And when I think of the bedrooms upstairs, I know a woman is up there with a small child sleeping, waiting for her husband's drunkenness to wear off, and that is all. There is no one in the master bedroom waiting for me, half-propped on pillows, surrounded by books, the death-look on her face being ignored by both of us. No, my beloved wife is gone from here, gone on to happier places, leaving behind a wish that I find happiness too. Who would have guessed I would go full circle and find it back here, the place I ran away from?" He nodded to his thoughts. "Yes, indeed, I feel as if I've come home again."

I poured him more wine and raised my glass to him. "Welcome home, Thomas." Our glasses touched with a tinkle.

Lizzie slipped from the room, taking some dishes with her.

Thomas took another drink and sat his glass down. His fingers moved up and down the stem, our eyes watching this.

"Where are you, Bess? Are you at home here?"

I nodded. "More and more it's becoming so. For years this was my workstation, but now our chapter of women have scattered, the back parlor has been returned to its original state, the new shelter downtown is taking in the majority of battered women. The Lighthouse is becoming less of a house, and more of a home ... I feel somehow attached. Could I be growing roots?"

"I hope so." He leaned toward me and his warm fingers circled my wrist. "Bess, you and I ... we're well suited, don't you think?"

I finally touched that floppy hair on his forehead and moved it over to his temple. I could only nod, so consumed I was by his intense green eyes searching mine.

"Bess, you may be shocked by what I'm going to say, but I've been waiting a long time to say this. There was so much in our way. We both had ghosts from the past we were running from. I ran for years, working my life away. So have you – I know you so well. But we were running in circles, with one foot always centered here. Center your life with me, Bess. I want you to marry me."

Had I only started blossoming at this moment? All my senses opened and leaned toward him as a flower would to the sun's rays, wanting to see and hear more. I reached for his hand and brought it to my mouth and inhaled its manly scent, my eyes watering, it couldn't be helped. I had dreamt and had nightmares of this - the reality of his present affection clashing with my past decisions.

He patted my hand. "Good then, you'll marry me."

I shook my head with regret, tears flowing. I pulled from his grasp and grabbed my napkin. The sound of my unrestrained sobs filled the room.

"I can't," I muttered between gasps. "I'm already married."

"*What?*"

My hands shook as I attempted to keep up with my eyes' salty production. "You don't know me as well as you might think, Thomas. I made one huge mistake that very few know about."

"Where is your husband? Why don't I know about him?"

I forced myself to meet his stare; his eyes were now the green in the ocean before a storm, but he was still leaning toward me in that concentrated way of his. I hadn't lost him yet.

I took in a deep breath to gain some control. I had to confront him with this and I desperately wished I had dealt with this on my own, before having to drag Thomas into the trap with me.

"Jere is in Tennessee."

"Why?"

"Because he lives there. I met him in Nashville through Mrs. Catt. It was while there that we finally realized our dream to win the woman's vote. Jere celebrated with us. I had reached the end of a chapter and needed to move on to another chapter and he was there at a very vulnerable time. I realized the mistake on our wedding night in his cabin filled with children. He kindly returned me to Nashville the following day. I haven't seen or spoken to him since." I didn't go into the details of Jere's lost love for my mother. The story was strange enough for Thomas to handle for now.

"Do you wish to divorce him?"

"It didn't matter until now, but yes, yes I do."

"Then I'll find a lawyer in Tennessee. The wine has given me a headache. I'll see you in the office tomorrow." He grabbed his hat and coat and was gone before I could say goodbye at the door. I certainly could have used a comforting kiss right then, but I had more than dampened his romantic intentions.

"I only have myself to blame," I muttered, watching his Duesenberg drive him away from his own home.

I closed the front door and leaned against it closing my eyes, his proposal of marriage slowly sinking in. I felt my heart swell and deflate in rhythm to my lungs as two thoughts repeated themselves: *Thomas proposed, I'm already married; Thomas proposed, I'm already married.* Poor Thomas thought all the ghosts were gone but found a skeleton in my closet instead.

I insisted on going to Tennessee alone and deal with Jere without Thomas standing in my shadow. The sooner the better because my conversations with Thomas had become stiff and stilted. Considering he was a reporter he asked few questions but instead was stern and snapped easily. I could only choke back my retorts and tears. I deserved his anger and disappointment; consequently, I felt secretly relieved when he kept his word and made an appointment for me with a reputable lawyer in Nashville. That was the best he could do and I told him so. The lawyer, Mr. McCorriston, finally telephoned to say the papers were ready to sign and be delivered to Jere. The difficulty would be in contacting Jere. He didn't have a telephone and to write him a letter sounded rather callous to me. I would simply have to find his place and talk to him in person.

Easier said than done. Mr. McCorriston picked me up at the train station and drove me to his office to discuss the divorce proceedings, but he did not recommend nor offer to drive me the hour's distance to Jere's log cabin. If Jere did not agree to sign, he could delay the divorce in the courts for years, Mr. McCorriston said, and that would lead to arguments, and Mr. McCorriston made it clear he was not serviced to police altercations. His tall lanky frame and paper-thin skin attested to that. I had no other recourse but to depend on him and resort to begging. I assured him that Jere was a calm, reasonable man and Mr. McCorriston would have to go no further than the dirt road that ended below Jere's property. I would walk the remaining way myself. The additional twenty dollars (worth four days of hard labor!) was the final bargaining chip and we were on our way, papers in hand. Jere had only a rural route address in the small village below his mountain, but Mr. McCorriston was familiar with the area. It was my duty to point out the road taking us up the mountain. I only hoped I could remember.

As we bumped along the town's pitted street, Mr. McCorriston played with his waxed mustache thoughtfully. He was a slow-talker and looked the part of the courtly southern politician.

"I got to ask you a question," he said, "that's going to sound personal, but better me than a judge in a courtroom full of people. Is there a chance you could be carrying a child?"

"Not a chance."

"Are you sure? Because if you find you are, then everything's thrown out and you'll have to start all over."

"Mr. Phillips and I did not … fulfill our marriage as husband and wife."

"You mean you did not consummate?" His eyes left the road and stared at me, his blond lashes blinking in astonishment.

"That is correct." I hoped my flushed face was not noticeable.

"Well then that's a whole different kettle of fish. Mr. Pickering never mentioned that when he called. Does he know that?"

"I don't know, frankly. I just assumed."

He laughed and returned to twirling his mustache. He pulled onto a side road and backed out, heading the other way. "We'll have to throw everything out and start all over, but it'll sure be a heck of a lot easier this way. All we need from Mr. Phillips is a signed declaration stating that the marriage was never consummated. Since your union's not validated, he can't very well contest it. I need the same declaration from you. We're going back to the office, draw up the two papers and then go to Mr. Phillip's place. It's a shame I'll have to charge Mr. Pickering for work you didn't need."

"Don't bill Mr. Pickering," I said. "It's my responsibility."

"Mr. Pickering was quite clear. I'll bill him. I wouldn't have taken this case if it was in a woman's name. Begging your pardon, but there's no guarantee of a woman's ability to pay."

I didn't care to argue with him over this and resigned myself to settle the matter with Thomas. Instead, I felt relief in knowing the divorce may be easier than expected, but I was also distressed that the simplicity and speed was based on intimacy, or lack thereof. I would never have dreamt of discussing my sexual conduct with Thomas. And here I was admitting as much with a stranger.

The trek to the cabin was a long one; we were lost and finally found by a man on horseback who led us to a cut in the trees that passed as a road. He pointed up and then with a spit of tobacco juice, meandered on down the main road. Our uphill climb did not look as familiar as I had hoped, my only guess being I was in a newly-wed stupor on that first ride. Early evening stretched shadows across the cabin and grounds as I paused on the rise above it. November gave its surroundings a scanty look that differed from last year's late summer growth and hushed the trees, although the weather was more an Indian summer. The squeak of the front porch swing drew my attention there where Mary Sue leisurely drifted back and forth, holding the youngest on her lap and an open book, her bare feet giving them a light push.

She read out loud, struggling through every one-syllable word, and didn't see me until I stepped up onto the front porch. "Hello, Mary Sue."

Her light blue eyes did not waiver from my face. "Are you coming back?"

"No - only for a short visit. How are you?" I dusted off the seat of a crude wooden slat chair on the other side of the front door and sat, the envelope clutched in my sweaty palm. I waved at the toddler and she released her thumb from her mouth long enough to smile back. She kicked her legs in some sort of shy exuberance.

"We're making it alright. Daddy and the boys are out in the field cutting corn stocks. Should be in directly. Did I make you mad?"

"Mad? Of course not. Why would you?"

"Daddy said that's why you left. Said I was hateful to you."

"That wasn't very nice of him to say that, Mary Sue. It was not your fault."

She shifted the baby on her lap and pushed the swing harder.

"What are you reading?"

"Nothing, really. I can't hardly read."

"How is school?"

She snorted. "What school. I haven't been to school since third grade. It's too far away. Why are you here?"

"I have a paper here for your daddy to sign. This will give him the freedom to marry someone else."

"He hasn't been anywhere to meet anybody since you left."

"He must sign this. I want a divorce."

"Daddy won't want a divorce. People around here will talk terrible about him, and they already had a prayer meeting to pray for your lost soul." We sat thinking about this, while the creaking swing continued. "But you got something in your favor. Daddy thinks more of us kids than what other folks think. I can help you. If we make a deal. Can you read and write?"

"Of course, Mary Sue."

"Don't say it like that. There's a lot of people who don't know how. You teach me how to read and write and I'll make Daddy sign."

"I'll teach you whether he signs or not. But I can't do that here. If you move into town, closer to a school, or if you ever move to Annan, where I live—"

"Daddy'll never agree to me leaving home. He needs me too bad."

"How old are you?"

"Sixteen."

"Then he can't keep you here against your will. You're a grown woman now. You certainly are doing the work of a woman. Isn't there someone else who can take over? One of the boys?"

"I do woman's work, so the boys won't do it. Elsie Price said she would, if we need her. She just lives down the holler from us. The church ladies said they'd take turns coming in too, but we never asked them before. But even if they did, it don't matter because somebody needs to be here all the time to cook the three meals and feed the chickens and haul in the water and wash the clothes."

"We'll talk to him together and see if he has any suggestions. Do we have a deal?" I walked over and extended my hand to her.

She shook it hard, her eyes set on determined. "A deal."

The boys were walking in from the field by then and Mary Sue carried the now-sleeping toddler into the house to "set the table".

Jere saw me and slowed his pace. "Boys go on around back and wash up. I'll be in directly." He wiped his face with the bandana tied loosely around his neck. Strands of hair had come undone from his pony tail and stuck to his face and neck. "Bess, this is a surprise."

"I had no other way of contacting you."

"No, I suppose not, although we do get letters in these here parts, believe it or not."

I held up the envelope. "I thought best to meet with you."

"Well, this sounds like official business, not a social call. Mary Sue?" he called through the screen door. "Fetch us two cold glasses of milk." He sat in the swing and focused his deep blue eyes on me. His dirty white undershirt and dusty denim trousers did not detract from his graceful yet muscular way of moving. He had thick legs and thick arms, but a narrow waist.

"Feels good to sit," he said. "I'm trying to work while the weather's good but I don't think days like today are meant for work. We're meant to pray that hell's heat hasn't risen."

He raised the palms of his callused hands to me, dirt in every crease. "I'd give you a hug or shake your hand but I'm too sweaty. You wouldn't like it." He wiped them on his trouser legs.

I heard a hint of irritation in his voice so I decided not to dilly-dally. "I understand, Jere. I won't stay long. I'm here to ask you to sign this declaration of annulment. The annulment will separate us legally. It means that because we did not—"

"I know what it means," he said. He stared at the floor beyond his feet. "Are you sure you want the stigma of divorce on your record? I don't think I do."

251

"An annulment says the marriage never happened in the eyes of the law, so there's no divorce. That's the way I see it, too."

"That's not the way I remembered it. We still said our vows."

Mary Sue came out with milk-filled canning jars and handed each of us one. She sat next to Jere, her hands under her legs as if to keep them still.

"Daddy, Bess and I had a real nice talk. She still wants to be part of the family. She wants to help us."

He raised his eyebrows to her. "What do you know, little missy?"

"She wants to teach me how to read and write and then I can teach my brothers and sisters."

His gaze turned to me. "Bribery, huh?"

"No, that's not how this started, but I suppose it is a sort of trade-off. Mary Sue and I made a bargain."

"Why is this so important to you, Bess? Are you wanting to marry another man?"

This was the question I dreaded and had tossed around in my mind for days. If I told him yes, he might not sign for spite. If I told him no, he might have reason to delay his signature. For sake of argument, I decided to go somewhere in-between.

"I hope to get married some day. But as long as I'm legally married ... well, really Jere, doesn't it look worse to be married but not live together, than it does to just admit our mistake and move on with our lives? And to prove to you I'm not a total write-off, I want to help your daughter." I paused here, desperate for some solution, some compromise that would make this work. Could I take her back with me? I could send her to school from the Lighthouse. We had plenty of room. Besides, I admittedly relished the thought of taking Mary Sue out of these woods and educating her into my own creation of a fine intelligent woman. She had the longing for learning; I could see it in her eyes.

"I propose that I take Mary Sue back to Annan with me and I'll send her to school there."

"No," he said. He locked his arms across his chest.

"She can live with me at the Lighthouse. I'll take good care of her."

"No, I said. I need her here." His stone countenance irritated me. I could be callous too, I thought as my will to debate rose within me.

"Oh yes, you need her here alright, to be your slave, to cook and clean for you. You, who spoke out in many a women's conference. You who said women should be treated equally and have a vote and a right to say what they need in their lives. Mrs. Catt said you spoke beautifully. Why do you preach but not let one of your own practice it?"

"Bess, I ask no more from Mary Sue than I do from the rest of my younguns. That's not why I want her here. My Cherokee mother only had boys and she taught us all how to cook and clean. I can do that myself if I have to."

Mary Sue placed her hand on his arm. "Daddy, I've worked hard for you, now let me go and do something for me. And sign that paper and let Bess go. You hang on to things you don't even need. You just don't like letting go is all. You all will be fine and then when I come back, I can pass my learning on down. We can't stay ignorant, Daddy."

Well said, little missy, I thought as I watched him struggle with his emotions. He took a deep breath and let it out slowly, tapping on the arm of the swing with his knuckles.

"I suppose you'll be wanting to take her back with you today?" It was more a statement than a question.

"That would be easiest. My driver is waiting for me in the car."

"Well, bring him in for supper. She's not leaving on an empty stomach. It won't take her long to pack. She's your sheep now, I'll let you wool it."

He walked past me to the screen door without meeting my eyes, his face blank, but his shoulders drooped in defeat. He must hate me by now, I thought, wincing as the screen door slapped shut behind him. I've given him nothing but I've taken a great deal away.

Mary Sue smiled the first smile I'd seen on her, timid and shaky as if her mouth muscles were out of practice and couldn't quite lift. "We all will be just fine," she said in that soft southern drawl of hers.

I had no doubt that she at least would be. I had doubts about me.

I'd brought on more than I bargained for. I hadn't thought things through clearly, so desperate was I to get that annulment signed. Mary Sue was far behind in education for her age, so the school principal recommended fulltime tutoring until January's new term. They would test her then for possible enrollment in seventh grade. I was responsible for getting her up to that level before then.

When I told Thomas about this though, he could not see the tremendous burden I had taken on. "Good girl, Bess. You've never been responsible for someone else before. You may learn as much as this little girl does." He closed the door to his office and took me into his arms. "You're a very good girl indeed," he said, his tone as soft as his gaze. His head dipped and his lips pressed mine gently. I blinked in wonder and saw his eyes were wide open as well. He backed away an inch and I reached for more, letting my lashes flutter closed, only wanting to feel him, touch him. The kiss lingered longer, me savoring the flavor as I would with ice cream. My fingertips traced his cheeks and jawbone and were lost in his thick hair. When he heard the soft moan, he pulled away. He squeezed my shoulders and returned my questioning gaze with heavy-lidded eyes, their green depths warm as summer grass. "As soon as that Tennessee lawyer calls and says we're clear, we're getting married. Or else I'm going to make a bad girl out of you."

At that moment, I had no objection either way. I held true love and I now understood its meaning. To long for someone physically, well, I didn't know this could be possible with Thomas but here I stood hungering for more of his lips.

"Kiss me again and I might marry you," I said.

He grinned and gave me a light peck. "Oh, you'll marry me. You have to. I'm the boss and you have to do what I tell you."

"Yes, sir," I said, batting my eyes, not the least bit irritated by his advantage. He squeezed my shoulders again and returned to his desk. "Besides," I continued in that sweet little girl tone, "I'd like to see more of those burning eyes and flushing cheeks. They're far more interesting than that business mask you just put back on."

He let out a short laugh but picked up a stack of papers in spite of me. "I'll see what I can do. In the meantime, stop flirting with me. It's distracting and we have a day's work to do."

He put his spectacles on the end of his nose and sat still for a moment. "Tell you what I want you to do." He pulled some papers out of his stack and handed them to me. "Take these company requests for advertisements and write them from the Lighthouse. From now until Mary Sue starts to school in January, work from there. You'll have a full day teaching her as it is. Do your newspaper work while she is studying."

He opened a file folder and began reading. I remained in place, in a state of disbelief. He finally glanced up and must've read the hurt look on my face at such a dismissal. He sighed. "Bess, it's only temporary. It will work out best for all of us. Tell Lizzie to pull out my wife's old school textbooks. She taught the same elementary years and reading, writing, and arithmetic haven't changed. Remember: teach, don't preach, so save women's rights for last, if you can. I'll come over for dinner tonight and meet your little scholar."

Thomas returned to his papers and I walked out, feeling rejected. I would miss the harried newspaper deadlines and political discussions on his upcoming election. I had hoped I added more value to the workplace than this. I shook it off, feeling particularly sensitive to Thomas nowadays. Didn't he understand that I'd not only follow him anywhere, but I wanted to be beside him, under him, one with him? Mate and have children, if children were what he wanted. I was his - I could only hope he would treat my enlarged heart with care.

Without a smile, Mary Sue made a place for me beside her on the front porch step, tucking her thin cotton dress around her legs. She jerked her chin toward our colored gardener, Eddie. "If your nigger'd mixed wood ash with manure he'd get prettier blooms."

Eddie was the house gardener for as long as I'd been around here. According to Thomas, he worked for "peanuts", just wanting a little extra money for doing something he loved. He looked older than dirt but he said gardening kept him going. Lizzie said "thank God" for him, because her slave days hadn't trained her to work outside. She'd been an inside darkie as a youth, many years ago.

"Eddie does what he can with what he knows," I said. "There's at least an acre here that must be mowed and trimmed. Any blooms are a blessing. This estate is certainly not like it used to be - flowers, rose bushes, rock gardens - but he can only keep up to a few nowadays." I patted her knee. "How are you today? Sorry I couldn't join you for breakfast on your first day here, but I met with your school principal and then went to the newspaper office to pick up some work."

Mary Sue remained quiet with her chin on her hand, gazing out with misty light blue eyes. "I'm homesick."

With hesitance, I placed my arm around her shoulders. She didn't tense so I relaxed a little. "You haven't been away from home before, have you?" I figured as much when she said her goodbyes to her daddy and siblings. There wasn't a dry eye in the house. Their sobbing had irritated me so that I was tempted to cry out, *she's not dying for goodness sake!*

She shook her head, her eyes becoming more liquid. "I want to go home."

"Give it a chance, Mary Sue. This squeeze for home you feel will ease up, you'll see. When I was about your age, I traveled to New York City for a few weeks and I experienced the same thing. At the time, I was taking classes here at the Lighthouse on how to lobby for the women's vote. Mrs. Catt took our entire class of fifteen to the big city to meet with the city council and participate in a women's march. We marched right down Fifth Avenue, if you can imagine. I was not only homesick but also terrified of so many people and so much noise. I missed Mama, as I missed her in any marches I participated in. When I was eleven I saw her in a July Fourth march. I'd never seen her look so alive before, her sign raised high, her step was high and keeping rhythm to the school band. She looked like a pretty canary who had been let out of her cage for a short time to sing." I gazed out too, thinking I should go pay a visit to Mama. *Ah, but wait a minute – this is Jere's daughter! This should be an interesting introduction.*

"At least you have a mommy," Mary Sue pierced into my thoughts. "And I heard what you said to Daddy that morning you left us. About him loving your mommy. That's a lie. He only loved my mommy."

How had she heard that? I felt a surge of guilt.

"Yes, I'm certain he loved your mother. He's a caring man. But don't be homesick. Here you'll have less physical labor and more mental exercise. You may not want to go back."

She jerked her shoulder. I got the hint and moved my arm away. "I'm going back alright. Maybe not now, but as soon as I'm smart. I'm not a quitter and I'm not a deserter either."

I realized then that she would be my penance for leaving her father.

Thomas took her under his wing, as if needing to nurture. I had no idea where his paternal instincts came from. He gave me money as a father would to a mother saying, "Those pitiful dresses have to go or she'll be the brunt of jokes at school. Buy her what she needs; take her to your seamstress or dress shop or wherever you girls go these days." His attendance at our dinner table improved and his attention to Mary Sue's learning never ceased. As a result, I developed a report sheet to show him her subjects and progression. School textbooks had questions at the end of each chapter and these I graded and entered into the report. Thomas reviewed these carefully, commenting on good and bad, but only in an encouraging way. This was a reprieve for her and me, for I had the tendency to lose my patience. I had three school years to cram into a sometimes slow-moving, slow-speaking stubborn sally who was accustomed to her own daily schedule 'back home'. She resisted my efforts more than once.

On one such day we sat in the front parlor, Mary Sue at the big oak desk and I on the sofa. I handed the marked arithmetic quiz back to Mary Sue and wiped my brow with my handkerchief. Opening a window, I said, "Study your times tables again, Mary Sue. Work on your flash cards after dinner tonight and then re-do this. Most of these answers are wrong. Take out your lined paper now and practice your penmanship." I turned back toward the sofa to work on an advertisement for Lux laundry suds, sensing her eyes boring a hole through the back of my head. I turned back to face her. "Yes, Mary Sue?"

"I'm tired of these numbers. Mr. Todd, my school teacher back home, said girls shouldn't worry about numbers. He said many girls had lost their souls to such study. Besides, I can't think when we're sweating here like pigs. Back home, we always had cool breezes coming through. Why do towns have to stink and sweat?"

One more story about 'back home' and I was surely going to scream.

"I suppose you'll learn why towns sweat in geography," I threw back. "Luckily for both of us, that's one subject we don't have to worry about this year. As far as arithmetic hurting girl's spirits, this is a common misconception brought about by narrow-minded men." From my stack of books on the table, I brought out a poem written by Alice Duer Miller in 1915 called *The Maiden's View*. I read a verse out loud:

> 'Though permutations and combinations
> My woman's heart allure,
> I'll never study algebra,
> But keep my spirit pure.'

"She used satire to bring out the ridiculousness of anti-suffrage sentiment. Now doesn't it sound ridiculous to say that girls' spirits will be damned by learning numbers?"

Mary Sue shrugged. "You swore just now. That's not right either."

I sighed in resignation. "Well, let's just move on with this then."

"That's what Mr. Pickering always says, but he never says it like you do. He says it nice but you're just too bossy!" She folded her arms across her chest, her expression daring me to move her. She had none of the dark Indian characteristics of her father and I could only guess her dark brooding manner, fair skin and light blue eyes had come from her mother's side.

I returned her stare, neither one of us willing to give in to look away. I was becoming angrier by the moment. I narrowed my eyes at her. "I do not sweat like a pig and you are one lucky hillbilly to have a town that is willing to take you in and teach you what 'back home' should have taught you years ago!"

"Maybe so," Mary Sue drawled. "But at least back home we don't just have a lot of hot air blowing. If we do, it comes from the weather, not from people."

I sat down hard on the sofa, my eyes not leaving her face. She at least had the courtesy to blush from this last insinuation and our flushed faces raised the temperature in the parlor by ten degrees, I'm certain of it. "Stop acting like an ignorant—"

A bell tinkled outside. Charlie's bell. A look through the window verified his presence on his bike, pulling his ice cream wagon. Good ol' Charlie with his white hair, white suit, and vanilla ice cream. He and his cooling balm would soothe the inflammation of our minds. I hesitated in rewarding her bad behavior with such a treat, but I couldn't, with any conscience, eat ice cream in front of her, so I swallowed my stinging - or, according to Mary Sue, *stinking* - vanity.

I motioned with my head for her to follow me. "We'll both feel better after an ice cream."

She stood up unhurriedly. "What is ice cream?"

I tried to calm my urge to run out doors after Charlie, before he got away. "You've never had ice cream?" I could understand her never riding a train before our trip, but ice cream?

"Stop talking to me like I'm ignorant. I ain't."

"Fine Mary Sue, you're not ignorant. Let's hurry."

I literally ran down the boardwalk after him, so happy I was for a cool treat and a break from Mary Sue's heated glare.

Charlie had mounded two cones and accepted payment before Mary Sue sauntered to the wagon. I made the introductions and Charlie and I both watched her expectantly.

She licked gingerly at it, like a cat might for water. "It's not as good as a snow cone."

"What is a snow cone?" I asked and then bit my tongue.

Her eyes lit at her opportunity. "You've never had a snow cone before?" She imitated the same unbelieving tone I had used.

Charlie patted her head. "With that accent, you come from the hills, don't you girl? Yesiree you do, and snow cones taste fine indeed. You bring in new-fallen snow, mound it in a bowl, and pour fresh cream over it." He winked at me. "It's almost as good as my wares but not quite. The only difference is I don't have to wait for winter's cold to make it. Modern technology gave me ice in warm weather when folks most want to eat frozen things."

Yes, try to top that 'back home', I thought. I smiled at Charlie's deeply wrinkled mug, and at our own small victory. I was snatching them however I could.

I was beginning to believe that Thomas and I would never wed. Our discussions became superficial, only surrounding our external events, never our internal emotions. I repeatedly played over in my mind his proposal to me and how much more romantic this could have been, if not for that one technicality. I had poured a bucket of water on his passion for me and I seemed to be having difficulties in waiting for that water to dry enough to start another spark. I hoped his flame hadn't died out altogether. A goodnight kiss on the cheek each night after dinner hardly gave indication he desired me.

He had not yet mentioned any calls from Mr. McCorriston and my pride in appearing too eager would not allow me to ask him. So I spent my time with him listening to everything I didn't want to hear and saying what I didn't care to talk about. I wanted to be grounded with meaningful issues, such as love and fulfilling my longings, but for some reason he was not allowing us to touch the ground. We were floating in newspaper facts and figures, campaign numbers and votes, school reports and grades. Perhaps he looked at me differently now, as a married woman already given to another man. Perhaps he no longer saw me as "an innocent dispassionate suffragist trying to right the homes of women but with little understanding, for the poor girl has no home of her own", as he'd once introduced me, wearing that mischievous grin. Perhaps he relished the idea of saving me, only to find out someone else had found me first. But I hadn't been saved then, and I didn't need to be saved now. Only loved. Perhaps his image of me was no longer of a virgin, pure and white, but of a divorcee, tarnished with Tennessee coal.

I could no longer pretend that all was fine with the world and none of it mattered to me. Thomas mattered and he mattered a great deal, more than I wished he had. I began to wish I didn't have such a strong attachment to someone so tangible, so real as to be physically painful. It was much simpler to love the floating image of Billy, who I could move to the front or the back of my mind at will. It was much easier to work the theories of suffrage, than to work the real life issues of caring for others. Love might fulfill me, but it could also bog me down and I certainly didn't want to drag and shuffle my feet when grounded, only walk lightly with my feet under my control.

These were my thoughts as I sat at dinner one such evening, only slightly aware of Lizzie and Mary Sue's chatter to Thomas over their plates. While Mary Sue sat erect and tense, watching every move Thomas made, he seemed as distracted as I, his eyes darting to my distant stare to see if I was still there.

"Bess, you're being quiet this evening," Thomas finally said.

"She's probably tired from pushing me around all day," Mary Sue said to Thomas, those woeful eyes looking for sympathy. "Thomas, help me with my arithmetic tonight. I'm having trouble with long division. You're the smartest person I know." She gave him her only smile of the day.

Lizzie's furrowed brow deepened. "Child, you say, *Mr. Pickering*, would you *please* help me. Make it a question and use your manners. Don't go telling Mr. Pickering what to do. You know your place."

I didn't know if Lizzie noticed, but Mary Sue seemed to always look straight through Lizzie like she was a large hole in the wall. Mary Sue's pleading eyes remained fixed on his face.

"Would you, Thomas? Maybe you could help me every night and I'd get to school a lot faster." Thomas hesitated and Lizzie appeared to read his thoughts.

"Child, Mr. Pickering is tired too. Miss Bess, I hope you're not too tired," Lizzie said to me, "I'll need help changing and washing that bed linen upstairs. Mr. Pickering, sir, that family of darkies you sent up here from Georgia – you know, the ones where her husband was lynched? Well that Mrs. Cosman had a time with her five children last night. That little Isaac, Miss Bess? Well, he wet the bed and that sent his brothers to sleep in the other two bedrooms too. She can't control her own children. She thinks because she comes up here, she's in high cotton now. I'm right glad, Mr. Pickering, that you found her a job and a place of her own. I can't sleep when there's so much foot-stomping above me. Who's this no-good man with them that Isaac calls 'uncle'? I found him sniffin' in the kitchen like a blind dog in the smokehouse. They're no-good niggers in my opinion."

"Lizzie!" I said. "Aren't you feeding them?" There's a sign by the front door for the coloreds to go around the back and enter into Lizzie's kitchen where they eat their meals.

She dipped her hand to me. "Don't go up on your soapbox, Miss Bess." She scooted her chair from the table. "I'm just tired like the rest of you. My day is gone. We'll change those sheets tomorrow. Goodnight."

With a worried brow, Thomas watched her hunched backside shuffle to the kitchen, her cane thumping a loud support. "She's not well," he mumbled. "She's getting too old to keep up with the Lighthouse." He drummed his fingers on the table for a moment. "Bess, meet me in the library. I wish to discuss a private matter with you."

As I followed Thomas, I felt relief in hearing the clatter of dishes. Mary Sue was going to wash the dishes on her own. Good; one less evening to prod.

Along side one table lamp, sat the only one winged-back chair in the small library, surrounded by bookshelves. This he sat in, while I folded my hands in front of me, at a loss as to what to do. He showed me by patting his knees. I raised my eyebrows in surprise, but he insistently patted his legs again. "Close the door and come here." I did just that. "Now sit here on my lap like a good little girl."

"No, Thomas, I—"

"Don't argue. Do as I say. You're my fiancé, aren't you?"

"Well, I don't know, Thomas. That's something we need to discuss, isn't it?"

He pulled me down to where he intended me to sit. He wrapped his arms around my waist and looked up into my eyes. "Don't look so disheartened. I still want to marry you. You're a free woman now."

"Mr. McCorriston?"

"He sent the documents last week."

"Last week? This is my life you're holding, Thomas!"

"I know very well what I'm holding," he said and squeezed. His eyes heated in that sensuous way of his.

"Thomas, don't toy with me." I attempted to get up.

"Sit still. We need to talk." He held on firm.

"I'm listening."

"Oh, so I'm to begin, am I? This is unusual. Fine." He gave my arm a light kiss. "Let's set a date, shall we?"

"A date for what?" I said coyly.

"You know damn well for what," he said.

There were questions running through my mind that I wanted answered, like why did he wait so long to tell me the news of the annulment? But to query him might only dampen his fervor toward me and I had done enough of that before now. I took a deep breath and relaxed. I returned his gaze and let his warmth come in. I smoothed his hair back, looking closely at the gray and blond strands, the gray undeniably taking over like weeds in a garden.

He backed his head away. "Don't look too close at this old man, or you'll change your mind." He pulled my chin down so that I would meet his eyes. "You do realize that I'm twenty years older than you, don't you?"

"That much?" I pretended surprise. Mocking Mary Sue's southern drawl, I said. "Then I reckon I'll have to call you daddy."

He laughed good-naturedly and squeezed me hard. "Ah, there's the Bess I know. Your spirit seemed strangely stifled here lately but it has miraculously re-emerged."

"All it takes is a caring hug, Thomas. Women are not so mysterious but you should know that, being the world-traveled reporter. You certainly are talking like a reporter. 'Spirit miraculously re-emerged'? Is re-emerged a word?"

"Don't doubt a world-traveled reporter." He flicked his thumb under my chin. "If you want a report, here is mine. 'Bess Wright, daughter of Mr. and Mrs. Robert Wright, has gladly, ecstatically, blissfully agreed to be the obedient wife to Mr. Thomas Pickering of 18 Pickering Lane. Her address was mysteriously not disclosed. The joyful wedding date is set for Christmas Day, in the year of our Lord, nineteen hundred and twenty.'"

"That's only two weeks away!"

His business mask surfaced straight away and his hold around my waist relaxed. "Because we should be married before the election. People are beginning to question our relationship, for obvious reasons. My dear old opponent, George, made matters worse today. He made some disparaging remarks on the radio. I suppose you haven't heard – I must buy a radio for this old house. But you'll read about it tomorrow." He paused and held firm to me again, as if tensed I might run away. "He claims I'm having an extra-marital affair with a married woman."

"But how can that be, Thomas? I'm the only woman you're seeing, right?" Thoughts flashed. He sent me out of his office to work here. I only saw him at dinner. I narrowed my eyes. "Or am I?"

Thomas chuckled. "He's talking about you, girl."

"*Me?* We're not having an *affair*. How extremely vulgar on his part. And I'm not married. Well yes, I suppose I could have been considered married, though I certainly don't look at myself that way. Oh my goodness, Thomas, did he give my name?"

"Not right away. At first he only referred to you as my assistant. But of course when asked who that was, he gave your name, yes. I think he enjoyed the suspense of it all. Luckily, or unluckily, he only knew your maiden name." He looked away, likely not wanting to see my head explode.

"*On the radio?* But oh my heavens, no one *knew* I was married and now *everyone* in town knows? Papa. He listens to it constantly. Now he and Mama know. How did George find out?"

Thomas shrugged, more I think to shake off my horrified stare than to show nonchalance. "Who knows? We work around nosy reporters. They can smell a secret. Maybe one was nosing around my office while you and I were talking. Walls have big ears in a newspaper office. I should have been more discreet, but I trusted my own staff. I hope whoever ratted, got a tidy sum from George."

He shifted my dead weight on his legs. I sat slumped - heavier with the weight of the world now on my shoulders. He cleared his throat. "I owe you an apology. If it weren't for my running for mayor, this would never have leaked out."

I turned straight ahead and stared at a shelf of books I had at one time coveted; Rousseau's *The Social Contract* ('Man is born free, and everywhere he is in chains'), a collection of poetry and ballads by Robert Burns (*'My love is like a red red rose/That's newly sprung in June;/ My love is like the melodie/That's sweetly play'd in tune.'*)

My love. Here. Not wanting him to see my disappointment, I waved a shaky hand at him. "Oh Thomas, that's not your fault. My supposed marriage is what has probably ruined your chances to win."

"Yes, I know. I was hoping you'd get around to thinking my way."

"What?" I turned to retort, but seeing his roguish grin return, I gave in to a laugh of my own.

"So, you owe me," he said. "You have to marry me now, to clear up both our names. We won't be able to face family and friends if you don't."

I watched his lips and those crooked teeth on the bottom and wondered why - the top ones were straight. I loved that mouth and what came out, and that grin that made me feel playful.

I sighed and leaned against him, laying my head on his shoulder. I examined the gold buttons on his vest contentedly. "I must go out tonight. But first I only want you to hold me."

"Go out? Where to at this hour?"

"Mama and Papa must be wondering about my marriage. I need to go explain."

He pulled out his pocket watch. "It's past nine. It's too late now. You can go tomorrow."

I took this from his fingers and touched the gold engraving. *Love cannot be measured with time. It is forever. Your loving wife, Cady.*

I pushed away the green-eyed monster. It seemed the more I cared, the more this monster sat between us. I switched my thoughts to my own past. "Billy sent me a watch on a wrist band from overseas. These bands were issued during the war so the servicemen wouldn't lose them. I've seen some men wearing them since. Perhaps I'll buy you one someday."

"This pocket watch works perfectly," he said and returned the gold disk to its vest pocket. "Billy, eh? Have you let go of your dead war hero? An ace pilot is something to be proud of."

"I'm not sure I had him to begin with. I never claimed ownership, although at times I regretted that. Billy was just always … there, in some form or another. Somehow this kept me attached for the longest time, knowing I could travel into the great unknown but have that line to guide me back. We all need something to hold, don't you think? But eventually Billy dissolved into thin air. Long after he died. When I realized this, I took the watch to his parents; they are the ones who are proud of him. They were far more appreciative than I to hold a time piece that had once wrapped Billy's wrist and absorbed his pulse. His mother listened to the ticking with her eyes aglow as if she were hearing his heart beat. I didn't give them his letters though – I burned those. That was my way of letting go." I wanted to add, *Could you do as much, Thomas?* but held my tongue. I was comfortable in his arms and didn't want to be pushed away.

Holding my tongue was the right thing to do. He held me tighter and lifted my chin to his. His kiss grew intense, his lips and tongue exploring and demanding. His breath and mine rushed and mingled and our nostrils flared for more but I dared not part with his mouth. I sucked and nibbled like a hungry lamb on a teat. His hand caressed my … well, he'd gone over the line and I was too heated to care. I felt his physical longing and my curiosity grew with it. I grew vividly aware of it all. To absorb his desire and give it back – was that love-making? I dared not ask; he would think I was far too presumptuous. We are not married, I reminded myself, and my immodesty may alarm him

"Bess, I want you," he whispered into my ear. "Would you—"

"Mr. Pickering, would you—"

I snapped to attention and stood up at the same time that Thomas pushed me. I stumbled a little as I brushed down my skirt. I had not the nerve to face toward the door where Mary Sue stood, but saw enough from the corner of my eye. I also spotted Thomas folding his hands across his lap to hide his bulge. I was mortified. Such an act of intimacy to be seen by such a young girl! Kissing – in his lap! I had not shared my engagement with her or anyone, waiting until the annulment was final. Any announcements before that seemed to smell of bigamy.

"Now I know why you left my daddy," Mary Sue said. Her voice was cold, monotone.

I turned to face her but she wasn't looking at me; she was staring at Thomas with an open hurt on her expression.

"Mary Sue, Thomas and I are only recently engaged. I told your father I wished to be free to marry."

"You're going to get hitched?" she asked Thomas.

"You and Lizzie will be the first to know, as soon as we finalize a date for the marriage ceremony." He stood up, obviously more suitable now to do so. "Bring your arithmetic to the back parlor. I'll see if I can't make it easier for you."

Excusing myself, I was decidedly relieved to have a task on hand to keep my hands occupied. I walked up the stairs to remove the bedroom sheets Lizzie had asked for. Until truly exhausted, I would not be able to sleep well tonight. There were too many questions banging around in my head wanting release. Thomas had mixed so much of good and bad emotions with black and white, in true reporter fashion, that all looked gray to me.

The slippers I had changed into muffled my approach to the back parlor. The bundle of sheets still in my arms, a scent of urine wafting to my nostrils, a hint of something more burning my ears, I stopped short before entering.

"But why do you have to marry her?" Mary Sue's voice came through in a higher pitch than normal.

"Keep your voice down, girl! There goes your education if Bess hears you talking this way."

"Why won't you answer my question?" Her tone had turned down to soft.

"Because, little one, the answer should be obvious. She is a dear friend."

"Friends don't make babies. Lovers do. She's too old for babies. I'm not."

I clamped my hand over my mouth to quiet my gasp of air. A pillowcase fell from my unraveling bundle. I stood nailed to the floor awaiting his answer. There was silence for a few moments.

"Mary Sue, this love you say you have for me, well I don't believe it. You miss your father and I am that father figure. You're also missing home and I perfectly understand homesickness for the south. That's why I go down there quite regularly. You're also sixteen and should be dating boys your own age. I meant it when I said I loved you back, but not like this. I love you as a daughter or niece. That's what we will do!" He said as if he had a bright idea. "You may call me Uncle Thomas. How's that?"

Another silence and then a muffled sound like two people –

"Do daughters kiss like that, Mr. Pickering?"

"Where did you learn that," he muttered.

"From a boy down the holler from me. I'm not as young as you think I am."

"I suppose studying arithmetic is out of the question now."

I heard rustling of papers and a chair scoot on the wood flooring. I attempted to back away but my legs were lead.

"Don't go, Thomas!" she loudly whispered. I dropped my load onto the floor and stepped forward, drawn like a moth to the fire.

"I will go, young lady," he said, his voice low, his tone blessedly scolding, "and you will go to bed and we both will forget this conversation. You are an attractive girl and I don't need any more frustrations than I already have. Remember that or Bess will not fill your head with matter, but have it on a platter!" He chuckled. "Not bad, eh? Chin up. Sit up straight. Give me that pretty smile of yours. That's a good girl."

"Will you kiss me goodnight?"

"You're a stubborn lassie, aren't you?" I heard a peck. "There's a kiss on the cheek for my little niece. Study hard. Nighty-night."

He almost ran into me as he came out into the hall, placing his hat on his head. His finger went to his lips to keep me quiet but there was no risk of that; I could only stand as a stone statue and stare at him. He took me by the hand and led me down the hall to the entrance way and outside to the front porch.

"You heard?" he said, still in that low tone of voice he used with her.

I nodded.

"She's just a homesick little girl, Bess. Don't look so stricken. You must pretend you don't know anything. The school year is only two weeks away and once she is in school and meets boys—" He squeezed my elbow. "You're not taking this seriously, I hope. You look pale in this moonlight."

"You kissed her," was all that came out of me, like a sleepwalker might mutter in a bad dream.

He scowled at me. "What would you have me do? Slap her?"

"No, that will be my job," I hissed. "But you could have told her how we feel for each other." His dark profile became blurred.

He peered into my face. "How do we feel about each other?"

"Well, I certainly know how I feel!"

"I don't. How do you feel, Bess? I'd like to know."

"Oh Thomas, you've opened my eyes and my heart so much it hurts!"

"That's a start. Go on."

"I love you." What a release this brought! I threw my arms around his neck and hid my flushed face in his neck.

He hugged me tight. "So, you love me then?"

I sniffed. "I must - I'm only happy with you. This house only feels like a home when you're here. I can't believe I'm saying this, but it's so true. And it feels so good to say it."

"Then say it again."

"I love you, Thomas."

"I love you, Bess."

"Then tell her, Thomas. Tell her how you feel and then I want to send her back home. That's all she talks about anyway."

He grasped my shoulders and pulled me away. "Bess, the jealous woman, I would never have guessed! I'm enjoying your sudden affections, but let's be mature about this. I think Mary Sue understands my feelings for you. If she is blind to it, then soon you and I will be living here as man and wife and she will have to see the truth." He lifted my chin to face him. His hat brim further shadowed his eyes and nose. I could only watch his mouth move in the dim light; lips that had kissed me so passionately so short a time ago, and then had kissed another. "She needs us. We can't kick her out now. Give her a chance to grow up."

I nodded. He leaned down to kiss me and I turned and gave him my cheek, not wanting residue from her mouth on mine. I could see the disappointment drawing tight around his mouth as he pulled away. He silently headed toward his motor car. The green-eyed monster was back and between us, only now he held both the ghost of Cady and a real live girl. I would have to think more about this.

I was grateful to have a mission the next morning. Mary Sue had been left to her own studying devices, papers and books strewn about her in the front parlor. School admission tests were only weeks away and I had little hope she'd pass. She gave me her customary scowl as I gave her the assignments and then I was on my way to Mama's house.

I walked in to find Mama feeding Papa his breakfast in their bedroom. Mama jumped up from the edge of the bed and turned off the radio as I said my hellos. Quiet settled around us and Mama's countenance relaxed with it. She rewarded me with a genuine smile. Papa eyed me accusingly as he chewed his egg. His skin had grown more sallow since last I visited, his eyes more sunken. Mama's worried expression and pallid complexion gave me further notice they hadn't slept well.

When asked how they were, Mama shook her head. "We had a long night." She brought a glass up to his lips. "Drink your milk," she said as to a child. "You need this."

He took one sip and then turned to me. "I heard about you on the radio yesterday. Perhaps you can explain why you're smearing the good name of Wright. What will the neighbors think now?"

Mama shook her head and sighed. She returned the glass to his tray. "I tried to explain to him it wasn't true, but you know how he is with that radio."

I sat in the chair on the other side of the bed and returned her sigh. Inhaling their weariness wore on me. "Some things are not true, some things are. It is hard to tell the difference. I wish I could say the radio was all lies." I came prepared with my handkerchief and this I fiddled with nervously. Telling them was going to be harder than I had anticipated.

Mama raised another bite of egg to Papa's lips but his attention stayed on me. She sighed again, not seeming to have the strength to finish feeding him. She removed his napkin from his chest and his tray from his lap and this she set on top of the radio cabinet.

That got his attention. "Ruby dear, do not take the chance of food falling onto my radio knobs. Take it out please."

She took the tray to the hallway floor by the door. Returning to sit again on the edge of the bed, she brushed off his sheet and smoothed his blanket. She moved methodically, as if out of a long habit, without thinking. From my youth I recalled how he had insisted on obedience from her and he would have it no other way, but at what cost? Did she love him after all these years of marriage? Did this question even matter to Papa? Did only her allegiance to him matter? Perhaps I wasn't to judge so harshly; this may be the course for all long-term marriages. Mates attached only at the hands, to lift and feed during the day, to pat to sleep at night. After my own fitful sleep the night before, with Thomas and little 'niece' spinning in my mind like a merry-go-round, marriage appeared bleaker by the moment. I would simply have to tell him I couldn't marry him.

"I know for a fact that the radio tells lies," Mama said, finally resting her hands in her lap and turning to me. "I heard advertised a beauty oil that if rubbed onto the face, would take away twenty years of wrinkles and lines." She touched these with her fingertips. "I am living proof this is a lie."

"Ruby dear, I told you that was a ridiculous purchase and if asked as I should have been, you would have been forbidden. Age is a natural progression and we're now in our old age. Why, at forty-eight I'm nearing my life expectancy. You dear, are not far behind me at forty."

"Fine, I'll give you another example. Mrs. Potts' Irons. Yes," she poked his leg, her spirit seeming to perk up in the banter. "Her Sad Irons were to make ironing so much easier than the old-style flat irons. This would reduce my ironing time in half so that I may spend more time in my well-equipped engine room of the home, my kitchen. Ha, the wooden handle broke in half! It reduced my time all right. To nothing! Now I must order another one. All lies, the radio is all lies."

I didn't have the heart to tell her I wrote that advertisement.

"You must send Bess out to buy you a Hotpoint Iron then. I just heard it advertised this morning. It has a cantilever handle that will save exertion all through your body. It requires electricity, however."

"You wouldn't allow a receptacle in the kitchen, Robert, remember? I suppose I could unplug your radio and iron up here."

"Now you're getting ridiculous."

"We could have a twin receptacle installed. Aimee has one in her kitchen in the same space as her single outlet and can plug in two appliances at once."

I was becoming restless. I had to jump in or Papa would be asleep soon. "Papa, what exactly did you hear on the radio yesterday that upset you?"

Mama glared openly at me, her puckered brow questioning my question.

I gave her a feeble smile but she didn't accept it. She turned her attention to Papa who cleared his throat as was customary when he felt he had something important to say. "A radio talk show. Most interesting. Candidate for mayor, Mr. Groves, said his opponent, Mr. Pickering, lived in immorality. He couldn't be trusted in public when he held such secrets in private. Something of that nature. Well, that sparked my interest. George Groves is a deacon in our church and I should vote for a man of God. However, bad judgment prevailed for I intended to vote for Mr. Pickering and since your mama has won such an important privilege, I directed her to do the same, trusting your judgment. He's always been good to you, gave you a home and employment. Your mama had assured me many times that he didn't live there in the same house."

"He doesn't," I broke in.

"Well, what I'm hearing is that the two of you – but that's not the worst of it ..." His hands clenched and unclenched.

"Robert, this is silly," Mama said, patting his leg. "You're going to get upset all over again over lies."

"You heard that I'm already married, didn't you?"

"Bess has an explanation for all of this, don't you Bess?" Mama said, her eyes pleading with mine to agree with her.

"I have one but you won't like it."

Mama's shoulders sagged a little. Papa closed his eyes. What if the news of my secret marriage to Jere weakened my father to death? How would Mama ever forgive me? How could I forgive myself? Besides, I hurriedly reasoned, I'm no longer married. Mr. McCorriston said the annulment meant the marriage no longer existed. I could live with that.

"You're right, Mama, it is all lies. Today as we speak, I am not married. But ..." My hand clutched my handkerchief. "Mr. Pickering and I are engaged to be married."

Relief wiped Mama's worried brow smooth. "Bess, you are going to be *married*! See, Robert, I told you she would marry some day."

Papa gave me a weak smile. "That fellow must be as old as I am. You certainly took a damn long time to do it."

Mama frowned at him for his use of language and turned a smile to me. "Bess, I'm happy for you. And to Mr. Pickering of all people. He is a respected man and he will make a fine husband. He certainly made Cady one; I remember envying her for his support in her fight for women's suffrage. Why, he had an open debate with this same Mr. Groves in City Hall Park just over that very thing, his arm fast around Cady, and their love for one another there for all to see. Oh and my first ride in a motor car was with Mr. Pickering. I can still remember the smell of the leather and the sound of that engine. We seemed to be moving so fast."

"Too fast for my liking, if I recall, dear," Papa said with a grimace. "You did not receive a warm reception when you arrived home in that contraption."

"We won't discuss that any further," Mama said. "I did what I had to do and you did what you had to do."

"What did you do?" I asked, glad to have the conversation switch.

"I spanked her," Papa said.

"Robert, don't," Mama said.

"Just like the spoiled child that she was," Papa continued, ignoring his wife's embarrassed blush. "If a wife doesn't know how to behave, it is the man's responsibility to teach her."

"Papa, you hit Mama?" More of a scold than surprise. I had heard as much coming from their bedroom when around eleven years of age.

"Bess, that was a long time ago," Mama said. "We won't discuss this any further. Your father and I both grew up after the birth of our Little Cady, may God rest her soul. This strong heroine medication your father takes is making him blurt out whatever is on his mind."

"It's a truth serum," Papa said. "Something you and Bess should be taking from the sound of it."

"Have you set a date yet?" Mama asked.

"Yes, it's set for Christmas Day. We haven't discussed the details." For example, can I go through with it? I added silently.

"Mercy! So soon and on Christ's birthday. I suppose you could wear your grandmother's dress. I was married in it. Light blue, blousy sleeves, high neck, lace collar, scratchy if I recall."

"How appealing," I said with a sardonic smile.

"Of course," Mama said, understanding. "More and more girls wear white these days."

Papa closed his eyes. A wedding for his oldest daughter; something he had waited for, for a very long time, and he would not be able to give me away to my husband. Of course he no longer owned me to give away, but any walk down an aisle would be impossible for him at this stage. I would have to think on this some more.

"Can I go?" asked Mary Sue.

"Definitely not," I said.

"After dishes," Lizzie said to her, "I'll help you study."

Mary Sue rolled her eyes. "Darkies can't *read*!" She ran out of the room.

A night out with Thomas alone! And to a movie house! What had taken us so long to do this? We were so accustomed to routine, as if marriage had already taken place.

Without discussion we turned toward downtown, instead of toward the motor car. We trekked the ten blocks that I took to and from the newspaper office, while Thomas gave me his day's campaigning events, brightly colored with anecdotes. "I challenged him on the facts in his story – his brain is like a coconut in a boxcar – and told him to stop pissing on my leg and telling me it's raining." He seemed more relaxed when not under the watchful eye of Lizzie and Mary Sue. They both appeared ready to answer his beckoning, but for different reasons. He seemed more comfortable as "boss" in the office, than as "master" of the house.

Outside the movie house stood a cardboard figure, as tall as I, of a man in baggy, tattered pants, worn down shoes that were ridiculously large, a coat and vest, and a weather-beaten derby hat, with the inscription I AM HERE TODAY. Charlie Chaplin dolls and comic books were in the shops so I certainly wasn't surprised he was here, too. Thomas promised that Chaplin's first full-length feature film, *The Kid*, would be well worth our walk. He was right as usual. Charlie as the infamous Tramp, finds a baby and raises him on his own until five years later when the boy's mother wants him back.

"The scenes of a man caring for a growing boy were absurd and I didn't know whether to laugh or cry," I said as we exited the dark inner room. I dabbed at my eyes with a handkerchief, blinking at the bright lights of the lobby.

"Looks to me like you made a decision," said Thomas. "Here, permit me to bring your smile back." And there on the sidewalk he imitated the comic walk of The Tramp, feet out to the sides, short struts, however Thomas reminded me more of a toy soldier whose wind-up march was winding down.

I laughed in spite of the passers-by. "I didn't know you were such a fan of this man." I tugged on his arm to stop, please. "You have succumbed to the 'Chaplinitis' going around."

He tucked my hand around his elbow and patted it as if to say, there, there, no more foolishness. "I've been watching his films since 1914. *The Immigrant, The Tramp, The Idle Class.* He loves to play on our sympathies for the poor, and our intolerance of the rich. He understands both. He grew up as an impoverished orphan in England and now is making more money than any actor in the world, perhaps more than any one person in the world, at ten thousand a week. He writes and directs all his films and his past continues to creep into those slum scenes, reminding me of Dickens novels. You haven't been to a Chaplin film?"

"I haven't been to a movie house before. I didn't understand the attraction to a silent movie. You know me; speeches are the best form of communication. But I was truly amazed at how he could convey emotions so well through facial expressions."

"I thought the story suited you. That's why I brought you here."

"On the contrary. Facial expressions are not my strong suit."

"I'm talking about Mary Sue, dear. She's much like this little boy, longing for love and attention, wanting to belong. Although you're not her mother, she needs your nurturing to bring out the best in her."

"Thomas, you're being as melodramatic as Charlie tonight. What Mary Sue longs for is to go back home and she'd love it if you'd go back with her. And not as Uncle Thomas either."

Thomas looked down at me with a father's disapproving scowl. "I think you, too, have the potential for melodrama."

"And I think you have the potential to look at her as a little girl when in fact she's a grown woman. And a mean-spirited one at that. She spells trouble, Thomas, and I don't like it." My tone sounded harsh. This conversation had slipped down into our first argument.

"And I think you are jealous, and this is very unbecoming. Particularly when the jealousy is of a poor little hillbilly."

"And I think you are insensitive, particularly when you want to be an uncle."

I had hit rock bottom and I looked up for a way out of this banter. I saw him smiling.

"I'd prefer to be a father. Do you think that someday you could help me out in that department?"

I smiled back, relieved he gave me a lift. "As a mother, you mean?"

"That would be the most enjoyable way, yes."

"This requires marriage you know."

"To keep the gossip down, yes. I'm prepared to do things in their proper order."

"I suppose I could accommodate your request. But do you think a baby should be placed in a sling, hanging from the rafters as Charlie did tonight?"

"No, but a sling would be necessary to hang from your back, so that the baby doesn't slow you down in marching for your next cause."

"Oh, but a baby would settle me down for certain, Thomas."

"I'm not so certain as you. I think when you were old enough to walk, your mother taught you instead to march. You may know no other way. We'll see."

The wintry night and the strong breeze cleared my clouded mind of the movie's events. We walked by Hullabaloo's where the music's blare and smoky stale air seemed in competition with its customers to get outside. We walked more briskly and soon the downtown stretched out and settled into sleepy homes and fresh currents of air.

We stopped on the boardwalk in front of the Lighthouse, aptly named tonight for its warm light reaching out through all the windows, more so than just the two on the front porch that always burned. Always a signal that one of us was out. The front door would also be unlocked as always in case a frightened woman needed shelter in a hurry.

"I've been thinking," Thomas said, his hands on my shoulders. "When this becomes our home, it will only be our home. Do you understand? No more Lighthouse. No more woeful women. No more debates. No more back parlor strategies to beat the men. No more war. I want peace. I've earned it and so have you. I'm entering the sunset of my life and I wish to spend it quietly with you over morning coffee and afternoon tea. No more speakeasies. Understood?"

"Not even the smallest smidgeon of drink at your birthday parties?" I asked, batting my eyes, playing the tease.

"If you like. But remember, you'll be my wife then and I won't stop at a kiss."

I gave him a light one on the cheek and whispered, "I'll hold you to that promise."

The wind whipped colder around my legs when he walked away, as if he held the only heat in the night. I gazed up to the white stone and blue shutters of his manor, the promise of warmth coming through the lighted windows, and thought of the many times I had hobbled up to the door in exhaustion from marches and petitions and travels. It had opened its doors to the weak and the weary, the tears and the fears, and to the strong ready to right the wrong. It would all be over soon. But it would always be a Lighthouse to me.

A letter arrived from the Annan Elementary School. January and seventh grade loomed ahead. I found Mary Sue at the back parlor's roll-top desk writing letters to her father and each of her siblings. These letters seemed to be getting longer and longer and her face told the story of another case of homesickness. Misty eyes and a down-turned mouth, one hand propping up the head as the other hand wrote in her large block letters. She had dressed in one of her two old "back-home" calico dresses, faded, loose around the waist with no belt. I hoped school and friends would make living away from home easier – if she passed the test. I thrust the letter out to her.

"This is the moment we've been waiting for, Mary Sue. Open it!"

"It don't matter," she said, at once irritating me with her southern slang. Her pen continued its slow movements of letters into words, words into sentences.

"Of course it matters, Mary Sue. We've worked - you've worked hard for this." I waited. My arm dropped to my side. Why was she always bursting my bubbles? "Don't you want to see if you passed?"

"I doubt if I did, and if I did, it don't matter."

"Why?" My voice had gone up an octave and I stood ready to shake her. She had labored through a four-hour exam. "Mary Sue, what is wrong?"

"Everything. I don't like it here, first of all."

Stupid hillbilly, horse's ass, stubborn mule … no matter what moved around her, she seemed determined to stand still.

I placed my hands on my hips ready for another debate. "Why do you continue to bite the hand that feeds you?"

She threw her pen down and folded her arms across her chest as always, accepting the challenge. Her light blue eyes met mine head on. "Because you might feed me poison someday. You don't like me. Lizzie don't like me either. You both just boss me around. Write this, Mary Sue. Wash that, Mary Sue. You look at what I'm wearing, you look at what I'm doing, but never at what I'm feeling. Daddy always asked me how I was feeling." This last statement brought on tears. "Besides, my daddy needs me. My brother is real sick." She sniffed noisily.

I had an urge to correct her grammar, but with one goal: to get Mary Sue educated and out of here. I hadn't realized until now I must go through her heart to do that. I felt inept as I looked down at her tear-stained face. I didn't know how to attach through emotion. My only way of reaching out to my sister was through a newspaper article, for goodness sake. How much better could I be to a stubborn mule? Somehow I needed to go deeper. This effort made me weary and I sat with a sigh in the chair across from her.

"Do they know why your brother's ill?"

"Doctor thinks he got polio."

"Oh dear, that is serious. But really, there's nothing you can do about it."

"Maybe there is. Maybe I can help. But I can't from here."

I leaned forward to where I could meet her at eye-level. "First we'll open this letter and see if you passed your exams. We'll write your father then and give him the news, and ask him what he thinks is best. Do you remember what Mr. McCorriston told us on our way back to Nashville from your home? He told us that new schools are

being built in Tennessee ever since the compulsory school attendance law was passed in 1913. If that's so, then perhaps within the
next year, you'll be able to continue with high school back home.
Let's not give up so soon, agreed?"

I waved the envelope in front of her as a tantalizer. "It may be
good news!"

She snatched it from my hands and opened with a faster speed
than I could have hoped for. Her mouth moved silently as her eyes
moved across each line. I expected the worst, while waiting for a sign.

Suddenly her arms were about my neck and she was crying.
Crying harder than I'd witnessed before.

"Oh Mary Sue, we'll try again. You'll study harder and take the
exams again."

She shook her head on my shoulder. "No, no. I passed, Miss
Wright, I passed!"

"Oh Mary Sue, yes, yes!" I squeezed her hard, feeling like I'd
passed the test, too.

She straightened and accepted my clean handkerchief with
a bright smile, her eyes glistening with fresh tears. "I'm not ignorant
after all. I'm as smart as any city folk."

"Yes ma'am, you are! We must celebrate." I ran to the door.
"Where's Lizzie? We must have a festive dinner and we can celebrate
with Thomas."

"Thomas," she said softly, her eyes on a distant view I sought to
block. "Thomas will know I'm smart now."

Desperate to talk with Thomas alone before dinner with Mary Sue,
I paced in front of the front parlor windows until his arrival. The
grandfather clock tolled seven times and supper was nearly on the
table before his Duesenberg finally pulled up. There was no time.
He looked more tired than usual, his hair disheveled and deeper
lines under his eyes. He paused long enough for me to give him
a kiss and smooth his hair, before rushing to the dining room.

He knew that Lizzie did not take kindly to late arrivals for dinner, although why he worried what our colored help thought was beyond my understanding.

"I do apologize much, Lizzie," he said as a preemptory strike.

Her feathers settled some at his sincere tone and she acquiesced with a nod and a shake of her cane.

"What do we have here?" he said with forced enthusiasm as he sat and laid his napkin on his leg. "Our best china and roses from the garden?"

"And I pressed our best linen table cloth," I said, showing off my contribution.

"I brought in the roses," said Mary Sue.

"This child is good in the garden," Lizzie said, placing the platter of roast pork by Thomas' plate.

"That's a good girl," Thomas said, slicing the pork. He sounded absent-minded, not giving Mary Sue his usual interest. "Bess, come into my office tomorrow. I've decided on another campaign promise to impose limitations on outdoor advertisements. I'm finding them everywhere; painted on rocks and trees, on the sides of buildings and barns. It's taking away from our natural scenery. You will also write a speech to the Women's Committee for Pure Foods. We'll need to add something about the milk—"

"I passed," Mary Sue called out.

He paused in his slicing. "Pardon?"

"I passed. That's why we have all this. We're celebrating!" She gave him a smile of expectation.

He looked to me for explanation. "We got the letter today from the school," I said. "Mary Sue passed her exams and is entering into seventh grade next month."

"Ahhh!" He gave her a wide smile. "I knew you could do it, little one. Piece of cake! Speaking of which, I do hope we have cake to celebrate."

"Yeah, but I had to make it," Mary Sue said in her pitiful tone.

"You volunteered to make it," I said as calm as possible.

Thomas lowered his brows at me and continued serving the pork. "Then I bet it is delicious. Remind your Uncle Thomas to give you a big bear hug before I go."

She jumped up and hurried around the table to him. "I'll give you one now." Her thin arms wrapped around his neck, her head to his shoulder, and she remained there. Thomas seemed at a loss as to what to do but soon dropped the serving utensils and patted her back awkwardly. "There, there, that is a good little girl."

Lizzie and I watched this demonstration carefully. We both understood her neediness by now, but she was a woman just the same. Lizzie's thick lips protruded in thought, hesitated to say something, then pinched closed. Instead, she chose to rock herself gently and hum a gospel tune as she was in habit of doing in troublesome times, this time it was, *Swing Low, Sweet Chariot.*

At last Thomas unwrapped Mary Sue's arms. "Soon we'll be feeding a new beau. Boys will come flocking, you'll see." She stood by his side waiting for more. He handed her a plate with a serving of pork. "Sit down, little one, and I'll give you a toast."

He held up his glass of iced tea and we followed suite. "To Mary Sue. A young lady who is going to prove to all those Tennessee hillbilly boys that she can out-smart them. The learning she'll take back and share with others will be immeasurable. We need more schools and more teachers. My favorite author, Mark Twain said, 'Every time you stop a school, you will have to build a jail. What you gain at one end you lose at the other. It's like feeding a dog on his own tail. It won't fatten the dog.' Here's to a future feeder of knowledge and a future teacher of Tennessee."

We all took a drink. He continued. "And while I'm on this subject, I wish to give a toast to our present teacher, Miss Pickering. Again to steal a Mark Twain quote, 'It is noble to teach oneself, but still nobler to teach others – and less trouble.' Here's to a noble woman who served Mary Sue well."

I gave the "less trouble" a mock frown but in fact appreciated Thomas' celebratory toast. A thank you from Mary Sue would've been nice but she only sat with her eyes glued to Thomas as if gold dropped from his lips and she was the gold digger. All the more reason to proceed with my plan – it's not my fault he came in too late to ask permission.

"I have – or rather we have – another announcement, don't we Thomas?" I reached over and squeezed his wrist.

His forehead creased in thought and his knife and fork paused in mid-air. Seeming to suddenly understand, his face smoothed and he shook his head. "No, we haven't discussed an announcement." His eyes remained focused on the plate.

"But Thomas dear, the event is only two weeks away."

"As you like." He waved his knife around the table. "Give them the news."

"Thomas and I are going to be married," I said. "We've set the date for Christmas Day."

"Praise be!" cackled Lizzie. "I've been praying for this news for the longest." She placed her hands together as in prayer and looked up to her heaven. "Thank you, sweet Jesus."

"You're happy about this," Thomas said. "Don't you deny it, Lizzie. You're as fine as a frog's hair, as my pappy used to say."

"Yes, sir, I am. I don't love a heap o' people, but I love the two of you, so I can die now knowing you'll look after each other. I can't stay here forever."

"You don't talk like the niggers back home do," Mary Sue said.

Thomas' eating utensils clattered to his plate. *Ignorant girl, to say this in front of Thomas!*

He pointed two fingers at Mary Sue, his index and middle finger, previously saved only for reporters bungling a story. "I hope I never hear you say that in my presence again. Understood?" Mary Sue had finally noticed his lowered eyebrows and an angry flash of green eyes. Good!

Lizzie waved her hand toward her as if to say it didn't matter, but her eyes snapped in their own fiery way. "No, but honey chile I shore have seen right smart of doze niggers, but dez not brought up by good white folk like me. Yes'm Thomas' wife Cady, God rest her soul, teached me how to read and do de 'rithmetic and how to talk right, and now I knowed who's white trash and who's ain't, and I's not shore which I's lookin' at right chere, but I's be 'spectin you to watch yer mouth or I's wash it fer you."

Silence. I had never heard Lizzie use such Negro slang but she spewed it fast, like the expressions were right under the surface. It became clear to me why she normally chose her words carefully and spoke slowly.

Mary Sue's eyes darted between Lizzie and Thomas. Her head nodded to both, her frame hunkered down from the scolding. This was going off track. What was important here tonight was that she understood that Thomas and I were to be married. I cleared my throat. "Thomas, I have a proposal to make concerning the location of our wedding ceremony."

"Justice of the peace is all that is necessary." He wiped his mouth with his napkin and scooted away from his unfinished plate, his appetite obviously gone.

"Of course, Thomas, the ceremony doesn't need to be more than that, but I wish for my parents to be there. I'm their first daughter to be married and –"

He shrugged his shoulders. "So they can come."

"They can't, Thomas. Papa is bed-ridden. That's why I wish to get married in Papa's bedroom."

He frowned at me and I sensed he did not like this discussion in front of others but I wanted our plans laid out, in front of Mary Sue. I wanted her to see our impending future as husband and wife and our love for one another. I had hoped, however, for a little more fervor and warmth from him to carry this out. I smiled to mask my growing uneasiness, silently blaming Mary Sue for switching the mood from praise to disapproval.

"Your papa's bedroom," he repeated slowly as if hearing it from himself would register in his brain. His index finger tapped the table in an irritating manner.

"Yes, Thomas, the bedroom is fairly large. Lizzie, certainly you are invited, and Mary Sue. My sister, of course. My brother, Victor, although he and I rarely see each other. My aunt Opal and uncle Jesse might wish—"

"That's enough." Thomas leaned toward me and likely read the alarm in my eyes. He inhaled deeply and then exhaled gradually. "Keep it short. Your parents, Lizzie, Mary Sue if she wants to, that's it." I felt chilled with his words and he felt this, too, when he took one of my cold hands. He looked into my eyes and held them there, intense and searching. He found what he was looking for because his eyes softened and he rubbed my hand between his own to warm my fingers. "If it makes you happy, then we'll be married in your papa's bedroom. But in the future, you will kindly refrain from such discussions with an audience, until we have settled it in private. Agreed?"

"Yes, dear."

"Now we have two witnesses to our commitment to one another. There's no backing out now for either one of us. I'll contact Judge Jacobs tomorrow to see—"

"Well, that's the other thing, Thomas. Papa wants Preacher Paul from his church to marry us."

He blinked in slow motion, annoyance clearly there. "He insulted my wife at the Women's Rights Convention."

For goodness sake, that was ten years ago! "Thomas, please. It matters a great deal to Papa."

"Anything else?"

"No. Yes. I'd like you to wear your white linen suit. You look quite handsome in it."

He backed against his chair to glimpse Lizzie across from me. "Lizzie, don't worry about that cake now. There's enough sweetness in here as it is. I don't think you and Mary Sue can take much more."

I had to agree. Mary Sue had grown pale, her eyes wide as if watching a play with a sad ending.

He bent forward so close, his breath moved my hair. "Then give me some sugar."

"Well, how much do you need? I have a few dollars put away but is this like a dowry—"

Lizzie's cackle blended with Thomas' chuckle.

"I'm not talking about money, honey, I'm talking about a good ol' southern kiss. If we're going to make a public display of our devotion, then we must publicly seal it with a kiss."

I had not planned for this. I backed away.

"Oh so now you wish to be clandestine?" He pulled my shoulders forward and planted a hard kiss to my lips. "Let's move on with it, then!"

Lizzie stood up and gathered the plates. "This will be like the old days in this house. Love doves have come back to roost. We can never have too much sugar. No, never."

Preacher Paul refused to marry us. Ever on duty, he preached to me during our telephone conversation that he'd heard "things" and that he'd never join a divorced woman with another man other than her first husband, it was against God's Word – I cut him off with an I-understand, and hung up the receiver. Fine. I didn't like him and his watery eyes either. I obviously had remained a "she-devil" as he had preached from the pulpit and in Mama's parlor when I was young. I had hoped he would think that, with Thomas, I had seen the error of my ways and finally was settling down with a shepherd who could lead me onto the righteous path.

Thomas looked relieved and immediately asked Judge Jacobs.

All was rushed and set and I had little to do with a ceremony that seemed to have a mind of its own. Too late I began questioning the setting – whilst standing in my parents' bedroom in my white skirt and jacket. When in the company of my parents, I vowed never to marry. Now I must vow in reverse and in the same bedroom where I'd overheard Papa abusing Mama when I was eleven. I must've lost my mind in agreeing to this.

In these surroundings, any matter of formality or ceremonious garnish like flower bouquets, were not only frivolous but foolish. Poor Pearl had bought me just such a bouquet but I pinched off the Christmas-red carnations and pinned these to the lapels of the wedding party, totaling eight. Mama and Pearl were our witnesses, Papa, Lizzie, and Mary Sue our only guests as a compromise to Thomas, although I questioned silently Lizzie's presence as a guest. Victor, Aunt Opal and Uncle Jesse would likely never forgive us.

The swiftness of the ceremony itself hinted of my previous one in Nashville and I prayed that the lack of preparation hadn't doomed this one. Doubts swished around in my head - an advertisement popped into my thoughts as we gathered at the foot of Papa's bed. *Tired of your marriage standing stagnate in a pool of water? Swish your worries away with an electric washing machine!* I smiled, as one must when going loony in the mind. I could only hope that this new road I had stepped on was paved as Thomas had wished all roads to be, and not pitted and bumpy as I knew mine had been.

Thomas slipped a new gold band onto my finger and I looked into his eyes skeptically. He returned my searching stare with a trusting gaze and a warmhearted smile. His warmth removed my clouds of doubt. He wore his white linen suit and looked oh so endearingly proverbial yet he spoke words I'd never heard him speak, promises that would last to our deaths. He seemed somehow out of the ordinary, holier, and I in my plain skirt was in danger of worshipping him. I repeated my vows, first spoken to Jere, but this time their significance caught in my throat and quivered my voice. My papa propped on top of the bedspread in his brown-suit and my mama standing with her hands clasped in front, wearing her ages-old cream and lace dress, disappeared as I focused on my new love. And yet this love had been ageless, years coming from an old friend. As I slipped the gold ring onto his finger, I marveled at the light freckles sprinkled on his hand, the ring's symbolism and his touch, personal and possessive.

It was done. He was given permission to kiss the bride. He did so with no embarrassing flushes on the bride's part, but only an inward glow and an outward willingness to move on with it then.

Mama's dining room table looked candle-light lovely with all her special dishes out, down to the tiny butter pats by each plate. The Christmas tree glowed in the corner of the room with its own set of candles. She and Pearl had gone to such great lengths and every piece of furniture, window and drinking glass shone to say this was not only a holiday. I ate little of the delicious wedding supper, so happy I was to be Mrs. Thomas Pickering and that he sat closely by my side, beaming as happy as I. Papa of course could not join us but he hoped to have a restful nap, and instructed us to return to his room for dessert and coffee. Lizzie presented the wedding cake displaying our names, joined together "in sugar", she emphasized with a mischievous sparkle in her eye. The evening glowed with smiling faces, despite Mary Sue's dour countenance. But with her, I expected nothing else and didn't really care if it was due to homesickness, unfamiliar family, or even her unrequited affections for Thomas. He was mine.

Nonetheless I was unprepared for her to throw cold water on the social event. It began with Mama's innocent question as she passed around the slices of cake.

"Mary Sue, how did you come to know Mr. and Mrs. Pickering?" She gave me a wink.

I recognized my error immediately in not preparing Mary Sue for this line of questioning, but we had spent little time together since my return to the newspaper office. Her presence had become blurred, as Thomas became my center of attention again.

"I first met her when she married my daddy."

Thomas and I froze, except for my hand searching for his under the table. He folded it in his in silent comfort.

Mama didn't see the connection and set a plate of cake in front of Pearl, saying, "Who married your daddy, sweetheart?"

"This lady right here." Mary Sue pointed to me.

Mama looked around, confusion on her face. "Whom did you point to, dear? Someone here at our table?"

"I pointed to *her*. Miz Bess!"

Mama sat down hard in her seat. Her hand went to her throat and she pulled at her lace collar. "Bess, can you explain what she is talking about?"

"She is talking about something I wish not to talk about during my wedding supper," I said.

Thomas turned in his chair and touched my shoulder. "There's nothing here to be ashamed about. You made a mistake that was easily rectified. Now let us confess our sins and be done with it. You are around family who will forgive and forget. I'll start."

I opened my mouth to protest but then clammed it shut. The cat was out of the bag and if Thomas wanted to stroke it, so be it. I wasn't the only sinner here; let Mama confess, too. If this wasn't killing two birds with one stone, I didn't know what was.

He turned toward his stunned audience. Mary Sue's eyes lit with sudden interest - oh the little witch!

"It's simply this," he said. "Women had just won the right to vote in federal elections. Our long-suffering suffragist, our devoted Bess, had walked through many layers of shoe leather – as she likes to describe it - to see this moment. She had lived and fought for this, but when the war was over, where does a battle-weary soldier go? Home? But what if you've given up your home for this sacrifice? Tired and unsure of where to go from this point in her life, she met Mary Sue's father, Mr. Jere Phillips, in Nashville Tennessee." He turned toward me. "You can take it from here."

"Thank you, Thomas," I said, without meaning it. I felt the cat scratching and irritating me. "*Jere Phillips*," I said slowly to Mama.

She looked blank and then sudden recognition lit her face. "Oh! Jere Phillips!"

"So you do know him after all."

"No, *I* don't know him. But I do remember you telling me last summer that you met him. So that's why you seemed so aggravated when you returned home! Pearl and I just couldn't understand it, since I hoped you'd be happy winning the vote."

Oh, I was going to disown her if this kept up!

"Mama!" I said, clearly angry.

Thomas scowled at me. "Could we get on with this then?" He looked around the table. "My new wife seems to be feeling the pressure of marriage already. So, let me finish for her. This gentleman proposed marriage to her, and she accepted this as a new direction to go in. They went to the justice of the peace and legalized their marriage and then he drove her to his log cabin."

I glanced quickly at Mama; now she'd have to know I'd married her old flame! Would her expression be one of jealousy? Of lost love? But no, not even a twitch! And I shook all over!

"At his home," Thomas continued, "Bess met Mary Sue and her brothers and sisters. Instantly realizing her mistake, Bess asked to be returned to Nashville the next day and the marriage was eventually annulled. Bess sought atonement through educating Mary Sue. While doing so, Bess and Mary Sue have become good friends and work on a common goal to prepare Mary Sue to teach back in her hills of Tennessee. I don't think Mary Sue will be truly happy until she gets back home. Isn't that right, Mary Sue?"

Such a revelation had to hurt Mama, for reasons that went beyond a secret lover: her daughter had kept her first marriage a secret. I smiled a satisfied smile to both Mary Sue and Mama as I slowly released of my vendetta. I'd gotten what I wanted and they didn't. Their betrayals and lies were doing them absolutely no good. Come to think of it, I had married the two men they coveted. I felt as smug as if I'd planned it all as revenge. Intoxicating!

Mama suddenly appeared distracted – her mind must have been spinning with questions – but I had to give her credit for respecting the inappropriate timing. She raised her glass of lemonade. "Here's to the bright future of Thomas and Bess, *and* Mary Sue! And to Jere Phillips!" She drank the entire contents of her glass and then set it down with a hard thud on the table.

"After you, Mrs. Pickering," Thomas said with a bow opening the front door.

We stepped inside to listen to the silent, dark rooms. My white cotton suit had been starched and stiff to wear and I immediately wanted to change, but I wasn't sure whether to go to my old bed-room behind the kitchen to do this or - I decided to let Thomas make the call.

He found his way in the dark to the library and turned on a lamp there. "I have an aged bottle of port hidden here from the Prohibition for just such an occasion as this. Will you have a glass with me?" He removed some books from a shelf and exposed a small door. Behind this door was a short-necked bottle; with it two tiny glasses. He poured a concentrated burgundy-colored wine into the glasses and handed me one. The taste was bittersweet and seemed to take any stray bad nerves down with it. I had another sip, willing my body to relax. He would have great expectations and I, as inexperienced with intimacy as a staked scarecrow, felt incompetent. One accustomed to detracting, not attracting, had attracted a beautiful peacock and how would I join him on the ground without hurting myself? Or worse, would I let him down? Would he be disappointed in me as a wife? As a lover? I watched him hold his glass to his lips and suddenly longed for his touch as he had touched me once before, sitting in this same wing-backed chair. How long ago that seemed, preserved then in chastity. Now he had opened the door and I was free to go inside and love him in the most intimate of ways. These were my thoughts as he refilled our glasses.

He touched his glass to mine, his cheeks flushed, his eyes intense and hungry.

"To us," he said.

"To us," I repeated.

He drank his down and then so did I. He lit two candles and handed one to me. "No electric lighting tonight, love. Let's take these up to our bed chamber."

I followed him through the dark hallway, shadows of the chairs and our figures looming large on the walls. Like a ghost I trailed him up the stairway, our white apparel glowing in the frail, flickering light. Light-headed now, my eyes played tricks with our silhouettes on the walls; my steps up the stairs exaggerating my shadowy form into marching steps. *Women's rights or War, What are we fighting for?*

At the top, he stopped and squared his shoulders as if preparing himself to face his foe. He opened the door to the master bed chamber and let out an audible sigh. He turned to me and smiled. "All is fine," he said. Walking carefully to the bedside table, he set his candle down and motioned for me to do the same on the other side. He met me there with a kiss.

A kiss so dizzying I wanted to lie down for it. He backed away, his lips deep red in the candlelight. His attention focused on my jacket buttons and skirt zipper until the suit lay heaped on the floor. My camisole slipped off over my head, my half-slip fell to my feet that I at least had enough sense left to step out of. He threw back the coverlets and picked me up and sat me down on the bed in what seemed one smooth motion. I watched with keen interest as a spectator would as he partially undressed himself, unashamedly. Silvery hair on his chest sparkled in the light as he bent over and blew out my candle, leaving his to burn. The light gone dimmer, my other senses turned up to high as he laid me down. I was the sponge, he was my water and I sought to soak him in. This sense of freedom to touch, explore, and bring our lips to private places was exhilarating. Instinctively I knew the ultimate outcome and I reached out to be taken and marked by him. The pain was brief and I cried out but ... soon forgotten in the surges of pleasure. To move with such abandon!

With a kiss to my neck, he rose up to his knees and looked down at the sheets.

"You are a virgin?"

"I *was*."

He patted my navel appreciatively.

"I wish *you* were," I added.

"No you don't," he said. He rested by my side, his arm possessively over my stomach. "I couldn't give you pleasure if I was fumbling and ignorant about it."

"Which means I gave you none?" I challenged.

"It's my pleasure to know I'm your first. Japanese men pay big money for virgin geishas."

His bare leg moved out of the way as I raised my hand to smack him. He snickered softly and placed my hand gently on his thigh. "We'll keep practicing until you get the hang of it. It'll be great fun teaching you."

"Maybe I can teach you some things, too," I said.

"Such as?" He yawned.

"Humility for starters. You are far too confident now, knowing you are my first."

"And last," he mumbled sleepily.

"And last." I repeated. *It is forever,* I added like a ghost.

CAPTURED, read the bold headlines in the next day's newspaper. *Our bachelor-about-town, our willful watchdog, our illustrious editor, our candidate for future mayor now has a new title as husband to a former suffragist, Miss Bess Wright ...*

"They failed to mention that you're the boss of the newspaper. Which goes in your favor, because there is no word of my former marriage or that I lived at your residence all these years. Do you threaten to wash your staff's mouth out with soap, if they don't give you a clean name?"

"Worse. I'll send one off to report on the filthy New York City septic system in the immigrant areas. I've only had to do that once, but all remember and want to stay clean, as much as I do."

We finished our sections of newspaper reading in peaceful quiet, with only the occasional clink of the coffee cup settling on its saucer and a crunch of toast here and there. Having breakfast brought to my – to our – bed was such a royal treat, I felt compelled to relay this to Thomas when he brought the tray in. I raised the top of my hand for him to kiss. He bowed as formally as one could in boxer shorts and an undershirt. I was tickled at our teasing. Such peace and relaxation I had never known. If it weren't for my virgin desecration causing such tenderness where I sat, I would have felt perfect. I could see calm and contentedness in my husband's (oh how I loved calling him that!) demeanor and I accepted full credit for it.

I was truly happy our wedding night had been spent here. From this vantage point, everything around me was new and different. No signs of his first wife were in the room; photographs and memorabilia had been replaced with a vase of fresh flowers on the mantle. I asked not where they were, since I wasn't supposed to know about them in this previously sanctioned chamber. The aged off-white lace coverlets had been removed from the stately four-poster bed and a wedding ring quilt – our gift from Mama's friend Phyllis - had been spread there on top of a thick feather mattress cover. Six or more feather pillows were there to prop us up in this early morning hour.

We were alone in the house, an added indulgence. While Thomas had been down in the kitchen, I had tiptoed naked down the hall to the bath room to wash and slip on my white nightgown. I had brought a damp cloth back to the bed to attempt to wash away the sheet's red bulls-eye, humming a gospel tune I'd heard Lizzie hum many times. I thought for a moment of the words, *Are you washed, in the blood, in the soul-cleansing blood of the lamb?* And giggled again like a school girl, absolutely light as a feather with giddy.

I wasn't sure whether to run about the house in my nightgown or stay in bed all day. Either approach would be exciting and fresh. Since Thomas had over-speculated my shyness on such a morning-after and thus eliminated my need to leave the vicinity, I threw aside the newspaper and opted for the bed covers.

God help me, I felt as young and pretty as a blossoming flower. I suppose one could think my bloom had been picked, but given that it was singled out by Thomas, I would happily sit in his vase as settled as those flowers on the mantle.

Thomas interpreted my inertia as a sign. He discarded his papers and rolled over onto his side. Kissing my shoulder, he grinned up at me under those bushy eyebrows as a young boy might from under a cap. His hand slipped under my nightgown and I flinched at first, but his crafted touch convinced me with tingles that I could take him in for yet another session in the art of lovemaking. I accepted what he taught with an openness I'd never experienced before and how wonderful to know I could do so without hesitancy.

Finally the mysterious key of love had opened my passage. Why Thomas, and not Billy or Jere I did not know. What I did know was that this felt so right that I clutched his back in a high rise of tingling sensations I couldn't control. He smiled down at me as he advanced his movements with a pleasurable smile that said to me, you are why I am here in this room, you and no other.

Thomas and I shared our own secrets in this shrouded bed chamber. I no longer stood outside looking in to another time. We made our own memories with I as his bride. His body became an experience in exploration, touching the blond hair of his thighs and learning the burning in his eyes when he reached for me. How his muscles tightened when we connected and how daring my kisses became. We sustained on our four-poster island with only an appetite for each other. Like Cinderella who arose in the castle of her prince, we lived happily ever after for three glorious days.

Then we hit the road running. Literally and figuratively. Reality forced its way through our door via the doorbell when long-awaited lawn signs and flyers were delivered on our third morning. Thus began a concentrated election campaign. We barnstormed our town of Annan with many of the same strategies I had learned in suffrage. Door-to-door we walked, arm-in-arm, asking for support, flyers changing hands listing his campaign promises, shaking folks' hands until our own hands ached. Permission was granted by scores of homeowners to post our lawn signs painted in bold blue letters, *Thomas Pickering for mayor: He's on the right road.*

Volunteers sprang up, Pearl and David among them, and our back parlor once again rang with incessant telephone calls and a collage of paper and people. We arranged for a last-minute media blitz through the newspaper and asked for a live debate. We knew our

opponent, George Groves, would have a stronghold over airwaves
as owner of the radio station, and some financial backing from the
businessmen of the community thanks be to such owners as Mr. Jones
of the textile mill who had a vendetta against Thomas for supporting the women's union. On the other hand, and for this reason,
we energized pledges from the women's groups. As the husband of
a suffragist, Thomas could prove his sincerity in addressing women's
concerns by introducing me wherever we went. We pushed the fact
that, thanks to women like me, all women could get out there and
vote and who best would ensure their voices were heard, with a good
woman behind him? There should be no wasted votes out there,
Thomas said over and over. To our pleasant surprise, the local chapter of the League of Women Voters agreed to sponsor an open-air
debate in City Hall Park and scheduled this for the day before the
election.

George declined. Not surprising that George preferred the
radio - his appearance as fat and pompous would not hold a candle to Thomas. Thomas rubbed his hands together in satisfaction.
"Now's our chance to give the press a good story. They're just itching
for one and they can't very well go out and make up their own. Let's
make his refusal as colorful and controversial as we can."

The next day's headlines gave Thomas what he wanted. *George
Can't Do It!*, read the bold letters on the front page. S*ome people question his ability to stand up to the big boys, when he refuses to stand up to his
opponent in the race for mayor, Mr. Thomas Pickering. Mr. Pickering stated,
"I believe I'm on the right road and my road leads to everywhere. Mr. Groves
leads to no where and I wish to prove that."*

Knowing we struck a nerve, at six on the nose that evening,
a group of us gathered in our back parlor around our new radio – the
one I remembered from his apartment – and fixed our eyes on its
dials, knobs and tubes, and listened to George change his tune.

"I'll tell you where Mr. Pickering's road leads," could be heard
George's tenor tone from the cabinet's gold fabric panel. "It leads to
the jazz joints where he's been seen consuming prohibited alcohol,
and it leads to his home where he harbors women who've left their

heart-stricken husbands. All led by his live-in girlfriend, only recently made decent by marrying her. I'm not afraid to stand up to such an immoral man. I accept the challenge of a debate with my opponent, Mr. Pickering. George *can* do it and will!"

We'd won a battle in this war, but hadn't come away without injury. George was going for blood and seemed more interested in ridiculing Thomas than upholding himself. Technically what he said had some tarnished, twisted truth. I squeezed my hands together, wishing his neck was in between.

"The challenge is on, my dear," Thomas said as he stood and turned the dial of the radio to off. He looked down at me with a hesitant smile. "He's giving us a hint of what is to be."

"We can fight back, Thomas. Eleven or twelve years ago, he wasn't on such high moral ground. Eunice, remember? He kicked her out of their home and brought in your ex-secretary, supposedly as his housekeeper. They married as soon as his divorce from Eunice was finalized. You must bring this up in tomorrow's debate!"

Thomas bit his lip in thought. "I don't necessarily agree with negative campaigning, dear, you know that. At any rate, public scrutiny can be brutal. Are you up for it?"

I stood and faced him, my hands on his chest, public affection for the group to witness, it didn't matter. "I was raised a suffragist," I said, lifting my chin to him. "I'll march beside you all the way."

Now you know some of my deep dark secrets, Mama.

Like I said, you first opened that bed chamber. Will you reveal all your own, during your year of awakening?

Katy's Chapter Four -- January 1964

L ife is a fragile balance between past and future. How do you like that saying? I made it up! The past taps me on one shoulder saying, *Remember me?* And the future taps me on the other saying, *Forget about her – it's me you've got to worry about.* And here I sit in the middle, not moving to the front seat, or the backseat. Georgia crippled me as much as it did little Jesi. I hadn't realized that until now. I pretend that everything is wonderful when the truth is, I tap dance over my damn nightmares as if tapping them down will keep them buried. They only immerge over and over to say, *Look at me! Look at me!* Like an unwanted child in a grotesque costume.

Mama says the Lighthouse has always been her haven. For me, it's a hide-out. Jesi and I came here in the middle of the night like run-away slaves and I've stayed hidden ever since. Hiding behind them telling me I'm needed here. Hiding behind them telling me Jesi's theirs. Hiding behind the fact that I gave up both of us far too easily.

Will this journey down Memory Lane help me understand why? Mama is a clever one – there has to be a damn good reason for all this writing. Silly me thought she's doing this project for me. Instead … all these years I thought I had been living at the Petticoat Junction and now, in sneaking into her wardrobe and reading her chapters, I find Peyton Place! You could have knocked me over with my feather ticking! My own mother *and* grandmother - this Jere fellow must have been one hunk!

Makes me damn curious as to why Grandmama Ruby said on her last page that she's heading to a greater judgment. Also makes me think that where my story is going may be easier to tell. You know how it is: it's a lot easier to throw shit into a muddy river than into a clear blue mountain spring.

Everyone is writing, even little Jesi. She looks pale and her limp seems more pronounced when she entered the dining room. But she only coils tighter if I prod and there's no revealing pages from her in the wardrobe. I want to yell Papa's expression, *Don't piss on my leg and tell me it's raining.* I mean really, what's this crap about planning to stay at a girlfriend's house for a long weekend? I want to yell, *What girlfriend?*

Best to leave her alone, let her write. Hopefully she writes about why she sneaks out in the middle of the night. Doesn't she think I notice?

1943

My feeble attempt at a Savannah birth control clinic is dropped like a hot sweet potato. I don't return Ellen's calls; she gives me a headache. And funding from eugenics? You've got to be kidding! I like Clary too much to stab her in the back with such a cut-throat, cut-ovaries organization. And when I tell Clary why Ellen is calling, Clary hangs up the phone on Ellen before she can finish asking for me. Clary looks so self-righteous and says, "That lady couldn't hit her ass with both hands!" I laugh til I cry.

So I kick it out of the way and I jitterbug on to the dance floor. There are some great boogey-woogey sounds with a beat I just can't sit on. It's a shame William can't fast-dance but never-mind; there are plenty of soldiers who can.

These fellows are here for the same reason I am: to forget why else we're here in this part of the country. "You're on furlough; I'm a Virgo," I say as a pick-up line. Why not beat them to the punch? Although I've heard some good ones at that *Bottoms Up* dance club or at its neighboring *Hug and Slug.*

Like *Love me tonight; my ship sails in the morning,* or *Do it for your country,* or *You know who else would look good in that dress? Me!"* or the one I laughed hardest at, *Uncle Sam wants you; meet Uncle Sam!*" We shake hands and I meet Samson for the first time. Beautiful sea-blue eyes (all sailors have this color after three months on open water, he jokes at my compliment), a sweet smile that easily breaks into a grin and makes his two front teeth that slightly overlap look adorable, like all guys should have crooked teeth. He could move his stuck-out ears up and down in line with his eyebrows after one of his jokes that remind me of a puppet on a string, like the recent Walt Disney flick, *Pinocchio.*

The best part is, I don't take these soldiers seriously and they don't take me home. William does. And I'm thinking he's okay with that. He has his own group of buddies and a couple of hang-on girls, one goes so far as being jealous. "Why do you call him 'William'?" she asks me, holding possessively onto his arm. "His name is Teeee-Jaaaay." She says it like I have a hearing problem. "It's our little secret," he tells her and winks at me and then the dead hoofer pulls me onto the dance floor for another slow one. She and his group patiently wait until his return and they once again talk about who's who like I'm not even there. He's popular enough with just being who he is, and I'm only his irritating poodle that has to be taken out once in a while.

So I learn to wander off.

I let the night take me where it wants. When I'm not being led onto the dance floor, I'm being led into another hometown story; soldiers don't like to talk about the war but they love to say they've got the best hometown sweetheart and the best mother. Sometimes I believe them.

"Hey Pinocchio, what's your sweetie's name?" I ask Sam.

"Cinderella." He gives me his grin and I roll my eyes.

"No, really," he says, handing me a beer. I guzzle it like a man; that last jitterbug took us flying around the floor and somehow Sam flipped me over and landed me on my feet like we'd been rehearsing all our lives. I still haven't figured that one out.

"Her name is Cindy but she works in my place in Pennsylvania's Mather coal mine. She's so brave to go down there, even though she knows my dad died down there in an explosion about fifteen years ago. Ever since I saw the soot streaks and those downcast eyes that first day she came up out of that hole, Cinderella's been her nickname. She burst out crying cause she'd never been so dirty before, she said. I reached down into the fireplace and rubbed some coal ash on my face and got down on one knee and asked her to marry this handsome prince."

"And?"

He took a long swig and then grinned and winked. "She will."

A couple of Sam's buddies join us for a few laughs and then meander off. The tempo of the band starts winding down for some slow time and one of my mama's pet songs begins. *Bye-bye Blackbird* makes me homesick and I begin to sway back and forth with my eyes closed, letting the melancholy take me over.

"Well, we might as well dance this one, too," Sam says, rather too nonchalantly.

I hesitate; some unwritten code tells me I'm stepping over a line with William. I've danced the slow ones with him only, even when the song isn't that slow, since that's all he knows how to do – that and sing the words in my ear (*Heart of my heart/I love that melody/ Heart of my heart/Brings back a memory*, oh that crooning voice of his! Even after all that he had done afterwards, this memory still sings so sweetly to me!)

But this is silly so I shrug it off and set my bottle down hard to indicate acceptance.

Sam's a little stiffer in such a close hold. Cindy had been his only sweetheart, this I knew from our few nights of talking, and I can tell that his experience is limited. He goes from being a limber puppet to a wooden stick. I laugh, he grins and we're both relieved to hear the song 'bye-bye' for good and get back to our bottles. I excuse myself to go to the toilet and the one tiny room is tucked beyond the u-shaped bar. Guys and girls that sit on this side of the bar are in the dark and are either serious sots or smooching. I glance over to see William sitting there as I stand in line behind other girls waiting to get into that stinking hole. I can hear him talking to his high school buddy, a guy who recently enlisted and had the fresh-shaved head to show for it.

"Yeah, you may be right, but she's a bitch." William sounds angry, his voice amplified by the three empty beer bottles in front of him.

"Hey, they're all a bitch but what can you do?" says what's-his-name. I'd been introduced but he has an undistinguishable face.

"There's things I can do." William twirls his bottle, looking deep in thought.

"Without your daddy's help?"

William snorts and gives his buddy a sarcastic smile. "Yes, without my *daddy*. He doesn't run my life you know."

His buddy gives him back a mocking grin. "Right," he says slowly, nodding his head. "Just askin'. Then what are you going to do?"

"I'm going to puncture that prized cherry of hers, that's what."

What's-his-name whistles a long low sound. "With or without her consent?"

"What do you think I am – some kind of animal?" They both chuckle. "What better place to get her consent than here? Some of these drinks work as better panty-strippers than I do."

By that point, I've moved far enough in the line that I can't hear much beyond their chortles. I'm feeling sick to my stomach. Who's William talking about? I have a sinking feeling that I know.

I return later to Sam, nervous and edgy. I had remembered while in the toilet that William has the car keys and I'm stuck with him and his plan. I can't keep quiet about it but I don't know Sam well enough to confide. "I have a friend who knows this guy," I begin, and then tell him what this guy has planned.

Sam looks so serious and concerned, I want to hug him. It's not until that moment that I realize how alone I feel, like I'm an island surrounded by sharks called Uncle Joe and William.

"One thing I've learned in this war is," Sam says pensively, "you've – a person's got to go on the offensive. You don't wait around for your enemy to attack; all you have to know is: Who's your enemy." He bangs his fist on the bar with each of these last three words. "When you know that, then you go in for the kill." He leans toward me, his reserve gone, and places his hand on my shoulder. His sea-blue eyes are deep, fathomless. "This friend has got to give this guy some of his own medicine. Get *him* drunk."

I see the sense of it right away. Once William is drunk, I can get the car keys and skedaddle.

I nod and tell him I have to go and he nods understandably. "I'll be here for an hour or so more," he says casually, intently eyeing his bottle.

I wind my way back around through the clusters of people, through another crowded night, and find William where I saw him last. Four empty beer bottles now line up in front of him and he's nursing another. I come up behind him and place my hand on his shoulder - imitating Sam's gesture gives me strength. "You going to go bowling with all those pins?" I ask, jerking my head toward the bottles.

He looks up at me with bloodshot eyes and I'm thinking *this won't take long*. "Buy me a drink, will ya?" I say.

That's his buddy's signal and he salutes us soldierly and walks away with such a creepy grin, I almost lose my nerve.

William gives himself away with a "Sure, doll!" but then as if he remembers something, he straightens his expression. He orders me a whiskey sour - whatever that is - and I insist that he drink the same. I take a sip, he drinks half the glass, and then his previous beer drinking kicks in and he goes to "drain a snake". I pour part of my drink into his glass and pour out the rest onto the floor next to my bar stool. No one notices, there's so many mugs and glasses sloshing around. He comes back and drinks his down and orders another round. He lights a cigarette and hands it to me. He squints through the smoke I blow toward him. "I don't like you dancing with other guys."

"Friends don't care who I dance with, as long as we're friends," I say. "Your buddy is over there trying to get your attention." He turns and looks off into the crowd and I pour my drink into his glass and onto the floor again.

I'm able to get by with drinking only a few sips through four glasses of whiskey sours, while I watch William sway and wave like he's under water. I'm feeling quite clever. Except that William is feeling quite cocky.

"Would you like to dance?" he asks with a slur.

I nod, not quite knowing what to expect – the band is playing *Boogie-Woogie Bugle Boy*, requiring fast kicks.

"Then I hope somebody asks you," he says. He snorts like he thinks he's funny, but I'm starting to see a mean drunk come out in his squinted eyes and dead stare. I'm hoping I haven't taken on more than I can handle.

The crowd is beginning to thin out and the bartender is watching William. "Last call," he says to William, in response to William moving his finger in a sloppy circle for another round.

William smirks and gives him the middle finger. "Fuck you." He leans toward me and almost falls off the bar stool. He catches himself by throwing his arms over my shoulders. "And fuck you."

"What did I do to deserve that?" I ask calmly, even though I'm ticked off by it.

"It's what you're *going* to do," he answers slowly. He lays his head on my shoulder. "You're going to ride me hard, a-a-a-all night," he says in my ear.

I've had enough. I pretend to hug him, while my hands search his jacket pockets and find the car keys. I clutch them tightly. Boy, what a relief!

I push him back up into his seat and prop his elbow onto the bar to steady him. I whisper into his ear, "Wait for me. I'm going to go water the lily." I head toward the toilet and then lose myself in the crowd and turn back to the front doors. I'm outside in a foxtrot for the car when I hear someone call my name. I freeze in fear.

I turn around and see Sam. It looks like he's been waiting, watching. I give him the thumbs-up and he grins and returns the same and heads back inside. He grabs hold of William just as he stumbles out. I hear Sam saying, "Whoa, fella, slow down!" William swings at him but Sam easily ducks and William falls. Sam gives me the bye-bye of the hand to get moving while he's bent over William. I start the engine of my Duesy and I ride her hard, just as William planned.

Jesi's Chapter Four -- January 1964

C hristmas has come and gone and I got new fishnet stockings and a shirtdress. I guess the New Year's resolution is to pretend Jesi doesn't wear an ugly leg brace. I don't get it. In 1963 I'm five years old; in 1964, I'm twenty-five? When did My Mamas decide I'm all growed-up and haired-over?

And more and more, it's not just Mama avoiding me. Like we all have the cooties. The four of us are writing more and more from our bedrooms, as if we're all getting to the hard parts. I walked by Mama's partly opened bedroom door last night and like always, her lights are on – she always sleeps with a light on, like she's afraid of the boogey man. I looked in and there she sat with paper scattered around her, shrunk by her fluffed-up feather mattress that she "can't live without", looking like she's sinking into snow, her face looking so miserable you'd think she's coming down from an LSD trip.

But not me, no way, man. I have to say that I'm writing the best part. I had a blast with Isaac last night. I thought Mama would go ape-shit this morning when she saw my hickey but she hung loose and asked me if I wanted to go on The Pill. I had to remind her I already was. Not that I need it with Isaac. We don't go All The Way. He's the sweetest lover and we just make out mostly. He doesn't even cop a feel unless I want him to. It's all upfront and giving. Love For Real.

Why don't I just quit being a candy-ass and write about it? You know I want to talk about it and I know you want to read about it. I think I'll treat this like a diary, since I never got one from Mama. The tradition of mother-to-daughter diaries stopped here for some reason. Maybe Mama thinks I don't have a life.

He's got bucket seats in his car that he calls Birth Control Seats. It's really hard to make out there. So we drove to City Hall Park and walked to that big white gazebo. So Romantic in the dark there, like on our own planet. Everything around us was dark with little pinpoints of light in the distance, so I started making the doo-da-doo-doo sound in the opening of *Twilight Zone,* my favorite TV show. But then we hear voices.

"Follow me," he said in a whisper. He ducked behind the gazebo, pulling my hand in such a squeeze, you'd thought I was his five-finger discount (who would steal a cripple anyway?). We crouched low and headed into the field of high grasses. The full moon made his white shirt glow ghostly that moved in the dark by itself, the rest of him disappearing into murkiness. We were also stepping over that murky line we had drawn between us in the name of friendship and race. Our black and white disappeared and we mingled as gray as he sat me down in the grasses and the moon watched him give me the sweetest kiss I have ever known. His breath hot on my cheek, he rocked me then, stroking my bum leg in a comforting way. No other dude had touched my brace before; they pretended it wasn't there, so I had pretended too, ignoring the elephant in the room. This moved me, man, in a new way. I clung to his sleeves like he'd just pulled me up on shore, safe from drowning. Fingers unbuttoned my blouse while I listened to our air hurriedly rush in and out of our bodies. Time stood still, or more like, we had run out of time and we had no time to lose. Once upon a time, I imagined I would stop him when it came to this, but no way now. When his hand slid inside my blouse, it was freaking amazing and I sought his large lips all on my own. I'd never felt turned-on before, not like this, it was just make-believe before this, trying to make-up big time for my deformity (how bummed out is it that I was like saying, *here, take this part between my legs, it's not messed up?*). I opened up, even opened my eyes and looked straight into his, dark depths like eternity. Gently he pushed me back, and I found myself lying on my back and him above me, the moon now a halo around his head, the grasses circling us, rustling with our secret. It was as if he had found the switch to

307

a motor and I heard a tiny hum release from my lips. Like a mushy movie love scene, I was tempted to say, *where have you been all my life?* But it sounded damn corny so instead I wrapped my arms around his neck and rocked against his hand; I couldn't stop now, the urge took me over. His hip and its clothed hard spot moved against my thigh. We soared to the moon together, gasped at the dizzying heights, and fell lightly back to the earth, now lying on our backs weak from the flight. This was my first orgasm, the first time I got off. What a rush.

And we didn't even do IT, man, no intercourse. How cool is that?

I reached for his hand, now lying limp by his side.

"I'd follow you anywhere," I said.

"Then follow me to Nashville."

Ruby's Chapter Five -- 1910

Summer's Growth

*T*oday is the convention. Those were my first thoughts as I laid there in the early morning in total terror. Too early yet to get up. My mind began its journey yet again of reciting the words of my poem, memorized by now, but like reaching for the hand of your mother, I was comforted.

Then I prayed, but I couldn't even imagine what to ask for, what the day would hold. Of course we discussed this at length at our last tea, but once I told them I'd written a "silly" song, I was asked to teach it to the others and now it will be part of our entrance into the park, and Oh My Lord, I didn't know where to begin!

My little inner voice said, *Then begin where you know.* Yes, of course, I would take this one step at a time. *Arise. Move about my kitchen. Light a fire in the stove.*

By the time the others came thumping, mumbling down the stairs, I had prepared their breakfast and started dinner. I was a mess, my apron showing every ingredient, so much my shaky hands had dropped or spilled, and a blister had formed on my finger. I couldn't seem to focus on one task for very long; the cornbread was missing some ingredient, my crust too brown, my poem too long, too many eyes I imagined on me, Robert's eyes on me.

Robert's eyebrows raised in question when he saw my disheveled appearance but he said nothing. He ate little and his only words were a request for apple cider vinegar mixed with water to settle his upset stomach. He seemed as distracted as me; that should have been my first clue.

I wasn't so naïve to believe he didn't know about the Women's Rights Convention; the ladies had posted signs around town stating so. Cady's husband, Thomas, had announced it in the newspaper. Carrie Chapman Catt's planned attendance, as president of the National American Woman Suffrage Association, had added credence to the convention, and I was certain the topic had come up in Robert's shoe shop, but he made no mention.

Nor did I. We had not spoken about women's rights since the morning after the preacher's visit. Nor had he made any more physical demands, as if his emotion was all spent. His non-intrusiveness had allowed me to move him into the background, becoming part of the furniture I must wash and care for. Now for the first time since then, I wondered what he was thinking. By the end of today, would I find myself without a home again? There was enough to be terrified of, without thinking of his reaction. *That* I would deal with *after* the convention. I couldn't back out now.

As if this wasn't enough, Bess gave me a scare. Robert had only departed for his shop a moment before and just as I felt some relief, Bess cried out "Mama, come upstairs, I'm bleeding!"

I sat down heavily on her bed at the discovery. "Oh my little Bess, you are not so little anymore," I said sadly. I felt I had lost my little girl in that very moment.

"What is wrong with me?" Bess sounded frightened.

"Nothing ... and everything," I answered, wishing I had warned Bess sooner; I'd seen woman's signs during Bess's Saturday bath. I, who wanted more freedom to speak openly, didn't wish to do so with my own daughter.

I sighed like the coward I was. "Well Bess, some call it a woman's curse, but I say you will be happy to see this, more times than not."

"I am *supposed* to bleed?" Bess asked, looking incredulously at her spotted pantalets.

"Sorry, Bess, Mama is talking in riddles. Yes, you are supposed to bleed every month, and will do so, unless you are married and with child – carrying a child in your stomach – well, actually the word is pregnant, although you are not to say that in public, though only the Lord knows why, since women have loads of babies. You won't bleed when you are pregnant. But otherwise you will for many years. So let us start your womanhood off by showing you how to layer rags and cotton and pin them to your pantalets. I'll prepare you a cup of lavender tea to ease your tummy."

Somehow she sensed the change immediately. When she came downstairs for breakfast, her hair was not braided; instead the top half was pulled back into a barrette, its long brown length meeting the tied waist in the back. She wore her longer white-laced church dress and stockings. Somehow Bess looked much older, her lips more pronounced, her cheekbones more defined, her face more drawn. It would not be long before I must introduce Bess to another curse – the corset. I didn't ask Bess why she was dressing up. She was a woman now and women didn't discuss such things.

But I could take her to the women's convention; what better way to introduce her to the world of women?

One step at a time, I walked closer to the City Hall Park. Step by step Bess and Aimee walked with me. Aimee's mother babysat our boys.

Women were beginning to congregate around the park gazebo and we set to work our tasks at hand. At last, our Cady arrived in Thomas' automobile. We all worried if she could. And oh what a shame if she hadn't, since without Cady, the convention, no, not even the Legion would have happened!

She has a disease, honey. It is in the womb. Ate up any chance of her having a baby. Or having a life for that matter, Lizzie had whispered to me at our last tea.

I shyly approached as Thomas assisted Cady from the passenger side. Lizzie stepped out from the back seat. Already Cady's appearance had changed, aged, bent slightly, her thinning frame leaning heavily on a cane.

She seemed to sense my dismay. "I look worse than I feel."

Yet her eyes were shining as she looked up and saw the streamers and banners around the top of the gazebo, the signs from our

Fourth of July march stuck in the grassy dirt around the bottom of the gazebo. She waved at Phyllis who was handing out flyers to people as they approached, laughing and talking as if she knew them all, flyers that read her 'Seven Reasons Why We Fight For Our Rights'. Cady waved at Eunice who was, along with two unknown gentlemen, putting the final touches on a booth they had put together a few yards away from the gazebo, with a sign across it that read 'Sign Our Petition Here!'

With theatrical flair, Mr. Whiting, the school principal, walked to the booth and signed the petition with flourish. He raised the pen in the air and we all applauded.

"Another man bit the dust!" called out a man strolling by, a woman on his arm. She laughed with him.

Thomas shook his head, his hand clamped firmly on Cady's elbow. "You shouldn't be around this negativity, Cady darling, you could get hurt. Ruby, don't let her fool you. She shouldn't be out today, but she doesn't listen to a word the doctor or I say to her."

No bright smile lit his eyes today and his dark blue suit only seemed to emphasize his somberness.

Cady patted his hand. "This is far enough, Thomas. I can walk the rest of the way with Ruby and Lizzie." She looked up at him with beseeching eyes, as if to say, *don't make a fuss, please.* He looked unwilling to let go, but relinquished his hold over to Lizzie.

"Don't you worry, Mr. Pickering," Lizzie said. "We'll look after her, won't we, Ruby?"

I flanked Cady's other side and tried to give a reassuring smile to Thomas. "Cady will be fine with us, Mr. Pickering. She is at her best when leading our little group to victory!"

I looked back to see Thomas still standing there, hat in hand, watching, trepidation written clearly on his bereaved face, as if already feeling a widower.

Ah, but my wicked thoughts were in envy, for I thought that Cady, even at her worst, was experiencing the best, with such a husband as Thomas.

Aimee nudged me out of my reverie. "Ruby, that must be the woman president!"

It certainly was. Cady introduced her as "Carrie Chapman Catt, president of the National American Woman Suffrage Association. We are so pleased she could be here!"

We women applauded and I felt quite privileged to be here. To think if I hadn't agreed to attend my first tea at Cady's home, what all I would have missed, standing in my kitchen, thinking in darkness, and not seeing more clearly through the light of others who had so much to offer! I loved Mrs. Catt's large intelligent eyes – they looked so kind, as if you could tell her anything and she would not be shocked but nod in understanding. Mrs. Catt wore the colors of the Legion, in a black and white wide-striped dress, and this subtle significance signaled respect that added prominence to our cause. She alone took away some of my nervous jitters.

Eventually my group of women gathered at the back of the expanding crowd, more women having joined after the convention was advertised. Cady and Mrs. Catt stepped up into the gazebo and sat on the backbench. This was it! My heart fluttered wildly and I could barely breathe, walking through groups of people standing about. Some eyed me suspiciously, others curiously, and I heard one whisper, "there is one of them!"

Lizzie draped a white satin sash over my head and onto one shoulder that read down the front in black letters, 'Women's Right to Vote'. "Made these myself!" Lizzie whispered.

I practically jumped out of my skin at a drum roll right behind me and turned to see Frances, a lady I'd only met briefly at Aimee's tea, with a snare drum secured around her neck by a wide ribbon that read, "Women's Vote" repeatedly down its length to where the drum rested below her waist.

"Ladies, in line, please!" she called out.

I grabbed the hand of Bess. "Come on, Bess, it is time you learned to march and sing for women-kind!" Bess fell in line behind me and we all marched in time with the drum.

This brought more people into a tighter group around us, many craning their necks to see what was going on. I guessed there were at least a hundred people or so, probably a good deal more on the outskirts of the park milling about.

"One, two, three, sing!" Frances shouted and we began singing the song I had written. Save for my children's births, this was the most exciting moment of my life.

> Wo-men are people, too!
> We are no less than you!
> Equal rights will see us through
> To share where freedom reigns!
>
> Wo-men are not as lambs!
> Take me just as I am!
> Let me speak for all wo-men
> And vote where freedom reigns!
> Voting rights will lend a hand
> To share where freedom reigns!

We marched through the crowd, singing loudly, proudly, facing the crowd boldly, not needing to read the music sheets. Around the gazebo we marched, splitting into two groups, one on each side. The drums, the song, the affect met their purpose; people crowded in around the front of the gazebo.

Thomas stood on my side of the gazebo, a megaphone in hand, eyeing the crowd of mostly men as if they were carrying weapons. When all was quiet, he handed the megaphone inside the gazebo to Cady, who then walked to the front railing without assistance. She faced the crowd, shoulders back, chin up, her stature of one defying defeat. She lifted the megaphone to her mouth.

"Ladies and gentlemen! Welcome to Annan's first Women's Rights Convention! The purpose of today's convention is to urge men to vote in November in favor of a proposed amendment to the state constitution to give women the right to vote. We come in peace and ask that you open your minds and hearts."

Her voice seemed to carry to the very length of the park and echo through the trees. Many of these faces watching Cady were not friendly, some were sneering, others shaking their heads, or worse, some looked indifferent, one lady hid a yawn behind her gloved hand. *Why?* I wondered for the umpteenth time.

One face stood out in the crowd; his was not sneering, his head cocked to one side, listening attentively, his deep-set blue eyes watching Cady closely. He wore a yellow rose pinned to his vest to signify him as one of the speakers. His head turned as someone bumped him in the crowd and his side to me revealed a short black ponytail. He was in the front row, close to where I stood, and his friendly, and yes, even intense, interest somehow comforted me.

I couldn't help but stare – something about him. Was he part Indian? Certainly not all Indian with those eyes and straight nose, but his blue-black hair and square jaw were certainly Indian traits. Was his skin naturally dark or did the sun darken it? He was dressed casually but certainly not in buckskin, of course there was that leather vest he was wearing –

I flinched at the change in voices in the gazebo. Phyllis was up there now reading off her 'Seven Reasons'.

Shame on you! You must concentrate more on what is going on.

Fear gripped me again. I'm next! How in the world could I face this crowd at such close range, I who wouldn't meet people's eyes when I walked to my church pew? I searched the crowd again, and again rested on the ponytail man – he had an air of prominence about him. He shifted his stance, straightening his arms and hooking his index fingers in his belt loops. As he did so, his eyes shifted to me and my cheeks burned in embarrassment. I shifted my gaze down to my hands, only to see them shaking.

Before I could think clearly, before I could calm down, I heard my name announced. My little group applauded around me, opening the way to the gazebo. My shaky legs carried me up there, although for the life of me, I didn't know how. The wood planks of the flooring beat my footsteps like a heartbeat as I walked across to where Cady stood applauding, her megaphone clamped under one arm. Cady then handed this to me with a warm smile. I attempted to smile back but my bottom lip quivered in other directions. Cady squeezed my elbow and then left me alone to face the many upturned eyes. I suddenly wished I'd brought my written poem, for then at least I'd have something else to look at, some words to read rather than reading these many expressions on so many faces. I grasped the megaphone with two hands and looked out at the sea of hats and bonnets. Alone, and oh so afraid – could they hear my heart?

I was floating, swaying, oh I needed an anchor! I thought surely, surely I was going to faint when once again I saw the man, the ponytail man, step forward into my view. He smiled reassuringly and nodded as if to say, *Everything is fine and I want to hear what you have to say.*

I reached out to the railing and steadied myself.

"Cat got your tongue, little lady?" some fellow piped from the crowd and with it followed some snickers.

I glanced back over to the ponytail man, and he nodded and smiled again. Such kind eyes! I returned his smile shakily, and slowly raised the megaphone to my mouth. I was amazed at the voice that came out the other end of it. It didn't sound like my own, and so much louder, bolder. Hearing myself talk so, gave me strength, and the feeling of fainting finally subsided. From my heart, my words came:

> Let my voice and my hands
> Reach to others in need.
> Give me the right to be counted,
> Good deeds feed, not just breed
> A door to a freedom,
> Of vote, of choice.
> More than a cry in my home.
> To be community's voi—

Gunshots choked words in my throat. I shrunk away from the deafening blast coming from the side, while others screeched or squealed. Then another blast that moved the crowd as one body away from the sound. Through the gazebo opening I could see a horse, its rider aiming a rifle at the trees. He fired a shot again and echoes could be heard in the deafening silence. I held onto the gazebo railing trembling, needing to sit down but too shocked at what I saw. Preacher Paul sat on that horse, his face red with anger and breathing hard as if he'd come in on foot. He rode closer to the gazebo, parting the silent and stunned crowd while I stood frozen on the spot, watching him in horror.

"Ruby!" he shouted, and he pointed a finger at me. It startled my heart so, the pain might not have been different than if he had shot his rifle at me. I clutched my chest with one hand and dropped the megaphone from the other hand.

"I've been sent here on God's errand to beseech you to leave here at once!" He pointed to the stairs. "Now go! And save your soul!"

I felt all eyes turn to me expectantly.

Numbed and shamed, I turned and walked toward the stairs.

"Let the lady stay."

I looked over the railing to see the ponytail man striding toward the horse. He moved as if in slow motion. I had never seen such a beautiful graceful creature – and I'm not talking about the horse. I stared in awe.

"Let the lady stay," he repeated, calmly, without shouting, yet I believed the outer edges of the park could hear his ring. "Her poem's asking to be heard. Let her speak."

Preacher Paul ignored him and faced the crowd. "Now you've heard from a woman and an Injun. What next for this devil's meeting – a darkie? Listen now to a man of God. Folks, here's what this man of God is telling you to do. Go home. Take your women home. Tell everyone who didn't come that this legion of women is of the devil. Brethren, we are in perilous times when we see mothers, wives, and daughters who no longer wish to abide by the Holy Word. We must, as masters of own domains, fight this Eve and her venomous vipers and protect what is rightfully ours. It is my *duty*," he pointed toward the heavens, "to stop this wormwood, as prophesied in Deuteronomy, before it eats our town of everything good and pure!"

From behind his horse came his deacons. I knew all of them of course but seeing Robert shocked me further. I gasped and the ponytail man glanced up at me questioningly. Preacher Paul leaned down to his deacons. "Now you go ahead and hand out God's Word to these good folk." The deacons began working their way through the crowd passing out papers, those taking the sheets looked stunned enough to do as they're told.

Robert ignored them. He was facing the ponytail man, glaring at him. Like some western stand-off, they stood facing each other in silence until Robert at last stepped around him.

"Ruby."

It took me a moment to turn my attention to where Robert stood at the bottom of the gazebo stairs. It seemed as if my body turned, but not my heart.

"Ruby," Robert repeated. "Come on down. You're going home."

I stepped slowly down the stairs, my head hung, not wanting to meet any eyes.

"Sir, you have no right to disturb this convention!"

I stopped on the bottom step and swung around.

Cady had picked up the megaphone I had dropped. With one hand on the rail to keep her steady, her arm rigid, she shouted, "If you wish to be heard, you should do so from your own pulpit!"

I had never seen her angry and shaking before.

"Sister, I appreciate what you are saying there," the preacher called down to her from his high horse, "and I'd be more than happy to preach to you this Sunday morning! Might do you some good! When was the last time you stepped foot inside a church, ma'am?"

Laughter rippled through the crowd. Thomas stepped forward and grabbed the reins to Preacher Paul's horse with such rage, I winced in fear of what he might do.

"That is enough, Paul!" Sheriff Porter came into view, mounted on his own gray mare, his rifle in plain view across his legs. "This is a public place and you are disturbing the peace."

"Are you, as a fellow man, going to stand by and let these men-haters destroy our families?" Preacher Paul called back across the crowd to him.

"As the sheriff of this town, I say they are breaking no laws and doing no wrong. Let them be and have their say. You'll have your own soon enough, I'm sure." Sheriff Porter placed both hands purposefully on his rifle. "But it won't be here."

Preacher Paul raised his empty hand. "As I said, I'm not here to cause any harm. I've said what I have to say and I'll say no more. Let our brethren finish passing out my declaration and then we'll be on our way."

Sheriff Porter shifted on his saddle. "They're not disturbing the peace but you are. I'll have to ask you to leave – now."

"Now sheriff, you and I go way back. As God is my witness, I don't understand-"

"*Now*, Paul." Sheriff's tone was deeper now, more foreboding. Thomas let go the reins and smacked the rear of Preacher Paul's horse so hard, it startled and jerked forward, causing the preacher to lose his cap and focus his attention on trying to stay on, while he trotted away.

Robert took my elbow and silently we walked to the edge of the crowd. I could hear Cady's clear voice behind me, introducing Lizzie to recite Sojourn Truth's *Ain't I a woman?* Oh, how I hated to walk away from hearing that. And how heartbreaking it would be to miss Mrs. Catt's *Ballot for Bullet* speech, too, such a famous suffragist. I wanted to cry.

"My God, Bess is here! Are you trying to corrupt my daughter, too?" I had forgotten about Bess. She had obviously followed us.

My words were still stuck in my throat, and flooding with tears. I made no argument. We walked to the outskirts of the crowd, Lizzie's voice becoming fainter. I could take it no longer.

"Robert, please stop and listen to me. I want to stay!"

"Do as I say, Ruby. No more scenes. You are in enough trouble as it is." His eyes looked straight ahead, still walking, still gripping my elbow, his jaw muscles working. "There's the wagon. Now get on without another word and go home."

I looked over to where he was motioning with his head, and saw Opal sitting on the wagon, reins in hand, waiting like a prison guard. Their betrayal took away any strength I might have had to resist. With what defiance I could muster, I jerked my elbow from Robert's clinch and refused to step up onto the bench where Opal sat.

Instead I walked to the back of the wagon and jumped up onto the open back of the wooden bed. If I was going to be treated as a farm hand, I would look like one. Bess climbed up beside me, somehow understanding to keep quiet. We sat side-by-side, legs dangling over the flat bed, my arm around her shoulders. I stared straight ahead, not daring to give Robert the pleasure of seeing me cry. The wagon lurched and we rode silently home.

When finally Opal pulled in the reins in front of the house, I jumped down and turned to help Bess and there behind her I saw a large oblong box, a fabric-covered one that had made many trips with Opal to customers carrying their new wedding gowns, evening gowns, jackets and dresses. These must be her altered dresses. Did she think she could do the same to me? Cut me down to fit one person, when I was designed for another? I would've given my right arm to have heard the ponytail man's speech.

"Keep your dresses," I called back over my shoulder to Opal. "I prefer black and white."

I approached slowly, watching Eunice pick up pieces of the booth, boards splintered and scattered about. The two clay pots of thick climbing ivy Eunice had so meticulously placed through chicken wire over the booth as an archway yesterday, was broken, dirt and vines scattered. One of the signs from the gazebo had been moved over here and stuck in the dirt by the broken booth. The sign had been altered with a big red 'R' in 'Fight', to read, 'FRight for Women's Rights!'

"What happened, Eunice?" I asked, placing my dinner basket on the ground.

Eunice flinched, startled. "Oh Ruby, I'm glad to see it's you. Seeing this sort of destruction at someone's hands makes me skittish, being here alone." She straightened and put her hands on her hips. "What happened here, I believe, is a coward from that church came in the night. Look at this!" and she kicked at a splintered board, anger showing on her flushed face. "Now I don't know what to do. We announced yesterday that the booth would be open every after-noon for two weeks, to collect signatures. Here you are, our first vol-unteer to station here, and I have nothing..." she kicked at another board, harder this time. "I hate men. If I could just get my hands on the man who—"

"Whoa, whoa, don't take it out on all the men!"

We turned to see the ponytail man walking through the oak trees toward us.

He ducked under a low-hanging branch. "So, we had more than one enemy in our midst yesterday, did we? Could've been worse – I've seen women shot at for asking for fairer wages at a bicycle factory. Annan is actually a peaceful little town."

"That's comforting," said Eunice, in a tone of one not impressed. She continued to look at the damage around her.

I could only stare, not quite believing he's standing here, just as I had fervently hoped for but thinking such a wish wouldn't happen. My face flushed crimson in being so impolite and I quickly bent to examine a piece of vine, its roots exposed.

"We can have a new booth built in an hour," he said. "If one of you can come with me and show me the way to the lumber mill or general store."

"I appreciate your thoughtfulness, er ... Mr. Bluemountain, isn't it?" said Eunice.

"Jeremiah."

"Well, I must be frank here, Jeremiah, and say I have no money left to buy supplies. What little I saved went into this," Eunice said, waving her hand around to the damage at her feet.

Money? I dropped the vine. I hadn't put in a penny for any of this, or for the sashes or the signs - worse yet, I suspected Robert had done this damage; he hadn't come home until long after I'd gone to bed, soaked to the bone from the night's thunderstorm.

"I think I can swing a few dollars for a good cause," Jeremiah was saying.

"No, I'll pay!" I blurted out, standing up. I met Jeremiah's eyes and couldn't look away. The warmest blue I'd ever seen. Silence circled around us.

Eunice was gazing, too, as if seeing him for the first time. "You'd do that?" she asked, almost in a whisper. He turned his attention to her and she blushed and began stacking board pieces by a tree. "While you're gone, Ruby, I'll take the petition and banner over to the gazebo and if anyone wants to sign the petition, they can do so there in the meantime."

Jeremiah gave me a sweet smile. "I have a borrowed buggy here," he said. "Is that alright? That you go with me, I mean?"

I could only nod and follow.

I stepped up into the buggy and sat before the questions came: Alone with this stranger? A married woman? Is he married? Will Robert see me? Can I breathe naturally? Will Jed's General Store let me use Robert's account?

He climbed in beside me and I decided, no, in these close quarters I cannot breath. "Ruby Wright, isn't it? Pleased to meet you." He reached out his hand and I watched my tiny white hand disappear into his larger brown one.

While he maneuvered the horse onto the street, I had a sudden urge to know everything about him. "Bluemountain – must be a meaning behind that name."

Am I being too forward?

"Well, I come from the Blue Ridge Mountains of Tennessee. When you see the mountains from a long way off, they look blue.

When my daddy died in a coal mining accident, my mommy, in Cherokee Indian custom, decided to change my last name to what I loved best. I believe I'm in safe keeping surrounded by all those giants. I come up here to walk on flatter ground, all open like this, and I feel naked as a baby." He tipped his hat to me. "Pardon the expression."

An image suddenly appeared in my mind of him without his shirt on and I blushed.

I don't know where you are heading, Ruby, when you turn red from your own thoughts.

Jeremiah turned the horse around in the park and we headed down Main Street. I caught sight of his hands holding firmly to the leather straps. Nice hands, I thought. Clean; not stained.

"Tell me what your speech was about," I said, just wanting to hear that sweet southern drawl talk to me. "I'm terribly sorry I missed it – the rest of the convention."

"It's a shame, for certain." He gave me a questioning look, not unlike the one he gave me yesterday when I gasped. "You look fine today though."

I blushed and suddenly felt that *yes, everything is fine today.* "Please," I said. "Just a little of what you talked about yesterday."

His words were lyrics to his melodious tone as he told me that where he came from, women work right beside men, hunting, skinning, planting, harvesting … and where would we be without their hard work and soft voices, their tender hugs for their children and their ferocious protection? How his daddy told stories about how women fought for the Union Army in the war, disguised like men and earning an honorable discharge. And many more who didn't fight but stood along the roads where the weary soldiers traveled and handed out bread and cheese, or nursed those soldiers who collapsed. That when all was said and done, we're asking for no more than what a man has and why should we be denied, when men depend on us for helping them with everything else?

The center of town came too quickly. The story ended and panic began. Robert's Walk Wright shoe store was only a few buildings down from Jed's General Store. Why had I only now remembered that?

"Pardon?" I asked. I sat back further, thankful for the sides to the buggy.

"I asked if we were heading in the right direction," Jeremiah said.

"Oh, yes," I answered. "The store is on this street just a few minutes away." I resisted looking at his face and those blue-blue eyes – blue eyes from blue mountains.

We entered the business district and no one took notice of us. There were many more wagons, buggies, bicycles, and even a few horseless carriages rumbling along here.

I dared not glance over to Robert's shop window as we plodded by far too slowly. I pointed and he pulled in his reins in front of Jed's General. I jumped down and rushed inside.

"Is there a sale on something here today I should know about?" Jeremiah called from behind me.

I waited for him inside the dark entrance. He had that same broad grin from yesterday. He brushed closer to me as he stepped aside for a woman exiting the store and my heart beat faster. I needed to concentrate better on why we were here.

"No, it is just cooler here, is all," I answered. I breathed in the familiar smell of cinnamon sticks, pickle barrels, and axle grease. Jed sold it all.

"Well, hello there, newcomers! How can I help you today?" called out Jed from behind the counter. I faced the counter, adjusting my eyes to the gloomy room and Jed's dim bulky figure. He could have no legs for all I knew; only that very round belly. He always sat behind the counter directing young boys to "stock, sweep, and sweat – that's what I pay them for!"

"Why, it is Mrs. Wright!" Jed shouted to the rooftops. "I hardly recognized you all dressed up in your Sunday best! But then you are a household name now, aren't you? I'll tell you what I did. Curiosity got the best of me and darn if I didn't walk all the way up to City Hall Park and watch a bunch of women bellyaching!" He slapped the counter. "Ha, I'm only kidding!"

His countenance quickly changed. He pointed his finger at me. "But I'll tell you one thing. You'll never see me put my signature on any kind of petition. No, siree-bob. City Council would be on me faster than a rattler, raising my taxes and what ever else they can think of. You rock their boat, they'll tip yours over."

He pointed to Jeremiah. "Hey, I saw you up there, too! You're from away, now are you?" He sounded like he was making an accusation. Of course he knew Jeremiah wasn't a resident.

"I'm from Nashville Tennessee, sir." He walked over and shook Jed's hand. "Where are your wood planks?"

I sensed he didn't care for Jed any more than I did. Jed was always too loud, too nosy, knew everybody's business. Probably would pass around that I came in with a strange man.

"How much wood do you need for the booth, ma'am?" Jeremiah asked loudly, as we headed to the back where Jed pointed. He must have picked up on Jed's gossipy ways.

Out of earshot, I turned to Jeremiah with my hand to my mouth, feeling foolish. "Why, I don't know! Eunice handled that yesterday." Why didn't I ask Eunice before we left? Scatterbrained, indeed!

"Well, I'm sure I can figure it out, Ruby. Don't look so embarrassed. Eunice did what she knew how, you did what you knew how. You contributed your own fair share. I know – I was watching. That was a mighty touching poem you started quoting yesterday. Did you write that?"

"Yes siree-bob!"

We laughed together!

And he asked me to recite the whole poem on the way back.

It was as if he really cared what I was thinking.

Jeremiah added up the cost easily and a new and stronger booth was standing by the noon hour. The cost on Robert's account had risen to eight dollars when we included cardboard and paint for more signs. To avoid suspicion I had asked Jed for my own account but he had refused. Somehow I would have to figure out a way to pay for this, and very soon before Robert found out.

I stood back with one hand on my chin, its elbow propped on the other arm across the stomach, a common stance for me, and looked at the finished product. I glanced over at Jeremiah. He stood in an identical pose. I burst out laughing. He looked at me quizzically and I raised my fingers from my chin and waved them. He did the same. He laughed easily, loved to talk. And I loved to hear him tell his stories of "back home".

He told me about how he and his "daddy and us eight boys" built their log cabin and called it Smoky Creek, because the creek that ran behind the place had a mist that rose above it about every morning. "I spent my spare time in the hills, stomping around every inch of it, loving every minute of it. Just like some ol' mountain lion.

"I had a girl there, we were sweet on each other, mostly from a distance for a few years, until her Daddy caught us holding hands walking up the hill behind her place. He said he wasn't going to have any half-breed grandbabies running around his place, so that was the end of that. He whipped her with a switch, and he would have done it worse next time, so she did what her Daddy told her to do."

He said he left home shortly after that to look for work. "There's no way I'm going to work in a coal mine and spit up blood like my Daddy." He moved down from the mountains into Nashville and got a job at a bicycle factory that he nicknamed 'Wheel and Deal' because the owner was a clever man who set up bicycle races on rocky terrain and threw in free britches to attract the girls. Even more cheap than clever, he wouldn't pay good wages to his workers, particularly the women. "I got paid more than women who had been there for years. It wasn't fair and I told him so, so he lowered my wages to theirs. He added coal to the flames then, I'll tell you. So we organized ourselves a little group and did what you did here. We made some signs and paraded back and forth in front of the factory, declaring unfair wages.

"The women there listened to one strong-willed gal, Dellafay, and if she told them to miss work and hold a sign instead, that's what they did. At first we didn't get the attention we wanted – like being shot at from the hill beside the building and one poor girl falling dead. Word got to the town newspaper and they sent a reporter to talk to us and Dellafay told him we demanded a town meeting. He put our story in the paper, and then the mayor agreed to the meeting. The reason he agreed was because his wife insisted. As it turns out, the mayor's wife had been reading up on Mrs. Catt and women's rights and this was just the sort of event she was looking for. So, she sent a telegram to Mrs. Catt, asking that she speak at the meeting. Mrs. Catt was so good, she got a standing ovation – well from the womenfolk anyway. Mr. Kinsley was told that if he didn't increase his wages, no one would buy a solitary bicycle from him. Well, he got scared and agreed to pay more to the women. But I didn't get to stay to reap what I helped sow.

"That meeting is how I met Mrs. Catt and that is why I'm here. Mrs. Catt asked that I escort her, first by train to Syracuse, and then by wagon these last twenty miles or so. We'll take the wagon back to Syracuse tomorrow or the next day, and then head on to New York City by train. I'm a volunteer escort, I guess you could say, but she makes sure I have enough to eat and have a roof over my head. She gets paid little or nothing for this and she and her husband put a lot of their own money and time into traveling all over to be the woman's mouthpiece. Her husband will meet her in New York City, when he gets to feeling better, and then she will get me a train ticket to go back home.

"I sure miss my mountains. Now that Daddy and Mommy have passed on, I'll take over the home-place and farm what I can. I'm a pretty good carver, too, so maybe I can make some money selling my carved birds and such. Instead of Wheel and Deal, I can Carve and Starve!" He laughed pleasantly at himself.

I found him so easy to work with, me holding boards for him as he nailed, explaining his measurements to me as if I was as smart as he and understood it all. In the heat of the day, I watched wet strands of hair falling from his ponytail; I watched the muscles in his arms expand through his white muslin shirt when he lifted the wood. I memorized his profile. Sometimes his hand would touch my shoulder; his arm would meet my arm. Out of the blue, an image came to me of the two of us building our own house, working side by side. I shook my head in amazement and then in shame.

He rolled his white shirtsleeves up higher and wiped his brow with a red bandana from his back pocket. "Let us sit for a spell and take a rest. There isn't a soul in this park now."

I hadn't noticed. I remembered my dinner basket shaded under a tree.

The only seating was the gazebo's backbench and he followed me there. I had taken my bonnet off to cool down and now attempted to smooth my hair back as I took the stairs. The sound of my footsteps across the planks of the wood flooring brought back memories and I stood frozen in the middle of its round structure, staring at the front and its lawn beyond, where no one stood today, where every-one stood yesterday.

"I was so frightened yesterday, I thought surely I would faint," I said softly.

"I thought you might, too," he replied, his voice as soft as mine. "Where did you get the courage to be a speaker?"

I turned around to where he sat on the backbench, and boldly looked into his eyes, thirsty to drink them in. "From you," I said.

Our eyes locked and his eyelids drooped ever so slightly as if to shade the shine coming from behind the blue. I looked away as I placed the basket between us and sat down.

"Well, this isn't fancy, but there is plenty for the both of us. Let's see, I have a jar of water, a jar of my twelve-day pickles, and some chunks of corn bread with apple—"

"You have corn bread?" he asked, incredulous to this, as if he asked, *you have gold?* He handled a piece like he had discovered the nuggets himself. "I haven't had corn bread since I left home two weeks ago! Didn't know Yankees made it up here." He paused with the piece at his mouth. "May I?"

"I wouldn't dream of breaking your heart with no, now!" I replied with a giggle.

Did I just sound flirtatious?

He munched down, gazing dreamily far off. He finished it in seconds. "Good," he said, rubbing his hands together to wipe off the crumbs. "What's next?" His hand halted in mid-air over the basket as he spotted my hair.

I was combing back the hair around my face, the same comb whose teeth had held my roped bun in place. The rope had quickly run its course down my back.

"Your hair – it's beautiful. May I touch it?"

I nodded and tensed.

I felt his hand touch my back and stroke my hair gently. "My mommy had long hair like that and she would braid it and leave it hanging down. You should do that, too – you'll look like my people."

If it were only that easy, to be his people.

I resumed combing. "My hair is a bear to work with, though; too long and heavy, especially in this heat it feels like a horse blanket on my back. It desperately needs a cut."

"Well, which is it, a bear or a horse? You know us Indians, we'll just name you Horse Hair, or Bear Head."

I smiled coyly, enjoying his attention as I twisted the rope of hair around my hand, and pinned it down at the nape of my neck with my hair comb.

He watched me closely. "You do that quickly and with such grace, you make it look easy. What is my little horse tail back here, maybe three inches?" He turned his head around for me to see. "One leather tie and it is finished." He turned back to face me. "That's men's work for you, but women amaze me how much they handle every day and still manage to look as delicate as a butterfly and as pretty, too." He smiled at me, his eyes softening, shining again. "You smell of lavender."

I couldn't turn away, even with a blush coming on. "Yes we are pretty tough cookies." I wiped a crumb from his mouth with the corner of the dishtowel that had covered the basket.

I would do no differently with one of my children.

The City Hall bell tower announced one o'clock in the afternoon. "I must go home soon. I left the children home alone for the first time—"

His eyes came closer, his lips. "Ruby?" He touched my face and moved his palm along my jaw line, his fingertips awakening my senses. Time suddenly stood still. This structure around me became our island, only eternity surrounded us out there, the only sound was his breathing, the only sight was his eyes, like stars brightly shining. I tilted my head and looked at his lips, then looked into his eyes, watched them as they closed, and his mouth was on mine, feeling as soft as a butterfly landing on a flower. My eyes closed, my lips reached for more, and he brought his mouth fully onto mine, giving me my first lover's kiss. Was it for only a second, or was it a lifetime, I couldn't be sure. But in that space where time didn't exist, I loved him forever.

I walked home on air, fingers gently touching my lips ever so often, my other hand holding the wild flowers. In my mind's eye, he's still here.

"Here, Ruby, before you go," and he had walked behind the line of trees to the open meadow beyond the park and picked the indigo and coneflower, tied them with the leather string from his hair, and walked back to me with his broad grin, his hair falling forward, touching his shoulders. "My gift to you for a most pleasant lunch. Best cornbread this side of the Blue Ridge. Are you sure I can't give you a ride home – at least part-way?"

I longed to say yes, to not say goodbye, but I would be traveling along the same street that Robert would be taking and it was crucial I reach home before him. But I hope to be here tomorrow afternoon, I said – to help with petition signatures of course.

I wondered how I would fill up my time before then. The evening, the long dark night and then the morning, it would take an eternity before I could walk back to the park. I decided to prepare him a linen sachet of my lavender flower blossoms.

I opened my front door to the smell of smoke. A piping of this was coming from the kitchen. I could hear Bess scold and Pearl cry out, the boys yell. I ran to the kitchen to see Bess throwing a bowl of water onto the stove, flames licking their way out from under the round inserts for pots, the lids red-hot.

"My God, what—" Fire caught onto Bess's sleeve and spread up her arm. I screamed, "More water!" as I jerked her to the water pump, pumping frantically with one hand and smacking her arm with the other., and splashed the little remaining water on her. It didn't completely go out and I smacked Bess's upper arm to put the flame out on her dress sleeve. Bess screamed so loud that the boys hushed and stood terrified. Water took an eternity to come through and out it out for good.

"Hush, Bess, it's gone now, Mama got it all, darling. You're a brave girl." I saw the bubbled skin under the charred sleeve and began to cry. "Mama is so sorry, Bess, Mama is so sorry! I should've been here, I'm not a good mommy, no!"

Aimee ran in from the back door. "I heard the screaming."

I ripped the sleeve open more, to give more air to the burns. "I think Bess needs some salve, Aimee," I said as calmly as possible. "Could you run get Doctor Hughes?"

"Can you walk upstairs, darling?" I asked Bess. She was sobbing but no longer hysterical. "I need to take this dress off." Bess nodded and we exited the kitchen in small steps and headed through the parlor toward the stairs.

I looked behind me; the boys and Pearl were following closely, mute, coughing, their eyes wide, red and wet. "Bess will be fine. You go outside now and get some fresh air, away from this smoke. You can come up and see her in a little while."

I looked down and almost stepped on a small bunch of wild flowers tied with a leather string. Fresh tears came as I stepped over them and I walked Bess bit by bit up the stairs.

I sat outside on the front verandah, my rocker creaking with each push, taking in deep breaths of fresh air. After a fitful night and a strong powdered heroin elixir, Bess was sleeping again. Robert had left earlier than usual that morning without disturbing me sleeping with Bess, another day's reprieve. Aimee had come over later in the morning with bread, cheese, and roast beef. I'd sent the other children off to the creek with a picnic. I simply couldn't cope with them.

Aimee had offered to take my place at the petition booth so what could I say, but *yes, thank-you?* And off she went … toward town, her footsteps on the boardwalk fading …

My last chance to see him … fading.

I clutched the arms of my chair to keep from running after her, my bandaged fingers stinging in protest.

Back and forth the rocker creaked his name. Each creak amplified the sound of my heart slowly breaking. He's was so close and yet … fading.

After today he would be gone forever and I hadn't said goodbye. Or said *come back and visit us* in a light airy way. Or *keep in touch.* Or *I love* … I had so much to say and yet could say nothing. These balusters might as well be my prison bars. I reached inside my apron pocket, found the leather tie and once more held it between my fingers, searching for solace there.

I looked up at the blue sky. So blue…I'm feeling blue without you, blue eyes…oooh, a whole new meaning to 'out of the blue'. I listened to the quiet around me and to the steady clip-clop of a distant horse. Like a school girl, I closed my eyes and imagined his lips on mine – oh to be kissed on your mouth so completely! Our lips were pressed like two pie crusts sealed together, the cracks no longer there, to make the perfect pie. I licked my lips for the sweet taste.

From the sound of it, the horse was coming closer. I opened my left eye to the street and a man on a horse came into my vision. He was two houses down, peering closely at each house he passed. He turned his head from side to side - I opened both eyes wide – he had a pony tail! My heart flew into my throat and I sat unmoving, watching in disbelief. And then I was up and running, down the stairs and down the boardwalk. I stopped dead in my tracks in front of my other next door neighbor's house, one hand at my throat to soothe the throbbing there.

What am I thinking of doing – throw myself into his open arms?

I bounced on my toes to keep me in place and instead threw my best smile as his horse approached and he drew back on his reins. He looked down at me, giving me his own, the sun shining blue tones to his black hair. We simply gazed at each other, me not quite believing he was really here. The horse shook its head and snorted and this brought me out of my trance. I stepped down from the boardwalk onto the cobbled street and patted the horse's neck. This was as close as I dared get, my hand longing to touch his boot, but touching the horse made me somehow feel closer to him, as if touching an indirect part of him.

"I came as soon as I heard." He motioned to my bandaged hand. "Aimee told me what happened when I asked where you were. I know I shouldn't be here, but—"

I looked up into his eyes and the neighbors disappeared. "I am happy you are here."

He swung down from his horse in one powerful movement and I suddenly found myself face to face with him. There was not enough air between us to breathe.

Touching my bandaged hand lightly, he asked, "Does it hurt?"

I glanced at it, not quite remembering why it was bandaged. "Not anymore."

He grinned broadly at me and I let out a soft laughter that felt so good. There had been nothing but pain since I had left him at the park yesterday, and now the pain was all gone. I had the urge to grab his hand and run through the fields beyond the houses; run with our hair blowing freely behind our backs. Running ... freely ...

"Your daughter? How is she?"

"Much better, thank you. It will take time for her to heal, but heal she will. May I - may I invite you to join me on the verandah?

I can make a cool drink – I think I have some lemons and there should be some ice left in the ice box—"

"I don't think that would be proper," he broke in, but he wasn't glancing around at neighbors' windows. His eyes didn't leave my face. It looked as if he was trying to memorize my features. "I'm not here to cause problems for you, Ruby. You have children; you would have to make explanations. You might have to lie and that would only make something ugly out of something beautiful. That is how I will remember you – something beautiful." He took in a jagged breath. "We didn't say goodbye yesterday, and I can't leave without it. I can't explain it." He reached out to touch my cheek but then having second thoughts, quickly withdrew his finger. "And I know, to be the proper gentleman, I should apologize."

He leaned his arm against the saddle and looked beyond me, his eyelids drooping heavily … dreamily. I loved that look about him. Into my memory, I etched and branded every line of his face, shoulders, his arm against the saddle, the deep reds and greens of the horse blanket underneath, his white linen shirt, his chest moving with each breath.

"There is no need to apologize," I said softly to his lips. I hardly sounded like myself, and yet I felt more like myself than ever before.

"It felt so right, didn't it Ruby?" He said, encouraged by my words, my tone. He tilted his head down and studied me earnestly.

"It did, Jeremiah." I felt a surge of happy blush in saying his name.

"I love it when your eyes shine like that," he said. "No wonder you were named Ruby – you glow like a gem. You ever been told that before?"

"No, but then I've never felt like this before." I felt out of breath; as if we had in fact ran through the fields and only just now paused.

"I made something for you." He turned to his saddlebag, unbuckled the flap, and brought out something hidden in his large hand. He opened his palm to me. A wooden carving of a dove sat there looking at me. Its head was smooth and round, its feathers carved in careful detail.

"Mommy believed that when a dove rested at your home, it brought love and peace. That is what I bring to you."

I picked the dove up carefully, as if grabbing it might startle it into flight. "I will treasure this always, Jeremiah. I wish I had something for you."

"Yesterday was the best gift you could give me, Ruby. I can understand what a sacrifice it must have been, to be there. I'll never forget it, or you."

"Jeremiah, how can I say goodbye?" My vision blurred and I looked back down at my dove, wishing my heart were made of this wood.

"This can't be goodbye forever, Ruby. Let's think of it that way. I can't stand the thought of it." He patted the horse's side as if it had just given him an idea. "I know what I can do. I'll come back through on my way home from New York City. I don't know how long it will be but when I do, do you think, Ruby, that maybe we could meet again in the park? We could just talk – there's nothing wrong with that, now is it?"

"I would love to sit again and talk with you, Jeremiah. That would be wonderful!" I felt a tremendous relief at not having to face forever. "This is not goodbye then. What a horrible word! Let us just say, what was it your mama used to say, win-na-de..."

"...ya-ho," he finished. "Win-na-de-ya-ho."

"Thank you for this day," we said together.

"I love you," I whispered to the dove and gave it a small kiss on its tiny beak. I laid it back in my lap and continued rocking. I looked down the street to where he had, only hours before, tipped his hat to me, mounted his horse, and rode away. I had watched until he had disappeared. I continued to watch now, as if he would magically appear again. Why not? Wasn't the last appearance only a dream? No, I had his dove, real and mine. I clasped it to my heart and rocked some more. I heard the distant clip-clop of a horse. I sat up straight, intensely squinting toward the sound.

Finally I sat back, weighted down by disappointment. Buggy wheels, too, not just a horse. I watched, disinterested, as Aimee stepped down from Eunice's buggy and Eunice waved and rode on. She joined me on the verandah.

"You're still here rocking away!" she said. "Goodness, it is terribly warm today!" She waved away my offer for a cold drink. "I shouldn't be here," she answered. "But first I must tell you what all happened today." She opened a folded fan from her handbag and waved it front of her face, her strayed blond hair in frizzy curls moving slightly in the hand-made breeze. "First I must apologize. Mr. Jeremiah Bluemountain showed so much concern for your accident, I felt I had no choice but to give him your address. When he left in such a hurry, I grew concerned that it may not have been the appropriate thing to do."

I saw curiosity, not concern, in Aimee's expression. I didn't blame Aimee for wondering. I tried desperately not to blush, as I said as off-handed as was humanly possible, "No need to apologize, Aimee." I wished to hear more about him; just hearing his name was exciting. My mind scrambled to think of another question about him. "So, why was he there?"

"You tell me," Aimee answered, shrugging. "He arrived shortly after I did, and quite honestly, from a distance I thought he was stalking something, the way he was watching, hunting for ... I don't know. Maybe it is because he looks so...Indian. I was uneasy until I recognized him from the convention and remembered he did a good job speaking on our behalf. It's so terribly unfortunate you couldn't have stayed. That preacher–"

"I don't wish to discuss that. Please continue about the Indian."

"Well, then Eunice told me about how you and he had rebuilt the broken booth - another tragedy, really, why such hostility? Anyway, she said Mr. Bluemountain was very kind to do so in the spare time he has waiting to escort Mrs. Catt to New York City. You should know that Mrs. Catt has been holed up in Cady's home ever since the convention. Cady collapsed that evening and hasn't been out of the house since, so Mrs. Catt stayed a little longer than planned to keep

Cady company. We must pray for Cady. Where was I? Oh, yes, well, when Mr. Bluemountain approached me, asking for your where-abouts, and well, I know I shouldn't say this but," she leaned toward me and murmured, "I was quite taken back by him. He has very nice eyes and a soft accent – he must be from the south somewhere."

She became quiet for a moment, curling a strand of blond hair around her finger. "So, did he?"

I flinched slightly in spite of my apparent calm. "Did he what?"

"Did he come by?"

"Oh Aimee, I just feel terribly guilty about the whole thing!" I blurted out. I had to tell someone what nagged at my heart - but not so foolish to tell everything in my heart. Although what I said was foolish enough.

"Guilty? Why?"

"Because if I hadn't been there building that booth with Jeremiah, fighting for women's rights and all, Bess would not have been here alone, fighting for her life!"

Aimee stopped twirling her hair and she sat up straight. "Bess is fighting for her life?" She glanced in the parlor window.

"No, not now. She is much better. But it is my fault she is burned in the first place, and if I hadn't returned home when I did, well I shudder to think."

"You think it is your fault because you weren't home? Oh, come on, Ruby, accidents happen! And you can't go on blaming yourself when … " She stopped when she saw Robert coming up the steps.

I hadn't seen him coming either, so absorbed I was under my blanket of shame.

He nodded toward Aimee. "Good day," he said coldly. He gave me the same cold expression. "Ruby, did I hear correctly that you weren't home yesterday?"

Aimee jumped up, patting around her skirts as if she had a bee under there. "Well, I must go. Good day, Robert, good day, Ruby." She ran toward home.

Robert's eyes hadn't left mine. "Ruby?"

I raised from my chair slowly and faced him, my judge and jury.

"Yes, Robert, I was not home during the afternoon."

"This has gone on long enough, Ruby. Get inside and go upstairs now."

"It is supper-time, Robert, and I must feed the children."

"How are you going to cook with a burnt hand, Ruby?" His tone bit accusingly.

"Aimee kindly brought over some food."

"Then place it on the table, and go to your room. I'll ensure the boys eat." He followed me inside. "Take some food up to Bess, first."

I obeyed, praying he did not make a scene in front of the boys, or raise his voice to where Bess could hear.

I sat with Bess and Pearl on their bed, nibbling off our plates, and remained there like a coward until evening darkened the window. I couldn't insist that Pearl sleep on blankets on the floor while I slept with Bess yet another night. When I heard the boys come up for bed, I decided to face my foe. I opened the door and answered back to the boys' goodnights, blowing them kisses. Robert stood at our bedroom door. He snapped his fingers and jerked his thumb to that dark place. Yet, I refused to scurry to him like a scared rabbit! I held up a finger for him to wait a moment and turned to the girls' bed and kissed them goodnight. I was determined to have a civil conversation with my husband.

I entered and he closed the door behind me. He slapped my face so hard that I saw spots. I put my hand over my mouth to silence my cry. He slapped my other cheek, harder this time and I tasted blood. I raised my hand to block a third strike and he grabbed my wrist and pulled my arm behind my back. There were no words; only heavy breathing and choked sobs. He pushed me onto the bed and fell on top of my back, smothering me deep into the feather mattress.

"No more, do you understand me?" he growled into my ear. "No more or I will surely beat the living hell out of you!" He jerked hard at his handful of hair at the nape of my neck. "Do. You. Understand. Me."

"Yes!" came my muffled cry. I could not breathe and kicked my legs in panic. He lifted himself off and I raised my head to breathe in air. Blood dropped off my chin onto the white chenille bedspread. I clamped my bandaged hand to my mouth and ran over to the wash-bowl. The bandage was turning red. I poured some water from the pitcher into the bowl.

Robert stopped pacing and watched me in the mirror over the bowl. "My God, you are bleeding," he said. He joined me at the wash-bowl and grabbed a washcloth. He clutched my chin, causing me to recoil.

"Hold still," he muttered. He dipped the wash cloth into the water and roughly wiped. "The inside of your lip is cut." I winced with pain and drew back. "Hold still, I said!" He continued to wipe but more gently now. He poured water into a glass. "Rinse." I obeyed and spit red into the bowl. He turned my shoulders to face him and wiped some more. "I want you to listen to me, Ruby. And listen good."

Fine, I'll listen but I don't have to look at you. I focused on his flared nostrils.

"You are no longer permitted outside this house, without my permission. You will remain here and look after the children as you are supposed to do."

I raised my eyes to his. They were examining my mouth with concern, but his lips were pinched and stern. He let go and threw the washcloth into the water. I stared down at the water slowly turn-ing pink.

"I'm going downstairs to read. You stay here." He turned his back to me and headed toward the door.

To see him turn from me, cut me off, what was he thinking? To leave me here, to *imprison me?* From deep within my gut, a low ember caught flame and I felt the heat quickly spread through to my very fingertips and toes.

"Robert, talk to me!" I cried through clenched teeth, spewing through my swollen lips.

He paused at the door and looked back. "Why should I? I no longer trust you." He turned to the door and twisted the knob.

How dare he! I snatched the washcloth from its reddened pool and threw it at his back with many years of pent-up anger behind it. It slapped loudly in the middle of his back and he arched as one might in being shot. He turned and looked down at the limp rag at his feet.

Fear seized me but it was too late now. I raised my chin. I walked toward him, hands clinched in fists and spat out, "Talk to me, I said!"

He picked up the rag and rolled it into his own fist. "Fine," he said. "Fine!" He came toward me and my body steeled itself for the blow. He shook the fist at me. "I'll talk to you! I'll tell you this! My shop has lost a good deal of business, did you know that? Of course you didn't! And do you want to know why?" He was up in my face now, his cheeks splotched, his brown eyes glazed with fury. "Because of you, Ruby! Ever since the parade, I've had to deal with comments in town about how I can't control my own wife, my own household, so how can I manage a business? Some men stopped buying from me altogether, saying they go into Syracuse now, where they can trust the merchant to know what he is doing. And the jokes about your women's group parading yourselves around town. Here is one for you: What is black and white and read once a month? I'll give you a hint; it is not the standard punch line, newspaper. The punch line is, marching women on their periods! Understand, r-e-d? Ha! Not so funny, is it? Jokes are one thing, which I hear plenty of, but there's more. Do you want to hear more?"

He began pacing the floor. "Of course, a parade was just getting your feet wet, wasn't it? You had bigger ways to disobey me. You had to go on public display and air out our personal problems into a damn megaphone for the whole town to hear. About how you want to reach others in need, when you can't even fill the needs of your own children? Hell, you haven't even spent time with your children, I bet this entire summer! Your idea of spending time with them is to drag Bess to a convention so she can watch her mama berate men with a bunch of bitches!"

He raised his hands up in the air. "And that's not all, Ruby, no that is not all. You may be quite proud of your little group but let me tell you what it did to *me*." He stopped and glared at me. "You remember me, don't you Ruby?" He jerked his thumb to his chest.

"I'm one of those men you hate. Well, I'll have you know that I lost my biggest contract because of *you!*" He pointed his finger at me. "For years I had a contract with the textile mill for steel-toed boots. After your public outcry in a God-forsaken convention, the owner of the mill comes to me and says he didn't realize that my wife was part of the petticoat rebellion. That's right, *petticoat rebellion!* You are a laughing stock! He said that, thanks to this group of women, he has several women now crying for better work conditions, and more money. It may run him into bankruptcy. He blamed *me* for what *you* are doing out there and canceled his order. I now have a stock of one hundred and twenty-eight pairs of boots and no buyer."

He walked back to me, his bottom lip trembling. "Let me explain that to you in simple English. That means that I have a hell of a lot of money spent on stock, but no money coming back in. Do you see what I mean, Ruby, do you?"

He turned away and I stared at his white shirt – at the large wet spot blotched with red. His shoulders were lower now, his head down, his energy spent.

I felt stronger somehow, as if in relinquishing his words to me he had relinquished his strength to me.

"Robert, how would I have known this, except that you – why, I had no idea!" I touched my swollen lip wishing that this of all nights I could speak clearly. "You and I live in two different worlds. You don't know mine any more than I know yours. But my world is much more confining. Sometimes the walls are closing in on me, Robert. I don't mind my chores, I just want to do more! Don't *you* see? I could help you in other ways, too – I could earn wages, if you are having financial difficulties—"

"This is exactly why I didn't want to tell you, Ruby," he said, his voice tired now and void of emotion. "Now you look at me as a man who cannot provide for his family. And I can. And no wife of mine is going to work outside this home."

He sighed, shaking his head. "Let me put it to you this way. I've thought a great deal about this here lately. I've given you everything my parents worked for; this house, this furniture, and I've given you everything that I have, money for food on the table, clothes on your back, the children. All I ask from you is that you maintain what you have been given. That is all. If you don't remain inside and do what God intended you to do, what you made an oath to do when you married me, then by God, I will divorce you. That is my right as a man. I will divorce you and you will have nothing; no home, no husband, no children."

He threw the tightly clenched rag into the bowl, water splattering the mirror. "Anything else you want to talk about?"

Divorce ... no children. I sat down hard on the bed and shook my head. I could think of nothing else to say.

Note from Bess: Mama is not well. "Writing took its toll," she explained from her bed. She asked me to use her diary excerpts to finish her year of awakening. She marked these pages:

November, 1910: I had a dream early this morn: Maple leaves fall around me, golds and deep reds, on this densely wooded hillside. One red lands softly on one of my two thick braids, braids dangling long below my breasts. My horse snorts loudly, jingling the harness that straps her head, chewing at the bit in her mouth. She receives a pat on the head, but a pull at her reins, for we must climb faster. I must keep up with him. I look ahead to see his backside walking beside his own horse, watch how nimbly he steps over a rock that I must soon climb, his sheepskin coat adding thickness to his broad back and arms, the thick piled collar pulled up slightly against the strong wind, his ponytail long now, dangling down his back. I don't see him speak but I hear his voice in my mind saying, "Don't stop, Ruby, you must keep moving." I bend my uncovered head against the wind and push forward up the steep incline. On we go, across a small plateau, and down the other side. We reach the bottom and come to a clearing. A wide fast-flowing river is revealed. A hundred yards across and on its other shore, sits a log cabin, smoke breathing life up its chimney, a mist shrouds behind it. I walk along the shore of the river looking for a way to cross. I see the cabin clearly but it is so far away. I long to be there but my steps only take me farther away. I stop. The mist thickens to fog and stretches across the surface of the brown water. The fog reaches our shore in front of him and he walks into it, is absorbed by it and slowly disappears, his horse's back end disappearing last. "Don't stop, Ruby," he says again. "But how do I get to the other side?" I cry out to him. "How do I get there from here? How do I ..."

Robert woke me. I was "whimpering". I reached up, half-expecting braids, but only found my shortened hair. Yesterday I sold my three-foot long braid through Aimee, my only connection to town, who sold it for enough money to pay off Robert's account to Jed's General for the booth lumber. What little hair I had left I pulled back this morning into a tight tiny bun and tucked this into a white Amish cap, appropriate for Opal's wedding.

Robert said grace at breakfast: "We can give thanks, children, to your mother, for her public shenanigans this summer that cut my shoe contracts in half." He folded his hands together in mock prayer and closed his eyes. "Thank you, Ruby, for this food we are about to starve on." Victor laughed but Jonathan knew better. He nudged his big brother.

Bess immediately stood up and spooned eggs onto everyone's plate except hers, saying she wasn't hungry.

He squinted at her like she was too bright. "And I suppose you weren't hungry last night when your mother served chicken gizzards? And the night before with eggs and potatoes? All charity from her brother." I'm guilty as charged. And embarrassed about my measly vegetable crop; it didn't seem I had enough time this summer to jar much from my garden. The children became quiet, picking listlessly at their food. Robert tapped his fingers on the table and finally sighed. "Bess, you will eat eggs with the rest of us. We will all go to the wedding where we will all eat a delicious Amish feast. We will survive and soon enough my business will pick back up." He smiled and winked at Victor. "Your mother needs to lose some weight anyway."

The wedding ... dismal. How beautiful Opal would've been as a Baptist bride! Evil thoughts while watching the three-hour ceremony: Remember, Opal, to give yourself to him is to lose yourself to you. Goodbye my little sister for you will be a changed woman tomorrow. Submit, give, love – but keep some for yourself. Tonight as I write this I can imagine Jacob in their new bed smothering, pushing, taking, and she losing her girlhood to his needs, opening, clenching, giving.

I am guilty and evil and alone I have these thoughts.

December, 1910: Cady's funeral was today. Her last words to me go over and over in my mind. *Ruby, don't fret it. Do what you must do.*

Thomas sat on the front pew, his head hung low. I didn't know men could cry so.

I clutched the side of Cady's eternal bed and I didn't recognize her with her eyes closed and her lips sealed. Lying down is not how she would want to be remembered. It seems almost indecent.

I dropped the carved dove down into the satin where it rested by Cady's side, red eye blinking in the candle light.

I left the church and walked on to Main Street, heading to the park. The town center looked different at night. It had its shutters and shades closed like every building felt the grief. It's hard to imagine the sunny festive air of the long-ago 4th of July parade here. I pulled my cape tighter around me.

A sheepskin coat appeared at my side. "You almost stepped out in front of my horse back there at the church," he said with a misty breath as if the ghost in him came out through his mouth. Here I was saying goodbye to memories and now I must face my most beloved ghost alive. He was robbing the air that I breathe with that smile.

He kicked away a mound of snow in my path and talked of his travels with Mrs. Catt but I heard little, only felt his presence. "You're taking steps through the snow as carefully as if it's piles of dung," he said.

"I must be careful not to fall."

"I'll pick you up if you do."

"I'm heavier than I used to be."

He stopped at a street lamp and held my arm to face him. He saw then. "You are carrying a child?"

"To be born in March," I answered with a nod.

He dug his hands into his pockets and looked away to the distant gazebo, where I had planned to sit in the cold with his memory. To have his actual body there radiating heat and stirring sensations was like lying under a very heavy woolen blanket. "Walk with me there?" I asked.

Within the gazebo, I felt braver to face those eyes, now a dark velvet in the meager lamp light thrown in here and there. "I dreamt of you." And then I told him about the dream and ended it with saying, "The mist reached for you and you disappeared into it and to the other side of the river but I couldn't find the way." I touched his sleeve. "You were wearing this sheepskin coat – how did I know that?"

Magically our space had become one and all else ebbed away. How does he do that? He reached into his pocket and with his other hand reached for my own. "Every creature deserves a mate of its own kind." The carved dove he placed there was slightly smaller than the first one. I knew this immediately for I had held that one many times while rocking on the veranda, always looking to my left, always making a wish that he'd appear on his horse as before. "Keep this with your other one and somehow you will find a way."

I wished he hadn't given this to me – better to be buried with its mate, but it was too late now and I knew it would go home with me to live a lonely life. I did not have the courage to tell him this.

Instead I hugged him, laying my cheek against his chest, wanting to crawl inside his heart. I felt his cheek on my head. He breathed in deeply. "Ah, your scent of lavender."

"Then take these," I said and handed him the sachet of lavender seeds. I had meant these for Cady, too, but had forgotten. "Plant these and I'll be there." Then I lightly kissed him – yes, it was I! I pulled away then and stepped down the gazebo stairs one step at a time, with a heavy heart and darkness all around me, not light-footed as that summer day. Life takes such unexpected turns.

Oh Diary, I must continue on. I must say that I knew he'd followed me home, staying at a distance like a dark angel. Again, that sound of his presence. <u>You must keep moving, Ruby.</u> I didn't turn around. Snow began to fall. The wind picked up and whipped my cape around my skirts. I bent forward, tucking in my chin, pushing my feet through the higher snow drifts. My legs became heavy and stiff from my wet woolen stockings. My skirts blew out like storm-swept sails, my bonnet's strings let go and away my bonnet flew. Ears, fingers, feet frigid with cold. <u>You must keep moving, Ruby.</u> As if in slow motion I marched higher and higher through the rising white, the wind pushing me back in a whisper to give up, to stop. Tears froze on my cheeks. "I must keep moving," I said out loud through chattering teeth. I rounded the corner and out of the blue I see Robert's home. No, <u>my</u> home. Warm light shone yellow from the parlor window onto the snowy lawn. I had an urge to lie down in it. What a welcoming way to bring a lost soul in.

Robert would be sitting in his chair there, reading, scowling – I was returning later than I had promised him, this being my first outing on my own in months. My stiff fingers still clutched the dove, its carved lines etched with sorrow, its weight grown heavy. I opened my fist and the dove fell into the soft snow and sunk deeper until it was covered completely.

At a snail's pace I reached the railing to the veranda stairs and looked up at the door. Whether he opened it or not, I resolved to make changes for the good.

I took it one step at a time and knocked softly.

The lock clicked and the door opened. He reached to where I stood and grabbed my arm and pulled me in. He looked down at my red, swollen face and ever so slowly his arms circled around me and he held on.

April 5th, 1911: I painted my parlor walls a misty blue today – like the mist in the Blue Ridge Mountains! No more gray! Next I will tear away that thick twenty-year old wallpaper with the damask patterns in the dining room. All that dark dreary mahogany wainscoting and staircase – white! Those heavy red flannel curtains that his mother treasured? Gone! In their place will hang white shears with black lace trim!

Next? Lavender paint for the bedroom walls! Robert has been carrying home a gallon of paint every Friday.

With my near-death during the birth of Little Cady, Robert developed a soft spot not unlike Little Cady's, on that hard head of his and had agreed to the alterations. (It didn't hurt that he got a large contract with the textile mill for work boots.)

Oh it wasn't easy, I'll admit to that. Every time he'd say, "NO, I like the way things are!" and deny my requests for wall paint, my stomach felt like my washing tub wringer was attached to my navel, cranking my pulled skin tighter and tighter and I'd suck in my breath and hold in what was trying to come out.

But come out she did, assisted by one such argument and a forced intimacy that made me hope that the baby had a hard head like Robert.

So upset I was that I ignored tending to his breakfast that morning and instead went to my favorite place here and rocked away, going nowhere fast. I'm here now as I write in my diary.

The March weather felt only cool enough to require my black shawl and I could watch spring come to life through birds and buds on the tree branches, crocus, tulip beds in the next yard ... that's when I saw it. There on the edge of the boardwalk laid a familiar shape. The sun's rays caught a red eye and I was down the stairs and next door as fast as I could waddle. Not a dead bird, but a wooden one with ruby eyes. Lying in a slush of melting snow. Wooden, just like my heart, we belong together.

How ironic that it was this same spot where he had handed me the first one. (It's certainly a good thing that the neighbors on this side don't know me!) Seasons change, all that was, goes away, and life begins again. I wiped it clean with my shawl (and today I continue to hold it while I write and Little Cady naps).

As I was saying, that day I brought it back to the house and as I climbed the stairs, I was seized with a gripping contraction that gave me cause to squeeze the poor bird until surely its wings would splinter.

My well of knowledge earned in last summer's "shenanigans" didn't help here knowing now that pregnancy causes more deaths than any other disease, except tuberculosis. Twenty-five thousand women die every year from this. I sputtered these statistics between contractions to Dr. Hughes who said this was only a wife's tale. He left me alone while he went away to deliver another baby from a woman much older in much more need, saying that my baby will come, with or without him, and he was right about that.

Women do love to talk in depth about their deliveries but I don't have much time before Little Cady awakens. Suffice it to say, Bess and I delivered Little Cady, while Robert paced the parlor. He did assist a little before that, when I insisted he read to me, to distract my mind from body. He appeared at the bedroom door, his eyes darting about as if he'd never been here before. "For God's sake Robert, you were here when the baby went in!" Can you imagine me saying such a thing? I wasn't myself –but maybe I shouldn't be - he did my bidding! He scooted a chair over to the bed and began reading from his newspaper about President McKinley. I kept the sounds of pain to a bare minimum for him, sounding like a trapped mouse. The newspaper rustled and with his head hidden behind it, he said, "Politics are more than you can understand. Here's one you will enjoy. It's not one I'd bring to your attention under normal circumstances–"

"Just read!" I gasped.

"Very well," he said in his maddeningly calm way. He read that history has shown that suffrage is not the way. That as far back as the Civil War, Susan B. Anthony and slave-born Sojourner Truth petitioned the government for emancipation of slaves with the belief that, once the war was over, women and slaves alike would be granted the same rights as white men. However, when the time came, Abraham Lincoln declared 'This hour belongs to the Negro'. "Pity," Robert said. "Abe was your hero and now we find he's betrayed you too."

Anger bore down hard and I sent him away. I had work to do.

Dr. Hughes returned in enough time to save my life and send Robert the bill – as Robert described it. I was bleeding profusely – as the doctor described it.

Oh! Here comes Aimee in a beautiful fur shawl and matching hand muff – looks like another apology from her husband.

April 6th, 1911: Aimee told me yesterday that when she heard me shouting out my window during the labor pains, she at once ran to fetch Phyllis. She brought her here with her midwife skills and basket of teas and tonics only to be turned away by Robert, who told them that no more than a <u>real</u> doctor was permitted in his home. I had no idea he was so protective! I will send a letter to Phyllis to explain this. How I would love to see her – not since Cady's funeral have we spoken. In my letter I will tell her my marvelous idea. It came to me during the night while pacing with Little Cady. My idea is this: We need a place to run to in the storm of a husband's drunkenness. And we could use the Pickering manor. Phyllis told Aimee and Aimee told me that Thomas no longer lived in the manor and was looking for another use for it. We could call it the Lighthouse.

Little Cady is crying.

April 15th, 1911: Phyllis loved my idea so much, she answered my letter in person. "Do this," she said and she gently stroked the baby's nose from the bridge down to the nostrils as I breast-fed her. "Do this several times while nursing to clear the mucous." I hope it works and that Little Cady will begin breathing easier and sleeping more.

He paces with Little Cady during the night as much as I do. His mother hadn't allowed him to hold our first four infants. As I watched him pace last night I had an amazing revelation – Robert was growing up. Had he struggled these last two years without his mother telling him what to do? Does a mother have that sort of power? It's true I tell my children when to eat, sleep, and what to wear – I could also tell Bess where to go and what to believe in! She's such an obedient child. I could have Bess pick up where I left off.

And Robert would never be the wiser for it. He'd pay no attention to the teachings of a mother to her daughter. And aren't I only doing what Preacher Paul preached - about God's hierarchy and the natural order of man?

He handed Little Cady over to me so very carefully while saying, "She's a cute little thing. Were the others this perfect?" Actually she's quite frail but I dare not bring that home to him. Instead I unbuttoned my gown and brought her to my breast. She hungrily moved her head back and forth until her mouth found her connection. Ah, that sweet tugging – what did Phyllis call it? Yes, <u>stimulating</u>, that's it. Never did I feel so close to my babies as I did in breastfeeding them. To be able to give nourishment like no man ever can. For the first time, I feel sorry for Robert.

"You look happy now," he said. "I prayed that another child would bring you back … your smile. Well, to be quite honest, I thought I was losing you. First to another man."

Dear Diary, I thought I would faint! With my heart in my throat, I glanced over to him. He was inspecting his hands, rubbing hard at the permanent shoe dye stain in his cuticles.

"But then you explained that he was Cady's husband, Thomas, and he was simply giving you a ride home in his blasted motor carriage.

"And then I thought I'd lost you to those high and mighty women and their damned cause. I had to bring you down to where you belong – with me. I did things I'm not proud of." He cleared his throat – the only thing customary in this dialogue, I assure you.

"Then I almost lost you to death and I would be partially to blame, for it is my child that would've killed you. Only then did I realize." He paused and finally met my astonished eyes. "I love you. There. It's said. That might be the first time I've said it but." He slapped his hands on his knees and looked around helplessly, finding himself in a realm he wasn't accustomed to.

"Paint the rooms!" he suddenly announced with a proud smile. "Paint all the damn rooms you want!"

Bess's Chapter Five -- 1920

What is Family?

Mary Sue had stayed at Mama's for four days after my wedding. On the fourth evening she walked home smelling of lavender. Handing me a sachet she had made - *Thomas and Bess* cross-stitched with our wedding date on one side - she smiled shyly. Her expression revealed no criticism of me. This was short-lived.

She took papers from my hand and pulled me to the front parlor as if someone important were there waiting to see me. No one was there; the house was quiet with Lizzie on an errand and Thomas at the office. Mary Sue pushed me down onto the sofa.

"You have to sit for what I'm about to tell you," she said. Her expression had changed - her eyes wide, her mouth tightly turned down.

I dared not let my mind guess so I folded my hands in my lap and waited.

"I just came back from your mommy's house," she said, sitting beside me and patting my arm. "I stayed longer to help her wash out the bedding. With Pearl gone so much of the time, and you here doing Lord-knows-what, your mommy just can't do all that lifting on her own."

I knew in my bones this had to be bad news.

"Last night your mommy asked me to sit with your daddy while she went next door to visit. He was in a state for shore. Like my daddy says, nervous as a long-tailed cat in a room full of rocking chairs."

She spoke so slowly I prayed silently to keep from screaming at her.

"I knowed what was wrong right away. I told him he didn't need to worry about you marrying again. You love Thomas a lot more than you loved my daddy, I told him. 'Course I told him it wasn't right you leaving my daddy after just one night, like we had cooties. But you couldn't help yourself. You thinkin' my daddy loved Miz Ruby more than you just ain't true, so I told him don't go worrying about that either. Daddy loved *my* mommy the best. Your daddy kept asking questions and I kept telling him not to worry. But. Well. You know your daddy's been real sick and he took a turn for the worse last night. Your mommy woke up this morning with him cold as stone beside her. Sometime in the night he drew his last breath."

I absorbed her meaning, feeling each line like a dagger, gawking at this impassive child. I wanted to kill the messenger. No, I wanted to kill the murderer! "What are you saying, Mary Sue? That my father *died?*"

She nodded gravely. "He just couldn't go on anymore," she said in a monotone, her eyes dazed. "Your wedding took what little he had left in him. He didn't want to eat anymore, talked out of his head like he was still working in his shoe store and your mommy was a customer. He—"

Rage took me to my feet. I grabbed her collar and jerked her to her feet. "Do you realize what you've done?" I shook her. "Do you? You vindictive crazy bitch!" I shoved hard and she fell back down onto the sofa.

She sat where she fell, limp as a rag doll. "Don't blame me for your sins," she said in that same monotone. "You think you can treat—"

I slapped her mouth shut. "Shut up you fool!"

Papa is dead, oh my God, he's dead. Mama! Poor Mama! I have to go to her!

"Straighten up!" I shouted. She obeyed, holding her cheek, her expression slowly changing to fear, as if she were coming up out of a bad dream.

"Mary Sue, do you know how to use a telephone? Do you? Answer me!"

She had the audacity to scowl. "Yes. I'm not stupid!" This I was beginning to see.

"Then ask the operator to connect you to Mr. Pickering at the Annan Newspaper. He's scheduled for an important interview and can't leave now. I'll run home, but just tell him what happened and to drive there as fast as he can. Can you do that? Can you?"

Her shoulders lifted as the bearer of such important news to Thomas. Her mouth relaxed into a martyred smile and she nodded. "Don't you worry. I'll let Thomas know."

I rushed toward the front door.

"And Lizzie, too!" she called out.

A block or so away, I waved down a taxi and finally reached my childhood home. The house already looked different. The threatening rain clouds fitted the occasion and the worn-out three-story wood and fish-scale siding had a doomed grayness surrounding it. Its second story window blinds were pulled down like eyes closed in death, the grief of another life lost here prevalent. It was like facing brother Jonathan's death all over again. Gloom settled around my heart and slowed my steps. I didn't want to walk into this grief I knew permeated these walls, grief which would bring tears of loss and worse, guilt. Damn that Mary Sue to hell! Already I wished I had been a better daughter to him as I took the steps to the verandah.

"Bess, he's gone."

I turned to see Mama in her rocking chair, partially hidden in the shadows. I rushed to her side and hugged her, relieved I wouldn't have to go into the darkness of the house just yet. "I know, Mama. Mary Sue just told me." If Mama only had a telephone I would've known sooner.

"No, I mean he's gone. The undertaker just left with him ... his body. They'll do whatever it is they do to a body, and then will bring him back here. Those were his wishes; to have his funeral in the parlor, just as we'd done for his mother. He'll be buried beside her and his father, as his mother had planned. Everything in this house seemed to go as his mother planned. Sometimes I'm not sure if I ever got the reins." She continued to steadily rock and gaze ahead of her as if her rocker was taking her for a ride through the past. "Look at that poplar tree there. It used to be so small I could see through its branches when I used to bring Little Cady out here and rock. Pearl believes Little Cady was born and died out here, but of course you know better than that. I feel like I can just think better out here. I can barely see around its trunk now, it's grown so big. Everything's grown, except me. Everybody's leaving, except me."

She paused in her rocking and turned her gaze down the street as if her ride took her to a scene to reckon with.

"At one time I wanted to go; when I saw him riding down my street right there, sitting tall on his horse, knowing he was looking only for me, I wanted to go with him. I dreamt about it but I couldn't get to the other side. There was no way to cross that river."

Her rocking resumed and she faced the tree again.

"My journey remained on this side of the river, to raise my five children, to see them move out into the world, to lose two to death. Little Jonathon; how I miss him and his arguments with his big brother Victor. Robert tolerated his two boys, but his girls, well, they seemed to have minds of their own he couldn't understand. But he tried in his own way. A day or so after your wedding, he said, "Ruby, I believe Bess has grown up to be a good woman." He gave Pearl his blessing for her marriage to David, too, and for the first time said he was proud of her. She was respectful enough to pretend she needed his permission.

"But I think you and Pearl were good women before you found a man to marry you. I taught you both to have your own lives, your own thoughts, and I never apologized to Robert for that, even if Pearl did get a little wild. She'll be fine. She and Victor have gone with the undertaker. Victor and your papa had money put aside for this, he said. I don't know how much or what the plan was. I'm told not to worry, they'll handle it. And so now I must see Robert go and this, too, is out of my hands."

I'd never heard Mama talk so, her eyes dreamlike and misty, but not teary. It wasn't only the December wind that chilled me. Mama felt it, too, and pulled her old black shawl tighter around her.

"Were you in love with him?" I asked.

"With all my heart."

She wasn't looking ahead any more, but down the street. I almost expected to see a man on a horse there.

Victor and Pearl's return from the undertaker brought Mama out of her trance. Victor looked so much like Papa it was as if Papa's spirit had simply moved down a generation to have another go at life. He looked stiff and uncomfortable surrounded only by his womenfolk. His big brown eyes – cow eyes I used to call him in our younger days – were red-rimmed and his square jaw was set to tolerate, as I'd seen Papa do so many times.

"The wake begins tomorrow night," he said as we sat around the table munching leftover bread and fried chicken, our family tears sufficiently subsided enough to eat. "We'll be up all night for the wake when his body gets here. Bess, plan to spend the night then. You can sleep with Pearl. Caroline and I will sleep in my old room on the third floor. The funeral is the next day. Preacher Paul will preside over the funeral. He'll be here tomorrow for prayers. Don't cook anything. I would imagine tons of food will be brought in from the church ladies once word gets out. Thomas can put this in the paper, Bess. Write something nice for the obituary, or better yet, I'll talk to Thomas about it. He'll know what to do."

I had chosen to forget Victor's domineering demeanor. It all came back to me in double irritation. But more so, I wondered where Thomas was at this late hour. He should have been here by now.

Victor leaned his chair back to look out the dining room window. "There he comes now. Beauty of a car. Has a darkie with him, though. With a house like that, I suspected slaves all along. Or could it be he has a mistress already?"

I ignored his feeble attempt at humor. At that moment, I wouldn't have cared if Thomas brought a flapper girl. I needed him - and at last hugged him tightly to tell him so.

"We would have been here sooner, but that little missy didn't tell us until after we ate supper," Lizzie said, deep lines in her dark brown forehead telling me of her fury.

"She didn't call you, Thomas?" I asked.

"Only to tell me to come home early for dinner."

"She sat in your place at the dinner table, Miz Bess," said Lizzie, "like she was Queen Victoria. Said she didn't want to spoil our appetites until we'd had a good meal. That girl wants to rule the roost, I tell you. I left her there to clean the kitchen," she added, looking quite pleased with her retaliation.

I had enough to worry about at the moment and did not wish to air out any more of our home laundry. "The funeral is day after tomorrow," I said to Thomas and Lizzie. "What time is the funeral, Victor?"

"One in the afternoon. After the funeral, we have an appointment at the lawyer's office to hear the reading of the will."

He scowled at Mama's stunned look. "He didn't tell you he had a will?" He shook his head when she shook hers. "Pity. He should have told you." As if giving her further clues, he added, "This is the same lawyer who drew up the papers for the Walk Wright shoe store transfer to me. We had an agreement. I thought you knew all about it."

"Your father told me little about his business. I thought *you* knew that." She sounded as if she felt like me; I wasn't appreciating the suspense either.

"Do you know what's in the will?" I asked.

"A little." His attention remained on cutting fat from his beef. "But I'm not obliged to say. It's legal jargon you wouldn't understand. Best left to the lawyer to explain." He placed his knife carefully on the left-hand corner of his plate.

A chip off the old block in every way.

The wake droned on and on and was putting me to sleep. I felt suffocated in the hugs of the crowds of people who came in and out of the parlor. Uncle Jesse and Aunt Edith squeezed me hard at the same time.

"Your papa and I didn't have much to say to one another," Uncle Jesse said, "but he was a good enough man, I believe."

"Every wife's fear, this is," said Aunt Edith, sniffing and shaking her head.

Aunt Opal and Uncle Jacob quietly patted Papa's hand – an unnatural manikin color, made worse by being manicured - old stain from shoe polish gone now – as if comforting him. I couldn't touch him. The man displayed in the coffin was a skeletal version of the papa I remembered from youth, even different from his sickly pallor in his last few years. I no longer wanted to be reminded of the years gone by and how death sneaks up on a loved one.

He wasn't going to wake; this old custom of staying with him in this cramped parlor suddenly seemed horribly morbid. The stroke of midnight coming from the mantle clock was the last strike and I sneaked out when Victor went to the privy. How I missed Thomas!

Shivering and exhausted from the long walk, I finally found my way through my front door. Without the aid of lighting I fumbled up the stairs to our bedroom. The door opened of its own accord and I stood face to face with Mary Sue, a candle in her hand illuminating wildly frightened eyes at seeing me there.

"What's the matter, Mary Sue? You look like you've seen a ghost," I whispered. It sounded more like a hiss. "Why are you coming out of my husband's bedroom?"

"I-I thought I heard something. I-I was afraid."

My borrowed nightgown covered her bare feet but she was shivering. I had a hunch she wasn't afraid until she saw me.

I grabbed her arm and squeezed hard. She whimpered and tried to get away. "You tell me now why you are here!" No longer a whisper but I didn't care.

"Let her go back to bed, Bess." The bedside lamp came on, revealing Thomas propping himself up in bed, bare-chested. He rubbed his eyes.

"Not until she explains to me why she's coming out of our bedroom!" I began to tremble, too, although more from seeing his nonchalance than from seeing her.

"I think she was sleep-walking. I woke up to find her standing here beside the bed, just watching me. The candle coming close to my face is what woke me up. Gave me quite a fright."

"Why did you think I was Bess's dead sister?" she asked.

"I didn't," Thomas said, smoothing back his own unkempt hair.

"You called me Cady."

"Cady. Oh yes," he glanced at me and then looked down and picked a thread off our wedding ring quilt. "I thought you were a ghost."

I examined her tousled light brown hair and her red lips. "You kissed him, didn't you?"

She backed up and shook her head, but her eyes belied her denial.

I shook her. "Tell me the truth!" Wax spilled from the candle onto my bare toe but I didn't care.

"He kissed me back!"

I decided to deal with him later. I pointed my finger at her, dismayed by its trembling. "You have gone from bitch to whore. You have betrayed me for the last time. I will write your father tomorrow to come immediately and take you back where you belong."

She sucked in her breath. "No, I don't want to go back!" She turned to Thomas. "Please don't make me go back. I'll behave. I promise. I love you, Uncle Thomas. Don't punish me for that!" She put her face in her free hand and sobbed.

I thought I had left the sobbing back at my parents' home. I'd have no more of it.

"Stop crying now you foolish woman-child. Why do you love another woman's husband? Are you stupid? Ignorant? Don't you see anything wrong with that?"

"He wasn't your husband when I fell for him. I know this is wrong and Daddy would wring my neck if he found out. Please don't tell him, Miz Bess!" She wiped her eyes with the back of her hand and nodded to me willingly. "I think tonight has cured me once and for all."

"I can't let you live here."

"Could I live with your mama? I start school in a few days. Just for a few more months. Please, Miz Bess, we got this far!"

Yes and how far would you have gotten if I hadn't shown up tonight? I thought but didn't ask. Her pleading eyes, hair laying softly about her shoulders, the white gown glowing in the candlelight, all gave her an angelic look. An angel who had fallen with Lucifer, I reminded myself.

I shrugged. "That is up to her. As long as you're out of here. You certainly don't sound homesick to go 'back home' these days." I mocked her hillbilly accent with this last line and felt at once ashamed for being so catty. Abruptly drained of emotion, I wanted no more of this scene. I felt nauseous. Mary Sue seemed to bring out weaknesses in all three of us.

I stepped out of her way and pointed down the hallway, imitating Victor's tone. "Go to bed, Mary Sue. Go to school tomorrow. Don't come to the funeral. Give Mama a few days and then ask her."

She nodded and ran down the hall. I stood still until her door had closed behind her.

"Come to bed and I'll explain," Thomas said, patting beside him.

"I don't want to talk about it anymore," I said and prepared for bed.

He snuggled against me under the quilt but I could only lie on my back, stiff and unfeeling as Papa was, lying in his parlor. My husband's face appeared above me, his body moved against, around and from within me. He moved rapidly, lurching his shoulders as if trying to get someone off his back. I wondered which one of them it was.

"I have to talk to you, Bess."

"Of course, Mama, come in. Did you walk here?"

She nodded and wiped at her swollen eyes with a scrunched handkerchief. "Your papa never did buy a motor car – death contraptions he always said they were. Sorry to interrupt your supper, but I had to talk to somebody."

"Come into the front parlor and sit down. You look exhausted after such a long walk. I apologize for having to leave right after the funeral today, but Thomas and I were scheduled to talk on a radio show at three and this kind of publicity must be taken when offered."

We sat together on the sofa.

"You were on the radio," she said as if trying to bring good news through her shroud of mourning. "Your papa would have loved to hear that. Maybe he did. Preacher Paul said his spirit is amongst us if we ever wish to talk to him. Mercy, what I would say to him now!"

I patted her hand. "You miss him, I'm sure."

"I'm not sure what I feel. What I'd love to say to him right now is that he did a terrible thing!"

"Is this about the will, Mama? The lawyer read the will to you this afternoon?"

She nodded and looked for a dry spot on her handkerchief.

"Victor certainly was being evasive about it," I said. "Obviously for a reason, now that you're so up—"

"He willed the house to Victor, Bess!" Mama cried. "Can you believe it? He gave away the house I shared with him and cleaned for him, and birthed five children there. I painted that old place and gardened around it and it became my own, only to find – no, to be *reminded* that your papa considered it *his* house and then his first-born son's house. It's a man's world, no matter how hard a woman works for it. Women have a right now to vote? Not me. Mercy! I didn't have a say!"

"This is legal?" Another damn statute I thought.

"Oh yes, the lawyer assured me of that," she said with a dry chortle. "But of course Victor was quick in pointing out that it remains my house, too, and I'm expected to live there, just move to a smaller bedroom is all, says Victor. He and Caroline and my grandchildren that she can't control, they're all moving in next week. If Jonathan

360

was alive, he would've put a stop to this. His heart was so like my brother Jesse's, but Victor is more like … " She paused.

"Papa," I interjected. I knew this to be true. Although Victor was only one year older than me, his teen years brought him into bossy manhood that "vastly" exceeded my years in "higher knowledge", a term he enjoyed using with me. Jonathan was four years younger than his brother but kindly stood his ground, or walked around Victor. He laughed at his brother's higher knowledge and told Victor: *the only way you can get higher than Bess is to climb that tree and live with the birds, and although you're a bird brain alright, you don't belong up there so high and mighty, but down on the ground pecking for food like the rest of us chickens.* Memories of Jonathan tugged at my heart and I wished Mama hadn't brought his name into this.

She exhaled slowly, visibly relaxing her shoulders, her resentment deflating. Her tone became more matter-of-fact. "Victor hasn't thought this out. I will likely have to move to the third story bedroom, since the second story only has the two bedrooms, now that the sewing room was renovated into the bath room and you know Pearl is in the other – well at least for the time being. I would imagine she'll want to get married sooner now, rather than later. Oh, but she and David postponed their wedding date, and of course Victor's children will need the third story …" Her voice trailed off, her misty dark blue eyes staring through the window at some distant image. "I don't know what to do," she said softly.

She looked about her as if just realizing where she was. "Do you know that the first time I came here was for an afternoon tea with the Ladies Legion? It was my first meeting and I sat on this same sofa. Mercy, that had to be more than ten years ago and nothing much has changed in here. Everything looks a little more tired is all."

I viewed these same faded fabrics and rugs with indifference. The furnishings were usable and I needed no more than that. "Well, as you very well know, the Lighthouse and suffrage brought in a good deal of women, but none of them had decorating on their minds. I'm afraid I'm not any better, having never really settled here until very recently. I still have to move some of my things from my old bedroom up to the master bedroom. I'm accustomed to being transient. I suppose I should start thinking differently as the wife of our future mayor. But that gives me an idea. My old bedroom will be empty and Lizzie is in the next room – why don't you come stay here for awhile until you know what to do. You always said you loved this house."

Admittedly I had another reason: I needed another pair of hands. Lizzie couldn't keep the place tidy any longer and it was starting to show, even to me. How timely that Thomas had put a stop to battered women staying here.

Even as she said, "Oh, I can't do that," a hopeful inner spark lit her eyes.

"Now you're free to live where you please, Mama. You once told me, 'Bess, I'm so tired of watching life through my window.' But you had no choice with Papa. You should know that I stayed distant from men and marriage because I was afraid of your entrapment."

"Oh, Bess, you've done very well, whatever the reason behind it. I believe that I have at least done one thing right: sending you here. Only with you do I feel I've accomplished something on the outside. My own daughter could march in parades and petition without serious repercussions. And have no one at home to tell you not to. I thought it only modesty that prevented you from boasting, but now I find no pride here, only the word 'entrapment'." She stood up. "I've had enough shock and disappointment for one day. I'm going home."

The more rooted I became, the more opinionated. Growing a heart wasn't necessarily a good thing. Saying what was in my heart wasn't either. Neither one of us was ready for the accusations I held inside. I decided to lighten it up a little. I gave her a mischievous grin.

"You have to admit, you didn't make the marriage bed sound too tempting with your birds-and-bees talk."

Her ancient ankle-length black wool dress made her look as worn and tired as our surroundings. She sighed in such a defeated way, I felt more forgiving. "Mercy, Bess, what are you talking about." She sat back down.

"Do you remember when you thought Billy and I might be getting married? Only there were no birds and bees in your description, but bulls and cows. Does Ruffenreddy ring a bell?"

She gave me a weak smile. "My own wedding night was a difficult one. Naivety can be a curse. I wanted you to be prepared."

I doubt I could have prepared for intimacy based on Mama's version. Taking me to Uncle Jesse's dairy farm and comparing the mating of a man and woman to the shocking scene of a bull mating a cow was frightening and overwhelming to a young girl. Ruffenreddy was the name Uncle Jesse had given to his stud bull and Mama used this analogy to describe the man's physical urges. I had a terrifying image of me on my knees and this huge red appendage ...

"Fortunately I have had sufficient time between then and my own wedding night to forget the fear I once had at being roughly mounted like a cow," I said. We both blushed. It was at that moment that I realized how to spell the bull's name: Rough-and-Ready.

"I should go home," she said sounding undecided. "But ... I don't have a home to go to." The tears returned. She dabbed at her eyes and smiled feebly. "I really am having a pity party, aren't I?"

"You're not going home. You are home. You'll feel better after you've eaten. Remember what Grandmama used to say, 'You can't fill your mind with thoughts if your stomach is empty'."

"I hate imposing ..." but allowed herself to be led into the dining room where she received a warm welcome by Lizzie, Mary Sue, and Thomas. They each cared for her at different levels but all agreed she must come and stay for as long as she needed.

While Lizzie and Mama discussed bedroom arrangements, I spotted Thomas letting out a long sigh as he poured himself more red wine. He must have wondered if he would ever be able to shed himself of the Lighthouse.

Even more disturbing was Mary Sue's happy face; she wouldn't have to move to Mama's house after all.

Thomas and I prepared for the open-air debate with jittery hands. Buttons and bow ties, cups and papers, were handled with tremors extended to the object in hand. Tension grew heavy in our room and down at the breakfast table where we found only a plate of scrambled eggs and bacon warming in the oven. I questioned Lizzie's sense of responsibility but Thomas ignored me and had no appetite. I had never seen him nervous before. I reacted to his terse comments and constant movements likewise and finally I could take no more.

I let my fork fall with a clatter to my plate. "Really, Thomas, you're acting as if you have ants in your pants."

He chewed for a moment. Eventually he said, "Wool makes me itch." No doubt; he no doubt forgot about the Dress Reform Movement and insisted on woolen long-legged underwear, starched shirt collar, high shoes and a new black Sack Suit with a matching vest with silk piping. What had happened to the casual confident Thomas in his light linen suit? He looked out of his element.

At least he would be warm enough. A blanket of February clouds hovered above our walk through City Hall Park to the large white gazebo, promising a long lack of sunshine and a possibility of snow.

Fortunately, warmth beyond our own capability to provide each other was given generously by those who came to offer their support. Their applause was like a good shot of prohibited whiskey. Gaiety mounted as the band struck up the tune, *Oh, you great big beautiful doll!* and Thomas highlighted the moment by directing a wink and grin to me.

Until I counted the small number of people in attendance – approximately seventy-five or so, when we had hoped and planned on two hundred or more. The aisle down the middle of the rows of wooden folding chairs divided sides and it seemed that more than half of the folks were on our side – the right side of course – but biased perception seems like truth at the time.

The audience – far more women than men – began settling and clucking like hens in a henhouse. Support primarily by women could do more harm than good. It got worse. With people taking their seats, I had a view beyond the crowd and gasped at what I saw: Lizzie and Mama were passing out signs that read, *Thomas Pickering paved the road for women!* and another that read, *Mr. Pickering is in Union with all women,* and yet another with his own slogan, *T. P. for mayor: He's on the right road.*

I hadn't authorized this! I stepped up into the gazebo to notify Thomas but George Groves had beaten me to the punch. His sprouting eyebrows met in the middle of his red forehead, his small eyes flashing anger.

"What the hell is your next act, Thomas? Why is that damn nigger woman marching up and down the aisle with that sign? Perhaps you could have her sing 'Mammy' next?"

Sure enough, Lizzie was indeed coming down the aisle with a sign. A colored woman should not be doing this; Lizzie had forgotten her place and Thomas would lose votes over this.

I began expressing my dismay to Thomas and George but George shook his head and hand at me like he was shaking off a pesky fly. "If she doesn't pull a Houdini and disappear, I'm walking off the stage!"

Not certain if he was referring to me or Lizzie, Thomas gave me a jerk of his head and I exited. I took no chances. George didn't want this debate in the first place and Thomas couldn't have one without his opponent. Thomas gave a slit-to-the-throat sign to the bandleader, who in turn pressed the air with his palms as if trying to push the music into the ground. The music faltered and fell and the ladies hurriedly found seats as if playing musical chairs. Someone took Lizzie's arm and pulled her to the last row of seats. She looked confused and out of place around all these white people.

George and Thomas each had five minutes for their opening statements. The moderator, Mr. Gibbons, posed the pre-planned questions. All was going well. Thomas answered the questions in a clear, clean manner I was proud of. The debate had not elevated to a shouting match.

Then Mr. Gibbons appeared to have lost his place. "Let's see," he finally said, his cough an exclamation point. "It's Mr. Pickering's turn to answer our next question first. Mr. Pickering, if you are elected Mayor, would you run your office ethically and morally? That is, would you be willing to close down the jazz joints and women's houses that sway our youth and our mothers into jumping ship and drowning in alcohol and divorce?"

I tensed. This question had been added unbeknownst to us and Thomas was stuck between a rock and a hard place – between boozers and women, alone in the middle of the aisle. It was well known he was against Prohibition.

"Freedom is a five-syllable word," he said. "It is Let-The-People-Choose. Jazz joints are legal in themselves, lively with dance bands and innocently serving soda drinks. Hullabaloos and Classy Jazz are reportedly packed with town folk every night. If these town favorites are closed down, you only satisfy some of the people, but not all. Those who wish not to go and dance to the great Al Jolsen or laugh with the Ted Lewis Jazz Band's *When My Baby Smiles at Me,* can stay home with their Victrolas and listen to the sweet lullabies of Lucy Gate singing *Mammy's Song.* Neither choice is wrong. The important thing in our town is freedom of choice. Give folks options of entertainment. We're in the heat of the Twentieth Century, the war is over and gaiety can be a part of our lives. We have the motor cars and new roads to travel to places not thought possible before. And to bring in folks from far away who can share their own culture. We just recently had the privilege of the Golden Jubilee Singers colored gospel group right here at the City Hall Park. Their beautiful harmonies matched those of the original Jubilee Singers of the 1870s singing, *Swing Low Sweet Chariot* and *Steal Away.* What if some people took exception to colored folks singing in public, and said, No, close them down? Shouldn't those who love gospel music have a say? I say the same about jazz music and dancing. Some love it, some hate it, but all should have the choice to go or stay away. Let-The-People-Choose. Mr. Groves, over to you."

"Thank you, Mr. Pickering," George said. "Considering you have one Negro vote here, that speech should do you a world of good. Ladies and gentlemen, did you notice that my friend here,

Mr. Pickering, failed to answer the second part of the question? This is why." He paused for effect, having captured everyone's attention. "He has directed his home over the years under the disguise of a women's house. Married women indeed hide here from their estranged husbands, but in fact Mr. Pickering has taken advantage of this to his own personal pleasure. I have very recently learned that his house is no more than a harem."

He held his hands up to the disturbed crowd, murmuring and moving about in their seats like the hens were suddenly awakened by a fox.

"That's right. Wives, women relatives, concubines, and Negro slaves have lived there. One little girl living there now is only fifteen years old and is willing to testify that Mr. Pickering made inappropriate advances toward her. His second wife lived in Mr. Pickering's home for years under the disguise of taking care of these supposedly-battered women but the truth was she had a husband somewhere else, too, while carrying on an affair with Mr. Pickering. What must our Christian town of Annan think he's been doing with all these women? Now he claims he's settled down, if you can call it that. Oh yes, Mr. Pickering is married to a divorcee. A divorcee with a criminal record, arrested and jailed in Washington for her suffragist antics."

I sat on the front row, mortified into staring straight ahead. The rumblings behind me became louder, the hens turned into hornets and George had thrown a rock at their nest. His hands clutched the gazebo railing hard enough to make his knuckles white. He raised his voice to be heard.

"Ladies and gentlemen, you should know that I am a deacon of the Clover United Church, a solid citizen who believes in right and wrong and if it's wrong it shouldn't be allowed. What message are we relaying to our children? What do you think they would choose, if told they could have the freedom to choose between going to school and staying home? Wrong is ugly, plain as the wart on your nose—"

"I've heard enough!" someone shouted. I twisted around in my seat to see a woman in the back row work her way around knees to the aisle, her long blonde braid bouncing like the reins of a mare.

I saw then it was Aimee, Mama's soft-spoken next-door neighbor. Her high pitch shook as if unaccustomed to these elevated heights but she projected her voice for all to hear. "Mr. Groves, I am one of those supposedly-battered women you refer to and if it weren't for Mr. Pickering's generosity of the Lighthouse, I would be dead! You are being brutally unkind, Mr. Groves. Mr. Pickering did not direct his house of women. He *gave* his house *to* women. He saved my life and many other women who had been beaten by their husbands. No one else would have done such a thing in those days. *And* I can testify that in all the time I worked and lived there, Mr. Pickering did *not* sleep a night there."

"And I can testify as a *former* slave," called out Lizzie as she stood, "that Mr. Pickering never slept there a day after his first wife died, until he married Miss Wright." She jerked an indignant thumb toward her heaving bosom. "*I ran the Lighthouse,* Mr. Groves. Only Mr. Pickering would trust a poor old Negro woman to do such a thing."

Phyllis of the original Ladies Legion stood. "I, too, worked there for years and can testify the same."

"So can I," shouted Mama. "And I," shouted another.

George raised his hands in surrender. "I apologize, ladies, if I have offended you," he said in a patronizing tone. "I only thought it proper to let the public know what I've been told – by what I considered a most reliable source, since Miss Mary Sue Phillips also lives in this same house. She is also willing to testify, but to quite a different story I assure you."

"Your time is up," Mr. Gibbons announced abruptly. "Mr. Pickering, your rebuttal, please."

I sent a subliminal message to Thomas: *Do some negative campaigning for once - please bring up his "housekeeper" and divorce from Eunice!*

Silence followed for a pregnant moment. I could almost hear Thomas' thoughts gather and rearrange themselves. My own thoughts screamed against the silence, *Mary Sue, you're going to wish you had a Lighthouse to run to, when I finish with you!*

"Mr. Groves, ladies and gentlemen, I've been a resident of Annan for thirty years, and for that thirty years I've spent my time reporting to you all of the town activities, whether that be crime, corruption, war deaths of our men, or suffrage for our women. Never, in all that time, was I accused of falsehood or dirty dealings. You be the judge. Let-The-People-Choose."

With that, he stepped down from the gazebo, grabbed my elbow and we walked away, leaving behind us a silent crowd and the sound of camera flashes popping.

I clung to the notion that Thomas would win the election right up until the announcement was made that he didn't. The night after the debate, I sat there numbed from exhaustion and comprehended nothing. Shocked from the news that George had won by a tight margin of eighty-nine, I absent-mindedly patted Thomas' shoulder. I looked around our crowded parlor and entrance hall to family and volunteers and felt as if I had personally let them down. Their eyes of disbelief trailed into pity and I hated this road we were on. I wanted to get off and get away from the "I'm-so-sorry-I-can't-believe-it".

But somehow Thomas carried this with strength of character, raising his arms as if lifting this weight above his head. "Folks, can I have your attention, please!"

He stepped up onto an entrance hall chair and the group immediately hushed, looking up to him for relief. He bestowed on them his heartwarming grin. "I'm the luckiest man in town so let's not have a pity-party, shall we? I say that because I see love and support that I didn't know before that I had. I want to thank you from the bottom of my heart for that support. You're what gave me the votes I got – I have no one else to blame but myself for the votes I didn't get. Insisting on a debate the day before the election was a political faux pas on my part."

Uneasy titters circulated around. "The point here is the majority ruled that George would be the best man for the job and we'll just see if they're right. He's a conservative right-winger who took the moral high ground promising closed nightclubs, strong business, and less union. My scales of equal opportunity were no match to his lead bottom."

He grinned and raised his hands to the guffaws. "In a nutshell, what this means to our little town, is now it will be all work and no play, and more signal lights telling us to stop and go on roads too bumpy to go anywhere."

"Pos-a-lootly!" said David.

"I could be wrong, I could be wrong," Thomas said, shaking his head. "We'll just have to wait and see. If not, perhaps David here would be interested in running?" Rumbles of laughter ran through the group. Pearl put her arm through David's, smiling hopefully up at him, proud he received the attention. David's chest rose as if inflated.

"In the meantime, I intend on heading south for awhile and enjoying my old age a great deal more before the Almighty votes me outta here for good. I'm sorry I can't serve you from the mayor's office, but today let's just celebrate life and let me at least serve you tea and butter biscuits in my humble home. No more sad faces, agreed?"

I analyzed his composure and his gestures as they emphasized his words, and he was as cool as a cucumber. Not only had he lifted that weight, but he had thrown it off. He actually looked relieved. "Again, I want to thank all of you, I don't have to name names because all of you are here. Well, I guess I better recognize one. Bess come over here. Bess was the wise woman behind me, telling me what to say and when to say it." He placed his hand over his heart and looked directly down at me. My heart soared up to meet his. "Bess, honey, thank you for your devotion and trust. Now can we live our lives in peace?"

Everyone looked my way, laughing easily. I pretended to think about it and then nodded. They all applauded, including Thomas.

I was amazed at how he had switched the mood from dark to light, as easily as turning on a light switch. The air became almost festive, definitely light-hearted, for they saw what I saw: Thomas was as happy – if not happier – without the added responsibility of political office. Why hadn't he told me this before?

I asked him this precise question that evening as my head settled on his shoulder in the privacy of our bed.

"If you'll recall," Thomas said, "it was not I whose eyes lit up at the thought of campaigning. You were most eager to step out and petition for another cause, albeit for opposite reasons than before, in bringing in yet another lowly man into political power over women. Not nearly as exciting as saving women from men, I wager. I thought my being mayor would make you happy. I'm sorry I have failed you."

"Oh, stop it Thomas. You haven't failed me at all." I thought about my unhappiness in the midst of celebrating the women's vote. "Besides, I think I'm most happy in the journey, not at the end of the road. Where shall we journey? South?"

I was thinking short-term as I snuggled in against him, my hand moving down his stomach. We hadn't been intimate since the night Mary Sue encroached on our most private space. He grasped my wrist.

"Not tonight," he said to the ceiling.

My hand rolled in on itself to hug my stomach. I desperately needed a hug; Thomas had been less than affectionate these last two weeks. A moonbeam coming through our window lit checkered patterns onto the Wedding Ring quilt, leaving half of some circles in the dark. I turned away, onto my side.

"We're at a crossroads, Bess, if you want to know where we are. I'm not sure which direction I'm taking. For now, I'm heading back to my southern roots, if just for a few weeks. This town has taken everything I have and I need to replenish these old tired bones."

"I understand you're tired, Thomas, but couldn't you rest here?"

"I have trouble sleeping in this room." He paused and caught his breath as if wondering whether to finish his thought. "I have strange dreams."

"About your first wife?" This was a natural guess since he had called Mary Sue by his first wife's name that nightmarish night.

371

"She's either dressed in all white with a sickly face not unlike her last days, or in all black and looking most healthy. Either way, she's propped up in this bed and watching me pace the floor. In these dreams my role is to enter the room and pace the floor. Sometimes she only watches, other times she says things like, "stop moving", or "you must settle or you'll be sick like I". Once she said, "I love you, Thomas" and I looked at her as I walked by the bed and her face changed into Mary Sue's."

"She was likely wearing black in that dream," I said.

"Yes, she was!" he said, sounding surprised.

I wasn't.

"I've had this dream in one form or another about four or five different nights now and it's to the point that when I enter this room, I half-expect to see her here, propped in bed. I'm haunted by this. Can you understand?"

"Yes. After I received word of Billy's death, I dreamt one night that he was running toward me on the street, his clothes were ablaze and he was yelling, 'The British are coming! The British are coming!'"

Thomas chuckled. "Sorry, I shouldn't laugh. Were you frightened – in the dream – or mistake him for Paul Revere?"

"Yes, of course, I was frightened – he was on fire for goodness sake. But I also realized that I'd combined several facts into one dream. First of all, his body was burned when they found him and his aeroplane. Secondly, he wrote a great deal in his letters about the British folk, and thirdly, although I hadn't thought about this until now, he was warning me he had fallen in love with a British woman.

"So, if that were so," I continued, "then Cady is giving you a warning to rest. She represents white and goodness, and the face of Mary Sue represents darkness and evil. Easy interpretation." So easy I hoped he would have another dream to tell him to settle down here.

"Speaking of Mary Sue, have you heard from her?"

"No, she told Mama that she's staying in hiding at a friend's until she's prepared to explain her conversation with George Groves. She claims he twisted what she said to him."

"He has a knack for that, you must admit, Bess."

"We can resolve this problem with Mary Sue together. Don't leave me alone here, Thomas."

"You will be fine with Lizzie, just like the old days."

"I don't want to journey backwards."

"I do. I need some time to think, reflect. I think I'll start a journal. Why must old age make you look back to where you came from? To measure the distance we came? At any rate, I need to be alone. People have swamped me for months now. Since I've been courting you, come to think of it. You're a loner like I, yet you seem to bring in an entourage of people for one reason or another. Most of them, like your first husband or Mary Sue, you don't really know or care to know, and it's hurt our reputation. You're like a magnet."

"Then you won't find peace with me, then, is that it? I attract chaos?"

"Your voice is shaking, Bess. I've upset you. Once again I say I'm sorry. I'm not really blaming you. I'm not leaving you for good. I'll be back in the spring. But just so you'll know, I'm heading south the first of March."

Lost election, the bedroom, the dreams, Mary Sue, me – I could close my eyes and throw a dart at any one of these as a reason he was leaving. I swiftly felt shallow and chilled as if a wind had blown me backwards, as easily as tumbleweed.

Listless as I felt as his Duesenberg pulled away, there were still some areas of my life I wanted to take control. Areas that drove Thomas away, and if fixed, might bring him back. I closed the front door and headed to my roll-top desk, its opening like a large mouth willing to tell all. I began writing:

Dear Jere,

Here's hoping this letter finds you and your children well. Your oldest daughter is doing well academically and her health seems fine. But her emotions are in turmoil and this has caused strife amongst those who care for her. To be more specific, I recently remarried and Mary Sue has developed strong immoral attachments for my husband. She is relentless in displaying her affections for him and in coming between us. This has made our living conditions difficult to say the least. I could attempt to ignore past indiscretions but recently publicized mis-communications have taken this too far. I can no longer allow these living arrangements and ask that you come to Annan to take her back home. In the long run, she will be happier there, as she never really outgrew her homesickness for her hills of Tennessee. I can only hope that schooling is available there for her so that she can graduate from high school and teach, as she had planned to do. I do apologize that I cannot help more than I have, but my marriage must come first.

I ask that you make the trip here to escort Mary Sue back to your home at your earliest convenience, preferably by springtime.

Warm regards,

Bess (Wright) Pickering

"Howdy Miz Bess."

I flinched so that I gave a curly-cue to my last name, making it look like Thomas' signature.

"I see you've come out of hiding."

"I wasn't hiding." She came over and stood beside me, looking at my paper. "Are you writing another speech for Thomas?"

I placed my hand over the letter. "No, there will be no more speeches. You must have heard that Thomas lost the election? Doesn't your friend have a radio or read the newspapers?"

"Yes, I know he lost. But you're always writing speeches for one reason or another. Maybe a Goodbye-I-Lost speech."

I narrowed my eyes at her. "You do realize you're part of the reason he lost?"

"You blame me for everything!" she said, putting her hands to her hips. "Now I get the blame for the way this stupid town votes, too?"

"You made Thomas sound like he was chasing you, rather than the other way around."

"That's not what I told Mr. Groves. He got it all wrong. On purpose, I bet."

"Safe bet, Mary Sue. But what did you tell him?"

"Where's Uncle Thomas? Is he mad at me? I can explain everything but I want him here because he'll believe me."

"Thanks to you, he's gone away for a few weeks. You're stuck with telling only me."

"Uncle Thomas is not here?" Her smug expression fell. A touch of fear watered her eyes. "I told him that Uncle Thomas kissed me when Mr. Groves asked me if he had made a pass at me while I lived here. That's all I said, but it seemed to satisfy that dirty old man. He just nodded and smiled and said, 'Just as I suspected!' People were talking about you and Uncle Thomas anyway. So don't blame it on me."

Forgetting about the letter, I folded my arms across my chest. "Really?" I challenged.

She saw the unshielded letter then and snatched it from the desk. She backed away from my attempted grasp, reading it. "Oh. Oh! You *sow*! You *harlot*!" she screamed. "I'll get you back for this! I will!" She ran from the back parlor, the letter clutched in her fingers.

"I'll simply write another one," I called out to her, proud with the satisfaction of sounding calm. I pulled out another piece of paper from the cubbyhole, my hand trembling to spite me.

Thank goodness Mama and Lizzie were out of earshot in the backyard, standing in patches of snow trying to resuscitate the old wooden washing machine with the annoying squeak in the crank. But this reminded me that I must concentrate more on the domestic necessities around here. I had no access to my husband's funds and he had given Lizzie her monthly allotment for household goods as if nothing had changed, including my status here. I hoped to have enough money put away to buy a new washing machine with a stainless steel tub, one that ran on electricity. The Eden Washing Machine with the Sediment Zone. *You can buy as you like and pay as you save*, I remembered the advertisement read. I wished I had written that. A new machine would make Lizzie's job easier – and eventually these duties would pass to me as Lizzie was becoming more feeble and bent, as if always ducking some imaginary doorway too low for her height. Mama helped where she could but hadn't officially moved in although she slept here most nights. She was bringing in a couple of items at a time, like a squirrel taking a nut or two to its hideaway.

Biting on my pen tip, I looked down at the blank sheet of paper, wondering if I should be so blunt this time. Perhaps being vague would suffice, but still insist on Jere coming to the rescue. I once thought of him as a sort of knight in shining armor. He could be so again, only this time to rescue me from his daughter - and vice versa. No, flattery wouldn't be appropriate coming from a married woman, and Jere would see through it. I began writing and the words flowed same as the first, showing my desire to say what I wanted to say for so long. I took in a deep breath as I signed my name again, glancing toward the door and her likely reappearance.

I smelled smoke. I sniffed the air. I was sure of it. Had Lizzie resorted to building a fire to boil our clothing? Surely not. That was backbreaking work and I would feel terribly guilty for not dealing with that machine sooner. I walked to the parlor doorway and sniffed again. It smelled like more than just wood burning. Hurrying to the back door proved only that Lizzie and Mama hadn't given up on their wooden friend, bent over it with an oilcan to its wringer rollers like feeding a child.

"I smell smoke," I called out through the screen door.

Mama straightened and looked around. Her gaze rose above me to the second story windows and her eyes enlarged in a frightening way. She touched her throat. "Lizzie, grab that watering can. There's a fire up there!" She grabbed a bucket and dipped this into the washing machine's filled belly of water. She and Lizzie took off running through the back door, down the hall, into the entranceway, and up the stairs, water splashing about their skirts and floor.

I followed suit, my fear of fire since being burned as a child coming back to me in spades. Mama threw open my bedroom door and we all gasped at the flames eating away at the bed's feather mattress and climbing rapidly, licking at the lace canopy. The extra oxygen brought in by the open door lent itself to the fire's hunger and the bed and its four posters were quickly engulfed.

We swiftly threw what was left of the water in our buckets onto the fire. I rushed to the bathroom and turned on the faucet in the bathing tub and here we replenished over and over. Mama, Lizzie, and I would fill, run, and throw, fill, run, and throw, all the while coughing through the smoke and bumping into each other in our haste. Oddly, no one shouted, or even spoke, expressions intense and tight-lipped to the dangerous task. They were braver than I, working much closer to the flame. At one point, Lizzie wet a towel and beat down fire that was rapidly covering the large fluffy pillows, her walking cane thrown aside somewhere. Sparks flew into her hair and caught hold of her dress and for one terrifying moment, I feared for her life. She became our center of attention until she was safe again. We labored hard until at last, after an eternity in hell, there was only smoking ash.

Blackened bedsprings, exposed now, looked like the innards of a large overcooked animal. All fabrics including my beloved wedding ring quilt had been grotesquely shrunken into small black scrap pieces. The wooden headboard and footboard, and the night tables were deeply scarred. On the floor by the bed was a partly charred piece of paper. On closer inspection I recognized my penmanship. It was what was left of my letter to Jere.

We tucked strands of singed hair behind our ears and began the long arduous task of cleaning and mopping. I knew better by now than to threaten Mary Sue, force her to clean this up, pay for the damage. She would only be intimidated, stay low like a smoldering ember, and then flare again. Evening fell before we collapsed, reaching a point where there was no more to do – in the bedroom that is. I had one more mission to complete before I would retire for the night in the spare bedroom. I returned to my desk and wrote a telegram. To hell with letters and waiting for spring. Tomorrow I would take Mary Sue back myself.

"What do you have to say for yourself, little missy?" Jere asked Mary Sue. I had asked him to meet me in town at the same boarding house of last summer and we sat on the same front porch where he had proposed to me. I suddenly felt that for all that had happened since, I hadn't gone very far.

"Nothing," she answered, her eyes remaining down as she and her father pushed the swing with their feet.

"Nothing," he mimicked. "Is living in a beautiful house with clothes you would never have seen otherwise, with schooling we could only wish for, *nothing?*"

"It don't mean nothing to me. I kept telling Miz Bess I wanted to go home but she wouldn't let me go. I was some pet, being trained to do tricks."

I opened my mouth to dispute, but only knew too well that Mary Sue was baiting me. Her daddy was here now; let him handle her.

"Little gal, I can tell you're getting too big for your britches. What *does* mean something to you."

"You, first of all. You weren't happy and Miz Bess made it worse. I hate her for what she did to you and not wanting anything to do with us kids. I wanted to get even with her for leaving us like she did. I watched you and you treated her good and was so patient. But she came to our place all high and mighty and looks down her nose at us like we're pigs in a pen with uncurled tails, and then she takes off after one night, like she was afraid of getting dirty or something. She hurt you real bad, Daddy."

"It's not like you think, Mary Sue."

"I know what I saw, Daddy. When you came back from driving her to Nashville, you moped around, yelling at us kids for the small-est things, sitting by yourself outside, rocking in the rocking chair like you was some old woman or taking off in the woods overnight. You even said it was our fault she left because there was too many of us. Or that we was mean to her. But we didn't treat her mean at all."

Jeremiah shook his head. "I shouldn't have done that. I was blaming everybody but me. I blamed your mommy for leaving me alone to raise you younguns. I was blaming you for looking and act-ing like your mommy: you forget nothing, you forgive nothing. I was mad at Bess, I was mad at all you kids, I was mad at the world. I've been simmering inside for years. But when I put it all in the pot and boiled it down, the only thing left was my toughened heart. It was my fault and nobody else's." He leaned forward in the swing, its needlepoint backing making him look out of place with his leather vest and weathered boots. He seemed in deep thought, rubbing his chin as if contemplating something.

He smiled apologetically at me. "Well, I hate airing out my dirty laundry here but since you've had to wear some of it, I reckon I owe you a glimpse behind the clothesline." Elbows on his knees, he looked toward the street like it was a road into the past.

"I know what my daughter has done here is terribly wrong but she came from two parents that should never have been and we made her what she is today. Let me go back a ways.

"As you know, I escorted Mrs. Catt to women's conferences and meetings throughout the northeast, from Tennessee to New York City. From about 1909 to 1911, I did this quite regularly. I had a few speeches up my own sleeve and being part of a minority, I could talk the talk because I'd walked the walk. I knew what it was like to have the white man view you as inferior. But what kept me doing it was my true love."

Mary Sue snapped to attention, that familiar scowl between her eyes telling me she considered this news another force to reckon with.

"I couldn't shake that sweet, dimpled smile and how her eyes shone when she recited her poem at the Women's Rights Convention. She spoke with such conviction when she started her poem and when she wasn't allowed to finish, I, well, I decided to speak for her. Every time I spoke for women, I'd think to myself, 'Ruby, sweetheart, this is for you.' Sad thing was, I became so lonely after that, like something was missing all the time. At every convention I kept doing double-takes at someone resembling Ruby, thinking she might have shown up."

He scratched his sideburn and I noticed then how much silver had been penciled into his black hair since last I saw him. Yet and still, his face showed little aging. "Around about 1911 I spoke at one such conference right here in town. A girl I'd been sweet on in my younger years came up to me afterwards, telling me she thought I spoke to her heart. She said she had no rights as a woman and I could tell her daddy was still a no-count moonshiner because of her pitiful sack dress and holey shoes. Rosemary had a pretty face though and I wanted her smile to fill up that empty space I had. If you want to know what she looked like, my little girl here is the spit-tin' image. Those big blue eyes the color of the sky on a hazy day.

"When I look at them I think of what my mommy used to say: if you have brown eyes, you're as shallow as a mud puddle. But blue eyes show you're as deep as a spring-fed lake. Of course I knew that wasn't true because Mommy had those Cherokee brown eyes that could see right through Daddy and me, blue eyes and all. As it turned out, Mommy and Daddy knew Rosemary's family, the Lorry's. Over the ridge and in the next holler is where they lived. Always mad at the world, feuding with somebody about all the time, the Lorry's were. Didn't believe in worldly things, they said. Didn't allow a deck of cards, liquor, or a bad word in the house. You were either a devil or an angel and the world – which only went to the head of their holler where their church was posted to keep out evil spirits – was short on angels. They wanted to make sure Rosemary turned into an angel. So they wouldn't hardly let her go out of their sight. She hated them for it and the best way to get even was to marry the half-injun her daddy chased away a few years before. We didn't have much time for courting and besides, as Bess can account for, I court fast and marry fast. Rosemary was eager to elope and that's that, daddy's good girl went bad.

"We were scratched out of her Lorry family Bible. Their daughter had turned wicked for spite and had gone to live with the devil in a tee-pee. The more children Rosemary had, the madder she got because her mommy and daddy wouldn't look at them. She dwelled on this and festered. I didn't help matters none. She'd yell at me or bawl about the kids, or fume about her daddy, and I'd do what I saw my daddy always do: take off for the woods. Hunt or fish until I'd think she'd cooled off. Of course she always just seemed madder when I got back."

Jere looked over at Mary Sue and studied her expression as if determining if she should hear the rest. She indeed looked more grown-up in behaving and listening.

"One day, when Rosemary was expecting our youngest, she up and dressed the younguns like they were going to church and waltzed the three hours to her daddy's house. Sure enough, her daddy run her off, her little savages with her. This was right before harvest time in the heat of summer, so Rosemary stopped a ways from the house where she couldn't be seen, and struck a match to her daddy's cornfield. Mary Sue saw the whole thing. Then Rosemary sent him a note: 'If you want the fire out, say you're sorry and I'll do a rain dance for you.'"

Jere sat back in the swing and his hands became more animated.

"He lost his crop and Rosemary went into labor from the long walk back, and bled to death. The worst of it is I could have stopped it if I had been there but my oldest boy and I was on a three-day fishing trip. I should have seen it coming. For days she had been on the warpath about her family having a reunion and she wasn't invited. I didn't want to hear anymore about how I was not a red man but colored yellow because I was afraid to go down there and scalp every last one of them. So I took off. I come back a day too late with a mess of fish, only to find a dead wife, seven motherless children, and a whole houseful of angry family blaming each other. Rosemary's mommy was blaming Rosemary's daddy, Rosemary's daddy was blaming me, and I was blaming Rosemary."

He beseeched me with his lake-blue eyes. "Mary Sue came from a long line of 'vengeance is mine, sayeth the Lorry's'. But I say, forgive her, for she knows not what she does. Like I said, it's my fault."

"I don't need forgivin'," Mary Sue said, pulling on a thread on her smudged school jumper. "And you don't either." The same dress she had worn the day she set the fire. I had gone to her friend's house and practically dragged her to the train station direct from there. We'd been traveling all night.

"It's Bess' fault," Mary Sue said to Jere. "If she had been our mommy, this wouldn't have happened."

Jere and I both sighed audibly, but mine came from relief.

Vanessa Russell

I returned home to the truth about Lizzie. Mama explained that Lizzie had developed serious infections from the burns to her calves. Mama had been applying salve but Lizzie had told her too late and now red streaks were moving up her thighs. Lizzie began running a high fever and talking out of her head and only then could Mama call a doctor. Otherwise Lizzie flat refused to see one. She had no trust in doctors; had seen enough leach-sucking quacks, she said. She would only allow Phyllis to call on her, but a midwife was limited in healing burns. The doctor was on his way and would I please talk with him?

I went to see Lizzie first: stretched out on top of her sheets, eyes closed, swollen legs loosely bandaged, barely visible in her red cotton nightgown.

"She doesn't want a lamp on," Mama said from behind me. "Only all of these candles."

Her wheezing was a sound I recognized as possible pneumonia from my ambulance driving days during the war. Men who had lain too long from serious wounds and had breathed in too shallow. Now Lizzie. I could hardly believe my eyes as I held her feverish hand.

Lizzie's eyes fluttered open and she licked her large lips. "So your mama told you. She wasn't supposed to unless it was life or death. You being here tells me something." She spoke in her deliberate way, only lower and full of air, like she had just run in from the clothesline with an armful of laundry. How many times had I seen her do that? I now longed to see her do that again, healthy and humming her gospel tunes.

"It tells me you're being stubborn as a mule," I said. "Why did you wait so long?"

"Because I's weary. Because there's nothin' no one can do. Because I's nigh on eighty years and I's not asking the Lord for any more. I's done took more than I had a right to. So let it be. The doctor, if'n he's worth his weight in salt, will tell you the same thing." She closed her eyes.

"Would you like a drink of water?" I asked, now really worried because she wasn't concentrating on her words anymore.

"See, you won't let it be."

"You're not being reasonable—"

"Sing to me. Sing me *Swing Low, Sweet Chariot,* like Mr. Pickering talked about in his speech. I's been thinkin' about that song ever since. I saw dem. The Jubilee Singers. All been slaves befo', black as coal. When I saw dem, I'd gone into town with my misses and dere dey was, standing on boxes in the square, a-singing proud, dressed up in fancy white folks' garments. That's when I knows I could be free too. I'd stayed on at the plantation after the war that freed us 'cause I had nowheres else to go but den the Jubilees' songs told me better. Not long after, Mr. Pickering, he found me along side the road with whip marks 'cause I'd run away before." Her voice dropped down lower and lower as she spoke and I eagerly leaned forward to hear her rare monologue. She attempted to lick her lips again, her tongue resembling a strawberry in the midst of chocolate. "Mister can't save me now. But I knows one thing. You's not his first love, but you's his last. He jes don't know what to do with it and you's got to show him."

She paused and licked her lips again. "Miz Ruby?"

Mama leaned forward into Lizzie's vision. "Yes, Lizzie?"

"The first time I met you was in this house," Lizzie said. "You sez den you's tired of spectating. Now you's come back and don't have to do that no mo'."

She linked her large-knuckled hands on her stomach. "Sing to me."

We did as best we could, each remembering words the other had forgotten until the doctor arrived.

She was right about the doctor. He had little hope for her. "She's old," he said. "Just give her what she wants."

We sang every gospel song we knew, Mama knowing more than I did. For two days we sat by her side giving her what she wanted. Except one thing; her last words to me were "forgive the chile".

I sent my second telegram of the month. I had a post office box address to Thomas's childhood plantation, now owned by his brother. He had said he was headed there. I could only hope he got the message and had begun his trip back to New York.

On the third day, I heard the front door opening and I took off running from my bedroom down the stairs, my heart heavy at the knowledge that Thomas had come home too late. And yet my heart beat strong in my chest at the thought of seeing him again.

His looked somber in his black suit and the deep lines around his mouth made him look years older than he had when he left, less than a week ago. Most of that time would have had to have been on the road.

"Thomas, you're home!" I said hoarsely, holding on to him tightly. His coat was cold and damp from the late evening air.

The staff from the morgue had carried Lizzie away that early morning. Mama and I were in shock and had hardly spoken or known what to do, any discussion sounding loud in this death shroud. Thomas would look after everything.

He patted my back. "I came as soon as I got the telegram, but with the roads ... where there were roads ... " He faded off and I nodded in understanding. "How is Lizzie?"

"She's gone," I said into his coat.

Grabbing my arms, he pulled me away and peered down into my face. "What do you mean, she's gone?"

"She died early this morning, Thomas. She said to tell you she loved you like a brother."

He saw my tears then and brought me back to his chest. "Oh my God," he whispered. "How could this happen. How?"

Another death; the same girl to blame.

Thomas stood in the middle of his large bedchamber. The bed was gutted now; only the scorched headboard and footboard remained, connected by iron railings with blistered paint. Black marks etched the floor boards, one particularly bad spot looked as if it had rained oil, reminding me of where Lizzie stood, the hem of her dress burning, sparks flying, as Mama and I flapped and fought the fire.

"Everything about this house I loved, is gone now," he said. I wished his tears would match mine as I stood in the doorway, but instead his eyes were dazed, and his mouth and shoulders sagged. His poor posture pouched his stomach like he'd overeaten. The weight of his sadness hung heavily in my chest. I longed to relieve us both.

"We could sell the house," I said.

He shook his head at me, unbelieving. "You love this house."

"I love you more."

He raised his eyebrows in surprise. "You'd move from here? You seemed so entrenched I thought I'd have to dig you out of here to bury you."

"You're what I'm attached to. I can live wherever you are."

"You don't know what you're saying, my dear. I should never have married again; I can't settle here. And now that Lizzie's gone …" He shook his head and shrugged his shoulders.

Fear clutched at me as I grasped my hands together to keep myself from running and clinging to him. "Thomas, have you forgotten I've traveled for years?" I felt better then, my own calm voice reassuring me. "I only rooted here because you asked me to. Old memories have bogged you down, not I, so please don't blame me. This old place is too much to maintain on my own. I'd be just as happy in your old apartment. You are what makes me happy. I thought you knew that."

I prepared myself with a deep breath to ask what was really weighing on my mind. "Don't I make you happy, Thomas?"

He folded his arms to match mine and nodded his head, eyes on the floor. "Sometimes so much, it scares me."

"No need to be scared of me, Thomas. I'm not a ghost but I am your wife and I fully expect to live with you. Wherever that may be."

His mouth protruded in thought, reminding me of Lizzie's. "Well, then, let's just see if you do," he said to the floor.

I accepted the challenge. "Tonight is a good night to start. Our bedroom is down the hall; third door on the left. I'll be the warm body lying on the right side of the bed."

He gave me a small reminder of the glorious smile I'd missed so much. "Let's move on with it, then." His heart seemed missing from the words but I didn't care.

Ah, to have his full attention on me, on the tiny pearl buttons on my nightgown, unbuttoning each one slowly with bright eyes as if anticipating a wonderful Christmas gift hidden inside. I gave him all I had, nude that I was. Worry and waiting had been replaced with want and need and I took control. If I didn't learn to lead, I'd fall behind and lose him.

I at last fell exhausted onto his chest and listened to his heart beat at a reporter's pace and then slow to a writer's steadied measured state. I held on as I slid to his side and heard him sigh. And I held on even tighter as later in the night his head cradled between my breasts and he cried like a baby. I knew then that he had come home to me for good, no matter where we were.

Lizzie's tombstone epitaph read what Thomas wrote: *Helped many women who fled to her door/Liberated now to sing to her Lord.* Its marble effigy of an angel stood as tall as any prominent name carved into stone in the cemetery. I had no doubt such a remembrance cost Thomas a pretty penny but 'she's family', he said. Papa's was only a few plots away and his plain headstone and gathered withered leaves tucked around the hard mound looked forlorn and ignored next to Lizzie's brightly flowered resting place. Standing at one gravesite with recent memories of another was the saddest moment of my life. Poor Mama looked as if she couldn't take any more.

So much grief and guilt swirled around me till I was in a dense fog. Sobbing rang in my ears and I had to stop it. I grouped together the remnants of the old Ladies Legion and we sang, *Swing Low, Sweet Chariot.* The song brought comfort to us all, just as Lizzie would have wanted. Somehow I believed she was watching, rocking and humming along with us.

The fog lifted. I felt light on my feet. I saw Thomas clearly, standing by an oak tree, hands in his pockets staring back at the gravesite with his head tilted in his reporter fashion, like he wanted to ask Lizzie's spirit a few questions. The sun filtering through the branches highlighted blond strands of his hair that age hadn't captured yet. I felt a strong urge to hold him and squeeze out any left-over sorrow.

I walked over and hooked my arm through his. "Penny for your thoughts."

"I do believe Lizzie just spoke to me," he said. "I heard, plain as day, Lizzie's voice in my head saying, 'I'm going home. You will, too.' Home is Georgia. I'm moving back home. *We* are moving back home. We'll sell the house here. The Pickerville Herald offered me an editor's job and by God I think I'm going to take it."

He nodded toward the fresh heap of dirt that would eventually settle down around Lizzie, as if to say, thanks for the tip. He took long strides toward the motor car and I had to advance my pace to keep up. "Lizzie was a wise old gal," he said. "She knew the only way to get me out of there was for her to leave first."

I thought how Lizzie served this man like he was her master. "Why did Lizzie never marry?"

"She did."

"Lizzie was married?"

"She didn't speak of this? Perhaps I shouldn't either." Thomas opened my door and shrugged. "Oh well, doesn't matter now. Lizzie was forced to marry another slave when she was thirteen. To make more slaves, naturally. She started running away after that, saying one master was enough, and she sure wasn't going to answer to two. She said all her life she was a lady looking for liberation." He motioned for me to get in the car. "Looks like she finally found it."

I glanced over and saw Mama laying flowers on Papa's grave. She wiped some of the fallen leaves away, reminding me of how she used to tend to his bed. She straightened and, wiping her hands on her long black woolen dress, joined her legion of ladies with a smile.

In that moment, it seemed to me that death, especially such a painful one, was necessary to free the living.

Spring winds whipped in and around our front seat of the Duesenberg as it motored toward Savannah. Behind the wheel highlighted in the morning sun, Thomas shone like a golden angel in his cream-colored shirt, tan trousers, and gold wedding band, blond and silver strands of hair carelessly blowing about. When sitting alone now and my thoughts turn to Thomas, this is the first image that surfaces, always radiating and fresh as a spring thaw.

Thomas was saying, "You may not like my brother at first. You may never; I'm not sure that I do, but Joe's an interesting enough character that someday I might write about. But I'll wait until he passes on, because he'd kill me if he knew the truth. For the truth is, he's hot-headed, cold-hearted, and lead-bottomed. He looks behind him so much, he knocks down every opportunity in front of him. I tell him he's too busy looking at what could have been if the South had won. He loves to talk about himself, even if it's bad, and he'll tell you what he's doing to make himself better and what you can do to make yourself better. But don't you remind him of his sore spots. You're a Yankee and wouldn't understand. He has a sign at his gate that reads, 'Welcome To The South, Now Go Home'.

"You'll like Harriet more. Only she can get away with telling him he's dumber than a hoe handle but built like a Greek god. Then she gives him a hug and sends him back outside. She's a strong woman who holds that plantation together with thread and feathers. She raises geese and ducks and stuffs their feathers into sewed mattresses and pillows. Joe says soon she can stuff them with dollar bills, if business keeps growing like it is. They're living on that for now since Joe's lost most of his cotton crop to boll weevils."

Two days later we pulled into their long winding driveway, weeping willows tiredly lining the sides. The one story white clap-board house rambled east and west of its center entranceway as if additions were added as family grew. Inside and directly across this large entrance hall was another formal entranceway facing the river. People used to come in that way when traveling by boat in the early days, explained Harriet, so it was considered the front of the house for many years until roads were better traveled.

Joe and Harriet gave us welcoming hugs, Joe telling Thomas that he 'looked like the rear end of hard times'. He had barbed-wire manners but I wasn't surprised by what he meant. Thomas was not fairing well. My man of the world had not handled this trip the way he used to and looked exhausted. The night before was spent sleeping on the front and back seat of the motor car, what with no lodging within several hundred miles of Joe's home. Not to mention mud splatters on our clothing from several events of pushing the metal beast through nature's deterrents. We had experienced three flat tires but Thomas was prepared with sufficient inner tubes, an air pump and patches. Gas fumes permeated our skin from the gas containers required to travel with us to cover the long intervals between gas filling stations. This being my first long trip by motor car, it was no longer a wonder to me why there was so much discussion and campaign promises to build more roads. I was ready to march and petition myself for this worthy cause.

Joe was not exactly a Greek god but more like a good example of the adage that beauty is in the eyes of the beholder. He was muscular enough through the arms and shoulders, a necessity in running a plantation no doubt, but too well fed by his doting wife who referred to him as 'my ol' man' and whose shadowed brown eyes followed him everywhere. She claimed he ran her ragged, and quite literally her bony structure looked that way in her patched house-dress, moving from one room to the next with cotton ticking in her hand. I suspected her once-upon-a-time good looks had been worn thin from over-use.

The only similarities I saw between Thomas and Joe, was the jaw line and wide smile, but Thomas looked much more the southern gentleman, whereas Joe with his waxed hair and mustache and small blue eyes squinting against the smoke of his ever-constant cigarette pinched in the corner of his mouth, looked more the part of a salesman. And in fact, he was gradually "herding" motor cars into a field that no longer proved profitable for crops. These he would make like new again, he claimed.

"I've sold these at five years younger than they really are," he said with a wink. "Speculating the age of a motor car is like figuring the age of a woman; it hinges on how much she's fixed up. One coat of enamel cosmetics and she's sold for a hundred dollars more. I got the idea from a billboard on the side of a barn outside Atlanta. Now if I could only fix my wife up like that." He smacked her buttocks like one might with a well-behaved horse.

"Charfin' on you," she said evenly. She took his cigarette, placed it to her own mouth and inhaled deeply, and returned it to its owner's corner. She seemed unaffected by him as if he was the lame leg she had grown accustomed to but wouldn't dream of amputating.

I lost sight of why we were there. Thomas wavered between being lethargic and nostalgic. He began to lose track of his story, the worst thing possible for a life-long reporter. Two weeks went by and still no news about a job at the Pickerville Herald, but I was more concerned that he wasn't actively making inquiries.

I read controversial newspaper articles to him, using them as sticks to stir his blood in the southern views of, *no progress is the best progress.* The news would read: *Improved roads would only bring the northerners in and let our children out.* The headlines boldly declared: *The Ku-Klux Klan Hit Again.* "Women were barred from the voting booth," I read loudly.

I tired quickly of southern patronage and even more so of their expressions. But Thomas only made it worse with, "Darlin', you've come to the cow's barn lookin' for cotton." He seemed content to remain in the bedroom of his youth reading Mark Twain or writing in a journal I'm not privy to, nor can I find where he's hidden it. Or he reminisces over dinner and alcoholic drink with Joe and a cigar. On several evenings Joe and Thomas went to town, saying they had business there and did not return until much past midnight.

Joe's expectations of his wife had also become contagious. Evidence of this was revealed one night as I excused myself from dinner for bed. I had had enough of memories and how the future would never make up for the past.

Thomas paused long enough in his rendition of the battle at Gettysburg to drawl, "Run my bath for me, darlin'."

His accent was bearing its native tongue more and more, especially with the drink. I turned in surprise just in time to see Harriet wear a smirk. She and I had already run out of things to talk about, being that her favorite topic was same as Joe's: Joe did this and Joe did that. The sun rose and set on him and I was just too blind to see.

"Yankees simply do not know how to take care of their men!" she'd said once during her sharing of assumed knowledge that the divorce rate was higher in the north. "Of course I'm not surprised," she added, "since women suffrage began there."

"Mrs. Thomas Pickering," Thomas later called from the bathing tub. This was behind a screen in the corner of the ample bedroom, added there with a small sink as an afterthought of modern plumbing.

"Isn't it enough I assumed your last name, without taking on your first too?" I answered.

He handed me a cloth as I approached. "Have it your way. Wash my back, Bess Pickering. Come to think of it, start at my head and wash down as far as possible, then go to my feet and wash up as far as possible. Then wash my possibles."

I paused. "Pardon?"

He laughed. "That's what my mother used to call our privates. Possibles."

Another endearing expression to endure but at least the subject had changed. This energized me. "I'll show you my possibles if you show me yours," I said and pulled my gown up over my head and let it fall to the floor. I stepped into the millions of tiny bubbles, feeling his slick legs move aside to make room. I sank slowly into the tepid water, thousands of bubbles bursting around me in whispers.

He grinned, obviously pleased with his woman. "This is getting interesting," he said. I bit back my retort that our baseline for interesting topics had reached rock bottom in the world of Joe but I was determined to wash it all away and bring us back our own little world.

I soaped the cloth and started with his face, moving down, as his hand roamed around. "Do as much as possible," I teased. I cherished his hard-earned focus on me: intense eyes, swelling member, moisture on his upper lip. I licked this and tasted soap and salt. I dropped the cloth, desiring instead to touch and taste his slippery skin, the hair with the smooth, the hardness and softness of it all, the clean mingled with the sweat. The water sloshed and cooled as our movements and breathing quickened and our bodies heated. The tide rose and washed over us both, leaving us trembling and then shivering.

"I love you. I want you to know that," he said as his hand fell away and he closed his eyes. He looked totally spent, his once flushed cheeks now cooled to insipid. I stood dripping water from goose bumps and shriveled nipples, and helped him to stand, feeling closer to him than I had ever felt before, as if our pliable wet flesh had molded like clay on the potter's wheel. I embraced and warmed as I dried us, limp and loose he was but enough of an upward turn of the lips to know he was contented. He remained naked and fell into bed. I tucked in beside him, still needing him, my recent awareness of such married pleasures yearning to make up for lost time.

Katydids sang me to sleep and katydids roused me, carried on the cool night air blowing through the window sheers. I reached for him, enjoying his exposed buttocks, fondling, knowing now how to touch to bring him to me. Soon he was over me, in me, watching me, until I gasped, before he gave in to his own. He collapsed on top of me and finally I was satisfied.

"What you want to do is—"

"How do you know what I want, Joe?"

Joe rubbed his cheek hard, calluses against whiskers, like sandpaper on splintered wood. "What I *do* know, little lady is that your *husband* told me to teach you to drive an automobile. *Au-to-mo-bile.* Remember that is what they're called down here. That is what I do know. And if you know more than that, then I'll just stop wasting both our time."

That tweaked a memory of what I read once in the New York Times: *The new mechanical wagon with the awful name automobile has come to stay.*

I sighed and tapped the steering wheel. All I knew was that I wished Thomas hadn't gone into town. Or that he had taken me with him and we were searching for our own home, apartment, anything. I was reaching my limit with the haggard southern belle and her overbearing hankering-to-be Confederate soldier.

He took my silence as surrender and continued. "Now this steering wheel you have a hold of is hard for a woman to manage. Your weak little hands will need leather gloves to get a good grip and use your whole body weight to press down on the foot brake. It can go as fast as fifty miles an hour if we want it to. This long stick sticking up here in the floor is to shift gears as you go faster. You have three speeds in this here transmission – well I don't mean to use big words to a girl, but all you need to know is you have to shift three times." He brought up three fingers, in case I didn't understand.

I went from lady to woman to girl. Why did I get younger in his dialogue? He wasn't the only one who referred to women as girls nowadays. Why were we perceived as being more childish since we earned the vote? It suddenly became obvious to me that we must prove ourselves all over again just because we get to vote.

"Joe, it may amaze you to know this, but I drove an ambulance during the war and although motor cars have changed over the years, I do know this is a Pierce-Arrow. Did you know that Pierce-Arrow trucks were used during the war? I saw them in the New York harbor, being shipped to England and France. As then, the headlights continue to be set inside the wings that give it a stately look in my opinion but the embroidered seats are a new fashion I think. Being a mere woman, I've also noticed that this particular Pierce-Arrow is well balanced, yet is slightly ostentatious, don't you think?"

He blinked in reply and I took this as surrender. "Do you see these windshield wipers, Joe?" I pulled the lever to operate them. "Did you know that a weak little woman's hands invented these? Mary Anderson was on her way to New York City when she saw street-car drivers opening the windows of their streetcars in order to see through the rain. She invented a swinging arm device with a rubber blade that the driver could work from within the motor car - excuse me – au-to-mo-bile. Isn't that something?"

He scratched his stomach and focused on the remaining herd of vehicles. "Should have put you in that old 1908 Buick and see how well you do with the steering wheel on the right side. Or in that old 1919 Oldsmobile 37 dash B model, I see that right now. But I wouldn't do that, you want to know why? Because it's un-roadworthy with bad brakes and steering, that's why. And I wouldn't do that to my brother's wife. I can still get twenty-five dollars for it, although old Franky ran it into a gatepost because his wife was sitting in his lap. Should be a law against that. Fords go for more but I'm getting tired of the black bugs. They're everywhere, like fleas on a mangy dog. But I bet you don't know what Ford said about that. He said, 'Americans can have any kind of car they want, and any color they want, as long as it's a Ford, and as long as it's black.'" He said that last line as if not everyone in America hadn't heard that one over and over. He took a long draw off his cigarette and flicked it out the window. "Well let's start her up and see what you can do with her."

I did so, lurching forward. The horses in the corral beside us jumped and whinnied. Wisely, they moved to the other side of their pen.

"You're going to give my horses distemper if you keep that up."

I ignored this statement as I concentrated on maneuvering the clutch and gas pedals with the stick. I had suffered through Joe and Harriet's raised eyebrows when I appeared that morning in my one pair of trousers, but was now appreciative of my choice of wardrobe as my legs worked in unladylike fashion. I slowly motored through the rutted grass, steering toward the lane way.

"You should have seen these horses when I drove these mechanical beasts in here. They took off running, one jumped over the fence, and I almost lost three of them to sickness within a few months. I think they sense that the automobile is replacing them. Can't be helped. Folks can call them new fangled if they want but you don't have to feed and care for these babies as much as horses, and automobiles are cheaper. I had trouble keeping hired hands here for a while though. They were as afraid as the horses were. Everybody's getting used to them now. The town is pretty much split between horse and automobile. We now have four feed barns, three black smith shops, and three gas filling stations. I expect the gas filling stations to increase and the feed barns to decrease. The automobile is taking over and all we can do is step out of its way. Like Tom said, we're in a new era. But it'll be fine because right now our only physical contact with the rest of America is over dirt roads, what don't come in by boat. We've now got a paved road all the way to Savannah. There's even talk of an airport to bring in our mail. Ol' Pickerville is only got about ten miles of paved streets. We need gutters and drains real bad. People can't walk in the streets anymore and the children can't play there so we need more walkways. Of course this road will go both ways and what goes out of Pickerville can come in. People are already complaining about outsiders who are coming into town and robbing and then getting away fast by motor. Hey, did Tom tell you that our town is named after our grandpappy? He just about ran the town himself, through his newspaper. Told everybody how to think and how to vote, just by writing propaganda. Tom could have done the same thing if he wanted to but women keep drawing him up north. First his first wife and now you. This time he says he's here for good. Did you know that?"

I was concentrating on the main road by now. Attempting to steer clear of the wagon wheel ruts, deeply channeled from many years of travel and the hardened craters from *automobile* wheels that had spun in the mud. The massive size of the vehicle handled it well, yet still I had trouble keeping it on the road.

"Hold her steady," Joe said. He slid over to me and reached his arm around my shoulder to the steering wheel and placed his other hand over my right hand, gripping the wheel. "You could use a strong hand," he breathed into my ear.

"I have one, thank you Joe, and it's going to punch you in the eye if you don't move back over to your side."

He did so quietly.

"No, I didn't know that," I finally said to his question. "We must still sell the Lighthouse. It's advertised for sale now. And then we must pack and say our goodbyes–"

"When you learn to drive," he continued and then paused to light a cigarette, "you should go to the soda fountain in town. It's our social center, now that the Prohibition is law. It's right with the confectionery shop – can't miss it. But shy away from town at night – it's no place for a wife. I don't know about Tom's rules, but Harriet's not allowed to go. The dance hall is open every night and there's a speakeasy behind it, though everybody pretends that it's not. Of course I don't see anything wrong with it myself. Making alcohol illegal is only making people want to drink it. It's like Adam and Eve with the forbidden fruit. Those Yankee government politicians are so confused, they don't know whether to scratch their watch, or wind their butt. Hardly anybody is tee-totaling anymore. The rage is to take drink.

"Turn into the Warner's laneway right here and I'll show you how to reverse. We have to get back. People's tongues will wag if they see me out with another woman. Especially Ethel Warner who lives right here. She'd complain if Jesus Christ himself came down and handed her a five-dollar bill. The last time gossip of another woman hit home, Harriet's weight plumb fell off."

With the warm sun and wind on my face and my hair blowing freely, I was tempted to argue and keep driving, enjoying this sense of having control over both these large beasts, but as his guest

I decided to cooperate and show my manners even if I was a Yankee. I pulled into the laneway.

I grabbed the ball of the stick and scratched gears a few times before Joe laid his hand back on mine and we found reverse together. A motor car honked its horn as I began to pull out and we saw it was our Duesenberg. Thomas slowed it down to a stop and got out. My heart lifted upon seeing him. My, he was handsome to me as he sauntered over in his tan suit, wearing his big grin.

"This metal looks good on you," he said, leaning in the window. He smoothed my hair down and patted my head. "How's my girl? Is Joe behaving himself? Are you learning how to drive alright?"

"I think it's more of, she's teaching me she's in the driver's seat, not I," Joe called out.

"That's my girl. Get out, Brother. I need to talk to you a moment." He gave me a wink and walked back to his motor car, Joe following behind. I could only hear murmurs and squirmed in frustration at the intended secrets. After some time of heads shaking and nodding and quick glances my way, Thomas came back and opened my door.

"We'll ride together. We're going to Savannah and we've only got an hour before night fall. Joe will follow."

"What about Harriet?" I asked, half-running to keep in step with his long strides.

"Joe wouldn't allow it. She'd only be in the way," he said. He gave me the once-over. "You're wearing trousers. Perfect."

We soon faced each other in the front seat. "Thomas. She'll be in the way of what? Why so mysterious?"

"We have a job tonight and I need your help," he answered, diverting his eyes to my hand and plucking at my fingers.

"Did you get a job, Thomas? Why that's wonderful! How soon can we move from—"

"It's not a day job, or one you can do in the open, I should say. It's the midnight shift, I guess."

He turned and released the brake, steering onto the road toward east. His business mask was on and his mouth pinched tight. I simply waited; if he needed my help, he would have to tell me what it is eventually.

Eventually was a long run through Pickerville where he pointed out the train station, the hotel, his old school, friends' well-appointed homes, the popular soda fountain, and the dance hall. Thomas boasted of their movie house, the marquee gaily claiming Rudolph Valentino in Four Horsemen of the Apocalypse. I couldn't resist gently reminding him that we (and most people in New York) had seen this film of the Great War melodrama months ago.

He nodded solemnly. "Everything moves slower down here but that's not necessarily a bad thing. It hasn't yet hit the South to censor dances, like they have up there, now that the New York state legislature passed the law saying the state commissioner could do such a thing. But it'll be just a matter of time before it will creep right down here, like a snake on a slippery slope. Now that those religious zealots have pushed Prohibition through our Constitution, their power is supreme in pushing forth their certain beliefs. They think that if our Creator disapproves of any pleasure and only tempts us with desires, we can please Him by refusing to go along with them. It's ridiculous. If a few men over-indulge in drink or in dance, then all mankind must give up the right to indulge at all. Now they're advocating that Jazz music, card-playing, and dancing be tabooed. Should we just sit in a somber way and wait out our days pondering the joys of heaven? Will we be able to dance in those streets of gold with David and his harp, when we can't do so now?"

He smacked the steering wheel. "Look at these streets here! They used to be filled with gaiety, music pouring from the saloons, parties and barbeques in many a home. Now any laughter is hidden underground. Those that rise to the top, lose their fizz."

I couldn't resist chuckling at that last line. "You should write that down."

He nodded grudgingly with a smile. "I believe I will."

"Add that perhaps we should lock all men up, because a few commit crimes."

He squeezed my hand, his humor returning. "Excellent. I'll add that in."

I delighted in seeing some of his passion return.

One main street and we were out the other side. Into darkness we drove until finally we pulled up in front of a quaint Victorian home in Savannah, on a street much like Mama's, flourishing gingerbread design and wide verandahs. A sign out front said this was *Mama Mia's Italian Eatery*. With white tablecloths and cozy rooms, the three of us dined on homemade ravioli and sweet iced tea, all the while enjoying this rare occurrence, with gossip around who's who here. Thomas was his old charming self, flirting with me, teasing the waitress, and arguing with Joe. I'd never felt so beautiful as I did that night basking in candlelight and Thomas' green eyes.

Then some signal came from behind me that Thomas acknowledged and he extended to Joe. Too soon we were back in our dark chilly motor cars, bringing on a somber mood. Thomas pulled out a hidden flask from under his seat and threw his head back for a long drink, his Adam's apple bobbing in the dim light from the restaurant.

He extended this flask to me. I shook my head. He took my hand and placed it on the flask. "Drink this, you'll need it."

I obeyed, shaken by the touch of his cold hand. He watched as I wiped my mouth with the back of my hand, the strength of the drink stealing my breath. "Take another," he said. "You'll need the warmth; it's getting cool outside."

"I'm not going to be outside. Besides, aren't you being presumptuous in drinking this hooch or whatever out in public?"

"It's against the law to sell it, not to drink it. Now take another."

I did but shook my head as I at last handed him the flask. I would refuse to drink more of this burning liquid. It smelled like rum balls but the taste was infinitely stronger and was lining my stomach like a rapid timber fire.

Yet my face heated and my body relaxed. I smiled my warmth back at him and and he returned his own smile. I could have gazed at him all night.

"This is not the place to seduce me, you know," I said, touching his hand.

He breathed a short laugh and flipped under my chin. "Seduction comes later, darlin'." His expression changed all too quickly and I suddenly felt saddened by this loss of romance. It seemed we'd had so little of it. He turned more to face me, his right knee up on the seat between us, his left arm slung over the steering wheel.

"Joe is a bootlegger," he said.

"Good Lord, Thomas!" I smiled in spite of myself, sounding so like Harriet.

He nodded with a wry smile. "We're hoping the Lord will be good to us tonight because Joe's in trouble."

"I would imagine so if he's a bootlegger. What does that have to do with us?"

"Everything. He's my brother and he needs my help. He's a broken man, Bess. He put every penny he had into his cotton crop and when the boll weevils killed that, he acquired that inventory of vehicles on an installment purchase."

I had written enough advertising to understand what installment buying meant but self-respecting families I knew rarely practiced it and then only for required items such as sewing machines. People did not openly discuss such things for it was as much as admitting they did not have sufficient income.

Thomas looked back to ensure Joe continued to wait in his own automobile. "But Joe's luck continued to turn sour. So many folks around here depend on the cotton crop and the boll weevils hit every plantation around. The south's right now in a post-war recession from job cuts from defense-related industries. The shipyard is running dry. No one can afford to buy another vehicle, so Joe's not selling, but of course the installment finance company still expects to get paid monthly. He's incurring debt, with bootlegging being his only way out."

"He has my sympathy, Thomas, but right or wrong, bootlegging is illegal and becoming dangerous. All you have to do is read the newspaper to know about the gang wars in Chicago and New York City."

He waved this off. "Yes, yes, but this is just a small operation in Georgia. No gangs, no one will get hurt, but he needs a second motor car to load the bottles coming in by boat. All you need to do is sit pretty behind the wheel and when we fill up the trunk, you drive back here. Two motors running for too long will look conspicuous and make too much noise. Joe's been distributing alcohol for months and I've already helped a few times, but this time he has a larger shipment coming in and it has to be moved quickly. The demand's been going up faster than a hot-air balloon, and the local speakeasy, The Blind Pig, wants most of it so it will be an easy drop off. It's right behind this restaurant. Joe says the harbor police have been bribed quiet by the distiller so everything is set."

Night had closed in around us and I abruptly shivered. Warm, inviting light made window patches on the lawns of homes down the street, reminding me of the Lighthouse's beckoning on many cold nights as I walked to its shelter. My chest tightened at my longing to be back there, safe in the arms of the Thomas I knew then. These strange surroundings filled in with Thomas's unfamiliar almost-pleading tone and alien words, bringing on a nightmarish quality. He had lost some of his self-assurance, instinctively telling me that he, too, was uncomfortable in the circumstances. But for his brother's sake, he was working hard at making this work. I took a deep breath. Then so would I. Resolve brought tears to my eyes, regret already there.

Someone tapped on the window and we both jumped. My heart lurched so, dredging my stomach to the point of being nauseous. We turned to see Joe by the driver's window. Thomas cranked the window down and told Joe to drive on ahead and we would follow him. "Is she ready? We don't want to take this machine off ground until we're sure she can fly."

Thomas waved him away irritably. "Let's just move—" but he didn't finish as he cranked back up the window.

Soon Joe's Pierce-Arrow appeared ahead of us and we followed behind through twisted streets, with me trying hard to memorize corner landmarks in order to find my way back. My vision had become blurred by the booze and I blinked repeatedly to distinguish a post office, a turn to the left, a bakery, three blocks, a hat shop, turn right, a boat repair shop, signs of a harbor with hoisted boats on land, a seafood restaurant, piers coming into sight, a turn and then we backed into a dark alley and stopped. The wooden slabs of the buildings on either side appeared ominous. My hands were shaking so, I felt tempted to bring back out the flask myself, but then decided I was in enough danger with the law as it was.

"Bess listen to me." He put on leather gloves and then placed his leathered hand to my cheek. I focused on his silhouette, wishing there was light enough to see his green eyes. "Keep the motor running but don't get out unless I open the door for you. The original plan was to ask you to help load, but now that I think of it, I don't want you to be identified, so stay inside. You'll hear the trunk being loaded. When you hear me tap on the trunk hood, that's your signal to drive slowly away. Don't rush or you'll draw attention. Joe and I will then load his trunk and he wants me there to witness the money transaction. I'll ride back with Joe and meet you at Mama Mia's. Do you understand?"

"Yes."

He opened the door and with one leg out, paused and looked back at me. "You're a strong woman, doll, you'll be fine," he said and then the darkness took him.

I moved over to the driver's seat, but sat on my knees facing the backbench and the small rear window, straining my eyes to see beyond the building toward the water. The moon shared only a sliver that night, selfishly reflecting meager rays on the water and this I focused on, knowing he was out there somewhere. I could make out crates and occasionally three different body forms. The trunk finally opened blocking my view but I heard no clinking bottles being loaded; only shuffling feet on gravel. Suddenly the trunk closed and a tapping sounded on the lid, though I saw no one. I turned hurriedly to face the steering wheel and then paused. What was I to do? I had no cargo; this was not as planned. I heard what sounded like a firecracker and then tapping again. Only when the tapping ended in one loud thud, as if a fist had dented Thomas' precious Duesenberg, did I comprehend his message. I put the car into drive and drove slowly away.

Mama Mia's had lost her warmth by the time I came to a stop in front. Closed down and covered in a dark shroud, her embellished verandah and embroidered furnishings were hidden and only straight cold lines and columns showed. It seemed days ago we were enjoying her warm food and southern hospitality, enjoying her drawled conversation.

The drive back had taken longer with wrong turns but I was grateful that the narrow streets were empty, save for my stodgy beast blocking lanes. I sat in the deafening quiet, feeling terribly alone and unsure. I could only guess that the time was around midnight. Questions raced through my mind but one thing became certain: something had gone wrong and I had been given warning to get out. Thank goodness Joe's automobile was there to bring them back.

A stretch of time passed. I shivered in the cold, only dressed for the warm day's driving lesson. I found the flask and brought it to my lips but then thought better of it; I would need all my faculties to stay focused. Instead I gave its small opening a sentimental peck, as only hours before Thomas's lips had been there. I wanted him there, in the flesh.

I banged my fist on the steering wheel. Where the hell was he? Damn you, Thomas, why did you get involved in this? Brother or not, Joe would have found another way. He was a tough old survivor but Thomas was not geared for the criminal mind. He only observed from a distance and wrote about them. Could discuss crime in theory but like the science teacher, putting his findings into practice took a different sort. Thomas skimmed the surface, scooping up details as they floated to the top. He would link them together to become a whole story, and then drop them back in and move on. There's always another story, he said. All you had to do was keep your chin up and look ahead, never look down or behind you or you'll miss what's out there. That was the Thomas I knew. Now he was looking down at his little brother with a helping hand, and fulfilling obligations of his past. Why had he gone in reverse?

I flinched when a branch of a magnolia tree landed on the hood. It brought me out of my trance into the dark space ahead, that sensation of suspension with no means to grab hold. My heart jolted and suddenly I was grounded again. I looked about the gloomy street and homes. I had to find help. They should have been here by now. I would go back and see what the trouble is. I clutched the steering wheel but then let my hands fall to my lap. Driving back there was tempting but too risky. Doing so could put them in further danger; two motors were conspicuous Thomas said. I might also miss their return.

It was then I remembered that Thomas referred to a speakeasy behind the restaurant. Perhaps someone from there would know what to do. I stepped out, stiff from sitting, and followed a brick path leading to the back of the restaurant, stumbling here and there over patches of grass growing between the bricks. My eyes finally focused on a back door facing the alley way but no lights came from its window. The door was locked and when I peered through it, saw a staircase leading to the basement, dimly lit from below. All was quiet though; no music or people milling about, no shadows of vehicles in the alley. Closed for certain.

As I approached the Duesenberg, headlights came my way and my heart soared at the sight of the Pierce-Arrow. Kissing and cursing them both came to mind but I merely waved and smiled. The motor car came to a stop beside mine and the window came down. Only Joe was to be seen and he simply said, "Follow me," and drove away. My hand and my smile dropped away. *Follow me?* To where, for God's sake? And where the hell was Thomas?

I was not to know for some time. Once again I traveled in question, just as I had with Thomas coming in. Through Savannah to Pickerville, through Pickerville and out the country road to the plantation I followed his tail lights. In doing so, it dawned on me that his number plate was not there to identify his vehicle. More than an hour's drive with Thomas not by my side as planned. I kept close to Joe, not wanting to lose my only way to Thomas. If he'd stopped suddenly for any creature crossing, I would have easily collided but I cared not. Joe was my lantern and I didn't want to remain in the dark any longer.

I pulled in beside him in the front yard and watched with rising frustration as he loped into the house. A lamp came on in the parlor as I entered.

"Sit on the divan, Bess."

Joe was pacing, running his fingers through his hair, his shirt tail out, one suspender hanging limp by his trousers. I grudgingly sat but needed to, my heart was racing so. I dared not question; something inside me didn't want to know. He turned to me then with a tear-smeared face and a blood-smeared shirt and I screamed.

He came to me with outstretched palms. "Bess, Bess, I got him to the hospital as fast as I could, but—"

"No, no, no!" I cried, clinging to his shirt sleeve, pleading into his eyes to tell me something different. "I want Thomas!"

"But then - but then, well, he got the bullet in the arm, didn't seem so bad—"

"He was shot, Joe, is that what you're telling me? Then we can go to the hospital, Joe!" I stood and pulled his arm. "We've got to go right now! Why did we come here, Joe?"

His body remained rigid as a tree trunk, his arm only a branch that swayed with me as I pulled. "Because Tom died of a heart attack."

His lips quivered as he said it and at first that is all that registered. A second later and I collapsed onto the floor, rocking, clutching my stomach, wanting to die with Thomas, my heart seized as if Thomas's bullet had found its way there. "No, no, no," I whispered. "No, no, no."

Joe's shoes were there, stepping toward me and then backing up as slippered feet came into view. I heard a woman crying, vaguely aware it was Harriet, her tears mingling with mine as she squatted and hugged my cheek to hers. Then she was gone and a blanket

405

came around my shoulders with appeasing masculine and feminine voices, footsteps, creaking wood planks. They became sounds of the storm and wind blowing around and around me, but I was in my own little spot in the eye of the hurricane.

I came tumbling to the ground as the storm ceased and quiet returned, when they lowered the coffin into the grave. A grief came over me too deep for tears. I couldn't move; my expression wouldn't change. I was gripped by this finality. I had become like Thomas was in his last days, only to look down and back. There was no future for me without him. I moved my body when someone told me to. *Stand up, honey, throw the rose into the grave, honey, time to walk back to the hearse, honey, eat something you'll feel better, honey, why don't you lie down, honey?*

I found myself facing our bed, crawling in, shoes and all and hugging his pillow, moving my knees up into a fetal position, staring at the bathing tub. I watched the shadows creep around the walls and deepen; darkening the room to black. The katydids returned as they had done every night, telling me over and over that life goes on. But I found my way to the window and shut it firmly. I wanted no part of the katydid's optimism.

Against my wishes the shadows lightened and brightened the walls. If I had slept, I wasn't aware, my eyes opening and closing at random. A newspaper came into view, slid under the door. Without hesitation, I was drawn to it like scripture to the starving soul. The newspaper was dated the day after Thomas' death. Circled was an article and photograph of a much younger Thomas, one I'd seen framed on their entranceway table, with Cady by his side. Here they had cut her away, displaying only his head and shoulders. We have both loved and lost, his youthful eyes seemed to say to me. But I had no sympathy for him; only this sense of betrayal in him leaving me. Now I bitterly supposed he was in heaven with his first wife smiling again that happy grin and I blocked his gaze with my hand as I read the article.

Pickering is Shot; Heart Finishes Him Off: Grandson of the founder of Pickerville News, Mr. Thomas Pickering, died in the hospital last night. According to Dr. Mooreland of the Civic Hospital Emergency Ward, Pickering was brought in by his brother, Joseph Pickering of Pick Plantation, with a gunshot wound to his arm. The doctor states that Pickering had lost a good deal of blood but his wound was not life threatening. Trauma and blood loss combined with an already failing heart caused the heart attack and Pickering was pronounced dead an hour after arrival.

Why he was shot is still under investigation. His brother, Joseph Pickering, made a statement to the paper that he and Thomas were strolling along the pier late that evening when they were attacked by two masked thugs demanding money. Thomas resisted and one of the attackers fired a .22 caliber pistol. The attackers panicked when Thomas fell to the ground and ran away without achieving their purpose. Joseph did not get a description of the two, nor could he give chase, he stated, with a wounded brother to attend to. Police report will not be released until the investigation is closed.

I read it again, having much to absorb. What stood out was his failing heart. Why hadn't he told me? How typical of Thomas to relay his story through the newspaper. One that only told half-truths. I jumped up and ran my bath. It was time to reenter the world and get some questions answered.

"Because he said he had convinced you he wasn't an old man, but an ailing heart would confirm you had married one older than dirt," said Joe. He took a sip of his coffee. "He had too much pride, that boy." He scooped more wet eggs into his mouth, churning my stomach.

I drummed my fingers on the newspaper article lying there between us on the table, evidence of lies and deception. And waited once again for truth. He gulped down his remaining coffee and continued. "He found out on his last trip here. Chest pains, being tired all the time. I didn't want a Yankee doctor, so I called Doc Williams, the same one that brought him and I into the world. Doc Williams came out and examined him and said his heart was weakening. He was directed to take life easy."

"And bootlegging with you was going to give him the easy life, Joe?"

His fork clattered to the plate and Harriet's cup clinked loudly with her saucer.

"How dare you insinuate that my husband—"

"Harriet, hush your mouth," he said and patted her arm. He rubbed his face hard, bringing my attention to the heavy bags under his eyes. "Bess, I take all the blame for this, I really do. I'm feeling as low as a toad in a dry well. I keep thinking I shouldn't have told him, but Tom is the only close blood family I got, and I tell him everything – well, told him everything. He knew things here on the plantation weren't going so good and he knew I owed money to our uncle. And when I went out on my runs, he said he'd come with me. He said he wanted to see what I got myself into. He wouldn't have taken no for an answer, he's my big brother.

"And, well, I don't mean to switch horses in midstream but there's another reason too. Tom owed me." He ate a biscuit while I watched him and wondered why Thomas's life was unfolding for me after it ended for him.

"You see, neither one of us wanted to grow cotton. Tom being the oldest was willed the plantation, Pa not taking no for an answer. He made us promise that we'd never sell the land. He was the second generation to own Pick Plantation, Grandpappy being the first. But that was before the Civil War and the slaves just about run the place. Grandpappy could manage this and the newspaper at the same time. But after the Yankees pillaged and burned, destroyed our crop and seeds, burned down the barns and sheds, and part of this house, Grandpappy and Pa had to start all over. Slaves were gone and that meant they'd have to work Tom and I to death.

Tom and I changed in different ways. While I grew to resent the Yankees for taking our slaves, Tom gained more sympathy for what the slaves had to do while they were working here. He grew to hate the plantation. We both know Tom's not the type to stay put in one place and do hard labor. He was a thinker and a writer, a reporter with wanderlust. He wanted out and he wanted to make a deal. He said if I took over, he'd see to it that little brother was looked after. So Tom got hired at the newspaper and saw to it that whatever we were selling got the biggest share of advertisement, and if I got into trouble he was there to bail me out, or lend a financial hand. But then while at college, he met Cady and that was all she wrote. They took off to New York and Harriet and I have been struggling to keep this place going ever since."

I wondered how one decision could linger for so many years without changing form, only to affect new decisions. Joe used Thomas as a freed slave, held by obligation.

"I understand," I said. "That brings us back to today and now that Thomas has …" Here I struggled to say the word but couldn't.

"Yes, passed away," Joe said, his chin on his chest.

"This has raised suspicion about your – your other means of income, so what now? Aren't you worried that an investigation could find you guilty, and, oh my God, Joe – I might be arrested as some sort of accomplice!" This had not occurred to me since his death. My world had stopped.

"No, I'm doing what I can to protect you, don't you see? That's what Tom would have wanted. No one knows you were there. I had taken the number plates off both automobiles. I've got connections at the newspaper – couple of cousins work there that have some control over what goes into it. I didn't mention you being with us and I already talked to the owner of Mama Mia's – he runs The Blind Pig too so he and I get along just fine. You weren't there as far as they're concerned. When Tom saw the gun, he wanted you out of there. He closed your trunk lid and gave you the signal to go. His movements scared – well, the gun went off and Tom fell to the ground. When your automobile didn't move, he wouldn't give up. He reached up as far as he could reach and continued to knock until you drove away. Thank the Lord you didn't find reverse."

I shuttered and pushed away my toast. "Why was he shot, Joe?"

"A rival came in. Wanted a piece of the action, he said, or he'd rat on us. We told him to go to hell, pardon my expression. He pulled out a gun and waved it around, it went off - meaning to scare us more I think - Tom fell, the man took off running. My business partner reloaded the crates back on the boat and cruised on down the shoreline, while I got Tom into my automobile and to the hospital. No traces. The investigation will find nothing. We look out for each other down here; everybody knows everybody, nobody knows nothing."

"Then you must know who shot Thomas."

His eyes darted to Harriet and then back down to his plate. He loosened his tie which had suddenly become a nuisance to him. "Yes ma'am, but we take care of our own. Don't you worry your little head about that."

"Do I know him, Joe?" Harriet asked, watching him closely. She, too, saw the signs.

He crossed his arms on the table and stared down at his half-eaten biscuit. "Oh, yeah, you know him," he said to the biscuit.

"I swan, it's my cousin, Louie, isn't it?"

"He's a bad egg, Harriet."

"Good Lord, Joe, he was probably drunker than Cooter Brown!"

Joe raised his right hand as if to swear. "I'm not going to hurt him, Harriet, no permanent damage. Just teach him a lesson he won't forget."

I hadn't driven to Georgia; I had driven to another world, one with twisted thorny vines so thickly intermingled, I couldn't see my way through them.

I tried to raise my head above it all. I took a deep breath. "So let me get this straight. You know who shot Thomas, but you're not going to report him to the police?"

He squinted his eyes at me as if I had shone a flashlight on him. The rueful blue eyes turned distant. "No, and no one else is going to either. I've already given my report to the police. You want me to go back and tell them, 'oh by the way, it was family that shot my brother'? And then tell them why? Do you want to go to jail? I know

I don't." He scooted his chair from the table, threw his napkin down and slammed the kitchen door behind him as he left.

Harriet jumped up and stacked plates. "You've done it now."

I stopped her with my hand and looked up at her pleadingly. "I haven't done anything except I tried to please my husband. I'm no different in that regard than you are."

She studied my face and then nodded.

"Now can you and I work together on this to clear our husbands' names and keep us all out of trouble? We need a clear alibi for when the policemen come around asking questions."

Caught in their thorns and scratched badly, I knew without any doubt I did not want to root here. I wanted to go home.

But home was not to be until the investigation was complete. Joe said it would look suspicious so I was to stay right there until he said I could go.

Rightly so, I sensed danger in Joe - the angry bear who would fiercely protect his own, including his own skin. I barely qualified as his own, hence I behaved myself and caused no more reason for suspected treason. Reluctantly I admitted to myself I needed his protection. Ironic, when it was he who put me in danger in the first place. He played savior and Satan and Harriet walked through fire for him and raised her eyes to him like he was God Almighty. So he saw nothing wrong with his logic. He could justify it all, including Thomas's death.

I bided my time.

Harriet and I made a truce. We agreed to tell the police that we were baking bread that day. Easy to believe because Harriet sold her bread to the local market. Everyone knew that, of course. But then I remembered that their nosy neighbor, Ethel Warner, might have seen Thomas, Joe and me during my driving lesson. If she had been watching her lane way, she would have seen me going from the Pierce-Arrow to the Duesenberg and heading toward Pickerville.

Thus a driving lesson and a quick tour of Pickerville was added to the story and then we would say that I was dropped off by Thomas to assist Harriet, and afterwards he'd joined Joe in Savannah.

I had nightmares about police dragging me away in chains; Thomas dressed in white being tortured in a dingy cell, a blood patch on his shirt just like the patch Joe wore that night; Harriet's hard brown eyes like buttons as she told me that refined ladies do not pronounce their 'R' harshly, like Yankees do. *Say Bah-be-cue*, she said. *Bah-be-cue, or you'll be cooked for dinner*; Joe was a constant roar in the background, of either wind or wild bear.

The policemen arrived two days later. What a fiasco their line of questioning was. I had worried for naught. They were only there to check off the box that said they interviewed all those involved. Since most of what I told them was true, and I didn't know about Thomas's demise until I was in Joe's parlor, the answers were easy, nor were they considered suspicious. In this instance, being a woman had gone in my favor. These were southern gentlemen whose etiquette were leftovers from pre-Civil War days, with 'yes ma'am, no ma'am, I beg your pardon ma'am' with a tip of their hats. The only thing amiss was a kiss on the top of my hand. I was the bereaved widow now and their visit leaned more toward paying their respects to a "like-able fellow, that Tom, my Pa went to school with him".

Harriet played the role of the mourning sister-in-law beautifully. Granted, she was sorry Thomas had died, but her grief was more prominent when going into battle for her man and she dressed in uniform to prove it. She wore black as she had every day since his death, but this day she included black lace gloves and black netting over her hair that blended in well with a shoe-length taffeta dress. The only other color was the white handkerchief she clutched in one hand to dab at an eye occasionally. I felt blatantly disloyal to Thomas as I stood by her side to "receive our guests" in my blue summer suit.

Harriet took it upon herself to clear my name for the sake of propriety. "You must forgive Mrs. Pickering, gentlemen. She brought few garments with her when she and Thomas came down from New

York. I assure you her grief is genuine. I've never met a more devoted wife than she."

I thought my ashen complexion and shadowed eyes would make this obvious, for I hadn't slept through the night, nor could I finish a meal, but loose clothing clearly did not compare well to black clothing. Harriet wanted my grief to be public, to somehow make up for my cold Yankee ways. But to flaunt my absolute loss was unthinkable. If they suspected I had lost my direction, that I was in the dark - for Thomas's light had shown me the way - if they suspected such a thing, I would have been appalled. Suspicions of wrongdoing were easier to abide, than suspicions of a shaky mental state. At one point I fumbled through words but Harriet recovered quickly with a pat on my arm and a "there, there, child, it will be over soon. I must ask your forgiveness once again gentlemen, as Bess hasn't been … well." I simply suffered through their piteous gaze with a stiff back and short answers, smiles given selfishly until they finally tipped their hats with goodbye.

I felt more than relieved to see their backsides for they were keeping me from going home.

"Go home? You are home. You married into Tom's family now. You belong here," Joe said at the supper table that night.

"Besides, you should never go backwards, Bess," Harriet said. "I don't mean to be cruel, but your own family didn't even come down for the funeral."

Good point and I had put aside my concerns about it. I had given Mama's address to Joe to telegram the news and funeral date. Instead of word from them, I received a telephone call from Victor who said Pearl had moved into the Lighthouse with Mama to keep it clean and orderly to show the home to interested buyers. He had taken the telegram over there only to find no one there, and no one knew where they were. He gave me excuses for his own absence from the funeral, saying he had no one there to look after his Walk Wright shoe store, but it was more likely that he was still miffed about not being invited to my wedding. To hear him talk, there was no one around but him in the whole world. But I had become numbed by it all, my only thought being that Mama did not need to attend a third funeral in so short a time.

I gave Harriet a brief explanation but I divulged little, knowing they continued to think my northern family scattered and uncaring, regardless. To say more, was to make excuses. It became evident my presence could not improve their views of the north.

Harriet turned her attention to Joe.

"Don't you want to know what the will says?" Joe asked.

"Thomas had a will?" I asked.

"He didn't tell you much, did he?"

"It seems to be so."

"Our lawyer is bringing it over in a week or two."

My, things moved slowly around here!

"Joe, I have a job on hold up in New York. If I don't go back soon, I'll lose it and I can't afford that. Can you please send him word to come sooner?"

"It's my responsibility to look after my brother's wife. That's the way Tom would have wanted it. It's not a woman's place out there in the workforce."

"Thomas himself assigned me this job, Joe. He's more liberal than you think."

"Did he give it to you before or after you were married?"

I faltered, getting his message. "Before. But, Joe—"

"That's what I thought. Tom was raised better than that. No respectable wife works away from home."

"I'm a widow now, Joe," I said softly. Where was his sympathy?

"You can work here. Harriet could use another hand and she makes money at baking and sewing. She can't keep up with all the orders for feather pillows and mattresses. She says you've been learning a little bit about it, helping her out at times. That's a good girl and I appreciate that. Harriet would pay you by the hour, and you get free room and board. Now it don't get any better than that. End of discussion."

He threw his napkin onto the table and walked out. This was becoming a familiar scene. He relished on getting the last word in. Words weren't coming to me at any rate. I sat bewildered. Was he going to hold me against my will? Did Thomas recognize the power his little brother threw around? I realized then that he had manipulated Thomas and he was trying to do the same to me. He was accustomed to having his way. His slave, indeed!

I turned to Harriet but, with her plate in hand, she trotted into the kitchen.

I followed behind. "Harriet, he can't be serious."

I couldn't read her expression, eyes like hard brown buttons. "Joe has given you so much and you appreciate so little. He's looked after everything for you, and paid Tom's funeral to boot."

"Harriet, I do appreciate what you *both* have done for me and for Thomas. Thomas dearly loved this place and was happy living here. I could have been too, with Thomas. But not without him. These are Thomas's roots, not mine. I belong with my own family."

She turned away and began running water into her wash pan. "If that's the way you feel, then all I can tell you is to give him his way for awhile and then maybe he'll let you go."

I could no longer stand being in her presence. I felt nauseated by their insinuations. I would have to think about this some more.

I lay in our bed – my bed – and bitterly wept. I resented Thomas for leaving me here in such a foreign place, where I, a former suffragist who'd fought for women's freedom, was now considered without any rights. Then I longed for him to be here and make my pain go away. I dried my eyes on his pillow.

Where was the Duesenberg key? When I drove it back here that terrible night, what did I do with it? I parked, I jumped out in a hurry to get word from Joe – it should still be in the ignition. I would drive back to New York on my own. I had assisted Thomas in changing those flat tires and I might be able to do it alone. If it rained, I wouldn't continue motoring through the mud and muck and get stuck. I'd pull over and wait it out. Sleep in the motor car a week if I had to. But then how would I find my way? Thomas had said that some day there would be road maps of wherever you wanted to go. I dearly wished I had one of those. All I knew to do was head north and thank goodness Thomas had a compass on the dashboard for just this reason. I would have to get that key and start preparations. And find money.

I slipped on my robe and outdoor shoes and tiptoed down the hall through the parlor and into the entranceway. Their bedroom was on the other side of the entrance, in the other wing, through the dining room and kitchen. They wouldn't hear me slip out. Their dog, Kipper, was on guard by the front door and gave a low growl until I let her smell my hand. Her tail wagged and I gave her a pat on the head. She escorted me outside and for this I was grateful, not thinking before how dark it would be. I waited until the half-moon came from behind a cloud and gave me a dim light to find the motor car. I found it where I'd left it, parked in the gravel beside the laneway. I sighed a relief to see it, like sighting an old friend who'd come to rescue me. Kipper and I walked quickly to its door and I opened it as slowly as possible to minimize any creaks and clicks. I sat behind the wheel and blindly reached for the ignition key.

It was gone. My hand groped around the dials, the dashboard, and the floorboard. I stepped out and checked the seats. In my panic, it hadn't registered that Kipper was barking. I leaned around the door to see that she was over by a tree barking at something rustling through the grasses.

"Come here, girl!" I whispered harshly. But she couldn't hear through her own warnings. I would have to make haste back to my room.

"What's going on out here?"

I closed the door too hard. Joe lit a lantern and held it up. There was a long pause as I stood frozen, hoping I had dissolved into the darkness. The gravel crunched as he walked closer.

"Is that you, Bess?"

I squeezed my hands together hard. "Yes it is, Joe. Sorry. I didn't mean to wake you."

He held the lantern up to my face, causing me to shade my eyes. "Why. Are. You. Out. Here?" he asked, so deliberate a question that I shrunk back a little.

Only his face was visible, as if floating above the lantern, needing a shave, deep creases around bloodshot eyes, his breath smelling of liquor, very much alert and sensing a menace. Lizzie came to mind and what she must have felt in being caught as a runaway slave, knowing a beating was coming. She was a strong woman and I could be too.

I shielded my eyes and smiled. "Put that lantern down some, will you Joe? You're blinding me."

He didn't move. Opening the door, I slid behind it using it like a shield. I spoke with obvious irritation. "I couldn't sleep, Joe. I miss Thomas. Plain and simple. I haven't been sleeping since – well, you know. I came out here to sit in Thomas's motor car. He loved this thing as much as a child. To sit here where he sat, to relive our last memories on our drive down here." I sat down hard on the driver's seat. I had spoken some truth and to hear how I missed him out loud was more than I could bear. I could conjure up the sound of his laughter as he steered here.

Joe let out a long breath and lowered the lantern. "Come on out of that automobile, girl. Get on back to bed before Kipper wakes up every chicken and goose I own. Don't do this again; it's not proper to be out here in your night clothes."

I stepped out and he pulled me close to him. "You're just a lonely woman who needs a man." He lightly smacked my buttocks. "Now get on back in there before I whip you like a child."

I kept my head down and nodded, thankful the veil of darkness hid my burning cheeks and smoldering eyes.

For the next week I worked without thinking, letting my mind race only at night without sleeping. Harriet said little, accustomed to working alone. I was given more and more of the house cleaning to do, while she concentrated on baking breads to sell, preparing meals, and sewing. Our work rarely required us to be in the same room and Joe stayed outside most of the day, and gone many evenings. I could only assume bootlegging took him away, but of course neither Harriet nor I spoke of this. Much of her time was spent in the kitchen, taking away opportunities to look for the key where it would most likely be. A large board hung on the kitchen wall dotted with half-exposed nails and here Joe hung keys for the various vehicles. A quick glance told me Thomas' recognizable pocketknife key chain wasn't with the others, so whether Joe believed me or not, he had hidden the key just in case.

In the night, I rummaged through clothes and pockets looking for money or another set of keys, anything to give me hope, only to discover Thomas's sweet musky scent stirred and rising, blurring my vision with more tears. Any money Thomas had carried on his person, must have been handed over to Joe at the hospital.

On the eighth night, my ideas for escape became more desperate. I'd telephone the police. But then what would I tell them - who would believe that I was trapped here? This town was politically incestuous and Joe one of their good ol' boys. He'd likely explain in that tired I'm-just-doing-my-best-by-Tom tone that I was bereaved beyond the ability to look after myself and he was just doing his duty, or I'd hurt myself. He'd already found me outside in the middle of the night in my night clothes "pining for her husband", I heard him say on the telephone. Harriet had previously made it clear to the policemen that I was not well. So whether I called them, or just took off running down the lane one night, I'd eventually be brought back to "where I belonged" to face judgment alone with Joe and Harriet as the ungrateful wench in a shaky mental state.

I pounded my fist into the mattress with frustration. I threw off my sheet and pulled my gown up to my knees, wishing there was more of a breeze coming through the window. The heat and humidity of the southern summer had become merciless just as Thomas had warned me. I flipped my pillow over to its cool side and then stilled. Wood floorboards were creaking out in the hall.

Someone stood at my door wiggling the door knob. There was a skeleton key inside the lock but I'd never had cause to use it. The door opened on a squeaky hinge and Joe's bulk emerged into the shadowy room.

"Where are you, lonely girl?" he said in a low sing-song voice. His body wavered as he stepped forward, like someone on a wind-tossed ship. He stumbled over my shoes and fell across my bed. He grabbed my legs. "There you are!" My struggle tightened his grip. "You'll not get away," he mumbled, slurred and slow. "You're mine now. Tom gave you to me. Just dropped you off and went on, like he's always done. Left me holding the bag, but this is one bag I'll get something out of." His hand slid up my leg like lightening and took hold of my panties and pulled. I clutched his wrist with both hands.

"Joe, I'll scream. Do you want Harriet to see you like this?" I hissed, not yet wanting to wake her, not yet wanting to believe why he was here.

"Scream, darlin'. She won't hear you. I gave her a night toddy that knocked her flat out. Then I stuffed cotton balls in her ears. If I can't sell the cotton, I'll stuff 'em." He chuckled at himself, letting out a burst of sour smelling liquor vapors. He suddenly jerked hard with both hands and I heard my panties rip. "Damn you woman!" he gasped. "Lay down!" He pushed me hard with his shoulder, pinning me to the bed, while he laid on top of me, partially on his side, trying to work his pants.

"Joe, no! No!" I continued to say, first in a whisper, then in a cry. His forearm came across my neck and pressed down hard, while his hand came over my mouth. With each struggle he pressed harder, until suffocation dulled my senses. Something inside said, *if you don't lie still, you will surely die.* With every bit of strength in me, I tried to calm myself, only my gasps of air and cries deep within my throat giving movement.

I vaguely heard his pants unzip and a cry bawled in my ears like a cow going into slaughter.

Something soft fell onto my leg and his hand moved against it over and over. "Come on, baby, come on, baby," he whispered down to it. Lying fully on top of me, he rubbed against my pelvis, hoping for a response from his lower member, but my breathing began to calm as I realized he could not conclude his violent act.

"Bitch!" he cried. He rolled over to the edge of the bed and sat up, his feet on the floor. He began crying, the silhouette of his shoulders moving up and down spastically.

"I thought it was Harriet's fault with that scrawny body of hers, not me," he said, his voice quivering child-like.

I watched without moving, fearing to draw his attention back to me. Finally his forearms came up to his face, wiping away the tears. Sniffing loudly, he arose and shuffled toward the door, pulling together his trousers and suspenders. The door closed softly behind him. I leaped from the bed and turned the key in the lock, my gown scurrying back down to my ankles.

If Thomas had come back, I would have thrown a bomb through his question of why his brother never had any children.

I walked into an unusually quiet kitchen the next morning. As I sliced a piece of bread, Harriet hobbled in, poured a glass of water and announced that a pounding headache would keep her in bed for the day. Joe had gone into town, she said, to deliver pillows to a customer. I could read in my room if I wanted, she added as she scuffled back out. I wondered why she never went with him, why she never left the plantation, and if she realized she still had the cotton balls in her ears. I sipped my cup of tea, my mind in a haze, many nights without sleep taking its toll. The telephone ringing startled me out of my bewilderment. The telephone box was on the wall by the kitchen door, across from the keys.

An angel spoke, "Bess, is that you?" Pearl's timing was beautiful and so was she, in spite of her dress code.

"Yes Pearl, it's me!" I forced myself to lower my declaration. "Pearl, it's so good to hear your voice." I breathed in deeply to control the tears, but she heard the quavering nonetheless. "I'm so glad you called. I … need … help!" This was easier to say than I thought it would be.

"Oh, Bess, I know. I'm so sorry about Thomas. He was a great guy. This might not have happened if he'd been elected mayor. This town—"

"Pearl, listen to me, it's more than that. Oh, so much more!" I paused, my mind racing, my eyes set on the board of keys. I began to focus on them as an idea came to mind. I wouldn't have much time before one of the two came back. The telephone box had been hung high, suitable for Joe, but not for Harriet. I tiptoed up to speak closely into its mouthpiece, cupping my hand over my mouth "Pearl, listen to me carefully. You're my only hope in getting out of here. You must come down by train to the town of Pickerville, Georgia. It's a small town about seven miles west of Savannah. Borrow money from Victor for train tickets and a hotel room for both of us."

"I've got my own money. Bess, what's wrong? What's going on?"

"They won't let me go home, Pearl! I'm trapped here, please, please help me." My whole body trembled so that I could barely breathe. I had allowed my fear to surface and it was all I could do not to throw the receiver down and start running. The panic in my voice relayed across the hundreds of miles.

"Oh my God … Bess … I've never heard you like this. I've never been on a train – but I can do it, I'm sure of it! I'll be on the next train down there, where did you say, Pickerville Georgia? Okay, don't you worry."

"I'll leave now, Pearl, and motor to the hotel. I'll meet you there. You can't miss it; it's right next to the train station." I silently thanked Thomas for pointing that out during our drive through the town. "Ask for … Lizzie Washington. Got that?" Using Lizzie's name was not in vain. I understood her more than ever.

I heard static, clicking, more than one breathing – damn it, this was a party-line!

"Got it," Pearl said. "But I might not get there until tomorrow or the next day. It must take a train a long time to go all the way down to Georgia."

"Whatever it takes, I'll be waiting. Pearl, thank you and I can't wait to see you."

I heard a noise and jolted around to face Kipper, stretching in the doorway. Joe obviously had her well trained to sense escape. I didn't pat her head this time. Not that I was superstitious but the last time I did that, I got caught in the act.

I returned to the board of keys, turning keys to look for any identification. Most were not marked from the motor car manufacturer, bringing to mind the question of stolen vehicles. I suspected the worst in Joe by this time. With trembling fingers, I reluctantly brought several down with no choice but to try them out on the twenty-five or so parked in the field.

Clutching these in my sweaty palms, I closed the screen door behind me quietly and entered the yard, scattering chickens and geese. They hadn't been fed yet and clustered around, pecking at my feet. This reminded me that I too would require food. With no money and a possible two-day wait, I would need to pack a picnic. Hardly the appropriate word for this state of affairs but I focused on it as such to search for the appropriate foods for my journey. With rising panic in getting out, I went back in and returned to the bread loaf, wrapping a tea towel around this. The covered butter dish was there along with a jar of apple butter. The icebox held only buttermilk and raw eggs.

I needed something to carry my "picnic" in. I glanced into the dining room and there across the back of a chair was a blue-striped ticking cover for a pillow. One end of the rectangle had been left unstitched for stuffing feathers. Silently thanking Harriet, I gratefully stuffed it instead with bread, apple butter, and peaches. Keys went in on top. I was ready to go.

Hustling past the fowl, my heart raced faster as I passed the barn. Joe had hired colored help but I saw no one. Perhaps the day was too hot for their kind. The sun blazed and I had no hat or gloves with me. Of course this was the least of my worries, but vanity does speak at the oddest times.

With trembling fingers I at last stopped in front of the first motor car, without care for its condition and brought out a key from my sack. It didn't fit the ignition, nor did any of the other keys I brought along. Just as I feared. I ran to the next one. In the bright sunlight I then noticed the name *Buick* etched into the key I grasped. It was God I thanked this time in enabling me to recollect Joe's comments on an old Buick where the driver's seat was on the right side. It was easy to spot. The leather top was down and badly worn and torn. I would consequently be easy to spot. But I had no time to pick and choose and no time to lose. The sputtering of her engine and its eventual grasp of gas-and-go was a blessed sound and we pulled away from its companions and out into the barn yard, chickens squawking our break out.

Somehow sensing that this was my last time going down the plantation's lane, I could almost visualize our Duesenberg heading in on our first day's arrival, dust billowing behind us as we neared Thomas's childhood home. How were we to know we were going the wrong way?

It seemed years ago. In a million years I would not have imagined this as my way of departure, but this old stutter had become my companion now and would take me away from here. The breeze cooled as we turned onto the road blowing a sense of freedom through my careless hair. Not since our arrival here had I felt this elation, as my blouse and skirt stirred and vibrated about, tingling my flesh alive. I pushed to the back of my mind who I was leaving behind. The good buried with the bad. I would have to concentrate on what lies ahead. I patted her large steering wheel, standing tall it was, on an exposed pole from the floor. "Let's just move on with it then!" I shouted above the sputter and stutter.

In due course, I could see Ethel Warner peering into her mailbox by the road. As I slowly puttered by, I could only smile and wave to her gaping mouth. I would be her next topic of gossip, of a woman motoring alone in the heat of day with a naked head and bare hands to bake in the sun. She could almost run beside me at the speed I traveled, or worse yet, jump inside, and this brought to mind Joe's eventual discovery. I could only pray that her tattle-tale was later rather than sooner.

Just outside of town the Buick exhausted, regardless of my increased pressure on her gas pedal. Steam puffed out from the cap on top of the hood. I could find no gasoline or water container inside. Just as well. I would not have been able to park this in front of the hotel and give away my hideout, so I patted her bench, as crusty and split as brown bread, and stepped down with my sack. She and I had gone as far as we could go.

The railroad tracks were off on the right and these I walked parallel to, guiding me to the hotel. Along the boardwalk, women discreetly eyed my disheveled appearance from under large floppy hats and umbrellas. My blouse was now blemished with perspiration, my breasts sagging shamelessly behind a loose-fitting camisole. I was thinking how easy I would be to identify - just when I almost ran into the back of Joe who was coming out of the general store carrying a sack of feed. His attention more on avoiding a passing motor car than of passing pedestrians, gave me time to step inside the dimness of the next door business. I watched him from the large front window, my eyes darting between bold white backwards lettering across the plate-glass reading, *Soda Fountain.* He walked across the street to his waiting truck, dumped his load and came back. I stepped back into the shadows while he returned next door and brought out another sack of feed. This he did repeatedly while I watched and waited, the room's interior giving me refuge and a place to cool down.

Or so I thought.

"May I help you, ma'am?"

I turned from the window toward the voice and could scarcely make out a large counter with a gentleman standing behind it. As my eyes adjusted to the diffused lighting, I noticed most of the stools in front of the counter, and small tables around, were filled with folks staring back at me. The room was oddly quiet.

"Oh dear," I said, my hands immediately going to my hair to smooth down. "I just came in out of the heat for a moment."

"Well, look here if it isn't Thomas Pickering's widow!" he said much too loudly, coming out from behind the counter. "You just sit yourself right down, Mrs. Pickering. Now what can I bring you?"

I opened my mouth to deny, but as he came closer I recognized him as one of the pallbearers at Thomas's funeral. He would know me for certain. I sat in the chair he offered. "Just a glass of water, please. I have many errands."

His thick sandy hair painfully reminded me of Thomas. He could be his cousin for all I knew.

"You must have come into town with Joe. He'll be in directly to buy his ice cream soda like he does every day he's here. It's good to see one of the Pickering women for a change. Joe keeps a tight rein on his wife; I haven't seen her in a month of Sundays. How is she fairing?"

Why is he so boisterous? I wondered as I nodded and answered, "Finer than a frog's hair." I wished Thomas was there to hear me say that.

Others returned to their melting desserts. "I'd rather be buried in a Croker sack!" a well turned-out lady whispered forcefully from behind. Everyone appeared as if they'd just stepped out of a bandbox. Coming to the soda fountain was a social event, just as Joe had said. *Joe. He could show up any minute.* Now that my eyes were accustomed, I glimpsed saloon-type swinging doors to the back. Natural lighting could be seen, indicating a back entrance. I drank down the water and while the proprietor's attention was averted to another customer, I scurried through the swinging doors, through a tiny storage room, and out the back door.

"Joe!" I heard from within. "I was just telling your sister-in-law here – where did she go?"

I ran through the alley to the general store's piled crates and dropped down behind these, afraid if I ran any further, I'd be spotted. It was only moments until I heard Joe's voice out there asking, "Are you sure it was her?"

"Sure as rain," was the answer. "Definitely not put together like she was at the funeral, but it was her alright. Falling apart, poor thing. Her hands were shaking. She's taking this hard, isn't she? She didn't come with you?"

"Nope." Joe kicked a box. "Damn! I told that woman to stay put!"

"Just calm down, Joe. She's not here so maybe she turned around and went out the front. You better go look for her. She must have walked all the way here from your place. Said she had errands to run so she's probably over at the dress shop. You know these women; once they get into town they don't want to leave. I'd say somebody needs to drive her home."

"She'll leave alright, when I find her," Joe said.

The footsteps faded and I waited a few more minutes to be on the safe side. I stood up straight and then froze. Mr. Soda Fountain's sandy head was peering from his doorframe and saw me at once. He brought his hand to his mouth and I had the horrible first thought that he was going to blow a whistle, like a policeman would in spotting a criminal. Instead, he put a finger to his lips and shook his head. Then his hand shooed me away. I understood instantly and took off running.

The alley ran beside the railroad tracks and this led me to the hotel back entrance. Tables sat out there as an extension to the dining room. Table cloths, lit candles, men in light suits and ladies in frocks and wide hats of many colors almost broke my heart in remembering our last dinner together and in what could have been and would never be.

My head down, I scurried past, praying these were all 'foreigners' that would not recognize me. Once inside the cool dark lobby, I registered as Lizzie Washington – and then scratched it out in remembering the telephone party line. I wrote the name Ruby Wright instead and asked the clerk to give Pearl Wright a written note with my room number on it when she arrived the next day. The clerk took forever and a lifetime, eyeing me warily because I had no luggage. When he finally handed my key to me, I avoided the elevator and took the three flights of stairs to my room. Once inside, I stood motionless, relieved and then alarmed. I would be forced to stay in this room until Pearl's arrival and I had forgotten my sack of foods at the Soda Fountain.

As I paced, there was a knock on the door. I paused, checked that the door was bolted, and then paced again. I could not answer, no matter what. I had only been in the room a short time so Pearl's arrival was out of the question. I wished for a radio or a book, something to do. I had tired of peeking down to the front street, everyone living his or her lives normally out there, walking freely. The slice of bread from breakfast had digested long ago, my stomach reminded me, although how long ago I didn't know. I wished I had Thomas's pocket watch, his first wife's engravings included. I had no keepsakes, save for this gold wedding band. His personal favorites, such as his first edition of Mark Twain's *What is Man?* were now unwillingly donated to his childhood home. I recalled one of its quotes that Thomas used often, once when I complained about Mary Sue: *Everything has its limit – iron ore cannot be educated into gold.*

How would I get beyond this grief and know my own favorite quotes, my own thoughts again?

More time passed, the shadows on the wall deepened. My stomach cruelly nudged when I heard trays clatter in the hallway. Perhaps later, when the lucky recipients had finished their meals, there might be a slice of uneaten bread—

A knock again upon the door. "Room service!"

I went to the door, longing to open it, but only leaned against it.

The knock repeated. "Room service, Miss Wright!"

He didn't know who I really was. I could answer. But I hadn't rang for room service. I heard the tray settle on the floor. I waited for silence. Moments later I pulled the tray in across the threshold and was about to close the door when I spotted my striped ticking sack beside the tray. Inside with my picnic items were chunks of fudge, a large bag of peanuts, a bottle of soda, and a note.

Your sack gave your intentions away, but don't worry, your secret is safe with me. If you need anything let me know. I owe Tom – he introduced my pretty wife to me. Enjoy your meal. Mr. Burton, proprietor of Soda Fountain.

He must have been the one who knocked first; perhaps throwing in what he had on-hand in his confectionery and soda fountain and then following me here. When I didn't answer, he had tried room service. It was a guess but it didn't really matter. My faith in southern men had been restored. The living ones were not all drunken blind pigs as the speakeasy's name had suggested and as Joe had attested to. How ironic I had been served pork on my dinner tray.

Pearl arrived the afternoon of the following day. Seeing her familiar family face was too much and I broke into sobs on her shoulder. Solitary confinement had made me think and reflect, regrets popping up unexpectedly, many over sister Pearl. Why had I given her so little attention, even during her many miles of walking door-to-door campaigning for Thomas? I had decided to be a more emotionally charged woman – passion was what Thomas once said I lacked - but this outburst was more than Pearl was prepared for.

She patted my back, speechless, finally asking, "Why are there so many good-looking bell bottoms around here?"

"You're close to a port," I answered, drying my eyes on my sleeve. "Where there's a port, there are ships. Where there are ships, there are sailors."

She gave me a pitying smile but I didn't care. I felt sorry for myself too.

"That whiskbroom down in the lobby," she said, looking out the window, "gave me a hard time when I asked for Lizzie Washington. It wasn't until I gave him my name that he remembered your note and then of course when I read it and saw you used Mama's name, I played dumb. Thanks for the change. I'm the one that ends up getting a lecture on how unhealthy it is for young ladies to travel alone."

"Whiskbroom?" I asked her.

"Yeah, you know, the fellow with the cultivated whiskers. You can see the handlebars from the back of his head."

I laughed, suddenly enjoying her slang. "I can't believe you're here."

"Nor I." She sat on the bed and bounced. "I changed trains three times to get to these sticks. Lucky me had a brush-ape sit beside me for the last part, telling me how fortunate I was to be in God's country and how northerners think they're such big shots. What do they think the north is, anyway? Hell on earth? I guess they don't bootleg down here."

She walked over to the side of the window again and barely moved the curtain to peek out, reminding me of a bimbo readying for a caper. "We've got to get a wiggle on. The train leaves in two hours and I've got to make some changes to your appearance before we leave. Policemen were walking around the platform and I heard one say your real name. And another one was asking around for a Lizzie Washington. How would they know that name? Did you really steal an automobile? Isn't that the same thing as a motor car? Gave me the heebie-jeebies. Whatever you've done, they're looking for you. I have to buy some things so I'll be right back, okay?"

I nodded, swallowing questions, resolved to trust her judgment.

Soon she returned, breathing as if she'd run up the stairs. "I had some trouble finding this, but it was worth it." She pulled out a wig, a wig of short-cropped hair and bangs, much like her own. That meant it could only be intended for me. "Don't look like such a wet blanket. Hair bobbing is so jazzy these days that the state of Connecticut says you have to have a barber's license to bob someone's hair. You learn a lot on a train."

I backed away. "I can't go out in public wearing that!"

"You will if you want to get out of here," she said, throwing the scalp onto the bed and reaching back into her shopping bag. "It's the real thing; women sell their hair all the time. You should see the cosmetics I brought to paint your face."

I began to dread what next came out. It was a straight, loose dress, banded around the hips like a waistline, in a flimsy, almost silky material. Matching flat shoes and a hat band with an ostrich feather completed the ensemble. The bright red color was ghastly but I again swallowed hard against my refusal, especially since Pearl wore bright blue of the same sort of garment. But at least, I encouraged myself, neither were sequined and frilled as I'd seen Pearl wear in the past. Nonetheless, we would look like a vaudeville act.

"It's so berry!" she said, sounding as if we were dressing for a party. "If we draw attention to ourselves and doll up, we won't look suspicious, you know?" She held the dress up in front of me. "Hmmm, you've lost some flesh. All the better that this might fall to below your knees and you won't get fluky on me. And nobody will say to you what I heard on the train from a hick with her teen-age daughter." She picked up the hat band and smoothed out the feather. "They sat across from me and were the perfect example of the nineteenth century bumping into the twentieth. She smacked her daughter's stocking leg and said, "Lord, child, pull that dress down. That lady can see plumb to the Promise Land!"

One thing was for certain; no one would recognize me, including me. I would have to travel through at least five states, walk through three train stations, and sit in open seating, dressed as a flapper girl.

Once again, she had beaten me at my own game.

As in days of old, Mama sat in her rocker, her black lace shawl about her shoulders, her head turned to her left, peering down the street expectedly. Only her location had changed. She stood as I stepped from the taxi and walked up the brick walkway to the Lighthouse, happy yet with a heavy heart.

The old two-story manor continued to impress me with its white-washed brick and blue shutters, an endearing elderly woman's face now in need of some cosmetics, her glass eyes promising inner warmth, the brightly colored band of flowers around her neck now being pruned by Eddie. He saw me and gave a big wave and a white toothy grin. Coming home was what I had longed for, yet dreaded too. I would not see Lizzie here; I would not wait for Thomas to come home later. But Mama stood here in front of me, Pearl walking behind me.

Mama squeezed me hard in her hug no different than if I had remained a child. "You need time to grieve, dear," she said.

I nodded and sniffed, relieved that I wouldn't have to explain.

"You girls must be famished. You've been traveling all night, haven't you?" she said, still in that soothing low tone she reserved for the battered women who entered here. She didn't ask about my costume but searched my face carefully. Now that my hair was under the wig, the exposed yellowing bruises on my neck glared and these she touched tenderly. "I would never have thought that someday it would be my own daughter coming into the Lighthouse battered and bruised. Come inside. I have food prepared."

I stepped inside the entranceway and memories flashed in my mind as if life-size photographs hung on the surrounding walls, waiting for my private viewing. I sat down hard on the settee. "This is all too much," I said.

"You'll start enjoying the memories after a while and wish there were more," Mama said. She lifted the wig from my head and began taking the pins from my hair. "I'm so sorry we couldn't have been there for you."

She sat beside me and pulled an opal-studded comb from her hair, combing this through my own, her fingers separating strands as if they were different colored threads for needlepoint. She moved unhurriedly. "I dreamt you were in danger. I was several stories up in a tall building. Down on the street I saw a sea of women roll forward as if of the same mind. Toward the town square they were moving, all dressed in the Legion colors of black and white, but carrying no suffrage signs. There, in the center square I saw you, tied at a stake. You stood erect, your chin jutted out stubbornly, your face impassive as I've seen so often. But the women were angry, chanting, 'Fight, fight! Fight for Bess's rights!' Over and over they repeated this, low at first, their voices rising with each chant. Your head turned slowly away from the crowd and tilted till your eyes met mine. Your expression changed to that of the eleven-year old little girl, when the sleeve of your dress caught fire at our old cooking stove. You screamed, 'Mama!' and I woke up paralyzed with fear. I woke Pearl immediately and told her to telephone you in Georgia. I knew then you needed me."

Braided hair fell over my shoulder and she reached for more strands.

431

"Did Pearl tell you David broke off their engagement?" she continued. "Word got back to him about how she had been violated in the mill's storeroom. He said she is now soiled. So terribly sad. Poor girl, now she is acting as her mama's chaperone.

"Bess, we didn't know until we came back here from Tennessee and Victor told us. He didn't know how to reach us and he was as mad as a wet hen. We were only gone a week or so but you know Victor. If I had told him where I was going and why, he would have done what he could to prevent me from going. He thinks he should be in control of my life. He loves keeping your father's memory alive but then he was the one who benefited from your father's death. I have yet to forgive either one of them."

I was having trouble with forgiveness too. "Why were you in Tennessee?"

"I was looking for someone."

I waved my hands in the air in frustration, further agitated by her calm state. "You taught me indeed to fight, fight, fight for women's rights, yes perhaps impassively as in your dream, but nonetheless I was out there. Where were you in those days when I needed you, where were you two weeks ago when I needed you? Now when you have the freedom to help me, you're not to be found."

"And neither was he."

"*Who?*" I almost shouted.

"It doesn't matter. And you're shouting at me." Her hands worked faster at my other braid, perhaps to prevent them from slapping me. "Besides, I have a confession to make."

Finally!

She remained quiet while she finished the braiding. "Opal and I had our best discussions while washing each other's hair," she said, patting my head. She sat next to me and it was all I could do not to scream, *say it, say you committed adultery!*

"I had no choices – marriage was my only future," she said. "Children were the next step with no choice. Oh, I was given *one* choice – your papa said if I didn't stop leaving the home and my duties behind for women's suffrage work, he would divorce me and take my children. Some choice. I wanted you to have more than that. And don't tell me you'd want that same kind of relationship with a man as I had with your father. You're more prudent. I'll not be any more disloyal to his memory than that, but you must be realistic here. I'll take some blame in reaching out through you. You could go where I could not. Try to understand as another woman. Billy understood and he was a man."

I had stood up by this time, antsy from my journey, my arms folded, pacing, listening, analyzing. I stopped in my tracks. "*Billy?* What does he have to do with Jere?"

She bit her lip. "*Jere?* Who's –" She waved her hand at me and said loudly, like I'd gone daft, "I'm talking about *Billy*. I probably shouldn't tell you this." Her eyes had trouble meeting mine. They darted between me and Pearl who had just joined us with a what-in-the-world-is-going-on-here expression.

Mama finally spoke. "Billy and I had a talk – a few months before he went to war. We were so close to winning the vote and you seemed so close to wedding Billy. I thought it best you do it in the right order. Your work for the cause was invaluable. Mrs. Catt told me that herself. If you had wed then, Billy would likely have forbidden you to do any further work."

"Mama, how much did you interfere here?"

"Quite a bit, I'm afraid. Or perhaps not at all. It was hard to read Billy. Relief and sorrow looked about the same on his face. You two were much alike in that regard in those days. It must have been a challenge for each of you to know what the other was feeling. Anyway, I simply asked that if his intentions were to propose marriage that he wait and do so after the war. He would have to go fight at any rate, and risk leaving you a widow with children. You had enough of your own battles here with marching, petitioning, weeks on the road. I wanted nothing to interfere."

I stood there, a statue of reproach staring down at her. So many emotions were bubbling but the strongest, anger, rose fastest to the surface and popped. "What's all this talk then about choices, when you took one of mine away?"

Mama grasped my folded arms, her eyes pleading. "I was only asking that choices be delayed. I rationalized that while he was fighting the men's war, you could be fighting the women's war. He showed me the wedding rings he bought."

My shock must have shown clearly, for then she said, "He didn't tell you." She looked distant. "He said he never disobeyed his mother and I was close to becoming his second one."

Another emotion arose and I giggled before my hand covered it completely. I scolded myself that I should remain angry, terribly angry, but instead I felt glad knowing that Billy loved me once. And I felt relief that I didn't marry him. In spite of everything, he would have met and most likely loved Christina while so far away in England. I might have been with child … who knows the regret we might have carried? As it was, I had the freedom to go work for Thomas, fall in love and share a much deeper relationship. As it was, I had no regrets.

I only had disappointment in Mama. But perhaps she had paid her dues as an adulterer, in having to instead look after Papa these last ten years. I would have to do my own interfering, starting with a letter to Tennessee. I knew how to find him.

But not so fast.

Perhaps not right away. After all, we have plenty of time. And now for the first time Mama can give one hundred percent to our cause – they must do away with the Comstock Law and allow distribution of birth control methods. If I bring Jere back into her life right now, she'll be useless again. In her own words, "nothing should interfere".

"Mothers are such powerful beings," I said. "I saw that myself in Tennessee with Mr. Harry Burns' mother. She won us the vote!"

August 26th, 1921: Dear Diary, I'm sitting at my desk and have finished my speech with a flourish.

Therefore, we must do away with the wording of the Comstock Law of 1873 that declares distribution of information about contraception is obscene and therefore illegal. Birth control is not obscene. Obscenity was helping deliver my aunt's tenth child and the weakened uterus remained outside her body. To declare this information as illegal has deteriorated the quality and quantity of birth control methods and devices, and has frightened many who would otherwise seek help, especially after seeing Margaret Sanger and then her husband, arrested for just such distribution.

Unlike animals, humans do not mate seasonally. Intimacies between a husband and wife are designed to bring pleasure, beside procreation.

I'm quite pleased with that last line. Out of habit, I straighten my heroine's photograph nailed on the wall next to me. My eyes look more like hers now; deeper set in determination and sorrow. It's been a year since we won the vote that she had paved the road for. What a year of awakening! I am still amazed I was elected President of our local chapter of the American Birth Control League. Mama said she had expected no less from our members. Of course I think her influence and vote and that of Pearl's helped the election quite a bit.

The letter from a lawyer in Pickerville is tucked in the roll-top desk's cubbyhole. It secured my family's future. My beloved Thomas had willed to me the Lighthouse and the Duesenberg, if I ever find the means to motor it back up north. The Pick Plantation is a more complicated matter, first willed to Joe until his death ... and then who's next in line? Once we're rid of him, Pickerville ... Savannah ... more branches to reach more women. Only time will tell.

But I have little time to dwell on it. I'll soon be on the train heading to the United States Capitol. We members of the National Woman's Party are angry indeed. Word came down that statues of Lucretia Mott, Elizabeth Cady Stanton, and my heroine, Susan B. Anthony, had been stored away in a filthy storage closet. So with buckets, brushes and soap, our 'mob' as Pearl calls us, is going to descend on our Capitol with a capital 'E' for Enough! No more hiding women's contributions. As Mama wrote in her song, women are people too. It's time to bring out our foremothers and let them shine. The next generation must know and honor our pioneers and must be taught that our fight is not over.

After all, I have a little one coming into the world. I think I'll name her Katydid.

Katy's Chapter Five -- 1943

I cry anyway. After all, William had become my friend. It hadn't all just been the Swing and booze scene. We'd gone to five picture shows together, he'd taught me how to use a slingshot, had some great laughs. Ate a great deal of malted milk balls, drank a great deal of Pepsi-colas. If he was fresh from the latest movie, he could quote practically a whole scene.

"With your memory to he says/she says, you should become a reporter," I said once, wiping away laughing tears.

"Daddy says our family doesn't need another – that is – a blab- bermouth."

He referenced his father like he was right under his skin. I couldn't tell if it was out of fear or out of worship. Reverence requires both, I guess.

"You really love your papa, don't you?" I asked.

"' If there was a law he's workin' with maybe I could take it, but it ain't the law. He's workin' away my spirit, tryin' to make me cringe and crawl, takin' away our decency'." William had quoted this scene from *Grapes of Wrath* with such passion, he could've replaced Henry Fonda himself.

"At least you have a daddy," I said. I thought any dad was better than no dad at all.

"I'd be your daddy if you'd let me," he said with a mischievous wink. I couldn't get him to talk any deeper than that.

Subsequent to the night he'd made the backseat of my car into a Struggle Buggy, and up until that last night that I left him stranded at the dance hall, he'd minded his manners. I'm talking a few weeks of good behavior here. His only method of coming on stronger was through another one of our movies, *Casablanca.* Outside the theatre that night, he took me in his arms in a slow dance, and with people gathering around with an ain't-that-sweet-smile and him loving the attention, he sang, "'You must remember this / A kiss is still a kiss / A sigh is just a sigh / The fundamental things apply / As time goes by. / And when two lovers woo, / They still say I love you / On that you can rely / No matter what the future brings-'"

Two could play that game. I stopped him with an animated shake of my head and open palms on his chest, and said (in my most sultry Ingrid Bergman voice), "' You know, Rick, I have many a friend in Casablanca, but somehow, just because you despise me, you are the only one I trust.'" I loved that line.

"Ugarte said that, not Ilsa."

"I knew that," I said, trying to cover up.

"Sure you did, kid," he said in his Humphrey Bogart voice.

So I cry and I miss the banter, the back-and-forth, the addictive challenge. He kept me on my toes and now I find myself flat-footed. I figure not even Papa's journal can let me down this low. I pull it from its hiding spot and clutching it to my chest, crawl into my feather bed sniffing and feeling lonely.

August 1, 1921: I was reading over my last entry and boy did I get on a tangent about the Prohibition and the women's vote, completely forgetting about my problem with my brother Joe. If Bess knew, she'd tell me to 'refocus', her favorite word these days, like I'm just staring off into nothing. It's not nothing; I just can't tell her what I'm looking at. It's a mess. Like I said in my last entry – and before I got sidetracked on the eighteenth and nine-teenth Amendments – my cousin, Jimmy, telephoned the other day. Jimmy's got a whole set of problems of his own and he's trying to dole them out like I need some. "Keep it in the family," he said. Hell, yes, keep it in the family. Or see a good number of family change residence to the local jailhouse. Puts a whole new meaning on 'family reunion' and frankly I think it's all wet baloney. God bless Pickerville Georgia.

Jimmy and his daddy – my uncle Willy – are involved in two things, and I'm split in two about it. One I'm one hundred percent against, one I'm one hundred percent for. The complication here is that one caper pays for the other and that doesn't sit well with me and my conscious. Yes, that's right, Dear Diary, I said 'caper'. Yours Truly has become a criminal of sorts. I even hesitated in writing that here but as I told Bess, if you can't say it, then write it down. Writing takes a load off the mind. It's the universe's way of giving you absolution.

Which is why newspaper editorials are so popular and why I was Edrite Formen.

Jimmy telephoned to say he needed my help. Seems that Joe has borrowed a chunk of change and has no way to pay it back. When the cotton crop went down with the boll weevils, Joe decided to invest in automobiles and use his barren cotton field as a sales lot. He claims this new venture made him busier than "a farmer with one hoe and two rattlesnakes". Turns out, he's not so busy. Brother or not, I have to say this: If Joe's brains were gunpowder, he wouldn't have enough to blow his hat off. His plan didn't pan out and he went all around Robin Hood's barn as to why, from blaming it on the locals who move too slowly to change, to blaming the stink coming from Harriet's chicken coops. I reminded him that it's Harriett's feather ticks and pillows business that's bringing their money in, so stop looking the gift horse in the mouth.

The scariest part of all I've just written is that I'm starting to talk like him. To quote my hero, Mark Twain, 'Let us be thankful for the fools. But for them, the rest of us could not succeed.'

Speaking of fools, there's Jimmy's little brother nicknamed Slingshot. He's a five-year old live wire that earned his nickname by killing every bird or squirrel that comes within fifty yards of their house. I'd forgotten about the pipsqueak until I was almost killed by him. I'd gone over there to talk business with Uncle Willy and Jimmy and there's Slingshot standing on their second floor balcony that extends across the front of the house above the veranda. "Take another step and you get it between the eyes," he said steadily, sounding overly menacing and convincing for his age. His dress shirt and suspenders added to his midget appearance. His slingshot stuck out between two railings and aimed at me. On the ground beneath the oak tree beside me, lay two dead Bluejays. How he could kill them in all that tree's droopy Spanish moss was an impressive mystery but it seemed rather sadistic. He always was an unpredictable brat and the rock remained in the sling and pulled back, aimed *at my head. Admittedly I broke out into a sweat. I raised my arms and said, "Okay, David, Goliath surrenders." We stood there staring each other down until his mother came to the rescue.*

Silver haired since her twenties, Marge stepped out onto the veranda with a tray of iced tea, still looking like a young Sheba even though she'd delivered Slingshot late in her mid-life. She said, "Thomas, why in the world are you standing there with your arms up like that." I rolled my eyes and jerked my head up and she immediately knew the cause. "TJ, you come down here instantly!" she called out, coming down the veranda steps and onto the grass. She shielded her eyes to look up to the second floor balcony but of course it's empty and now I'm looking foolish. She gently lowered my arms while saying, "I could shoot his daddy for teaching TJ to be so violent with that slingshot!"

I sit very still, reading no more. Just staring. At one word. *TJ.*

There could only be one TJ with a slingshot – he'd taught me to use one, with rocks aimed at Pepsi bottles. And only one silver-haired Marge – who now I know is my papa's aunt ... which makes TJ my cousin. Holey-moley we're related! I'd been making out with my cousin – and he'd asked me to marry him! I think I'm going to blow my top. But I have to think first. This must be why he didn't want his mother to know where I was living. But how could his last name be "Jackson"? And why would he want to marry his cousin? And why is Uncle Joe pushing us together?

"Clary, I'll take Uncle Joe's breakfast tray in to his room," I say the next morning.

"You're volunteering for abuse? I only do it cause I get paid for it," she says with a chuckle. Then she turns from the stove to take a hard look at me. "What's wrong, child? You look as weak as pond water." She pulls out a chair at her working table. "Take a sit and I'll bring you a cup of coffee." She sets this down in front of me, slumped and sleepy in my seat. I yawn loudly and don't eat. Big mistake.

"Clary, I'm all discombobulated. Did you know that William Thomas Jackson the Third, or TJ, is in fact my cousin?"

She stops fussing around me and returns to the stove, her back to me. "Don't ask me nothing."

I stare at her backside wondering why and what to say but then I figure if I say anything, she'll just high-tail it to her room behind the kitchen. I wait silently for the eggs from her skillet to be added to the tray and I take this out of the kitchen without another word.

I'm relieved to see that Uncle Joe has a little color to his cheeks this morning. I'd be more hesitant to pounce if he looked like he was dying.

I set the tray down on his bed table in front of him. His eyes roll over to me in surprise and he immediately attempts to sit up more, smoothing his scrimpy gray hairs. "Well, this is an honor, missy. You bringing me breakfast. That's more than I been getting from you. More than a wave and a spit of gravel as you drive down my laneway." His mouth slacks as he studies me. "What's wrong now? You look like the backside of bad weather."

"Yes, it seems I've been giving that impression all morning," I say dryly. I sit down and face him. "I haven't been around much because I was doing what you told me to do. And that was to spend time with William Thomas Jackson the third."

"That's a good girl," he says with a nod. "Did he ask you to marry him yet? I know he thinks you're cuter than a bug's ear. What you need to do is—"

"Why the hell would you want me to marry my *cousin?*" I blurt out, shocking myself. This isn't the way I planned it.

He plops his head on his pillow and closes his eyes, and I swear for the life of me, he's faking it. I become madder yet.

"Answer me!"

He opens one eye, a mean eye, like looking into the eye of a rooster. "Don't you talk to me in that tone, missy. I'm not so sick I can't get a switch after you."

"Now you're *threatening* me? What the *hell* is going on here? I want to know! I want answers *now!*" I'm shouting and it actually feels good; I didn't know I had so much pent up inside.

I've never seen someone so angry before; how his eye could turn redder from the inside-out, his face blotch red in patches. "This plantation is not going to some smart-ass kid and her bitch of a mother, I don't care if you are my next of kin. I'll do the right thing by your daddy, I owe him that as my brother, but on my terms. Do you hear me? On my terms!" He coughs a wicked deep-throated croup and truly does look sick now. "My terms," he says hoarsely and takes a jagged breath. "My terms are, you will marry TJ and keep the plantation on the south side of the family, the *right* side of the family, if I have to beat you every step to the church house! Do you hear me, girl? Are you listening to me?" The more he says, the more his mouth foams in the corners.

I sit immobilized, shocked, like watching a chicken turn into a vulture. He keeps saying *Are you listening me, do you hear me, girl?* as someone drags me out of the room. Suddenly Clary's face is in mine. "What are you trying to do, Miss Katy, get yourself killed? Don't you know what that man is capable of doing? He'd have you hanging from a tree, and there you are, taunting him, like holding meat up to a mad dog." She shakes my arm. "What's wrong with you, girl? Now you get on up to your room and read your papa's journal, or a book, or take a long soak in the tub. You want me run you some bath water? Come on."

She mutters under her breath the whole way up there, and then turns on the bath water faucets, and stretches a towel up to block her view of me. "Now get undressed," she says. "I'm not leaving til you do."

I do as she says and step into the tub. Papa's journal still lays on the bed and this she gets and thrusts in my face. "Don't say another word to anybody until you read some more and calm down." I begin where I left off in his last entry.

I've strayed with my thoughts again; seems I do that a great deal here lately. I think of one thing, then grab another … like a monkey swinging through the branches of a tree … should I have the operation … should I tell Bess … should I tell Joe to go to …

Oh yes, Joe. I was talking about Joe owing Uncle Willy money and plenty of it. And Joe using the green stuff for his investment in automobiles but not having much luck in selling them. Since Joe's hurting and can't deliver, he came to me for help. I can't help him until I sell the Lighthouse; what I mean to say is, my manor - damn women have taken over and I don't even think of it as mine anymore.

Like I said, I went over to Uncle Willy's to see if I could help in some other way. After the slingshot event, and after TJ ran off to kill a schoolteacher or something equally bad, Uncle Willy and I talked in his study and he convinced me that the best way for Joe to come even is to help Uncle Willy out with a few bootlegging deals. If we'd give him a hand with that, Joe is all square. We'd even come out ahead and I admit I could use some cash flow. The illegal part of it all bothers me but liquor shouldn't be illegal and I'm not with the Bible tappers who believe it's wrong. To quote Mark Twain, "Whenever you find yourself on the side of the majority, it's time to pause and reflect."

I told Uncle Willy we'd help him; for one thing you're either with Uncle Willy or you're against him, there's no in-between. I also knew Joe would have no scruples in breaking the law. But now in my reflection of it all, I'm getting a tight feeling in my chest over it all. If I get caught, Bess would lose all respect. And to support an uncle who makes a great deal of white sheets and black skin disappear - in other words, is in charge of the local chapter of the KKK – that part I'm totally against. I've always been a supporter of the Negro community and hire one whenever I can. Those I got to know, like Lizzie and the hired hand I got out here working and sleeping in the barn, are hardworking and caring folks just looking to get by, no different than the rest of us. The problem with James is he's not only working and sleeping, he's hiding. Hiding from the likes of my own people, who lynched James' brother, Chester, but James got away. Joe's not happy about keeping him here, but I think we owe him. I've decided to better protect him by sending James and Chester's wife and children up to the Lighthouse until James can find a job up there. James tells me Chester has five children and without their daddy, they're all working as field hands, even their two-year old Isaac. James and his brother were "caught flirting" with two young white ladies, daughters of the local klansmen. "The KKK is not singling out niggers," my uncle said, when I questioned him about it. "The KKK is spreading across the nation to protect Americans against immigrants coming in and taking our jobs, against Jews and Catholics trying to take over our religion, against Communists trying to take over our government." Sure enough, my research found that there's about three million men openly registered as members, as far away as California and Oregon, and it's growing because of the loose immigration laws. I quoted Thomas Jefferson to Joe, "Those who desire to give up Freedom in order to gain Security, will not have, nor do they deserve, either one." And further told Joe that these "knights" of the KKK were damn un-American but he didn't say one way or another. Plenty of fidgeting though, which made me more suspicious of his own affiliations.

As one would imagine, they're totally against Prohibition and that's where I come in with the bootlegging. Tomorrow night as a matter of fact. Tomorrow night. More to come.

I turn the page, eager to read more. Blank page. That was Papa's last entry.

I want to get to the bottom of this and decide that a five-party telephone won't do. Foolish me jumps out of the bathtub and drives over to William's plantation and asks their colored cook for William. Instead of seeing Teeee-Jay, here comes his father. This confirms my thinking that "Willy" is short for William. I'm shaking in my boots but he's sweet as pie and invites me in to wait for his son in the den, telling me that TJ and his mother have gone out to run errands. The place is unusually quiet and I'm flabbergasted by the old musty smells, the creaking worn patches in the dusty wood flooring, the threadbare sofa in the den, the clutter of newspapers, tea cups, a jacket on the floor, wall hangings crooked, like only the outside mattered in its manicured appearance. I remember TJ telling me that they could only afford a cook these days and I'm thinking she obviously spends all her time in the kitchen. He hands me a strong drink without first asking and sits across from me while we idle-chat. I can't imagine TJ's perfectly poised mother living in this. I reach the bottom of my bourbon with mint floating in it and this loosens my tongue. I finally blurt out, "Are you my Great-Uncle Willy?"

He sets down his glass and eyes me coolly. "You want to straight-talk, do you? Alright. Joe phoned me in quite a state a little earlier. Said you came in his room yelling like a sick hound, demanding answers. Said your attitude would make a preacher cuss. That's a sign of poor upbringing right there, especially when you've been offered a silver platter with your daddy's growing-up home-place and it's prime real estate that you and TJ could benefit from. You and TJ should get hitched and combine these two plantations and we can make the Pickerings strong again in the community." He lights a cigar like he's got all day to bullshit me. "But you don't want to rush this by killing your uncle. He's family and family looks after one another."

My back goes rigid and I'm feeling injured. I say no, of course not and why does he say such a thing. And he goes into a long speech about Joe's poor health and that if I'm only there to put Joe six feet under so that I can get his plantation, then I'm going about it all wrong and that I should be ashamed of myself.

I go from injury to anger in three seconds flat.

"Marrying my cousin is not the answer either," I say. "And I'm not the only one who should be ashamed. You and your KKK and your bootlegging killed my papa and I had to grow up without him."

His eyes go dark as if I've torn off the veil into his dark side and I jump up like the seat cushion caught on fire. Yet my do-or-die had to finish its say. As if I'm not standing in enough shit, I shovel more. "All I'm asking," I say in a shaky voice, "is that you call off the dogs, Joe and TJ, and your secret will be safe with me. I'm not looking for a husband, and if I was, I sure as hell wouldn't marry a self-centered, mean-spirited *cousin* to get what is rightfully mine. Like father, like son. You know what? I've had enough of this southern charm. I'm going back up north, where I belong. Someone can just mail me the deed when Joe dies."

I stomp out of the room and out onto the front verandah. My steps slow, though, going down the stairs as I notice the gigantic oak tree in the front yard and all of a sudden I can imagine, I can almost *see* Papa standing there beside the tree in a white linen suit looking just like his photograph, his hand is shading his eyes and he's looking up at the second story, just like his journal said. He's saying, *that's dangerous, get away from here*, and somehow I know he's talking to me.

I pick up the pace heading toward my Duesy when a hand clamps onto my shoulder. It's Uncle Willy. With a gun. "Don't be in such a hurry," he says in a low tone that gives me goose bumps. "I want to give you a tour." He motions with his gun. "Come on, Miss Priss."

Seeing a real hand gun for the first time in my life stuns me and things become unreal, like watching one of those gangster films TJ and I enjoyed. We walk behind the house and around the breezeway to "the kitchen house" and he tells me in a tour-guide voice that this plantation house used to be a grand southern belle, her long gown and train spread out for miles. "Damn war and runaway slaves took most of the cotton crop and my granddad was forced to sell off land until his southern belle was reduced to a church lady in an ugly skirt." We walk beyond the mowed lawn, cedar fencing around its edge, and as we pass some small gray timber buildings that look a hundred years old, he uses his gun as a pointer as he calls out their purpose: a smokehouse, a tool barn, a granary, a stable. He opens the door to the stable and I peer inside to empty stalls. We continue to an overgrown field and pause where in the tall grasses lay remnants of a foundation here and there, bricks, and partial fireplaces. "Granddad owned more than fifty slaves at one time." He shakes his head and I'm thinking I agree: that's terrible. Until he turns away muttering, "Damn war."

We enter a wooded area and through there we continue for some time, with his strong hold on my elbow, his other hand holding the gun as casually as he held his drink. A small shack suddenly appears as if growing there, practically covered by ivy, fern, and Spanish moss that's dripping down from tall, overhanging trees, the weight and sag in this humidity making it all look weary. Its tiny front porch is sunken with rotting wooden planks and I can hear something scatter underneath as we step up onto it.

"My daddy hid slaves here," he says, opening the door. "They'd work off their ten-year indenture and then he'd give them a piece of land." I'm now a tourist and step up to look through the door without hesitation. "Only TJ and I know about this place."

I'm in a stupid daze with only the word *gun* repeating itself in my head but this statement and the dark interior wakes me up into pure terror. I cry out "No!" and pull away but his grip tightens and his other arm comes around my neck and squeezes. "Since you're so against the KKK," he mutters in my ear, "maybe you and darkie ghosts can mediate." With this he shoves me in and slams the door behind me. I rush forward to grab the door knob but he's quick to lock with a key from the outside. I'm a prisoner.

I don't yell. I don't cry. My whole being goes into survival mode. After trying the door a few times, and after deciding that the one window is too small to crawl through, I stand quietly, waiting for my vision to adjust to murky gray. There's no sunlight that comes through; the place sits in total shade. I can make out some furnishings against the three walls: a cot, some sort of cupboard, and a bench. Everything is gray, even the musty mattress, and I can't bring in another color, more light – there's no matches for the lantern in the cupboard. Just a rusty can opener and a tin cup and, oh yes, a slop jar that eventually comes in handy for my ... wastes. I at last sit gingerly on the mattress, amongst the circles of darker gray stain, and I wait and listen. Panic rises up and I swallow it back down; I don't want to go crazy here. Of all the questions skittering around in my head, the one that is loudest is Why Am I Here? I find out much later, when the gray becomes dark and feels like the darker it becomes, the smaller my space is and I'm becoming afraid this darkness will touch me, wrap around me, squeeze me until I suffocate. I'm wishing I'd eaten breakfast that morning rather than delivering Joe his. Then I'm wishing I'm back there, even to be yelled at by Joe; he wasn't so bad, everything there had been looked after for me, no housecleaning or cooking, that warm massive feather bed ... and oh, Clary's sweet potato biscuits ...

Through the window I see an artificial ray of light dart about from tree to tree and become brighter as I hear footsteps on the porch. The rotting lumber creaks and cracks under the weight of more than one soul out there, keys jingle, the door answers back with its own creak as it opens and closes. The ray of light comes around to shine on me. I shade my eyes.

"Katy?"

I'm so relieved! "TJ! Why am I here?"

There's a long pause as the flashlight remains on me. "Daddy wants us to work things out," he finally answers, his voice sounding unsure. I hear the door being locked again from the outside but whoever is out there, stays there. "Stop asking questions!" he says, sounding forcefully gruff. "You'll speak when spoken to!" We listen to the sound of footsteps walking away.

"You don't have to shout, TJ. Did you bring some matches? Did you bring a lantern or a lamp or something?"

"I brought a candle," he said, lowering his voice.

I hear a bag rattling, smell food, a sandwich in wax paper lands on my lap, as the flashlight beam darts around from his other hand. I stand up and grab this to set up on the cupboard for better lighting. He yanks it out of my hand and with a force I'm not expecting, shoves his hand against my chest and I sit back down on the mattress with a thud.

"Sit still!" he barks and I sense some alarm in his voice.

I've lost my sandwich to the darkness below me. I want to eat, to cry, to demand, to beg. *Fight with honey*, someone once said. "Look, TJ, I don't understand any of this. I'm sorry but my sandwich dropped from my lap and I can't see it." I use my sweetest tone. "Can you get it?"

"In a minute." He continues fumbling through the bag and a bottle of liquor comes out. TJ takes a long swig; I can hear his throat swallowing drink after drink, I can smell the bourbon. He pushes the bottle into my hand. "Drink, then you can eat."

I hand this back to him after my attempt. "It's too strong."

His flashlight shines down on my sandwich and this he picks up off the floor and throws across the tiny room. "Drink!" His voice is shrill now.

I do as I'm told, now wanting the booze as much as he does. I guzzle and with an empty stomach, it hits hard. Back and forth we pass the bottle without words until I'm woozy. He seems to be drinking for courage, I'm drinking for cowardice. It's all I can do not to start screaming, fighting, clawing. The bourbon works its black magic and I relax and sway and watch his hands light the candle, now seeing two, no, only one, becoming glad for the cozy darkness around us. The flashlight is off and has disappeared into black and I feel I am disappearing, too.

"Why, why, why," I hear myself say softly. "Why am I here?"

This seems to give him the opening he's looking for. "For this, baby." And with a power and strength I can't reckon with, he grabs my shoulders, pushes me back and he's swiftly lying on top, moving hard and fast as if afraid I'll get away, his breath getting louder in my ear, hands pinching, groping, pulling, my dress and panties twisted, ripped enough for his mission. I struggle like someone under water, weight and motion a hundred times heavier. His weight is on me, then in me, then through me, like I've been skewered to the bed.

The impact of what he's done hits later, in the smothering closeness, blackness of the room, the candle now disappeared with the flashlight, and of him passed out beside me. I lie immobilized, trying to breathe in deeply, and with each expelled breath goes a *Why?* Finally the early morning light shows me the dark gray blood on my thigh, his unzipped trousers, and I become abruptly sick and run to the slop jar.

"Rinse with this," he says, now standing at the cupboard with a Mason jar of water. He's a stranger to me now; revolting, sloppy, his hair flat on one side, no shirt. He does his business at the slop jar while I drink thirstily. I'm as sick as I've ever been and can only lie down again to keep from falling in the shifting room. I face the wall and he spoons in behind me and soon I hear him snoring. I sleep in pieces, between the real, the unreal, the dreams, the nightmare. I'm not sure which I'm in when he begins to move against me. "Don't be upset with me," he mumbles, his hand coming around to squeeze my breast. "I love you." And soon he's doing what he did hours before and this time I just lie there, any movement causing more pain, just lie there and wait and it's taking longer and he's moving slower and he's talking to me, telling me how he loves me, how he wants me, how I need him to marry me. And all I can concentrate on is the burning, and how my energy had bled out and what's the use and just get it over with. Over and over, unbuttoning my blouse, kissing my breasts, and can't he see I'm not there anymore? Uncaring, unfeeling. Except somewhere in me, I hope he dies.

"Why" I ask him as he prepares to leave.

"I'm here to impregnate you so that you have to marry me."

I want to scream at such a horrid plan but I need answers more. "Why is that so important?" I'm relieved I sound as calm as he, but my trembling hands betray me and I place them under my legs on the bed as I sit there watching him bag the candle holder, food papers, empty bottle of bourbon. I feel sick to my stomach just looking at it. I'm showing signs of pregnancy already.

"Daddy and I need your plantation; it's more fertile land than this one and we need more land to grow more cotton. And. Love. I want you," he says like an after-thought. He looks at his watch and begins to move hurriedly.

"What is your real name?"

He sighs like I've gone too far. "Thomas Jackson Pickering."

"The 'William' part …"

He nods. "Is my daddy's name."

How original.

He picks up my sandwich that he'd thrown eons ago. He hands this to me. "Enough questions. Fill your mouth with this. I'll bring more tonight."

"Tonight? You're leaving me here all day?" I stood, shaky, at the verge of a breakdown. "Take me with you!" I shout. I can't bear the thought of another … I grab his shirt sleeve. "It's too dark here. I said, take me with you, you bastard!"

I heard footsteps returning outside and the door unlocking. Whoever was there remained to listen.

He gives me his cocky grin. "Oh so now I remember you. You're the rude bitch who left me stranded at the club." He drops his grin and pinches my chin. "You were a cock-tease that night, weren't you?" My eyes fill with tears and his expression changes with it. "I'm sorry, baby, but you deserved what you got. For all those weeks, I'd jump at your beck and call, take you where you wanted to go, save all my dances for you, I was a slave to your love, honey, and yet you treated me badly. Now you're a slave to my love, baby doll. Daddy said I can keep you here until you learn how to treat your man, because, if you don't, you'll have to learn how to obey your master. .But now that we're a couple, we'll treat each other better, right?" He kisses me on the cheek. "See you tonight."

As he opens the door I feel a dam break inside. I rush at him screaming, clawing, him fighting back and me not caring if he killed me. I have to get out of there.

Like the night before, something in him switches to high power and his strength takes me over. I'm thrown on the bed and he sits on top of me, his knees squeezed into my ribs. I thrash about like a mad woman until he slaps me into silence.

"I'm sorry, I'm sorry," he says, stretching out over me. He holds my face in his hands. "I didn't mean to hurt you, I swear to God I didn't." He's crying now, sobbing into my neck. "Baby, please forgive me, I won't hurt you again, just be patient with me, okay? I've got to work this out with Daddy. I'm his slave, now I've made you into one, and oh God, oh God ..." on and on he whispers.

"I'm pregnant now," I whisper. "So, you can let me go."

"You are?" he says, searching my face for signs. "How do you know?"

"I had morning sickness, remember?"

"Baby, it can't happen that soon. Unless." He becomes rigid and arches away from me. "Unless you've fucked someone else before. It was that man at the bar with the big ears, wasn't it?" He jumps off the bed and before I can get there, he's out the door and I hear the lock click over, saying *trapped again.*

I sit there in that damned shack, munching on that stale bologna sandwich, trying to make it last, trying to settle my stomach, trying to stay calm. I don't know what time of day it is when I hear footsteps and the door unlocks and opens. My eyes adjust to where I recognize the plantation's colored cook and she's motioning to me with her hand to come over there quickly. When I do, she whispers, "I got word from Clary to get you out of here. She's worried sick, child." She pushes me out onto the porch. "Now get going and don't look back and don't say a word to what happened here, or Clary will hang from a tree, sure as the world."

I stumble off the porch and turn left. "That way a-take you back to the devil," she whispers sharply. She comes up behind me and turns me right. "This way a-take you through cotton patch to a dirt road. Then turn left. Walk til you get to a brown rusty truck. My son will drive you into town and hand you money, sent by Clary. She said to tell you to buy a ticket and go home." She pushes me forward. "Remember, don't look back and don't say a word."

I do all she says, except buy the ticket. There isn't enough money in the envelope to do that, according to the train station teller. Not even close. And not enough for the hotel next door. But I have enough for a tiny room in the attic of a boarding house down the street for a few days. I look hazy-crazy and need a place to clean myself up and think what to do. The heavy-set lady there brings a pitcher of fresh water, and shows me the community bathroom down on the second floor, saying only old men board here, all the young have enlisted in the war. "You're lucky I have a spot for you, honey, there's no housing left and the hotel prices have gone through the roof. Hundreds have come in to work at the shipyard." The make-shift room consists of a twin bed and a night table, with a divider to hide attic storage stuff, and it's stifling up here. I can't get back down the two flights fast enough.

Dinner is the most delicious in my life and while there, two old men are talking about their new jobs at the shipyard and how they're hiring anyone, "even women". They laugh because the world's gone crazy, and they make jokes about women crying if they get a "boo-boo". They say the war machine is hungrier than ever, now that all the young men are over in Europe fighting, and factories are getting desperate. "My neighbor is giving welding classes to girls if you're interested. Has it all set up down in his basement," one of the old coots say, the same one who had teetered precariously over the table on one foot, pretending he's in high heeled shoes, crying in a high pitched voice, "oh, oh, I broke my nail!" and then falling to the floor with, "oh, oh, I broke my heel!"

"Nothing complicated," he continues, raising his hand as if to reassure me. "Figure the girls can handle the tack welding, as long as you can do it horizontally, vertically, and flat on your back. You ever been flat on your back, girl?" They both snicker and Mrs. Worthington gently scolds them like children and includes the other three odds and sods who sit there grinning, enjoying the show. I sense she's enjoying their jawing but I pay attention to none of them, except to ask questions. Their ridicule chalks another one against the male species and this is when I realize I've started keeping score and only speak to them when necessary (I only said hello and goodbye to the cook's son who drove me into town). Yet these bastards spur me on and admittedly I want to prove them wrong. Besides, earning a living appeals to me and I don't have enough money to go back to Mama and I sure as hell can't go back to Joe's, even if the traitor does have my Duesy. And now I owe Clary twenty-two dollars – I can't even begin to think how many months of her wages she loaned me. All good reasons and I ask the hunchback old man with the missing teeth where I can go tomorrow for the welding class. He offers to walk me there on the way to the Savannah River Shipyard and that's how I get started.

Like he says on the long boring walk while he beats his gums, the training is fast and easy, now that the unions have allowed the curriculum to be shortened to get new welders to the yard sooner ("but don't get to thinking that the girls can join the union; get that out of your pretty head right now" and he catches me rolling my eyes and he leaves in a huff, muttering "ungrateful bitch"). We're five women total in my class, all in various stages - some having returned from the shipyard to learn more than tacking - and we do some giggling and fussing but when it comes down to the work, we take it as seriously as making pie crusts. I nickname us The Girls (after telling them the old-coot story) and whenever one of us uses or calls out that term of endearment, we all stop what we're doing (if we're not holding the blow torch), put our hands on our hips and thrust our chests out. We carry this on to the shipyard too and other women catch on to it and call out the government slogan, *Working Women Win Wars!* We laugh until we're wiping the tears away. On our breaks we stick together passing around Lucky Strikes and talking about the passes men make and who's hotsty-totsy and who's all wet. The men call us bird-herds as they walk by but they don't dare approach us. Laughter is the best ammunition that a woman's got.

One such afternoon we're all standing outside and I have a heart attack when I see TJ walk by in his red cashmere sweater and tan slacks. His printing shop isn't far away and he looks like he's just out for a stroll. A couple of The Girls whistle at the "sheik". I pull my cap down over my face and tell them to can that shit. He halts briefly for one horrible minute but then only returns a blow-kiss and continues on. Shirley, our best atta-girl, puts two and two together and says, "Girls, girls. You know those rich types are about as useful as a screen door on a submarine." I ask, "Got anything more than that cig?" They seem to understand and, that night, they escort me out to the dance hall across the street and I get sauced.

I thought The Girls would be housewife types "flocking to war work", like the campaign ads illustrate, but most had worked before, even those who are married. It's just that the Depression years had kept them down, and the pay here is a hell of a lot better than wait-ressing or clerking at sixty dollars a month. Some say they're here for patriotic reasons but the major motive is the money, and when I find out I'm going to make two hundred and twelve dollars a month after five days of learning to tack-weld, I'm bedazzled. The yard even has a twenty-four hour children center for the white mothers.

I can't get to the shipyard fast enough and when I tell Mrs. Worthington I got the job, she says she'll wait until my first paycheck to get her boarding money because I'm a *lady*. She says loudly that she'll defy any man who'll cheat her but she has a knowing smile and something devious in those beady eyes. She makes me think there's only one letter difference between defiance and deviance. She's cheap, I know that. The first thing I buy is a feather tick for that prickly straw mattress in her attic. The tick has Harriet Pickering's name stitched on the tag.

The most difficult part is working while wearing the full protective gear in Georgia autumn heat. With heavy green suede-like overalls, men's suede gloves up to the elbow, and the helmet with the protective face shield, we're cooking inside and I don't mean in the kitchen. I come close to fainting a couple of times but would rather die than do that around these men. They'd never let me hear the end of it. They're wise-guys, mostly, and I learn more swear words than I knew existed. I love wearing the trousers though (even though I find I'm less likely to apply lipstick) and I love my job as assistant to a union welder, Dicky Rolletini, working on the frame of a submarine rescue ship. He doesn't have to wear as much protective gear as I do, so he gives me the easy jobs where I don't have to get into terribly awkward positions. With the clothing and Dicky protecting me, I don't have to worry about a thing.

Well, that's not entirely true. Three months into the job and I have to face something: I haven't had a visit from the *Red Baron*. I'm making excuses up to this point: more physical exertion than I'm accustomed to; I haven't counted the days correctly; doing men's work has made my body act like a man; I have a disease from the asbestos fibers coming off my welding rod when it comes in contact with the welding torch flame (Dicky told me about that danger). I know the real reason but I can't face it any different than I can face Mama.

I send her and Clary vague letters about doing my patriotic duty. I know Mama will like that and I know Clary will know better. I send her money and *mum's-the-word*, and she writes back that Duesy is fine and Uncle Joe is not. All good news.

Through December, Dicky's not so protective anymore: the boss is asking him why I'm gaining weight; the boss is asking him if we fool around; the boss is asking him if I'd go to the shipyard doctor to be checked for female weaknesses; the boss is telling him unmarried chubby women are less responsible; the boss is telling him I have a job until the end of December (because "nobody on his watch gets the ax at Christmas") and that's it. "Don't come back in January, kitten," Dicky says with a shrug of his shoulders and a quick glance at my protruding stomach. "The boss tells me that's why he hates hiring women. They always get knocked down or knocked up."

I'm hurt because I'm thinking he's my friend, but I know he considers himself lucky to have such a job with a hole in his heart and therefore not any good to the war as a soldier. The Girls give teary goodbye hugs and a promise that I'll be be-bopping soon, and I slow-waltz it back to the boarding house.

"No one will hire you, pregnant as a spring heifer," Mrs. Worthington states with hands on hips. I find out she's right and end up working off my boarding doing her kitchen work. There's nothing exciting to tell you about that – what woman doesn't know about kitchen work?

"A soldier no doubt did this," she says, coming into the kitchen one evening and catching me rubbing my lower back. "That's what a girl gets when whoring around town," she adds, referring to my few nights with The Girls at the shipyard dance hall. It isn't TJ's hangout but I'd stopped going out altogether, in fear of running into him.

I immediately straighten and turn back to the sink. I'd never admitted to her about my condition. "For fifty dollars I can get you a potion," she says casually, folding linen napkins at the working table. I turn to face her, eyebrows raised. "It's legal," she continues quickly, keeping her eyes focused on her work. "A menstrual blockage, it's called. Advertised in the newspaper but smart women know what it's used for. A simple drink that will cure you of female troubles."

I think about it. So there. I've said it. I'm tired of the shame and I want to go home to Mama. Men don't meet my eyes anymore and I figure my life is over in finding a beau, or even someone to dance with. Don't get me wrong; there are many women around that are pregnant but they proudly wear that gold wedding band as proof of decency, and talk incessantly about their husband overseas, like the women themselves wear the Purple Heart. A few have stayed here and their husbands come in from the ships and stay overnight and I have to hear bedsprings creak decently all hours of the night. I never know how to answer their questions on where my husband is fighting and sometimes I lie and make up a place. I'm getting good at lying through writing Mama. I've had dozens of imagined explanations with her and none of them are convincing. No matter what, she'll only tell me that if I'd done what I promised about the birth control clinic, I wouldn't be in this mess. She's right. So there. I've said that too. Yet my conscience is part of the problem and the other part is the fifty dollars. I'd spent most of my dough from the shipyard on rent and clothing. With what little I have left, I have to buy bigger dresses.

Alright, I was almost in another lie here. If I can afford bigger dresses, I can afford …The truth is, I hand her the money for the potion, she hands me a capped bottle of dark liquid, and she never mentions another word about it. I stand in my little attic room, slowly bring the potion to my lips, and then drink it quickly before I can change my mind. The stuff tastes awful with all that lead in it. I sit on the bed. I lie down on the bed. I wait. And then I grab the chamber pot from under the bed. God punishes me by making me upchuck everything but the baby for three horribly sweaty days. Blood, diarrhea … I want to cry out for help but I'm too ashamed. Every now and then I hear footsteps and think Mrs. Worthington is checking on me, but they go away without a knock on my door. I clean up my own mess and on the fourth, I'm back in the kitchen and the baby is kicking me good. And I'm kicking myself over trying to rid of my own flesh and blood, even if part of that blood belongs to a mean-spirited cousin. I'm beginning to think I'm no better.

In my eighth month, Clary sends word that Uncle Joe has died "in a croak" and the coast is clear. I cry for the first time that I can remember, realizing that relief is where my water tap is. I'm weaker in body but stronger of mind, determined to make this work to where

I can tell Mama about it. With Clary's letter, now I can see how to do that. First of all, Clary is a midwife, so when I show up at the Pick Plantation by taxi cab, and after her initial, "Oh Lord, child!" and my response by patting my stomach and saying, "Yes, it is!" I know I'm back to where I should be. Clary will look after that part.

Then I do the harder part. At Uncle Joe's funeral I wear Clary's bulky Kangeroo coat with large pockets that hide my condition. Only then do I feel comfortable facing TJ and his father, not wanting to see his father smirk at me for his successful plan. At least TJ has the propriety to look frightened when he first sees me. After the funeral I approach a very solemn TJ and invite him out to the house for dinner. I enjoy his shock and the glimpse of admiration as he nods a speechless acceptance.

I open the door to him in my one and only maternity dress; the style is tight and ties at the waist in the back and has ruffles down the front and sleeves, as if ruffles will detract. I tied it tight to stick out obscenely. His eyes enlarge, as if in need to take it all in and he blushes and stammers terribly, making this all worthwhile. He hands me a gift, a pair of rayon stockings - a rarity these days - mumbling something about replacing my ankle socks with these "much later", meaning when I can once again wear a garter. I say nothing about the obvious, pretending it's all perfectly normal.

Then, over Clary's sweet potato biscuits (which always puts me in a good mood), I ask him to marry me "for the baby's sake". To give him credit here, he could've said no - Clary had told me that Uncle Joe's dying words were cursing me and Mama and that he'd changed his will to give the plantation to TJ. Instead, a very contrite TJ grabs my hand and tells me I won't regret it. Our wedding will make everybody happy, he claims. "And even you'll be happy once you know that I joined the service. Yes, ma'am, I've enlisted for atonement. I feel plain awful for what I did. Hey," he adds, feigning chirpy, "if you're lucky, I'll die of trench fever like my uncle did in the Great War."

"Well, that's just whiz-bang," I mutter and take a large bite of biscuit. Not even TJ, looking his spiffy best dressed in a suit and tie could ruin my appetite these days. "I guess your uncle is my uncle, too?" This really isn't a question because I really don't want to know.

TJ jumps up, takes my cigarette and butts it out, and pulls my hands to lift my bulk to my feet. "Let's get married tomorrow. You said you won't leave the plantation again until after the baby is born. So, I'll bring an ordained minister out here and Daddy can be our witness."

"Why so soon?" I haven't thought this through, past asking.

"Yeah, what's the rush?" he asks, patting my stomach basketball.

I have to laugh. "Okay. But only your mother," I say. I have my limits.

"All right," he answers slowly. "I'll see what I can do."

He pulls it off and ends the vows by slipping a gold wedding band on my finger. He's wearing his service uniform; I'm wearing the maternity dress, only I loosen the tie in the back when I see the pinched lips on the minister. My first thought is, *now I can call Mama.*

TJ's mother insists I help her in the kitchen (much to Clary's surprise who had been peeping through the kitchen door to watch our ceremony), only to take me to the sideboard and whisper, "If it makes you feel any better, William is not TJ's father." I gasp and then my eyes become larger at the implications to my unborn child. "You know who I am," I state, admiring her wise blue eyes and silver hair framing her face. Even up close she has a porcelain complexion. She continues as if I haven't spoken. "TJ doesn't know but his father suspects. So understand this. TJ has always tried to please a father he's never had and who has never loved TJ, or anyone else for that matter. I hope you have a son who can love TJ back." She kisses my cheek and leaves the room, leaving a shocked daughter-in-law slash great-niece behind in an aftermath of Coty perfume.

He leaves for basic training at Camp Wolters, Texas the next week. Before that, we stay at the plantation house for the entire "honeymoon". I avoid the public, he and Clary avoid each other. He can't harm me any longer and the easiest thing to do to avoid conflict is to submit to his manhood every time he asks. And he always asks first. And he asks every night. He moves on top of me, trying not to apply weight to my stomach, and we avoid each other's eyes. The truth is there to see and says that the only connection we have is where he's entered me. After a few nights, he only enters from behind.

He does his thing quickly, sometimes clinging desperately. Night after night he pulls down the covers to my sacred feather bed and creeps in behind me. I keep to my side unless he taps my shoulder. "Please, baby, please?" he asks as he pulls up my ankle-length nightgown. I nod my consent, expose myself further and he's off to the races.

I cry when he leaves for basic training, and you remember the only reason why I cry, don't you?

Jesi is born the day after TJ leaves, as if it's safe now to come out. She is delivered about four weeks early and takes about the same amount of hellish time as my imprisonment in TJ's shack. I feel like I'm going through it all over again, in my room with the shades down during the day, and the all-night grips of black pain. What goes in one way must come out the same. "Don't leave me alone," I cry out to Clary, when she goes away to get more towels. "Don't turn the lamp off!" I cry when she wants me to try to sleep. Clary is changing her tune, when she takes my cigarettes away and tells me to sip her herbal concoctions or when she massages my legs, which tells me she is getting worried. At long last – and with what I think is my dying breath - I scream out and bear down while Clary pushes on my stomach and I feel Jesi slip out as if there's nothing to it. Clary cries out, "It's a girl!" and I try to joke by asking if my heart and lungs came out with her. Clary doesn't smile though and seems to be concentrating on what's going on between my bent legs. "It's a girl," she says, softly this time, "but she's a little damaged."

"Damaged?" I ask, trying to lift myself up from my pillows.

"Lay still," she says. She's quiet for a minute. "This little 'un's got clubfoot," she mutters.

"Clary?"

She looks over at me as if I've suddenly just showed up. "I'll get her cleaned up and bring her back. You lie still so I can get you cleaned next."

I'm somehow dozing when she returns, a doctor in tow. He lifts up my sheet and feels around like he knows me as wife, and gives Clary instructions on massaging my stomach to rid of afterbirth, and tells her to wash me down and change my sheets. She frowns at him for bossing her around and I can't say I blame her now that she's done the hard part, but she just says "yes sir, no sir". He tells her I should've seen a doctor during my pregnancy and that I should've been taken to a hospital, like it's her fault, and hoarsely I call out that I'm where I want to be and where the hell is my baby?

"I've sent her to the hospital," the doctor says, turning on a different kinder tone. "She has birth defects that may require immediate surgery. She's breathing poorly and she appears to have talipes equinovarus."

"Oh God," I say. It sounds serious. "Clary, bring me back my damn cigarettes."

One leg is four inches shorter and curved out, the other has a clubfoot that is surgically straightened and splints applied. This is after they clear up her lung infection. She's in the hospital for weeks and my breasts dry up like apples on the ground. I'm too tired to feel much of anything and I try not to think. Mama tries to change that.

"I was planning on coming down there for the birth," she says in *that tone,* as if I had intentionally planned time of delivery. I immediately start feeling agitated; she just has that gift I reckon. And Lord Child, all the questions: Why was she born so early? How many months along did you say you were? Why didn't you tell me sooner you were married last fall? Why are there birth defects? We've never had a birth defect in our entire family! What kind of family does this TJ come from? And she says *TJ* as if she doesn't believe that's his real name. Her being so smart always takes me by surprise although it shouldn't. Of course the more I tell her, the more she asks. "Why is Jesi's last name the same as ours?" *It's the woman's way of the future for war babies,* I try to explain. She's not buying any of it.

I change the subject to one of her liking, a long-time tactic of mine. "I've decided to pursue the birth control clinic." This is true; I want to do this more than ever. I owe this to Mama for all my lies. Besides, I have time on my hands now that Jesi is in the hospital and I don't want to think about her coming home. With the leg bandages and tubes, she's cumbersome to hold and always cries when I do. I know how she feels. I usually spend my time with her by holding her fingers and stroking her head. Her blonde wisps of hair, wide mouth and porcelain skin reminds me too much of how she got here. Many days I feign exhaustion and Clary goes in my stead. Marge starts going every day at noon "just in case".

TJ comes in after basic training for a few days, on his way to France. He looks older with his hair cut so close, and he's mean and lean-looking, too. He studies Jesi lying asleep in the hospital ward's metal crib, then glares at me accusingly and I snap, "The doctor says it's because we had too much sex while I was pregnant." I leave him there with Marge and drive my Duesy home. He spends his days at the hospital or at his parents' home and falls into my bed at night and begins snoring before I can say *don't touch me.* "Maybe we should communicate by walky-talky," he says one morning, before driving Duesy away. That's the last time I see her. "We decided Jesi isn't safe in a twenty year old Duesenberg and the war effort needs the scrap metal. Call Mother when you need a ride."

"Anytime you need it, darling," she says with a hug.

Two weeks later we get a telegram informing us that TJ is killed in the Normandy invasion. I feel badly for Marge.

With the deed to the plantation now in my name, I tell the estate lawyer who is reading the will that I want to sell it. "So soon?" he asks. "You should not make decisions while grieving."

"Sell it? That's preposterous!" shouts William, there in the lawyer's office with Marge. TJ had willed his beloved slingshot to William and William looks none too impressed. I'm all the more determined. Marge smiles that knowing Mona-Lisa smile at it all and calmly tells William that they must go see Jesi at the hospital. He leaves in a huff.

The sale doesn't take more than a week or so, with such prime real estate. Luckily for me, the estate lawyer says, he also represents civil rights cases and doesn't like William. This keeps William's lawyer and interference at bay and that's all the details my lawyer will "bother" me with. The sale goes for much less than I had hoped for and I never meet the new owner but at the end, I don't care. With some of the proceeds I rent a duplex on one of Savannah's park-like squares, with enough room for Clary and Jesi, arranged by Ellen Whitman and within walking distance to her home. She wants me near for her own reasons, I want out of small-minded Pickerville ("Pickleville" I nicknamed it, just to irritate TJ), and with no constant reminders of Uncle Joe, I love my new home. Clary fusses about the move but has become so attached to Jesi that I convince her to move with me, knowing she'll tend to Jesi now that she's home. She's almost three months old and admittedly I'm scared to tend to her on my own.

On the other side of the duplex, Ellen and I convert into office space and name it the Bess Birth Control Clinic, using only its acronym of BBCC on the front door. This is partly funded by the Planned Parenthood Federation of America and partly funded by private donations from those women who come in for contraceptive information. Laws like the Comstock Law forbidding dissemination of contraceptive information had finally been overturned, but the religious wings are a pain in the ass. I sit as receptionist and pass out pamphlets sent by my grateful Mama, and I hire a nurse who comes in a few hours a day to privately discuss birth control methods in the back room. Ellen is a tireless volunteer; she gets the word out, prints more pamphlets and brings in more funding and soon the waiting room fills daily.

I feel more useful here than at home. Jesi prefers Clary and we all only get frustrated with each other. I lose patience with Jesi's slow growth and healing. Another leg surgery and brace sets her back and she's not able to crawl and falls over easily when sitting. And that wide, bright smile of hers! I can't bear it.

"I'm keen on what I'm doing," I tell Mama. "The women look so relieved when they walk out of the clinic, knowing they have some control back in their lives. Most have four or more children and can't afford to feed another, the husband left or is killed in the war, or it endangers the mother's health, or a myriad of sad reasons. Some come in disguises, with wigs and scarves, and about everyone comes in with sunglasses on. I joke that I'm going to go on the radio announcing, 'Every day is a sunny day at BBCC'! Nurse Jones takes them into a private room and shows them how to use condoms or douches and for the brave and few, the diaphragm, and we discuss other methods like counting days until ovulation. We're secretly handing out free condoms and lubricants to those who ask for our *feminine hygiene products* – the term we've given to keep them disguised - but that's becoming risky. I'm afraid word is getting out and I'm receiving threatening telephone calls from religious groups telling me I'm killing God's children and this wicked sin must be stopped." I love sounding grown-up to her and talking her language.

"I attended the Chicago Birth Control Conference in 1923," says Mama, "and I remember one of our own, Eleanor Wembridge, saying there that it would be difficult if not impossible to teach the dull how to use birth control. In my experience, it's impossible to teach the deacons, not the dull. I'd hoped that when Preacher Paul passed away, the younger preacher would have fresh ideas, but that's not to be so. God never changes, he says. Church-going women remain afraid to prevent pregnancies. I'll send you her paper titled *The Seventh Child in the Four-room House.*"

I want to say that I don't want more papers, I'm inundated with them; I want Mama here. I want to say that one of the threatening callers sounds like TJ's father. But Mama is swamped with work at her clinic and the Lighthouse in Annan New York and promises yet again to try to free herself up to come down and help out. She recommends I screen my calls, so I begin giving out the code name of "Jesi" to only those women who come in.

The next morning a note is tacked on the BBCC front door, scribbled with *Neither repented they of their murders, nor of their sorceries, nor of their magic potions, nor of their fornication, nor of their thefts. Revelations 9:21.*

With a shaky hand I extend this note to Clary who promptly turns to her family Bible, its brown leather looking as spotted and worn as her hands. "I didn't think that sounded right," she says. "Now why in the world would someone add 'magic potion'? Ain't God's Word good enough?" she mutters, studying the note suspiciously.

I suddenly feel a wave of sickness not unlike those three days in hell up in Mrs. Worthington's attic. That's when I have my own revelation.

I stick this note under Mrs. Worthington's nose. "I don't get it," I say. "You support abortion but oppose birth control?"

She sits at her kitchen table and wipes her spectacle lens and reads it down her nose, through her glasses. "You should know better than to think that I judge what women do with their bodies. You can sleep with the devil for all I care." I see she's still angry with me for walking out on her kitchen work. "You remember Mr. Dotson, don't you? The one you call an old coot?" She doesn't look at me for an answer and I stand and wait. "Well, he's also an old snoop and I catch him sneaking around here all the time. He heard us talking about the potion I sold you, and he heard well we all heard – you vomiting all hours of the night. He told me so himself. That's how he justified peeping into your keyhole. 'Course that wasn't the only time I caught him doing that. He likes to call you a sweet tart. There's not much I can do about him. Don't underestimate his age or the men he runs with."

This same night after I return home from the boarding house, I'm awakened by the smell of smoke. In our robes, Clary and I find ourselves outside on the street, dazed, shivering and taking turns holding Jesi while watching the firemen put out the flames to BBCC. The three-feet high flaming white cross in the front yard they leave be, like it's a lawn ornament. Clary seems hypnotized by the cross, mumbling prayers. Usually Jesi is comforted immediately by her but not tonight. Jesi senses Clary's condition and screams in absolute terror.

A fireman approaches. "We think we've found the culprit," he says, holding out a blackened tool. "Do you know where this might've come from?"

"What is it?" I ask.

"Sorry, ma'am, of course you wouldn't know. It's a welder's torch."

We end the night with Jesi and me in Ellen's nursery on a small cot and Clary on a blanket pallet in Ellen's parlor – until Jesi fusses so much that I have to take her to Clary that is. "Go ahead and sleep on the floor. See if I care," I say, handing her over at three in the morning. I want her to snuggle with me, like I see other toddlers with their mothers, but she's so thorny.

"You're coming home," Mama announces, when I telephone her the next morning in a shaky voice and not caring if I sound grown-up. "I'll send someone down there to get you. He can get to you sooner than I can."

That afternoon a black Ford truck pulls up out front of Ellen's house, with a Tennessee license plate. "I'm Jerry," he says, taking his felt hat off at the door and bowing just enough for good old-fashioned manners. He has a full head of white hair, pulled back in a ponytail and I've never seen anything like him. He's beautiful and old at the same time. I immediately want to sit at his feet and ask him about the migration of birds or something like that. At first he looks like the silent Indian Chief type and I feel like everything is going to be okay and I wonder at the same time, how does he do that? His presence fills Ellen's parlor. But then after his cup of coffee, he spoils it by clapping his hands together and saying in a strong hill-billy accent, "Let's fire 'er up!" We all look at him in shock and watch his expression change from cheerful to sorrow as he realizes the implication. "My tongue twisted around my eye teeth and I couldn't see what I was saying." He bowed again. "Please forgive me, ma'am."

I shrug at the old hillbilly and mumble, *Thanks, Mama.*

I don't have much beyond some smoky-smelling clothing and I pack little, two suitcases. I had sold the furniture with the plantation house; all that old wood seemed to have grown roots there. The duplex apartment was furnished and now smoke-damaged, the office next door is destroyed. Not even Clary will come with us. "There's other white folks I can care for, and I'm gonna stay with my sister until I finds me one" she answers coolly, like this is all my fault for "running away". I see where Jesi gets her pigheadedness.

Marge comes around looking so distraught and disheveled, she loses goddess-status. I'm thinking she must suspect the same group I do. It doesn't help her age either that she's still mourning TJ, covered head-to-foot in black, so that I take pity on her and promise that Jesi and I won't be gone long; "just a visit with the other side". She and Clary cry anyway and Jesi intuitively understands and I have to wrench her from Clary's arms. I promise to write. I promise to come back. I think back to all those false promises.

We're heading north and out of Georgia before I can get Jesi to calm down. She basically just passes out. I miss Clary already.

In the silence that finally settles on us, I mumble, "So how do you know my mama?"

"It's a long story," he says.

I'm too frazzled to hear a long story from a man, especially one with a hillbilly accent. I want his silent muscular profile wisely making me a path toward home. If he talks, he might slow down. No doubt Mama knows him from one of her chapters or leagues or clinics. Who cares? He gives me an odd look and I'm not sure if I said 'who cares' out loud or not. "Nice weather we're having," I say with a yawn and we're distracted by the rain and hail. I hold hands with the passenger door and go back to sleep. Jesi lays stretched out on my lap or between us on the seat, like more luggage. She and I sleep a great deal of the trip, both exhausted from the trauma and sudden changes.

We're in Pennsylvania when he stops for his hundredth cup of coffee and asks, "What happened to her leg?"

I rub my eyes irritably. I'd scarcely woken from a short nightmare of searching for something unknown and running through fire trying to find it. I hesitate and keep to myself, *Could be the cousin who raped me*, and then continue out loud, "Could be from lying on my stomach in my job at the shipyard, could be the fibers from the welding torch, could be the magic potion, could be the wrath of God for my wicked sins. I've thought about it over and over, to the point that I don't want to think about it any longer. Mama will know what to do." I wonder to myself, *Why am I protecting TJ?*

He merely nods as if he's heard it all. "Your mommy and mammaw will take good care of both of you." Only a fleeting thought, I wonder how he knows that.

"Yes, ma'am," he said, like I had cared enough to ask him a question. "Now that your mammaw and mommy have done their work and women have got their basic rights, I'm giving civil rights their due attention. We sure got a lot of poor colored people in Tennessee who get a raw deal and every time one so much as complains or steps out of line, in come the KKK and shut him up for good ..." and on he rambles, not seeming to notice that I'd become deaf-mute and attached to the passenger door. I doze off and on.

Late in the night we at last stop in front of the Lighthouse – for the first time I notice it looks a bit rickety, like it's in competition with me to see who falls first. Looks like every light is on, Mama's way of saying Welcome Home. I want to run back in to its safe womb and never leave again. I didn't do so good out there on my own.

Jerry stares at the house, his hands motionless on the steering wheel, his body so still, his eyes distant, to the point that I'm thinking he's listening for crunching leaves or a breaking stick, like he's stalking deer. I don't like the idea of him doing that to my home-place.

"Thank you for a safe trip home!" I say as gaily as possible. That should scare the deer away.

"Win-na-de-ya-ho," he says softly but he's not looking at me.

Another old coot talking gibberish. I roll my eyes, gather up Jesi, and leave him in the truck without invitation. I decide to tell Mama he didn't want to come in. "Leave my suitcases on the sidewalk," I say above Jesi's whimpers.

Jesi's Chapter Five -- 1964

I'm writing this from the hospital. Long story. I'll get to it. First, here's what I wrote on the bus trip down to Nashville.

February 26, 1964: Isaac and I are on a Greyhound and will be traveling all night. Here we sit, heading to a sit-in.

"Sit-in will be easy with your leg and all," Isaac said, as we took our seat at the front of the Greyhound. "Now we both will be even."

"Even?"

"Yeah, we'll both have a handicap." He pointed to his skin. "Where we're going, my skin keeps me from doing a lot." I wonder again how old he is. There's something older about him, like his mannerisms and white shirt and tie, but it's hard to tell; his brown skin is clear and his forehead is as smooth as fudge.

"Did I ever tell you how old I am?" he asked. Yeah, he does that all the time – reading my mind, I mean. "I'm forty-four."

"Groovy," I answered. Forty-four? Holy Shit!

"Did I ever tell you that I've slept in your house?"

"Did we sleep together? Slip me some acid and now I don't remember?"

"You weren't born yet. I was only two years old. Your grandpa brought me and my family up here. After my dad was lynched. We stayed at the Lighthouse for a few days until my uncle and my mother got themselves jobs. Your grandpa helped there too. They still talk about it and drive me by your house and tell me never to forget about the good white people, no matter how bad it gets. I can remember wetting the bed there and getting whipped for it and I can remember that winding staircase and me sliding down those wooden stairs bumpity-bump in my pajamas. We moved to the colored section of town where I quit school and went back to Savannah looking for my roots.

I found out they're actually in the small town right outside Savannah called Pickerville. Ever heard of it?"

"Only on my birth certificate," I said, thinking how cool that he knows my birth place, but not surprised; he flips me out in knowing more about me than I do. Mama and GB would look all upset when I brought up anything about my birth, like it was JFK's assassination or something. So then out of nowhere GB said she'd work something out to where I'd know all about where I came from. Thanks to GG telling me where the key is to their chapters, now I know more than I want to know. I sure as hell ain't telling Isaac about that.

"You mean you and me were born at the same place?" Isaac asked, giving me his first grin of the day. "I knew you lived at the Lighthouse; that's why I sat behind you in Civics class. Did I tell you that I came back up north to finally get my high school diploma? We got more in common than we thought, white sugar!"

More in common than he knew; I still don't have my diploma. A Goof maybe, but I'm a hip Goof.

So we're heading south and the further down we go, the further back in the bus we sit. When we change buses in Kentucky, we go to the last row. "I got dibs on this here seat," he says with a weak chuckle.

"Why?" I asked stupidly.

"Cause I want no trouble," he answered as he flops down, hard, like someone pushed him.

"We could pretend we're back in the Passion Pit," I teased, referring to his name for parking in the back row of the drive-in movie.

He looked out the window, saying nothing. Out there was getting hotter and hotter, and darker and darker. Okay, it's getting night time but you get my drift.

"Are we driving into hell or something?" I asked, trying to lighten him up.

No smile. He looked out the window some more. He's not frosted but he's not happy either. "Very, very close," he finally answered, so softly I lean in to hear him. "So close, you can smell the smoke. And at night, if you're real quiet, you can hear the cries." And then he begins reciting a cool poem that he tells me later is called "Silhouette" by Langston Hughes:

> *Southern gentle lady*
> *Do not swoon*

They've just hung a black man
In the light of the moon
They've hung a black man
To the roadside tree
In that dark of the moon
For the world to see
How Dixie protects
Its white womanhood
Southern gentle lady
Be good!
Be good!

I look out the bus window into the black night and the whole thing gives me goose bumps. What's odder than what he's saying is how he's saying it. He's mumbling now and speaking faster, like he doesn't want anyone to overhear, and he doesn't want anyone to stop him. This tall straight proud man loses his posture, too, and stops looking me in the eye. But the thing most far out is, he's replacing "Yeah, man" with "Yes, sir". He's freaking me out to where yesterday I would've kidded around with something like, You wanna be my slave? Like maybe my sex slave? *But today I'm afraid he'd go ape. He's probably going to go ape-shit over me even saying "ape".*

It's morning when we get off the bus in Nashville and the day just gets freakier from there. Two colored men met us at the bus station and called me a "righteous babe" and Isaac got some of his confidence back and introduced them as "old room mates" and they all laughed like that's a good joke. Not So Funny when I pieced together that their living arrangement was at the Parchman State Prison. They called themselves Freedom Riders in those days. "Doesn't sound so free to me," I said uneasily and they laughed easily. They mentioned some sort of clan and how this clan set fire to a bus the Freedom Riders were riding in, like they were talking about a Sunday drive. "Weren't you scared, man?" One of them, Joseph, placed his large brown hand on my shoulder and answered, "I used to go to Martin Luther King's church and he preached that there is some evil in the best of us and some good in the worst of us. When you look at everybody that way, you don't get so scared."

We walked to the bus terminal lunch counter, where a sign was posted stating, *We Serve Only White Trade Here.* I turned to walk away and Isaac asked where I was going? "Somewhere where we all can eat," I said. The three of them laughed again, jolly laughter and I wondered why colored people have such nice white teeth. "Get with it, righteous babe!" Henry said.

They sat casually at the counter and I said, "That's cool," like we do this all the time. The waitress behind the counter didn't look so cool. "Everything's copasetic," I said to her. "I'm Goldilocks and this is the three bears and we would like some porridge please." She pretended like we weren't even there. Isaac put his finger to his lips to me and I clammed.

We sat there for an hour until I got so hungry watching her bring burgers and fries to other customers. "You need to eat," Isaac whispered to me. "I want you to stay here and me and the other two will go out on the street. Order some sandwiches and bring them out, okay?" He laid two dollars on the counter.

As soon as they left, the waitress brought me a menu. "My mother has polio and that's the only reason I'm serving you. You better find you a new batch of friends, people of your own kind, if you're staying here in this town." She shook her head, kind of like a mother who sees her child misbehaving.

I brought the food wrapped in wax paper out to the boys and they're all laughing again. "What gives?" I asked. "Goldilocks, I thought I'd lose it back there," answered Henry. "*The three bears? You are a trip!*" and they cracked up again.

We scarfed our tuna sandwiches down on the way to Kress 5&10. "We gotta keep moving if we want to start a movement," Henry said. They tell me they're all members of the NAACP and they're opposing segregation at restaurants through nonviolent direct action. They tell me they hope I'm not here for kicks. They tell me I'm not "hep" but I will be when this day is over. They ask Isaac if we're jacketed and he says I'm his white sugar to sweeten his bitter coffee and he gives me a wink. "That sounds easier on the ear than *zebra*," says Henry and they all chuckle and shake their heads.

At the Kress lunch counter, it looks like the sit-in is in gear 'cause there sat other colored folks at the counter. Isaac whispered to me that I could sit on the end of the counter if I wanted to, to stay out of line of any danger, so naturally I chose to sit between him and Henry. All of us sat calmly, all the men decked out in white shirts and ties, and me in my shirtdress from Christmas, looking like we were going to church next. People started coming up behind us and saying shitty comments about niggers and nigger lovers but I followed Isaac's lead and we never turned around to acknowledge them. In the mirror across from us, I could see a few of the taller flakes standing behind us, some greasers who had combed their hair into duck tails or wore flat-tops, and acting Elvis-cocky.

Isaac ordered coffee and we got the same eyeball that the waitress at the terminal counter threw us – and nothing else. We sat for four hours like that while the mob behind us thickened and I could feel the anger creeping down my back like molasses. Come to find out, it wasn't molasses but cream. I'm about to freak out, so I put my hand over my mouth and turned to Isaac only to watch in horror as salt, mustard and ketchup were dumped on my three bears' afro hair. They continued looking ahead, chins jutted out, mouths firmly shut, Joseph looking so sad. Isaac whispered, "These are probably local clan members. Don't sweat it. Remember: Nonviolent resistance." Sitting like that, our backs were to the wall – if you get my drift – and with nowhere to go, man, it was a bummer.

Isaac didn't set me up for this sort of bullshit hostility but hey, it's probably my fault since I was bragging about how I came from three women who fought in revolutions. I claimed I came ready as Superman but I sure as hell wasn't geared up for the cigarette someone put out on Joseph's arm. Joseph flinched, Joseph broke out in a sweat but Joseph was one badass in being able to take that and not lose it. It was all I could do not to turn around and give the asshole back there the bird.

"Maybe we should book it," said Isaac to Joseph. He was chewing on his lip.

"Tomorrow it's McCrory's lunch counter," Joseph said with a feeble smile.

No sooner than he said that, I saw caps and uniforms in the mirror and heard whistles blowing and someone yelled out, "The Fuzz!" and it all turned to mayhem.

I swear to Buddha, I've never seen anything like it – police pigs grabbing colored men off their stools and beating them with clubs. White racists spitting and yelling, like this is a legal dog fight. Someone grabbed my bandana I had wrapped around my hair and my cool choker I had beaded myself and dragged me off my stool. When I tripped over my bum leg and fell to the floor, the group around me noticed my brace and I heard, "She's a cripple, man, leave her alone." I crawled between pants, peggers, all straight legs, to the front of the place and huddled in the corner, shaking. I looked out the plate glass window and saw them handcuffing Isaac and I jumped to attention and pushed my way outside.

"Why are you arresting him," I shouted above the roar. "He's done nothing wrong! We were just sitting in there!"

"Disturbing the peace, breaking segregation laws, disorderly conduct, you name it, miss, we can pin it on him." The pig looked me up and down, like he was drawing designs on me, and finally said, "You don't belong here. Now get outta here before I change my mind." He jerked hard at Isaac's cuffed hands and I saw Isaac grimace. His lip was bleeding and he had a large bump on his forehead. So damn unfair!

"Why won't you arrest me, huh? I'm a cripple, right? I'm no good to you, is that it?" I slowly raised my hand and my middle finger popped out like it's been dying to all day. "Climb on this, Tarzan!"

Isaac turned around as far as he could to try to face me with his hands behind his back. I could see his eyes bugging out at my finger. "Cool it, white sugar," he said. "He's right, you don't belong here. You go on! Call David Lewis and he'll come get you."

"You can't tell me what to do!" I shouted. "No man can tell me what to do. Arrest me, too! Is it because I'm white then, is that it?" The policeman turned his back to me and walked away with Isaac.

That's when I noticed a riot had broke out around me and someone had set fire to the rag top of a hot-rodder and people were yelling "It's gonna blow!" and I have this unexplained terror of fire and I couldn't stay in this madhouse alone, to die, to burn in hell. I was going with Isaac All The Way. With all my limping might, I ran at the uniform and shoved him hard in his back. He tripped and almost fell to the ground, bringing Isaac with him. Isaac looked at me like I was a mad woman; I suppose I looked that way, maybe I was. "Arrest me, you racist pig," I yelled. "I'm a nigger lover and I love this one!"

"Alright! You asked for it!" he growled. Red in the face, he grabbed my arm with his free hand and hauled us to the first partly empty paddy wagon down the street. The first two wagons lined up were already full. All I could see were the whites of their eyes as someone lifted me up into the wagon. I had no idea so many colored people had shown up at the restaurant.

This same pig started to close the doors to the back of the wagon but then decided to yell something first. "It's damn un-American what you people did back there! Why don't you go back where you came from?"

"Hey, peace is patriotic, too," a voice from the darkness answered. I then knew Joseph was back there somewhere. The doors slammed hard.

There must've been fifty of us crammed into the jail cell, barely enough room to sit on the floor, some stood along the walls. I was given a small spot on the bottom bunk bed because they felt sorry for my bad limp. Falling from the stool had done some damage that I hadn't noticed until we settled in the cell but I didn't want the stares if I took the brace off. Legs from the top bunk dangled around my head. Joseph and Henry were there, too, and the three of them huddled at my feet, talking about how they wished they'd gotten more than a knuckle sandwich at the Kress lunch counter and how hungry they were for fried chicken. I love fried chicken too and we all agreed to break bread together some day.

"We'll go to Savannah next," said Henry, wrapping my bandana around his bloodied hand. "They're not so quick to arrest since half the folks there are colored registered voters." It's unreal how the three of them laughed so comfortably. Joseph said, "Man, you just don't quit, do you? You cruisin' for another bruisin'?" The raw cigarette burn on his arm looked like a red eye on his dark skin. It slowly closed a brown eyelid as it dried to a scab while we sat there all night. And, man, I swear, he never looked at it once.

With all those souls in this hell-cell, you'd think it'd stay warm, but the concrete walls, floors, metal bars, I don't know, but it got fucking cold. I started shivering in my thin shirtdress and I couldn't stop. Then I started coughing and I couldn't stop that. "What's your tale, nightingale?" asked Henry softly, looking up at me with warm coffee eyes. (Man, that's all I could think about, watching so many steaming cups being served and never getting one, and aren't you supposed to get water and bread in jail?) Isaac felt my forehead and stood up and stepped over the many bodies sleeping sitting up, til he got to the metal bars. "Hey," he called out in a loud whisper. "Anybody here?" No answer. We could only see more pukey-green concrete block walls beyond the cell. "We got us a sick baby in here, can anybody hear me?" No answer. I didn't want to bring any attention to me and I already felt like such a drag for fazing out that I sighed in relief when he gave up and came back.

Toward early morning, though, I was wheezing like a rubber ducky and no longer able to concentrate on their whispered plans of "jail-no-bail". For the first time in this whole freakin' happening, I see Isaac hacked off. He didn't care if he woke the world. He started yelling at the bars for someone to get their asses back here right now and let this white girl out so she can get back to Annan New York and see her doctor, or they were going to have a murder on their hands. I wasn't sure whose he was talking about.

"Can I help you, little girl?" I turned my attention to a white man, an old one bent down to me, with long white hair all the way down to his shoulders that fell forward and partly hid his face. *Why do Big Daddies treat me like an ankle-biter?* I sent him up a glare to mind his own bees-wax but he sent back a groovy smile and kind blue eyes. Kind of softened all those wrinkles, making me homesick for GG.

"Yeah," I croaked, attempting a half beam to make up for my glare. "You got a peace pipe you can pass around here?"

He raised his hand like a good television Indian. "How!" he said and gave me an open grin that made me feel warm inside. Since when did *those kind* have blue eyes? His weren't even dull like a lot of old men either, but twinkling like a Santa Claus.

The cell opened with a clang and we all looked over to see a uniform and Isaac brought him over to me. Uh-oh, the same one from yesterday; he'll keep me here til Aquarius aligns with Mars. With Isaac's blown up story of me at death's door, the Indian had a pow-wow with the fuzz and told him *he* could take me back up to New York.

"No, you can't," I called out hoarsely. This sent me into fits of coughs.

I might as well have howled to the moon.

"Aren't you getting too old to be doing this crap, Jerry? Why don't you stay home and watch the sunset?" the uniform asked.

"You might be right, sir," Jerry-or-whoever said, nodding solemnly like these were wise words. "Let me take this little girl home and, I promise, as the Great Spirit is my witness, you won't see hide-nor-tail of me ever again."

Wasn't anybody going to ask me? "Hey!" I reached up and tugged on Isaac's shirt sleeve from my bed roost, trying not to get too cranked to keep the lungs settled. "I'm not going anywhere. I don't know this man. Does that matter to anyone here? How does he know where I live?"

"I may be stabbing in the dark here," this Jerry guy said, "but I'm reckoning you live in a big white-brick house they call the Lighthouse?" And he started naming My Mamas' names and about how old they are and really freaking me out. "If you come from Annan, New York, and you're in this kind of pickle barrel, you could only come from one line of ladies, the strongest women I know of."

"I'm afraid I didn't inherit that part," I said after another deep-throated croup.

"They'll be very proud of you," he said, so kindly I had an urge to hug. "I'll see to that."

I wanted to ask him, *do you really think so?* I had another urge to say, *my heart soars like the eagle.* Would he laugh? My three brown bears here sure would. But we were interrupted.

"You two," the uniform said, "get outta here before I change my mind." Man, he needed new material.

I stood slowly. "Isaac … " I couldn't think of anything else to say; I knew they had me.

He touched my arm; I wanted more, like a goodbye kiss, but suicide in this land. "You go take care of yourself. I'll be up there soon. You hear?" I nodded, not able to speak, not able to take my eyes off his Sweet, Sad Face. "You's good people. Thanks. For everything."

The cop tugged at me to go then and everyone quietly parted a Red-Sea path to the cell door. Some patted my back or on top of my head as I limped out, with only the clink-clink of my shoe brace making a sound.

Then there was a long dark hallway that seemed to go on and on into eternity. My legs got heavier and heavier walking forever … clink … clink. Suddenly there was bright sun glittering off cars blinding me. Then it got dark. I tried to open my eyes and a car tire is eye-level. He's leaning over me, moving hair from my face, "You fainted, honey, I'm here, hold my hand tight" … blue eyes, Blue Mountain he says. "Your mommy and mammaw will meet you up there, I'll drive up" … to the top of the blue mountain? … a white cot … bright lights … up, up … heaven? … God, Jerry's an angel … how can he *drive* up? … helicopter blades? … loud noises … a low roar … down, down … GB's face … GG's face … Mama's face … *you had us scared to death!* … fading in and out, in and out, like bad TV reception. The trouble is not in your set.

I'm fine now, *copasetic,* Mama said, but she's a lousy liar. My writing's sloppy and I'm writing fast because they won't give me much time before they put this freaking plastic tent over my bed. "Cool. I'm finally going on a camping trip," I tell the nurse through my oxygen mask. I sound raspy and there's that rubber ducky sound again. Hard to hold a pen, hard to breathe. No one is smiling; sure would be nice to see some nice white teeth and hear his laughter … where are you?

BESS -- March 1964

We arrive at the gravesite and I simply cannot believe that our free-spirited Jesi is closed up in that box. I can't bear it. I can't. Mama is the one making the most sense, in just "zoning out" as Jesi would call it. I wish I could do the same. I'm so tired of being durable, but like any old shoe, I need mending. Doesn't anyone see that?

But what if Mama doesn't get her mind back? I can't bear to think of it.

Who can face this cruel reality? I'll tell you who. Katy. Jesi's own mother. I do not understand her. When we received news of Jesi's death, she fell to the floor of the hospital waiting room like a spiraling leaf and has been as brittle ever since. But not a tear to spare. No, not one drop. I had stopped reading her chapters after she had revealed why she hadn't originally opened the birth control clinic. She lacked commitment and drive.

But then I read more - what if I lose her too? I was going to bury our chapters with Jesi. So many secrets revealed. But I went back and took the stack of papers back out. I knew that Jesi had been reading them, as well as Katy. Just as I had hoped they would. Didn't they think I would've removed the chapters from the locked wardrobe otherwise? We needed an understanding of each other and I thought this project the best way. I wanted to understand Mama and Jere's love for each other and what had really happened between them that would warrant my belief in their wrong-doing. I find out that I'm the one wrong. I wanted to know what happened to Katy while in Georgia. She came back a changed woman and rarely has left the house since, and I had secretly blamed myself for pushing the birth control clinic. I find out how wrong I was. I wanted to know what was going on in Jesi's mind and where she was disappearing to, sex and drugs being my worst fear. Again I was terribly wrong. In the process I found my writing very therapeutic in telling my own truth. Now I'm considering putting it together for public consumption. I haven't decided – yet I can envision the cover: a medieval-looking tapestry of four armored women marching through their different eras, colorful threads linking past to present, on a background of deep green ivy, branched out yet intertwined at intervals, all growing from the same root.

It's inspiring and heartbreaking at the same time. This is not the ending I had planned. If only a writer could bring the dead back and make it a happy ending with just pen and paper.

Here am I, the cold one, the "Mount Everest", crying my eyes out. The only one. Can someone explain the sense of it all? I must make some sense of this or I will surely go mad. I so much want to tell Jesi I didn't mean to be cold, that I really cared.

The night of her death, a nurse handed me papers with Jesi's handwriting scrawled across like she had written this on a bumpy bus ride. I rushed home to find her remaining chapters stuffed into her night table drawer. What I realized came too late. I take full responsibility for not being more in tune with Jesi's needs, her mama's needs, and for harboring accusations toward my own mama.

Where is the love, man? Jesi had the right question there but I'm so damned upset with the rest of us Mamas for not having the answers. We thought ourselves above her and her substandard rebellion. Now I see she's no better or worse – just one of our kind wanting to have the freedom to choose.

Overwhelmed by the public sobbing around me, I walk away and up a small knoll. I look back down on the group circled around the hole in the earth, Jesi's coffin suspended above to give us one last chance at farewell. I see this hole as a gap in my chest, where my heart used to be. I had grown one and lost it during my year of awakening. Jesi had been the heart to us all, the one who felt the

481

most, the one who suffered the most, the one who shocked the most, and now such a vibrant life is to be buried like so many memories, harshly exposing my own one-dimensional life.

After all my struggles, why would one of my own choose civil rights instead? I've pushed Jesi too hard, is that it? What else could she do but break and fly off in a different direction? Perhaps she's smarter than I am; perhaps she saw the futility of my life. Frankly I'm tired of pushing for the Equal Rights Amendment. After forty years in draft, this ERA continues to be non-ratified. What is this all about, this life of mine? If not for women's rights, then for what? And if not for Jesi and her offspring, why go on fighting? I will not write another letter, attend another meeting! No more arguing, no more debate!

I begin pacing, my arms folded around me against the cold winds. One gust catches my head scarf like a sail and I watch helplessly as it takes to the air.

But wait! Why am I bickering about the ERA? Jesi lost her *life* for her cause! Can I not give more of my life for both my cause and hers? So that she does not die in vain? And so that my life has not been wasted? I must make sense of it all. I must or I will surely lose my mind.

I know what I will do: I'll table this at tomorrow's meeting of the National Woman's Party and discuss this personally with Alice Paul. The draft Civil Rights bill is going in front of the Senate this very year and now is the time to push gender inclusion. If the front door's locked, go around back.

I hear singing. I stop and look down there.

Prayer has ended and people are walking away. Remaining are mostly Uncle Jesse's sons and grandchildren and Aunt Opal's children and grandchildren. They alone can make a crowd and Jesi would have loved to see them. Yet Jesi's colored friend, Isaac, remains with my family and has brought his guitar from the church. He's singing Bob Dylan's *Blowin' in the Wind.* Wasn't it enough that he had sung Dylan's song, *Don't think twice, it's alright* at the church? How inappropriate. He hadn't asked permission to perform and who would want to hear such rebel trash? Yes, the two world wars took lives, but they saved many more. Jesi's generation doesn't understand! I start back down to ask him to stop, when I hear other voices join in, *The answer my friend is blowin' in the wind, the answer is blowin' in the wind.*

What draws my attention more so is, from a distance I see a man walking across the field toward the graveyard. His walk, like a graceful long stride, is vaguely familiar, but his head of white hair and stooped shoulders are not. As he nears the group from the side, I see something all too familiar: a pony tail. This could only be one man.

I hurry down the slope, thinking he's looking for me but when I call his name, he doesn't seem to hear but keeps searching, peering into people's faces. When he sees Katy he halts. He touches her shoulder and she stops singing and backs away, giving him an impatient frown.

"Miss Katy, I came as fast as I could drive after they put her on the helicopter but then my truck broke down and there weren't a gas filling station for miles." He still has that low tenderness in his deep voice that makes you feel like no one else matters to him.

Suddenly recognition sparks and she asks, "You're Jerry, aren't you?"

"Yes, ma'am and I'm so sorry I couldn't have done more. She was such a brave little girl."

Mama's back is to us as she faces the coffin, shoulders and head down, her pocketbook hanging limp from her hand. I see her head jolt upon hearing his voice. Her trembling liver-spotted hand touches her throat.

"Now I know who you are!" Katy turns completely to give him her full attention, and for the first time I notice she's not wearing her heavy make-up and thick eyeliner. Her pallor highlights the deep circles under her eyes. She looks beautifully pure to me. "This isn't the first time you've come to our rescue so there's no need to apologize." I'm pleased to see her eyes finally fill with tears and flow down her face.

"I'm so relieved to see you again and thank you," she continues. "Jesi spoke of her guardian angel but the description could only be the Jerry who brought us back up north when she was a baby. If anyone should apologize, it's me. To think what could've happened if you hadn't been in that jail cell. If she had died there, away from home–" She pauses and grasps his wrinkled hand, holding it between her own. She was giving affection to a man!

"She hung in there with the toughest of 'em," Jere said. "And me not knowing who she was until her colored boy tried to get help."

Mama had slowly turned around while he spoke, her hand still at her throat, her eyes as glazed as blue marble.

"Jeremiah?" Mama asks hoarsely, incredulously, as if expecting him to say no. I know I expected such an answer.

He turns to his side and sees her for the first time. "Ruby?" He looks visibly shaken as he touches her cheek. "Ruby. You are a sight for sore eyes."

She wraps her arms slowly around his waist, closes her eyes against his chest and holds on, beginning to weep. "She's gone, Jeremiah, our Jesi's gone." It's a sudden painful cry but I'm immensely relieved to hear Mama's old self again.

He stands motionless for a moment, his arms at his side. Then he seems to fold himself around her, his arms about her thick winter coat, and pressing his cheek to the top of her head, he rocks slightly, side to side.

Jeremiah? That is twice she called him that. Jere. Jeremiah. Jerry. This is all the same man?

Shocked I watch Jere back away and cup my mama's aged face like he's holding a trophy he'd won unexpectedly. She looks like a stranger to me, her hands on the waist of another man besides Papa, gazing up into this man's eyes as if they've picked up where they left off.

Jere's cheekbones protrude more than I remember, his skin wrinkles and sags some in places, his thick hair is white as snow and there's deep lines around his eyes and mouth that become more pronounced as he smiles at her. But his eyes remain vibrant and he still has that aura – that word used these days to describe such a strong presence.

Katy and others walk away from such a private scene but I stay in place, waiting with questions. I give a second-glance to Katy. She's actually allowing the long-time doting Mr. Dodds to put his arm around her shoulders. Jesi would be so pleased. *Let's get it* on, I can hear Jesi say. I shake my head at past and future.

"I can't believe you're standing here in front of me," Jere is saying to Mama, his voice threaded with emotion. "Flesh and blood, living and breathing, letting me know I'm not dreaming. Your eyes are as blue as when you were a young girl."

"Blue as the Blue Ridge, Mr. Jeremiah Bluemountain?"

"My God, I haven't been called that for fifty years. I'd forgotten how much I like hearing it. I shouldn't have listened to my wife and changed it back to my daddy's name, Phillips. I reckon she didn't want to go around with my mommy's Indian name to be made fun of."

We begin to walk slowly back to the parking lot.

"Your wife ..."

"Died many years ago."

"Children?"

"Thought you might have met my oldest girl when Bess looked after her up here. You didn't meet Mary Sue?"

Mama freezes. That confused glazed look she wore earlier returns and I fear we have lost her again. We can only watch as she struggles in a helpless silence.

She finally shakes her head "How can that be, Jeremiah? Mary Sue's father was Bess's first husband."

Yes, I want to cry, *you remember!*

Jere – Jeremiah - cocks his head to the side, naturally missing the point. "Yes, I'm Mary Sue's father." His silver eyebrows raise at what this implies. He would have to explain and this might put Mama back into a bad condition. How sad her day has clouded so quickly.

But her eyes don't become remote at all. No, they turn on me with such a storm of accusation, betrayal and hurt, I feel defensive.

"Mama, I can explain."

"You were married to Jeremiah?"

Jeremiah steps back as if too close to the fire.

"Yes. Do you remember when Thom—"

"And you didn't tell me?"

"I didn't know he was Jeremiah, Mama. I only knew him as Jere Phillips."

Why am I being defensive? I fold my arms in my customary debate way and state, "As a matter of fact, I asked you back in those days if you knew him and you denied it. I thought you were lying to me."

"I didn't know he was Jere Phillips." She suddenly looks hurt. "You've been thinking all this time that I lied to you? Your own mama?"

"Well, I thought you had reason to, being in love with a man not my papa."

"If you thought I was in love with him, then why'd you marry him?"

"Because I didn't put two and two together until after we married and went to Jere's cabin. I saw the carved dove and the lavender bushes. He didn't deny that I reminded him of you. That's the only reason why he married me."

She turns on him like an angry mother bear. "You married my *daughter*? How could you use her that way?"

"I didn't know she was your daughter." His eyes dart between us, looking as if he's stepped into an ambush. He takes us each by the elbow. "Let's walk," he says.

We reach the parking lot and finally he sighs deeply as if in surrender. He leans heavily against his truck frame, folding his arms across his chest. He stares down at his boots. "Well, I didn't know for sure anyway. That would seem too good to be true." He gives Mama his sincerely blue eyes. "To marry someone who looked like you and talked like you used to about women's rights. I thought you were gone forever and that Bess dropped in as a proxy."

"A *proxy*? Thanks so much, Jere," I say, my face flushing at the insult.

He raises his hand, still in surrender mode. "I'm sorry, Bess, I'm just trying to explain." He returns his blue gaze to Mama. "You

486

should know that nothing happened between us – like what would happen between a man and his wife. Bess is a smart gal and caught on real quick. She high-tailed it out of there after one night. I can't say that I blame her, even if my male pride suffered some."

For the next few moments we listen to the distant murmur of folks saying goodbye and driving away, as we all absorb these revelations about each other.

"You grow lavender?" Mama finally asks, her eyes softening in acceptance.

"Yes, ma'am, and I wish now I'd brought you a bunch and a carved dove to go with it."

"I still have your last dove," she says, taking one step toward him.

He regains his composure as he sees he's in safe territory again. "You do?" He gives her a side-long glance. "But I gave you two doves."

"The other one I dropped into Cady's coffin – that last night we spoke in the gazebo."

"No wonder we stayed apart all these years, Ruby. You separated the pair."

"I thought it best at the time. I had to do what was right by my family. I had children to raise – and a husband."

"How is he?" he asks, sounding obligatory.

"He died twenty-two years ago. Mary Sue was there at the time."

I could almost hear a squeaky door opening.

"I'm sorry." He doesn't look sorry to me. He's searching her face for signs of life, not death. Nor do any of us want to hash over the past regarding Mary Sue, I'm certain.

She nods. "I tried to look you up once but it doesn't matter now. We have some catching up to do."

Tears come to me and it isn't for sentimental reasons. I have become overwhelmed with regret and sadness. All those years wasted in unsuccessful ERA battles, when Mama should've been with Jere. Yet they do find their own happy ending as if it's all meant to be. I don't know how to find mine. *It is mind-blowing, Jesi,* I murmur as I look back and watch them lower the coffin down under. I feel like another crying jag is coming on in losing the point of it all.

Out of the blue Jere places his hand on my shoulder. "Bess, I want to thank you for taking on Mary Sue the way you did. I'm sorry I wasn't more appreciative with what you had done but, well, I had given up hope for her for awhile. She lost a husband and two sons to the coal mine and the hard knocks sure brought her a long way. Not only did she teach her brothers and sisters how to read and write and whip 'em right through high school, but she's become a school teacher and well-known activist in bringing in schools in the Blue Ridge Mountains. In a speech last week, she gave you all the credit. I never thought I'd say it but I'm right proud of her."

Mama isn't listening. She's walked a few steps closer to where the gravediggers begin the task of hiding Jesi from us forever. Mama's crying openly now, her handkerchief in hand quivering. I feel the loss too and with only the three of us remaining, I sing along to the saddest tune in the world.

Suddenly Mama subsides, wipes her eyes and nose, and puts her handkerchief back into her sleeve. "We'll just go with the flow. That's what Jesi wants us to do." Jere joins her and she tucks her arm into his. "Let's all go to the Lighthouse. I want to have a nice chat with Jesi's young man, Isaac. Jeremiah, you come too. We have tons of food everybody brought in and I don't want to lose sight of you just yet. Cady's funeral was the last I saw you. I don't want to lose Bess next, before we meet again. She's as healthy as a horse."

Epilogue

Annan Newspaper, July 2, 1964:

History is forever altered today in the landmark passage of the Civil Rights Act, signed by President Johnson. This act outlaws racial segregation in schools, public places, and employment. The bill was introduced last year by then President, our deceased John F. Kennedy, when he asked for legislation "giving all Americans the right to be served in facilities which are open to the public ... and greater protection for the right to vote."

In an interesting twist of fate, after 57 days in a filibuster, a weakened Act included "sex" in its title VII, added by its strong opposition, Howard W. Smith, as a means to defeat the bill by inserting objectionable amendments. However, Smith claims his sincerity and is reportedly close to women's rights activist, Alice Paul. The National Woman's Party had been actively promoting the amendment. The prohibition against discrimination based on sex was added at the last hour and quickly passed as amended.

An open-air celebration is planned at City Hall Park, with our own women's libber and soon-to-be published author, Mrs. Bess Wright-Pickering, as key-note speaker.

Made in the USA
Lexington, KY
16 November 2017